SAVING ME

SADIE ALLEN

Cover Design by Cover Couture
www.bookcovercouture.com
Photo (c) Depositphotos
Editing by: C&D Editing
Proofread by: Judy's Proofreading
Formatted by: Under Cover Designs

This work in no way glamorizes or encourages anyone to take their own life. I hope to shine a light on mental illness, which is something that should be discussed more openly in schools and colleges, especially depression and anxiety.

Suicide is an act of desperation.

If you or anyone you know is struggling with thoughts of suicide or depression/anxiety, please seek help immediately.
<u>Don't wait!</u>

Sometimes, our minds are our own worst enemy.

AUTHOR'S NOTE

This book is very personal to me. As someone whose life has been touched by suicide several times and has struggled with depression in the past, I have put a lot of my own feelings and experiences into *Saving Me*.

Everyone handles and battles negative emotions differently, so this isn't a representation of everyone's battle. Also, I don't think having a boyfriend or girlfriend is the answer or cure for depression or suicidal thoughts. I do, however, believe that there are people who come into our lives at the right moment who can make all the difference. My best friend did that for me over a decade ago. She stood by me when I didn't have anyone, and that made all the difference in the world.

I also encourage you to be that person for someone else. As the saying goes: we don't know what battle someone is fighting today, so be kind. Always be kind.

If you are struggling with depression or suicidal thoughts, I beg you, right now, talk to someone. *You matter.* You matter to me and many others you may not even realize. There is nothing weak in asking for help. Even the strongest people have their bad days. If you don't feel comfortable contacting someone you know, here is a list of organizations that will be happy to talk to you:

NATIONAL SUICIDE PREVENTION LIFELINE
1.800.273.TALK (273-8255)

National Child Abuse Hotline
1.800.4.A.CHILD (422-4453)
National Domestic Abuse Hotline

1.800.799.SAFE (799-7233)

RAPE, ABUSE AND INCEST NATIONAL NETWORK (RAINN)
1.800.656.HOPE (656-4673)

The Trevor Project
1.866.4.U.TREVOR (488-7386)
Veterans Crisis Line
1.800.273.TALK (273-8255) PRESS 1

This is an organization that is near
and dear to my heart:
TO WRITE LOVE ON HER ARMS
TEXT TWLOHA TO 741-741
https://twloha.com

To Rachael J.
Your death changed something inside us all. The world became a little crueler,
and we became a little less innocent.

"Most of us are imprisoned by something. We're living in darkness until something flips on the switch."
- Wynonna Judd

"Two roads diverged in a wood,
and I
I took the one less travelled by,
And that has made all the difference."
- Robert Frost

NOBODY

I stood at the top of the bleachers, studying the pill bottle in my hand and wondering if I should just chug the whole bottle or swallow a few at a time. If I choked, I guessed it would serve the same purpose. But that wasn't the quiet, peaceful passing I imagined.

I looked out at the horizon, where the sun was dipping toward the earth, and exhaled a shaky breath. This would be my last sunset. It was a more perfect one than I could ever have dreamed. The sky was streaked in oranges, pinks, and blues, as a light, cool breeze whispered through the air, causing wisps of hair to tickle my face and neck.

I wrapped my arms around myself as I watched the sky deepen into twilight, the last vestige of glowing warmth before the oncoming night. It was kind of poetic in a way ... I would soon drift away into the night myself.

I wiped the wetness that trailed down my face with one hand while I gripped the bottle tighter in the other. Was I really going to do this?

Now, you might be wondering why a girl like me, from a family like mine, would commit suicide in her track uniform while standing atop the bleachers at the football field. One word: desperation.

I knew it probably didn't make any sense, but at seventeen years old, I was just tired of life. I was tired of being used and abused. Of being raw on the inside, like someone had scraped out my insides with a rusty spoon and left me bleeding and hollow. The pain blazing up my leg from the tips of my toes to the middle of my back was the only indication I was still alive. That I could feel anything. I was a ghost before I was even dead ... which I was about to change.

I took a shuddered breath. A faint buzz filled my brain as memories flashed through my mind like some macabre slideshow.

I had a father who only started caring about me when I jumped my first hurdle on field day in sixth grade. Normal fathers would find this a proud moment, not change their purpose in life. It wouldn't change the core of the father-daughter relationship. For my father, Derek Everly, however, it was a life-changing moment for the both of us.

My father had been a college track star who held state and national titles in the one hundred- and ten-meter hurdles. After graduating college, his path had been set for the Olympics. He had the determination and the numbers to back it up ... until an ACL tear saw his dreams go up in a puff of smoke. So, on that fateful day, when his only child showed the same aptitude for jumping over obstacles, those dreams had reignited and became a blaze beyond my control. He was determined to live his dreams again ... through me. Now he was more like a live-in coach than a father.

Sometimes I wondered if I was just numbers to him. Numbers on a stopwatch, in a track lane, on the scale in the bathroom, or a place-holder at the end of a race. Was my value really based on a set of figures? Would he still love me if I could never run again, like if I was paralyzed? My stomach roiled, and a sour taste filled my mouth. The thought was devastating. My life *was* numbers.

In his bid to achieve his dream, he controlled every aspect of my life, from what I put in my mouth to who I let ride in my car. He had once literally forced my mouth open in a restaurant to fish out a bite of buttered roll. Who did that? And Heaven forbid I let someone who wasn't athletic, church-going, or white put their butt on the plush leather seats of my brand-new Toyota 4-Runner. Everything was about winning or how I made my family look in the eyes of our respectable townspeople.

My mother, her only crime was indifference. She allowed her husband to treat me like a possession because she was also a posses-sion. Unlike me, though, she was a willing possession who didn't under-stand why I chafed beneath the manipulation and control that were like physical bonds restraining me from living the life I chose. She didn't realize, or maybe she didn't care, that I was slowly suffocating, drowning in the sea of their expectations.

I shook my head in an attempt to hold the memories at bay.

However, his voice was a constant presence in my head. All I could hear were his cold, unfeeling words ...

"That was piss poor, Allison."

"How many calories are in that?"

"You look heavy."

"It's like you're running in molasses."

Finally, his words from yesterday were the metaphorical nail in my coffin.

"You're useless to me now! What am I supposed to do with you? You're broken!"

I *was* broken.

And now I was all *alone.*

Useless.

Nothing.

I wanted freedom from my gilded cage, the imprisonment that had finally broke me.

It wasn't just the controlling behavior of my father and the indifference from my mother.

My boyfriend, Miles, the lying, cheating douchebag, was banging my best friend behind my back. All my other friends knew, but none of them had said a word to me. They thought I was too stupid to see the way Laura looked at Miles, and the way he looked at her. Laura, well, she had not been very discreet regarding her feelings toward my boyfriend. She talked about him all the time, saying everything but "I'm boning him after your curfew every weekend."

None of my friends would care if I was gone. They would probably shed a few pretty tears, maybe Miles would get some comforting sympathy lays. Other than a memorial scholarship donation, I would be a distant memory for them.

And these were supposedly the good kids? The children of the upper middle class? The "cream of the crop"? The future of our community?

Give me a break.

They were emotionally bankrupt liars who only cared about surface appearances. As long as I gave them *that* smile and nodded in all the right places as they gossiped about who still wore the same clothes from last year, they thought I was perfectly fine, happy even.

I wasn't fine. I had been screaming on the inside for years, and no one had cared enough to ask me if I wanted to do something or be someone other than how *they* saw me. Everything was just chosen for me—my activities, my classes, my clothes, my hair, what colleges I was applying to, and my future career. My parents hadn't consulted me. I was on the fast track to success—go to college, earn my undergraduate degree, and then go to law school like my father before me and his father before him. Still, I was the disappointment because I had the audacity to have been born a girl. However, jumping over a hurdle quickly seemed to have made up for my lack of a penis.

Then, yesterday, everything had changed. The answers to all my questions were answered. What was left of my battered and bruised soul effing died.

The first meet of the year, the preliminaries for the one hundred-meter hurdles.

As I had leaped over that third hurdle and brought my trail leg over, something cracked and popped. Then pain, blinding pain, had shot from my hip all the way to my brain. My knee had crashed into the top of the obstacle, but it had been nothing compared to the hurt that had taken over my body from my hip and back.

I had gone down, taking the hurdle with me and knocking into the runner in the next lane. I had slid across the rubber track, feeling my skin tear and burn. My lungs had seized as the pain took all the air from me, and wetness had leaked from my eyes and down my face.

"Help me," I remembered croaking, fighting back a scream of agony as I tried to move my leg.

I didn't remember much about what had happened after that, except the pain. Just the pain. I had never felt pain like that in my entire life. I imagined childbirth was at that pain threshold.

Dad, as well as my mom, who I hadn't even noticed was with us until we were in the emergency bay, had rushed me to the closest emergency room. Once there, we were immediately rushed back. I figured that was partly due to the screaming.

Dad had set me on the bed carefully, while Mom smoothed her

hands over my face, pushing my hair back. If I had been totally coherent, I would have seen the tears shimmering in her own eyes.

The rest was a blur of going to the x-ray room, getting my scrapes cleaned, and then the doctor coming in. I should have known something bad was going to happen when my dad, a nurse, and my mother started to hold me down. Then the doctor had grabbed my hurt leg and maneuvered it in a way that had made the pain from earlier seem like a dream. A scream had ripped from my throat as, with a deft movement and the accompanying *pop*, my leg had been set back into place, and then it was all over.

"There, that should do it," the tall man wearing a lab coat had declared as he set my leg down gently on the table.

"Wh-wh-what did you do?" I had asked, panting, my breaths sawing in and out of my chest.

"Young lady, your hip was dislocated. And due to the bruising that's appearing on the back of your thigh, I also think you have a small tear in your hamstring. The dislocation I can fix, but the soreness from the dislocation and the possible tear is something you're going to have to take it easy on."

"Okay." What else could I have said? I was just glad the feeling of someone stabbing me repeatedly with a knife was gone from my body.

"What do you mean, *take it easy*? When will she be able to run again?" my dad asked.

"Run again? Sir, your daughter will need to see a sports injury specialist for that, but I don't think she'll be on a track anytime soon. I recommend one we hav—"

"Thank you, but we'll take her back home and have her doctor refer one," Dad interrupted.

I looked at my mom, whose lips were thinned and eyes narrowed. I could tell she was biting her tongue. Evidently, she didn't like my dad being rude any more than I did. That was new.

I knew the doctor had to have been annoyed, but his expression had taken on one of extreme patience as he said, "Again, she'll need to rest and ice her hip and leg for the rest of the week. Try to keep it elevated. I'll get her some pain medication just for tonight, but Tylenol or Aleve should work after that. We'll wrap her leg while you fill out the discharge papers, and then we'll leave you all to it." He then patted my non-injured foot and was gone with a swipe of the curtain.

"Derek ..." my mother said softly, but my dad was already on the phone.

"Russel? Derek Everly. Ally had an incident, and we need a referral." He stared at his feet as Dr. Black said something on the other end. "She dislocated her hip and possibly has a small tear in her hamstring." He nodded then looked up at my mom, extending his hand and snapping his fingers.

I guessed she knew what he meant because she pulled out her phone and reached over me to hand it to him. He then cradled his phone to his ear and started tapping away at my mom's phone ...

The memory was so fresh in my mind that it now haunted the present.

I looked down at the pills in my hand again. They were small, white, and round ... so innocuous looking. Then I again looked up and over the back railing of the bleachers, watching the sun as it slowly sunk into the horizon. I ignored the icy prickles that skittered over my skin, the tears that continued to drip from my face, the whispers of doubt that crept into the forefront of my mind.

Was I really going to do this?

The buzzing in my head was getting louder, like there was a hive of bees nesting there. Panic seized me in a vise as my body bucked with a sob, my breaths coming out in pants. I squeezed my eyes shut tightly and shook my head from side to side with such force that it wrenched my neck. The bees were relentless.

I *had* to do this. The decision had been made, and I had to stick to the plan. Finally, something was going to be *my* choice. This was going to be my emancipation.

I took a deep breath then lifted the hand holding the pills toward my mouth ...

A blur of movement flashed in front of me, knocking all my mother's Tramadol out of my hand. I watched in shock as the little white pills hit the metal with what sounded like dozens of little *pings* as they fell everywhere, most landing on the ground in the dirt beneath the bleachers.

I slowly turned my head to see who had dared to ruin *my* moment and froze. How had I not seen him? How had I not *heard* him? I stared into a pair of burning semi-blue eyes. And by semi-blue, I meant they were mostly blue with a bit of brown in his right eye. Unusual. *Beautiful.*

I was momentarily mesmerized, lost in a way that dulled the pain that was a living, breathing thing inside me. The buzzing bees were muted as I stared into those smoldering depths.

I knew those eyes. I sometimes felt them on me at school. They belonged to Sterling Chapman.

Funny, I thought distantly, that he should be the one to intrude on this moment. I had always had kind of a *thing* for him. He was insanely hot, hotter than Miles on his best day, but totally off limits. He was a theater kid with a lip ring. My parents would freak and lock me in my room if he ever showed up at our door.

Besides having a cool name like Sterling and the lip ring, he was tall with shaggy black hair and arresting eyes that felt like they could see right through you. He had a square jawline, high cheekbones that high-lighted his fantastic bone structure, and when he flashed his signature grin, you could see his perfectly straight, white teeth.

There was just *something* about him. It was in the way he held his body, so confident and sure that it bordered on cocky. If he was in the room, it was impossible to take your eyes away from him.

A twinge of something that felt strangely like regret tightened my chest. Maybe in a different life, I could have been the kind of girl who was free to make her own choices. One who could be Sterling Chapman's girlfriend. One who could pick out her own clothes, be friends with whomever she wanted, and who could eat whatever she wanted.

I rubbed my chest, right where my heart should be. *What would a life like that be like?*

"Hello? Allison?"

I blinked out of my musings as harsh reality intruded.

I *was not* that girl.

Never to be that girl.

I clenched my jaw. It felt as if ice was creeping, hardening, and encasing my heart, my body, rapidly spreading until I was hard and cold all the way through—a living ice sculpture.

Sterling had been speaking to me for a while, but I was so absorbed in my misery that I had failed to hear his words. His face looked pinched, and his lips were devoid of his usual, carefree smirk.

I didn't reply. I stared in stony silence, waiting for him to continue or leave. At the moment, I didn't care either way. I cared about nothing. Then something struck me ...

I narrowed my eyes. "Did you just call me Allison?"

"What's with the pills?" he barked.

I ignored him. "Did you just call me Allison?"

"That's your name, yeah?"

"Yeah, but no one ever calls me that. Everyone calls me Ally."

"Well, *Allison*, what's the deal with that bottle of prescription pills and you standing up here in your"—he gestured to my uniform —"track shit?"

I opened my mouth, but nothing came out. I then closed it and glared, only to open it again, hoping a sarcastic reply would miraculously fly out. Strangely, or maybe not so strange since I felt my icy shell cracking at the idea of him knowing my weakness, shame burned in my gut.

I focused my eyes away from his to a point over his shoulder. I wanted to tell him it wasn't what it looked like, but sadly, it was exactly what it looked like.

I sighed and looked toward the horizon again. The sun had disappeared, and stars were beginning to dot the sky. The security lights had flickered to life, casting an eerie glow over the stadium and the school in the distance.

I was very aware of Sterling standing next to me. My skin prickled, and my heart danced an erratic beat. I glanced at him out of the corner of my eye. He was still watching me like he was still waiting for me to answer.

"Got nothing to say?"

It was like he was taunting me. His face was hard, unyielding, and I knew he wouldn't believe me if I told him that I was just taking in the scenery.

When I still said nothing, he just shook his head.

"I thought you were better."

What did that mean?

Before I could unravel the knot that had formed in my throat to ask, he had turned away and was now on his way down the steps.

I watched him go, his broad shoulders stretching the fabric of his black T-shirt that tapered down to a narrow waist. The guy was built like an athlete, yet he didn't play a sport.

His last words caused something inside me to break, my icy shell a memory.

He thought I was better? Better than what? I wasn't better. I was nobody.

❧

After Sterling had left, I had tried my best to pick up all the pills he had knocked from my hands. I even went under the bleachers to pick up the ones in the dirt, using the light from my cell phone. It had taken forever, but I thought I had gotten them all. I would hate for a kid to find them and think they were candy.

I had then stuffed them all back in the pill bottle and stashed it under my driver's seat. I couldn't sneak them back into my mother's medicine cabinet because they were all covered in dirt, so they would just have to wait there until I could dispose of them without danger.

Now I was parking my car in the designated spot on the circle driveway in front of my house. It was late, which meant he was going to be mad. He always got mad if I came home after dark. Then I would have to hear another lecture about psychos who abducted women who had car trouble off the side of the road. Not only that, but I wasn't supposed to be driving at all.

I blew out a breath. He was going to be in rare form. The prospect left me feeling exhausted and empty.

Most teenagers thought having a license meant freedom. Not for me. I got a different kind of weight shackled to my leg. The morning I took the test to get my driver's license, I woke to find my bedroom door covered in newspaper articles. Newspaper articles about teenagers who died in horrific car wrecks, drunk driving incidents, people burned alive in their cars, broken necks, or ran over on the side of the road. I was surprised I had passed my driver's test that morning. I had already been nervous, but after scanning those papers attached to my door, I wanted to curl into a ball and never leave my room.

I unplugged my phone from the car charger and looked at the screen. It was full of missed calls and text messages. Most were from my dad; others were from my mom, Miles, and the girls. All wondered where I was—my dad was getting more belligerent the later it got. I knew he was going to let me have it as soon as I walked through the door.

The front lights were blazing, and it seemed like every light inside the house was on, as well. I leaned back against the seat and closed my eyes, trying to calm my breathing by taking a deep breath, counting to five, and then releasing it for five. I had read online that this breathing exercise was good for warding off panic attacks.

I tried to visualize my happy place—a beach with warm, white sand and sparkling, clear blue water. However, the only blue I could see were Sterling Chapman's eyes.

My heart sank. I didn't want to think about Sterling. I also didn't want to think about what awaited me inside that house.

What if I just cranked the engine and drove off? What if I just drove until I ran out of gas and disappeared?

I knew that would be impossible. My father was not a tolerant man. He would see my running away as a betrayal. If I left in my car, he would report it stolen and have me arrested. No one crossed Derek Everly, even his own daughter.

The knock on my window startled me. I looked to my left to see my father's scowling face. He couldn't even wait for me to come inside.

As I cracked the door open, he stepped back. Then, before I could even get a foot on the ground, he started in on me.

"What the hell do you think you are doing? You aren't supposed to drive!"

I opened my mouth to answer, but he cut me off.

"Where have you been? Do you know what time it is? We have an appointment with the specialist tomorrow."

I sighed. It wasn't like I had just come from a place where I thought I would end my life or anything.

The "specialist" he was talking about was an orthopedic surgeon who specialized in sports medicine. Dad had pulled some strings—a client who was an NFL player with a DUI record—and had gotten an appointment with the doctor on a Thursday.

Before I could answer any of his questions, he was already opening his mouth again, so I just stared at my feet and hoped he would get this over with soon. I really wanted to crash once I got in the house.

"Do you know what happens to young women who stay out after dark?"

"Nothing good?" I replied, concentrating hard on the bright colors that made up the outside of my Asics running shoes. I loved them because they look like hot pink paint had been splattered all over them.

I heard him make a sound in his throat and looked up to see his eyes narrowed, and his lips thinned until they disappeared.

I quickly dropped my eyes in an act of submission. He never wanted me to look him in the eyes. He might ask me to, but his stare would turn so cold I couldn't bear to hold it for very long.

"Don't talk back to me, Allison Marie Everly."

I sighed again because, really, when you asked a question, didn't you expect an answer?

"When we lived in Forney growing up, a girl was abducted by a serial killer off the side of the road. All they found was her sock. A sock, Allison! That's all her parents had left to bury."

I had heard this story from the time I was mobile and could wander away from them. I knew his next words before he even opened his mouth to deliver them.

"You have to keep your phone with you at all times. But not only that, you have to actually answer it, Allison. Do you want us to bury your socks one day because you weren't within reach of your phone? Cars break down all the time. Yours shouldn't, but you never know when you might run over a nail or a tack. We have OnStar for a reason. Even if your phone is dead, you can use the OnStar to call us to let us know where you are."

I wouldn't be surprised if he already knew where I had been. I wouldn't put it past him to have a tracer on my phone or even my car. Derek Everly was an attorney, after all. A defense attorney who kept most of his clients out of jail. He knew all the tricks in the book.

"So, where were you?" When I didn't answer right away, he snapped, "Answer me!"

I jerked my head up and stuttered, "Um ... I-I-I was at school."

Self-loathing burned a hole in my stomach, and my heart felt heavy in my chest. I hated myself for stuttering in front of him. I hated exposing that weakness to him.

"This late? And in your uniform?" Doubt was heavy in his tone.

"Uh ... I ... uh ... I wanted to make sure I turned in my practice gear before school tomorrow."

I winced at the lie. It was terrible. I usually did so much better. I had gotten adept at lying over the years. I felt like I did nothing but lie to him. I lied about what I ate, because I wasn't allowed anything that might be remotely bad for me. I even collected change just so I could have some money to buy Twinkies or a juice out of the vending machine. You wouldn't believe all the places I had hidden food or hidden myself so I could eat the food I had been denied. I sometimes lied about where I was just because I could. It wasn't like I was at a crack house or in some boy's bedroom. Most of the time, I would just drive out to the lake and watch the water.

He eyed me in clear disbelief. "In your track uniform?"

I was so stupid. In my defense, it wasn't like I had anticipated coming home and getting caught. As a result, I wasn't prepared with an extra set of clothes.

It took everything I had to control my facial expression. "Um ... I didn't want them to forget I was part of the team. What if it's the last time I get to wear it?"

It was supposed to be ...

He eyed me again like he wanted to call me out on my lie, but I held his glacial stare steady as it froze me in place. I made sure to slow my breathing, relax my face, and keep my hands open instead of clenching them into fists like I wanted to. Any kind of hitch or tension would give me away. I learned that quickly after I had been caught a few times.

He let out a sigh then said, "Don't think like that. Negative thinking only brings negative results. Just go on in the house. You're too late to eat anything tonight. It'll either turn to sugar or it won't digest enough for you to burn it. Can't afford to pack on the pounds now that you can't run."

I wanted to roll my eyes. Heaven forbid I stored any kind of fat.

I grabbed my crutches from the back seat and hobbled toward the house, through the front door, and straight to my room without another word. My dad didn't even call out a goodnight like he usually did when I opened my bedroom door. Still, I flicked my fingers behind me anyway without looking back at him. I knew my mother was already in bed because staying up late "gave her wrinkles."

I closed the door and leaned against it, my head making a *thunk* against the wood. Then I slid down as the weight of despair took my breath away. This wasn't how tonight was supposed to go.

I rubbed the thigh of my hurt leg, my eyes burning right before tears slowly started leaking down my face, feeling hot against my cold skin.

Sterling's words played on a loop in my head, even after I was in bed, staring up at the darkened ceiling. Five little words had had the power to steal the only activity that ever brought me peace.

I thought you were better ...

BODY LIKE A BACKROAD

I pulled into my assigned parking spot in the student lot and threw the car in park. My dad had finally relented this morning and let me drive again. I had missed school yesterday and couldn't afford to miss another day and keep my position in the top ten of my class.

Dread sat heavily in my stomach like a stone, and my eyelids felt like they had sand in them. How could I go back into that building and pretend like the past two days had never happened?

I leaned back in the seat and tried to breathe deeply. I closed my eyes and pulled air into my lungs for five and released it for five. The hysteria that wanted to claw its way up my throat made it almost impossible. I knew I had to get out. Everyone was inside the building, and the bell would ring soon.

"Sterling!" a feminine voice cried out from somewhere behind my car, and my eyes shot open.

There he was, in the row in front of mine, the guy who had kept me up last night with his parting words. He was leaning against the trunk of an older model car that was rusted around the edges and had no paint, just that matte gray color.

He was just as beautiful as he was yesterday, dressed in worn jeans, a faded navy-blue Nirvana tee, and a slouchy gray toboggan that covered everything but the edge of his hairline. He hadn't noticed me —thank God for small miracles—so I watched him watch a girl, who had shiny black hair that was so black it was almost blue and so long that it hung to her waist, strut up to him.

The closer she got to him, the darker his expression became. By the time she stood in front of him, his mouth was an angry slash and his brows were furrowed. What made my breath catch were his eyes. They were hard like marble and flat.

The chick's head was bobbing side to side as she talked, and the more she talked, the scarier he looked.

I felt like a creeper as I watched him with this unknown female. Was she his girlfriend? No, his body language screamed, "go away." Maybe she was an ex?

I shouldn't care. Technically, I had a boyfriend. He wasn't a good boyfriend, but I hadn't seen the point in stirring up drama right before I killed myself by breaking up with him. I hadn't bothered to reply to any of his messages, or anyone else's from our group either. I guessed, if I was going to live, maybe I should scrape him off. My mother would hate it since she *loved* Miles, but she wasn't the one dating the cheating jerkwad. I wondered what she would think of Sterling?

His eyes sliced my way like I had called his name aloud, and I froze, his unusual eyes pinning me in place. I could feel heat creep up my neck and hit my cheeks. *Crap.*

When the girl gave him a harsh shove to one shoulder, his eyes came back to her. He said something, and then it was her turn to spot me.

She looked over her shoulder and narrowed her eyes while her lips pinched together like she had just sucked on a lemon. She was familiar, but I couldn't remember her name. She was gorgeous in an exotic way that surpassed everyone in my group of friends, even with her face screwed up like that.

She then turned back to him, and there she went, the head bobbing again. This time, though, she added an arm stabbing in my direction.

Sterling's face shut down. I knew he was done with whatever this girl was saying.

I didn't know if I should try to make a run for it—not that I could —or if I should just sit there and wait for them to end their drama. Sterling soon answered that question by simply brushing past the girl as he made his way toward the building.

I berated myself for the small pang I felt when he didn't spare me another glance. Sterling Chapman was off limits, and I would do well to remember that.

The girl, though, she shot me a venomous look before running after him as she called out his name again.

When the last bell sounded, I blew out a breath. It wasn't even nine o'clock and all I wanted to do was drive away and never look back. I just hoped no one tattled on me to my parents about being tardy to first period.

I opened my car door and gingerly slid out before limping to the trunk and pulling my backpack out. With it hitched up on my shoulders, I slowly trudged up to the door, crutches digging into my armpits, cursing Sterling Chapman and his speckled blue eyes.

❧

The good thing about being late was that Miles was already at his first period class. I knew he would be waiting for me outside the door when the bell rang, as usual. This time, though, he would be demanding answers.

I had successfully avoided him since the accident. I hadn't answered any of his texts or calls. He had been busy with baseball, or so his text said, so he hadn't been to my house. Thank God. Now, I was going to have to finally deal with him.

Irritation and weariness battled for predominance when I saw him waiting beside the door, a scowl marring his classically handsome face.

"Why haven't you answered my calls or texts? I've been worried ..." He pushed away from the wall and came to my side.

I bit my lip to keep myself from calling him a liar. I wondered if I would have a permanent indention on my bottom lip from the sheer number of times I had bit it in a day. I always thought biting back my words was better than letting them spew forth. Honestly, I knew even if I did voice my thoughts, they would go unheard. So, what was the point?

Miles lifted his arm and tried to wrap it around my shoulders, which brought me out of my contemplation and caused me to stumble. Pain cut like a knife from the back of my thigh to between my shoulder blades.

"Shoot! Sorry, Ally." Miles' contrite voice broke through the haze of pain.

I gritted my teeth and held back the snappy retort I wanted to lash him with. Who in their right mind tried to put their arm around someone who was struggling to walk with crutches?

"It's okay," I grumbled.

We were quiet a moment, whereas the people around us called out greetings and Miles gave flicked fingers and chin lifts to his buds and teammates. I ignored them all. It was rude and out of character for me not to wave or say hi, but my freaking leg hurt, thanks to the idiot at my side.

"So, why didn't you call me?"

I shrugged. It wasn't like I was going to tell him the truth.

"I'm your boyfriend, Ally. You're supposed to call or at least text me back after something like this goes down."

Resentment welled up inside of me. Maybe if he was a *true* boyfriend, I would have called, but he wasn't.

"Look, it's all been a blur, Miles. My phone died"—a lie—"I've been doped up on pain medicine"—another lie—"and my dad has been pretty adamant about me getting rest. So, I just haven't had time." Which was actually the truth. It was always good to mix some truth in with a lie. In my experience, it made them more believable.

"Okay," he acquiesced.

See? Worked like a charm.

We made it to my next class and paused by the door. He kept his body between me and the people going inside. At last he was doing something right.

"Tell me you're okay at least." His lips were turned down, his brow furrowed in concern.

"I'm fine," I lied ... again.

"That's good." He cleared his throat. "So, I'll see you at lunch?" He flashed me a mega-watt smile.

"Sure," I said, focusing on the place over his shoulder, knowing what would come next.

When he leaned forward and kissed my cheek, it took everything inside me not to cringe away. It made my skin crawl to think about where those lips had been this week alone. When I got inside the classroom, I would discreetly clean my skin with hand sanitizer.

That out of the way, he loped off down the hall toward the Ag building. His next period was athletics, so I didn't have to worry about him waiting for me after next period. He would just meet me at lunch ... like always.

Sigh.

All morning, I felt the looks and whispers. Several people came up to see if I was okay and to give me awkward hugs in class. Most of the kids were nice, even sympathetic, and helped me with doors, getting stuff out of my locker, putting on my backpack, and getting a chair to prop my leg up on. It really was *nice*, but it was starting to grate on my nerves. I was looking forward to lunch, hoping people would be too preoccupied getting food to bother me.

A girl could dream.

I had set my lunch bag on the table and was about to sit down at my usual spot across from Miles, when a clear, sultry voice started singing Sam Hunt's "Body Like A Backroad" over to my left.

I turned my head to see Sterling standing at the top of the stage by one of the columns that winged the edge, rocking his hips from side to side. The rest of the kids surrounding him were still seated but started drumming to the beat of the song with anything handy, bobbing their heads along with their makeshift music. All except four—the girl from the parking lot and three others. She just rolled her eyes and walked off, the others following.

Sterling began moving his hand up and down like it was cruising over hills and valleys. Then he pretended he was gripping a steering wheel. When he got to the end of the chorus, he raised both hands and made the shape of an hourglass.

During the entire performance, his eyes never left mine, and I couldn't take my eyes off him.

A giggle coming from my right broke the spell. I looked around the cafetorium to see everyone watching not just him, but me, as well. My ears felt hot, and my chest constricted as I ducked my head, refusing to look back up at the stage area.

"Was Sterling Chapman singing that to *you?*"

I didn't like the way Laura emphasized "you," like I was some three-eyed alien who didn't inspire boys to spontaneously break out in song.

I turned my head in her direction to see her smirking at me, but before I could reply, Miles barked, "What the hell, Ally!"

I swung my head back to see a red-faced Miles glaring at me and grinding his teeth. I actually felt a genuine laugh bubble up in my throat, but I fought it back down. It wouldn't do to laugh at Mr. I-can't-keep-my-dick-in-my-pants when he felt threatened. I doubted he really felt jealousy over me. It was more like he was pissed that another guy was paying attention to something he considered his.

Swallowing repeatedly to fight back the laugh, I sat up in my chair and took in Miles' classically handsome face. He was good-looking with his wavy blond hair and blue eyes. Tall, but not as tall as Sterling. And where Sterling was built like a swimmer with long, lean muscles, Miles was bulkier. He spent hours in the weight room, adding to his already muscular frame, where Sterling just looked naturally in shape.

"Are you screwing him?" he asked through gritted teeth.

This time, I didn't hold in the urge to laugh. I let it flow freely. The giggles burst from my belly and mingled with a thousand butterflies at the thought of being with Sterling in that way. I wanted to say, "I wish." Instead, I denied his accusation.

"Of course she isn't," came Laura's unneeded input. "You know she's practically the Virgin Mary."

A chorus of female giggles accompanied hers, and I felt my laughter die a swift death.

I looked over at Laura and caught her giving Miles a knowing look. I peeked at him from the corner of my eye to watch his reaction, but he was studiously ignoring her, his focus solely on me. He knew I was a virgin, and it wasn't from a lack of trying on his part to change that status. I just didn't feel that way toward him anymore. That had died when I figured out he had lost his virginity long ago.

Again, I questioned why I was even with him anymore. There

wasn't any substance to our relationship. He didn't have a clue or just didn't care that I was unhappy, that I couldn't stand being under my father's thumb for a second longer. It was all so ... shallow.

I glanced around the table full of people I used to consider my friends and studied them. They were all the same. They looked the same, dressed the same, talked the same. The only difference was hair color and gender. The girls even had their hair styled the same, and I knew, if I looked in a mirror right now, I would see the same.

I would see my long, brown hair in fashionable waves, my eyes lined, my cheeks shimmery, and my clothes would be a variation of the girls around me.

Bile rose from my stomach and stole my appetite. I wanted to run to the girls' bathroom with a pair of scissors and hack off my hair. I wanted to wash this crap off my face. I wanted to scream and cry and rant. I could feel the pressure begin to build inside me, ready to explode.

Sometimes, I thought there was a beast living within me. I felt it rage and twist, writhing in agony, throwing itself against the steel bars of its cage.

I was that beast.

I didn't realize I was panting until I clumsily stood, knocking my chair over, and snatched my lunch from the table. I couldn't catch my breath.

"Ally ..." Miles' voice tried to break through the suffocating sensation that threatened to overtake me. Everything was too loud, too bright, too fast ...

Without looking back at any of them, I took off, hobbling as fast as I could until I was down the hall. There, I found myself a little alcove close to the gym, squeezed between two vending machines. It was dark and quiet since everyone was still at lunch. I felt ridiculous squeezed in there with my crutches, but I needed to escape. I needed the solitude.

I took a deep breath and prepared to start my breathing exercises, when I heard a clinking sound and a familiar hum echo off the walls of the small enclosure.

I peeked my head out and around the machine to see Sterling, eyes concentrated on the choices offered, his hand in his pocket, jangling the change there. He obviously didn't notice me because, when he came to a decision and moved to the change slot right by my face, he jerked back with a yelp.

"Jeez! What are you doing?" he puffed with his hand over his heart. "How did you even fit in there?"

He stepped in close and peered into the space from above my head, which placed my face an inch away from his chest. I really should have moved back, but I couldn't help myself ... I breathed him in. I inhaled and hoped he didn't realize what I was doing.

I didn't know if the woodsy smell was his cologne, soap, or the deodorant he used. Or maybe it was just him. Wherever it came from, I loved it.

When I took another sniff, the rusty rumble coming from said chest had me freezing in place.

"Whatcha doing, Allison?" he asked, laughter coating his tone.

Caught.

Feeling the blood drain from my face, I bit my lip and mumbled, "Um..." while still staring at his navy T-shirt covered chest.

"Did you just smell me?"

"Um ..." What could I say? I wasn't going to admit to sniffing his chest like some weirdo.

"I have to get a whiff of you now. It's only fair."

What?

Shock rooted me to the spot, but I quickly, and albeit reluctantly, lifted and crossed my arms as his words sunk into my Sterling-induced haze.

Would he try to bend down and put his face in my boobs since I sniffed *his* chest? I shouldn't find that appealing. Nope. Not one bit. One panic-inducing thought struck me, though. What if I stunk? I had started sweating when I made my mad dash from the cafetorium. Heck, I was sweating now just thinking about sweating.

"Are you whimpering?"

"N-no ..." I stammered.

I felt what I assumed was his nose pressed to the top of my head, which meant he wasn't going to be smelling my chest. I felt both relief and oddly disappointed.

Minutes that felt like hours passed as I waited for him to move or at least say something. Then I felt something press against my scalp that suspiciously felt like his lips before he lifted away.

"Mmm ... You smell clean, and your hair is so soft," he said as he reached up, fingering the strands near my face.

What was going on? Yesterday, he told me he thought I was better, and now, he was in my personal space, smelling me and telling me my hair was soft? What changed? Did he feel sorry for me now? Is that what this was about?

"What kind of shampoo do you use?"

Sterling was still touching my hair. I couldn't believe he was going to stand there and ask what kind of shampoo I used after he interrupted my attempted suicide yesterday and my witnessing his drama in the parking lot this morning.

I had yet to look at his face, knowing I would get caught up in his gorgeous multicolored eyes, so I kept my eyes trained on his chest as I whispered, "Dove."

"What was that?"

I coughed to clear my throat before repeating, "Dove," a little louder.

I wanted to ask him the questions that were burning holes in my brain, like why he had said what he said to me yesterday, why he had sung to me back in the cafetorium, or why had he touched and sniffed my hair. However, the bell rang, signaling the end of lunch, while I just stammered and stuttered like an idiot.

"Well, I'll have to buy that brand next time. Smells good." He gave me a wink, and then he was gone before I could collect myself enough to ask the questions that were on the tip of my tongue. He just left me standing between two vending machines, wondering what on earth had just happened.

A PERFECT TRAGEDY

After school, two days after the life-altering meet, I was sitting in the waiting room of the sports injury specialist/orthopedic that our family doctor recommended, staring at the cool blue walls, the smell of muscle cream heavy in my nose. I shifted in the chair and winced at the pinch in the back of my thigh. I was sore but not healed.

My phone went off in my pocket, but I ignored it. It was probably Miles again. He had been messaging me nonstop since after lunch. I didn't have the energy to deal with him, or the questions Laura and our friends would have if it was one of them calling, especially when I didn't have the answers myself.

"Ally, honey, your phone is buzzing," my mom whispered like I couldn't feel it going off in my pocket.

"I don't feel like talking."

"If you don't feel like talking, then shut it off," my dad berated.

Shutting it off required lifting my booty to slide it out of my pocket. I wasn't sure I had it in me to make that movement without yelping in pain.

When my phone went off again, my father cut his eyes to me. I drew myself inward against that look and was about to lift my butt when the nurse called, "Allison Everly?"

I blew out a breath. Saved by the nurse.

I grabbed the arms of the chair and lifted myself up as Mom handed me my crutches. Then I limped my way to the African-American lady dressed in rose pink scrubs and holding a clipboard.

"Hi, Allison. If y'all would just follow me." She held the door open with one hand until I felt my father's heat at my back, then she breezed past the nurses' station and down the hall. Mom hurried around and kept pace with me at my side like she was afraid I would fall.

"You okay?" she asked me softly.

I simply nodded.

We finally made it to where the nurse waited, again holding the door open one-handed. I squinted at the name tag that was pinned to her scrub jacket and saw her name was Athena. Cool name. I told her so.

"Thanks, honey. Now, if y'all will just step on in to exam room three."

Slowly, we made our way inside. Mom gestured over to the exam table, and I paused in front of it. She took my crutches, leaned them against the wall, and then practically lifted me up on the papered surface. Guilt stabbed me like a hot knife in my stomach. Mom had broken her back a few years ago in a car wreck, and it still spasmed and ached. That was why she had the prescription for Tramadol.

When I was situated, she stepped back then instantly started massaging her lower back. A sick feeling curled in my stomach that she might be hurting, and I had taken her medication.

My dad remained standing, leaning against the wall that held a poster of the inside of a knee joint, while Mom sat in a chair by the examination table and pulled her designer purse into her lap. With her taupe claws, she picked the zipper on the side.

When my phone went off again, my dad clenched his jaw and shot me a look under his heavy brow. Okay, I had to figure this out. I could lean back and slide the phone out of my pocket, but it would probably hurt. Or, I could stand up and pull it out, which would probably hurt, too, and would take a great amount of effort. Why hadn't I gotten it out when I had gotten up in the waiting room?

As the buzzing in my pocket continued, I heard one word. "Allison."

"Do you want me to get it out for you?" my mom asked with a note of apprehension in her voice. I didn't know if it was in the face of my father's annoyance, or if she worried I was going to hurt myself getting this phone out.

"No, I'll get it."

I gritted my teeth and went with what seemed like the fastest option. I lifted my hips up a smidge and sucked in a sharp breath at the pain that radiated throughout my back, butt, and leg. I slid the phone out and ever so gently placed my butt back in the seat. Then I gave Dad my own look before I peeked down and saw a plethora of notifications. I scrolled through them and saw several texts and missed calls from Miles, Laura, Ariel, and other people in our circle. There were also Instagram notifications, and two yellow Snapchat notifications from Miles. I made a face.

"What?" Mom asked, eyes big as she leaned forward.

I snapped my mouth closed hard enough that my teeth clinked together, and then I immediately hit the button on the side of my phone that darkened the screen and placed it face down on my lap.

"Nothing. Just a lot of people sending me stuff and calling."

"Of course they would! People love you, honey," she cried, patting my good leg.

I made a strange sound in my throat as I tried to hold back the chuckle that wanted to rumble out.

When Dad blew out a frustrated breath, I looked over, seeing him scowling at the door, still propped against the wall with his hands in his pockets.

"What's taking him so long?" he grumbled.

When Mom sighed and rolled her eyes, I felt mine get huge. She never said a word or showed any sign of impatience with my dad ... ever. He was a man who wouldn't appreciate nor tolerate it.

My eyes jerked back to him as he turned his scowl on my mother but didn't say anything. Probably because the door handle jangled then was slowly opened, revealing a tall, athletic-looking man dressed in a black polo and khaki pants. He held his hand out first to me and introduced himself.

"Hi, I'm Dr. Richards."

When I took his hand, he gave me a solid, firm shake then shook my mother's then my dad's hands.

"So, what's going on, Allison?" He grabbed the stool that was underneath the computer desk and rolled to my side.

I opened my mouth to reply, but my dad cut me off.

"She dislocated her hip—"

"No offense, Mr. Everly," Dr. Richards interrupted him, "but I'd rather hear it from the person I'm going to be treating."

My dad's face darkened, and the muscles in his jaw started working.

A sick sort of satisfaction welled up inside me. I felt the corners of my lips curve upward. I didn't think I had ever seen anyone put my dad in his place. He relished his role as master of his universe, and I knew it was killing him that he had no control in here.

I wondered, since his pride was stung, if he would make us leave, but the doctor in front of me was supposed to be one of the best sports injury specialists in the state. It looked like Derek Everly was going to have to stand there and shut up. I had to fight back a giggle.

"So, Allison, what happened?" asked Dr. Richards.

I told him everything. I told him about the popping sound my leg had been making for weeks prior to what had happened Tuesday. How it hadn't felt right, especially before the race. I told him about what had happened as I went over the third hurdle and the utter agony I had felt. And he just listened, nodding after almost everything I said like he knew exactly what I was talking about.

When I finished, he had me get up and walk—more like hobble—around the examining room while he squatted against the wall and watched.

"What is this accomplishing?" my dad asked, a petulant edge to his tone.

"I'm evaluating her injury and range of motion," Dr. Richards replied, not even looking at my father.

When he was satisfied, Dr. Richards got up and walked to the exam table.

"Now, young lady, if you'll just make your way over here, I'll help you back up onto the table."

I limped over as a constant burning pain shot up the back of my thigh, all the way up to my lower back. When I was close, he practically lifted me onto the table then had me slump forward—evidently slumping your shoulders was a test for nerve damage—and then lie back so he could lift my leg to see how far it would stretch. When I cried out after only lifting it less than halfway up, he gently lowered my leg back down.

All these things made the previous burn in my leg intensify to a flaming burn. My heartbeat pulsed in my lower butt cheek, sweat dotted my forehead, and I tried to regulate my breathing by taking long, slow inhales and exhales. I knew these were not good things. In fact, I could feel the building tension in the room swirl around me, almost visibly radiating from my father.

Dr. Richards then helped me turn to lie on my stomach. I dreaded the next set of tests he was going to conduct.

I tried to get comfortable, but every time I moved, the paper covering the table would make that crinkly-crunchy sound.

I heard Dr. Richards walk away, and then the sound of the door being opened. I looked over my shoulder to see him poke his head out as he called for Athena.

"Allison, get still," my dad snapped.

I looked in the direction of his voice and saw that he had moved to stand near Mom's chair.

She looked up at him, a scowl pinched on her beautiful face as she hissed, "Derek."

Athena bustled in with her tablet in hand, interrupting the potential argument.

Ignoring them, Dr. Richards strolled back to me, saying, "Now, I'm going to look at your injury. I may move your clothing around, but everything will stay covered."

I felt him move the hem of my shorts up then prod the area below my butt cheek. I jerked and sucked in a breath as a stab of pain jolted me.

"Tender there?"

"Yes, sir," I replied through clenched teeth.

"Athena, mark posterior compartment, biceps femoris."

He poked and prodded all around my thigh, my knee, and lower back, finding areas that weren't as painful but still sore. He had Athena make a note, and then had me lift my foot up so my knee was bent, and proceeded to pull my foot softly by the heel forward. I practically growled in pain as I gave him little resistance.

He was slowly lowering my foot back down when he asked Athena for the iPad. I closed my eyes and let my forehead drop to the white sanitary paper. I didn't know how much time had passed, but I was almost asleep when he cleared his throat.

"I just looked over the x-rays from the hospital and can confirm that you had a dislocation. That'll be sore for a while, but I can infer from everything that it was manipulated back into position correctly." He looked up from the iPad and gave me a small smile.

I tried to flip my body back over on my own so I could see him better, but both Athena and my mother hurried over and carefully got me into an upright position.

Dr. Richards chuckled then continued with his assessment. "Since it was promptly treated, there shouldn't be any lasting damage. The joint will be weak for a while, and you'll need to give it and the surrounding muscles adequate time to heal or your risk for another dislocation will significantly increase. For now, you'll need lots of RICE."

"Rice?" I asked in confusion, not seeing how the grain would help a sports injury.

"Rest, ice, compression, and elevation. R.I.C.E." He chuckled again, and I felt my cheeks get hot. *Duh, I knew that.*

I could feel my dad's irritated gaze drilling a hole into my head, but I refused to look his way. I already felt stupid enough. I peeked at my mother instead, who was again giving my dad a look. She now held a small notebook and a pencil in her hand, evidently taking notes on the doctor's orders.

"Will she be able to compete again this season?" Dad's hands were out of his pockets and curled into fists at his sides.

That was the million-dollar question.

I sucked in a breath and held it while I waited for the doctor to declare my fate. It was like waiting for a judge to pronounce a guilty verdict and the sentencing.

Dr. Richards cut his eyes back to my dad and answered reluctantly but firmly, "No, most definitely not."

The breath that I had been holding seemed to freeze in my chest.

The air in the room became stifling from the tension. I could feel the negative emotions rolling off my father in waves.

Oblivious to the death rays my father was probably shooting him, Dr. Richards turned back to me, his eyes filled with commiseration. "In addition to the dislocation, you've strained your hamstring. From my examination, it looks to be a grade two tear, so your leg needs to be kept elevated and ice applied to the bruised area for twenty minutes every two hours for the next forty-eight hours. I'm going to replace the compression bandage with one that will help with the bleeding and swelling before y'all leave."

"So, PT can't get her back on the track by the district meet? I don't believe that. We'll get a second—"

The compassion morphed out of Dr. Richard's face as he turned and faced off with my dad. His face looked as if it had been chiseled from stone as he said in a cool voice, "You put your daughter back on that track, I'll call Child Protective Services."

"Now, wait a damn min—"

"No, Mr. Everly, you wait a minute. Seventeen-year-olds do not dislocate their hips. It takes a tremendous amount of force to do so, usually something like a car accident in someone so young. But I believe both her hamstring and her hip were compromised by over-stretching and overuse."

"That's not—"

"Shut up, Derek, and listen to the man! You're not a doctor!" my mother snapped, her eyes slit as she glared up at my father.

My mouth dropped open at her unusual show of defiance.

I looked at my dad and could see the fury written in every line on his face and lit in his burning brown eyes like a blaze. He opened his mouth to reply, but then snapped it shut when Dr. Richards spoke.

"I'm the best orthopedic surgeon in the state—my clientele proves that. I've treated professional athletes and have orchestrated many returns to the sports they're paid to play. In my *expert* opinion, she's done hurdling for the year. That hip is going to take time to heal and her body probably needs the rest.

"If you put her out there too soon and her hip dislocates again, it could become a chronic problem for the rest of her life. She may even have to have hip replacement surgery before her fortieth birthday. Your decision could affect her mobility for the rest of her life, her quality of life when her days as a track athlete ends. Now is the time to think about what this could mean for Allison long-term, Mr. Everly."

"Fine. Mandy, get whatever else Allison needs. I'll meet you at the car," he gritted out through clenched teeth, not even looking at me again as he brushed by Dr. Richards and stormed out. The door practically vibrated from the vicious pull he used to slam it closed.

"I'm so sorry, Dr. Richards," my mother said quietly, her voice sounding far away.

I felt weird, like my mind couldn't process what was happening to me. I opened my mouth to say something, anything, but the words wouldn't come out. *Not run track ever?* That was still a foreign concept, an unknown entity. I was a hurdler. That was *me*.

When I had decided to end my life, it was a given I wouldn't be running again, but hearing it out loud from a doctor seemed to make it more real. Especially now that my demise had been waylaid.

Official.

"Allison," I heard Dr. Richards call.

I blinked my eyes back into focus and tried to concentrate on what he was telling me.

"Now, I see you already have a pair of crutches. That's good. I don't think you'll need them for very long. I want to keep you on an anti-inflammatory for a week, so I'll write you a script for that."

He handed me the prescription and, for some reason, that made me feel weirder. No adult had ever let me take charge of anything, even my own care. Everything was either dictated or handled for me. If my dad could arrange it and afford it, he would probably have someone brush my teeth for me every morning and night to ensure I was doing it correctly.

"I'm also going to call over to Jamie Saunders' office. She's a physical therapist my office works with. We'll get you set up with that over the next few weeks. My receptionist will get you on the schedule to come back and see me a month from now, so I can check your progress. Jenny can also make you an appointment with Jamie if you'd like?"

I nodded while my mother answered vocally. "Yes, that'd be wonderful. Thank you."

He tapped the screen of his iPad, likely making a note, then handed the device to the silent Athena who I had forgotten was even in the room. Then he moved toward the door.

"Don't forget, RICE, RICE, baby," he said in a strange hissing way, followed by funny beat sounds.

When my mom laughed, I knew he was trying to lighten the atmosphere.

"Don't tell me you've never heard of Vanilla Ice?" Dr. Richards exclaimed.

When I shook my head, he clutched his chest and sighed dramatically, which made Mom laugh even more.

"Now, y'all get out of here before you break my heart even more."

Then he was gone.

§.

The ride back home was somber. Neither of my parents spoke to the other. The tension felt stagnate in the air between them, thick and cloying, making my insides churn. Dad didn't ask about what Dr. Richards had said after he left, and my mother didn't tell him.

Unease slithered over my skin like a snake. I worked on controlling the pain and my unease by counting my breaths. I tried to suck in as much air as I could and expanded my chest until it was almost painful. I then exhaled it through my nose for as long as I could until it felt like my belly was hollow.

"Don't we need to stop by the pharmacy?" I asked when we pulled into our driveway. I had forgotten about it until I saw it poking out of the outer pocket of my mother's purse as she got out of the car. I had handed it to her before I had tried to get off the exam table back at the doctor's office.

My dad didn't say anything. He just got out and slammed the door.

My mom poked her head back in the car and said, "Just hang tight, and I'll come around to help you. Don't worry about the prescription. I'll get it tomorrow." She winked. She freaking winked!

What was going on?

When we got inside, instead of going straight to my room and wallowing in my bed, my mother parked me on the couch in front of the TV and handed me the remote. She even brought out my pillow from my bed and tucked it under my head then collected all the accent pillows from the furniture in the living room. It took a bit to figure out how to elevate my injured hip and thigh but in the end, we got it to where I could get semi-comfortable. No matter which way I moved, it either hurt or felt awkward.

"I'll go get an ice pack so we can start icing."

I didn't say anything. I just fired up Netflix and turned on my favorite show, *Gilmore Girls*. I wanted to be like Rory. She wasn't athletic, but she was really smart. Her mom was awesome, and she rarely saw her dad. The only pressures in her life were the ones she placed on herself.

"Here, lift up a little, honey. I'll put the ice pack under you."

After doing that, she pulled out her phone—I assumed to set the timer for twenty minutes—and then walked back toward the hall. I thought she had gone to the kitchen, but then I heard a door slam from the direction of my father's office.

I froze when the yelling started. Then I reached for the remote, paused the television, and strained my ears to listen. I could hear the high-pitched shrieks of my mother and the low-timbered fury of my father's bellows. However, I couldn't understand the words because distance and a thick wooden door muffled the sound.

My mind reeled, and a heavy feeling settled in the pit of my stomach. What on earth was going on? They never fought. My mother constantly bowed to the superior knowledge of her husband and made it her purpose in life to accommodate his every whim.

Finally, it stopped. Neither parent appeared for what felt like forever. The first to emerge was my father with a leather duffle in his hand. His face looked carved from stone, but his eyes were a burning inferno of rage. Fear skittered up my spine, and my limbs turned cold. Then, when he stabbed a finger in my direction, I jumped.

Through clenched teeth, he growled, "I have to leave for a while, Allison, but you need to remember your place. Just because you're out for the season doesn't mean you can start stuffing your face. You may be no good right now, but we need to start thinking about—"

"Derek!" my mom clipped over him.

As his eyes moved to her, the look of pure malice that came over his face took my breath away.

"You need to leave." She gave him a look I couldn't read.

My mouth dropped open when he spun on his heels and stalked out, slamming the door behind him. Then my eyes moved back to my mom, who was still standing at the edge of the room, her eyes closed and face pained.

"W-what's going on? Where is he going?" Not that I wasn't happy he was leaving. I was freaking ecstatic, but the whole scene was so bizarre I couldn't help asking.

She opened her eyes and rotated her neck to look at me. "He's going out of town on business."

"But—"

"I should start dinner," she interrupted, moving toward the kitchen.

I watched her go, a feeling, more like a knowing, washing over me. Something had changed. Something so huge that I knew my life would never be the same.

❧

After finishing icing my leg, I hobbled over to a bar stool in our kitchen and watched as my mother jerkily chopped up vegetables and threw them into the salad bowl with more force than was probably necessary. Her face was red, and the lines around her eyes and mouth were tight. She grabbed a cucumber and basically murdered it in front of my eyes. I was entranced as I then watched her stab into a tomato and all the guts shot out.

Have you ever looked at a knife and wondered: what would happen if you put it to your skin? Would it hurt or, in some sick way, would you find relief? Every time I looked at one, the temptation right at my fingertips, I wondered. However, fear of the pain always prevented me from doing it. Plus, I wasn't big on blood. The sight of it always made me weak in the knees and bile would rise to my throat. So, I just avoided anything sharp when I was alone. Just in case ...

I shifted my focus to my mother. She was an aging beauty queen and absolutely gorgeous. If Marilyn Monroe had lived to be in her forties, she would have looked like my mother. Platinum blonde hair with an hourglass figure that gave Kim K. a run for her money. She even had a beauty mark near her mouth.

I wasn't close to my mother anymore. She had become more like my father's second-in-command, his mouthpiece when he wasn't here. The enforcer of rules. However, something had sparked in her today. A new woman had emerged while we were in that doctor's office.

"Shut up, Derek, and listen to the man! You're not a doctor!"

My phone vibrated on the counter, taking me out of the memory. I looked down to see I had another snap from Miles. I rolled my eyes and ignored it. It was probably another shirtless selfie of him in his bathroom, proclaiming he "wished I was there." He hadn't gotten brave enough to send me a D pic yet, but I was nervous that was in my future. I was sure Laura probably had a collection of them.

"Who was that?" my mom asked as she used those claw-like utensil things to mix up the salad.

"Miles," I sighed.

She ignored the sigh, her eyes lighting up at the mention of Miles. She loved Miles. I would suspect him of sleeping with her, too, if she was married to any other man. I wasn't the only person my father had clutched in his iron fist. He was just as controlling of her as he was of me. They would have to be awfully creative to be having an affair.

"Tell him I said hi!"

"Will do," I lied, pretending to type him a message.

"We should have him over for dinner this weekend."

"Mmhmm ..." I replied, eyes still on my phone. I wasn't going to invite Miles anywhere.

I clicked on the snap, just so the alert would go away, and what do you know? Shirtless Miles, but no message this time, just his nipples and that arrogant smirk I had found irresistible once upon a time.

I eyed the picture dispassionately before it disappeared. He was attractive, but his looks had lost their luster. Why was I with him when there was nothing there? That question was coming up more and more lately.

"I just love that boy. So charming and athletic ..."

Oh yeah, that's why.

The last thing I needed was her in my business.

My phone went off again, and I looked down, expecting it to be Miles again. Instead, it was a snap from someone I didn't know. *Perfect-tragedy5.*

I opened it, seeing a picture of the lake as the sun went down. It was beautiful, even more beautiful than yesterday's sunset. The sky was painted in blues, pinks, and oranges; clouds soft and glowing warm; the light winking off the smooth-as-glass water. The text band read, "*Sunsets over the lake. 1 reason to stay.*"

My breath caught, and then panic squeezed my heart like a vise.

Sterling.

Before she could see my face, which probably advertised my panic, Mom's phone rang, and she walked over to where it was charging. When she answered, a dark cloud moved over her face. She turned around and moved to the edge of the room as she hissed into the phone, "I told you not to ..."

I kept my eyes down on my phone. The picture was gone, but the memory of it was enough to score my soul. Its beauty had sparked something inside me, a hopefulness I had never felt as I gazed into its glowing warmth. I had been numb for so long, and I didn't want to feel again, yet Sterling was making me feel with little effort on his part. I didn't even know him.

Being able to feel meant I could get hurt, and I couldn't bear the weight of emotion on my heart anymore. It was too hard, too messy. The people in my life had slowly leeched everything good from me. I was an ash casting, ready to blow into dust.

And now, if I had any appetite at all, it had just died. The urge to flee, to be alone was too much. I couldn't even make my lungs work, and I desperately needed air.

I peeked at my mother who had her back to me and was talking quietly yet angrily into her phone. Her posture was stiff and almost vibrating. She leaned against the doorway, and I saw her reach around to massage her lower back. A knot formed in my belly, tight and hot. She was in pain.

My throat felt thick, and tears welled in my eyes. I would figure something out soon. Maybe I could clean her pain pills up and put them back? I'd have to wait until I could get out to my car without her noticing.

I scooted my stool back, grabbed my crutches, and limped to my room. I didn't bother showering, I just changed into my pajamas and crawled under the covers. The sobs I had been holding back were choking me. The tears I had been holding at bay broke loose. I could cry here, alone in my room. The darkness, a blanket of security as I curled into myself and let them flow.

At one point, I heard the door open and close, but nothing else.

I was weak. So freaking weak and powerless. Why wouldn't God just let me die? Why did I have to even be born? The hollowness inside me was infinite. My heart felt heavy, like every beat was a Herculean feat. It, along with my mind and body, were sinking, too tired to fight the pull of the encroaching darkness. I wanted to slip under. I wanted the peace it would bring. To not feel a single thing ever again.

My life was just like Sterling's Snapchat username.

A perfect tragedy.

SUCKER FOR PAIN

I was in the parking lot at school, sitting on the hood of my car, waiting for my mother to pick me up for physical therapy. The doctor's office had called her that morning, telling her they had gotten me an appointment for today. She texted me after first period and said she would be here at lunch.

My eyes were still swollen and puffy from crying myself to sleep last night, and my head felt like it was full of cotton. The sun was high, but the air still held a bite of chill. It was track weather. I could feel it in the air. The crisp, coolness would grow colder as the sun set, and something about it invigorated me; made me anticipate the beginning of another season. I could picture the stadium lights glowing against the dark sky, the crowd milling about like ants, the sound of the starter gun cracking into the silence, and the eruption of cheers at the end of a race.

Only ... I wouldn't have another season.

I gazed around the parking lot and let my eyes wander toward the track that lay behind it. Memories of me standing in this exact spot flooded my consciousness.

My father would usually take me to school on meet days. He did this so I could ride home with him afterward and listen to him talk about what I could improve on or the mistakes I had made. Basically, things that made me want to bash my head against the passenger window. I didn't think he had really cared if I listened or not. He just enjoyed hearing his own voice.

I wouldn't miss that.

I also wouldn't miss the weigh-ins, the constant *click* of the stopwatch, or the overtraining and stretching. I wouldn't miss the sound of my father's voice as he told me how inadequate I was.

I wouldn't miss *him*.

Not wanting to think about him or track any longer, I was about to pull my earphones out of my bag and fire up one of my playlists when I felt the warmth of someone's body nudge mine.

"Hey," Sarah said as she dropped her bag on the concrete at our feet.

"Hey. What are you doing out here?"

"Doctor's appointment. Jean Adele is taking me to get my birth control pills."

I nodded because, well, she *needed* them.

Sarah Burns was a member of our clique, and the only one who was on the track team with me. The rest of the girls were cheerleaders or on the volleyball team. I had been a cheerleader my freshman year, until my dad wanted me to solely concentrate on track. In a way, I was grateful, since Laura and Ariel were cheerleaders.

When those two were together, no one was safe. They would pick a girl apart until she was a raw and bloody mess. I hated it. Hated how they would comment on a girl's looks, her clothes, her family, or even the way she talked. If they had a boyfriend, they made sure to flirt with him. It was disgusting.

Sarah could be like that when she was with Laura and those girls. Mostly, she was a chameleon. She would act like the people she was around and told you everything she thought you wanted to hear. That made her a favorite of Laura's because she loved feeling like queen bee, and Sarah supplied that crap.

She also supplied info.

"So ..." she drew out.

I held my breath and lifted my brows as I waited for the inevitable question.

"Why was Sterling Chapman singing to you yesterday?"

I studied her face and saw the open curiosity there. What I didn't like was the eagerness that laced her voice. She was like a dog shaking with anticipation of finding the bone her master wanted her to bring back.

I sighed and decided to search out my headphones as I said, "I don't know."

And that was the truth. I didn't know why he had sung that song while he looked at me. I had thought he didn't like me, if I went by the words he had told me after knocking the pills from my hand.

I thought you were better.

Would I ever forget those words? They crept into my mind when I least expected them.

I wanted to be better, but I felt like it was too late for me. My time had passed.

"He's so freakin' hot," she said dreamily.

I didn't say anything. I turned on my headphones, activated the Bluetooth on my phone, and then waited for them to sync.

"I'd do him."

My jaw clenched. I had the urge to shove her off my car because she would so do him. She had done most of the athletic teams at school, and maybe a few coaches, too. Her panties would be considered ankle warmers if she wore any at all.

When my phone finally connected with my headphones, I inserted one earbud as I told Sarah, "No offense, but I have a screaming headache and want to zone out." I made a show of fiddling with the other one.

Annoyance flashed across her face before she hid it with a pout. She wasn't going to let me off the hook that easily. There was gossip to be had, and she was going to be the one to dig it out.

"Tell me something; a guy just doesn't sing about a girl's body like that without getting in on some of that action. You hooking up with him on the low?" She waggled her eyebrows up and down and nudged me with her shoulder as she added, "I won't tell Miles."

I snorted. I wanted to say, "Yeah, I bet you know all about that," but what came out of my mouth was, "Nothing to tell. Like I said, I don't know why he sang to me." That said, I put the other earbud in my ear and hit play.

The first song on my playlist was from the *Suicide Squad* movie, "Sucker for Pain." I closed my eyes and tried to quiet my mind, but over the music, Sterling's words haunted me all over again.

At some point, I heard a car and felt Sarah move away, but I didn't open my eyes until I heard my mother's car horn.

I grabbed my crutches and my backpack, and slowly moved to what felt like my doom.

⚜

Hours later, I was lying on the couch, watching *Gilmore Girls*, now dressed in my black Lululemon tank that split down the back and a matching pair of yoga pants, when *they* arrived. Mom had gone to run errands, and my dad was on his trip, so I was alone in the house. My leg hurt from the electrode thing the physical therapist had put on my injured leg, which was why I was lying on two ice packs and letting the world of Stars Hollow and the quick-witted women on screen take me away.

I heard the front door open and my eyes flew to the doorway. Miles, Laura, Ariel, and Sarah stood in the entryway of the living room, staring at me.

I felt a knot form in my throat when I noticed the girls wore a variation of what I wore. We could have been an ad for Lululemon. Laura's tank was white and see-through, showing off the lavender Barre bra underneath. Ariel's was just a regular purple tank that fit loosely on her body, but dipped down in front. Sarah's looked like mine in the front, except she had knotted it so her belly showed. All three wore the same exact pair of tight stretch yoga pants that I was currently wearing, and I really wished for a blanket right about now to cover myself.

It was then I vowed, *I vowed* to raid my closet and sell every single article of clothing. If I wasn't going to die anytime soon, I was going to change *everything*. I just needed to figure out how.

A throat cleared, and I looked up into the face of my "boyfriend" who stood behind the trio, his tall bulk making them look small in comparison.

"How you feeling, baby?" His eyes looked worried, whereas I wanted to roll mine.

"Fine," I sighed.

It was a shame the guy was so handsome; the wounded puppy look worked well on him. He still didn't match Sterling's dark beauty, yet I could still see what I saw in him years ago. He was cute, and he could be sweet, but he just couldn't say no to other girls.

Miles moved through the line of girls. "You didn't answer any of my calls or texts."

It sounded more like an accusation than a statement, so I didn't answer. What did he want me to say? That I didn't want to talk to him? Likely not.

When he reached the couch, he sat at the end and carefully lifted my feet, putting them on his lap. I caught the flash of anger, or maybe it was hurt, that came across Laura's face before she and the others moved to the love seat.

"This okay?" Miles asked, and I nodded. Surprisingly, the movement hadn't hurt. My mom had reattached the compression bandage and had laid a new ice pack under me before she had left.

"I never understood why you liked this show so much. Rory is kind of lame," Laura cut in.

My mind blanked. *Lame?* Rory was awesome. She lived in Stars Hollow where the people were supportive and hilarious, unlike Oleander where they were indifferent and judgmental. She also dated a guy like Dean who was majorly hot and sweet.

Another tall, dark, and handsome guy flashed through my mind, but I shook my head to clear his image.

"So, are you going to the party tonight?" That was Sarah, the informant and brown-noser.

"No, I'm not supposed to move very much for the next forty-eight hours. Doctor's orders," I lied with a shrug. I should probably act a lot more bummed, but I wasn't. I didn't want to go. I never wanted to go, but Laura's was the one place where my father would let me go without an interrogation. Laura's father was in the same fraternity as mine, and for some reason, it gave anything that had to do with the Daniels family a stamp of approval. So, I normally went on the rare occasion that both her parents were out of town and she wanted to host a party.

"That's too bad," Laura said, though her tone contradicted her words.

"I could stay here with you. Veg out in front of the TV like we used to," Miles offered.

I looked at him from out of the corner of my eye. We never did that anymore, not since freshman year.

I was about to answer him, but whether I would affirm or deny his suggestion, I wouldn't find out since Ariel broke in.

"You can't. You told Gage you would give him a ride tonight."

Gage was Ariel's boyfriend. He was the catcher to Miles' pitcher. He wasn't as tall as Miles, but he was broader, stouter, and resembled an ox. They were best friends, and since Gage wrecked his truck last month, we all took turns carting him around. Not me so much because everyone knew how my dad was, and no one wanted to deal with a pissed off Derek Everly. Being an unapproved passenger wasn't something Gage wanted to try, especially since he was of the male species. My dad barely tolerated Miles coming around.

"Oh yeah," he replied, sounding genuinely disappointed.

It was times like these when I felt a stirring for him in my chest. Not love or attraction, but something akin to tenderness. That was, until Laura ruined it.

"Did Miles tell you he confronted Sterling about him singing to you yesterday?"

What now?

"You did what?" I asked carefully, quietly.

I could feel the eyes of the others on me as they studied my reaction, so I kept my face impassive. On the inside, however, I was a riot of emotions and questions. Did he only talk to him? Did he try to scare him away? Did he get physical? The thought of Miles hitting Sterling made me want to haul off and hit *him*. Sterling had been nothing but nice. If it wasn't for him, they probably would have found my dead body slumped in the bleachers. I had to fight the urge to do my breathing exercises as prickles of anxiety crept over my skin.

"He disrespected my girl."

Deep breath in, exhale out.

A strangled sound came from the love seat, and then a loud *thump*. My gaze shot to the girls, and I saw Laura's face was pink, her fists balled in her lap, the knuckles on both white. Meanwhile, Ariel's face held a grimace, and she was trying to scoot away from Laura.

Uh-oh, I guess Laura didn't like that so much.

Why were we playing this game anymore? Why hadn't Miles broken up with me for not putting out? Why didn't he just play the field or date Laura? Why have I gone along with this insanity for so long?

"Miles—"

"Baby, you saying he had cause to sing that to you?" he asked, wrapping his hand around one of my feet. I wanted to jerk it away, but I didn't, thinking I might hurt myself worse if I attempted.

I ignored the snort and giggles coming from our audience. "No—"

"Then I had to speak up. You're mine, and no one poaches what's mine."

Dear Lord. That was what all this "baby" stuff and wanting to hang around my house was about. He was peeing on me! Marking his territory! It was like I was some doll on a shelf that only he could play with, which I never let him play with, but still ... I was simply a possession to him.

I was going to have to break up with him soon. I would do it now, but I didn't want to in front of Flopsy, Mopsy, and Cottontail.

"He was just joking. You didn't hit him, did you?"

He narrowed his eyes, and his grip on my foot tightened. "No, but why do you care? It wasn't funny."

"It kind of was ..." Sarah chimed in.

I shot her a look that promised retribution.

She read that look and looked toward the TV that was still playing *Gilmore Girls.*

I reached over and paused it, cursing myself for not doing it earlier. Now I was going to have to rewind it.

"Well, Miles, we need to go. I still have some *supplies* to pick up for the party tonight," Laura said as she stood abruptly.

Thank God. I was grateful, even though she didn't do it with my comfort in mind. More like she didn't like watching Miles try to be sweet to me any more than I did.

"I could—"

"I need *your* help with some *things*." Laura cut Miles off with a hard stare and raised brows.

He sent her an unhappy look, but he didn't say no. Instead, he gently moved my feet and got up from the couch.

"We'll see you at school on Monday?" Laura inquired, and I nodded. "Good."

She led the girls out of the room like a mother duck leading her ducklings to water. One of them yelled, Ariel more than likely, "Feel better soon!" The sound of their giggles echoed in the hall before I heard the door close behind them.

Miles was still standing by the couch when my eyes left the doorway and turned to him. He just stared at me.

"What?"

"Why can't I figure you out?" he asked, seemingly more to himself. The tip of his tongue was lodged in the corner of his mouth as he sometimes did when he was concentrating on something, forehead furrowed, and his arctic blue eyes bore into me like they could penetrate my skull and discover the mysteries I had hidden there.

I shrugged. Not sure what to say since I wasn't quite sure where he was going with that question. What did he want to know? It wasn't like he didn't know the basic things. We did grow up together.

He opened his mouth to say something, but then the sound of a horn blared outside. He dropped his head slightly to one side and squeezed his eyes shut, his mouth tight. After a moment, he blinked them open and looked toward the television, his stare fixed on the frozen still of Lorelai's mouth open in mid-speak. His square jaw flexed and moved like he was grinding his teeth.

Before I could ask him if he was okay, he jerked his head back at me, his blue eyes searching.

"You know you're different, right?" he asked quietly, the sound of the horn bleating outside almost drowning him out.

I sucked in a breath. What did he mean by that?

Before I could ask, he stepped forward, bent down, and pressed his lips to my forehead.

I closed my eyes and breathed in his cologne. He smelled nice. He always did, due to the expensive cologne he wore. The contact of his lips was also nice, but it didn't make my heart race or my skin tingle. Still, it was comforting, familiar.

"Love you," he whispered.

I didn't say it back. I rarely heard those words so I was out of practice. That didn't matter. I wouldn't have said them anyway. I didn't feel that for him. Not like he meant them. I guessed I loved him as a part of my childhood, as a friend. Anything more, though? No. That had been gone for a long time.

He was just a label now.

When I opened my eyes, he was gone.

❧

Mom eventually came back with groceries, her face strained. She looked tired.

My chest constricted, wishing I could get up and help her with those bags, and guilt ate at my insides like a cancer.

I couldn't think about the pills she needed that were currently buried under the seat of my car, so I reached for my phone for a distraction, only to come up empty.

I scanned around the couch for it, but I couldn't find it. Panic swelled in my chest at the thought of my mother finding it and going through it.

After I lifted all the pillows and dug into the cushions, I called out, "Have you seen my phone?"

"Yes, honey, I put it on the charger in your room. It was dead," was my mother's reply. I heard her moving around the kitchen, the rustle of the plastic sacks, the sounds of cabinets and the fridge opening and closing.

A familiar sense of self-loathing reared its ugly head when I thought of my mom in there, lifting and bending without anything to take the edge off the pain she must be feeling. At the same time, I felt relief at my phone being dead when she had found it. My stomach churned, and my head began to pound from the conflicting emotions battling in my head.

"Do you want me to go get it? I'm sure it's charged by now."

"No," I shouted, hastily getting up. I began limping back to my room double time.

I saw my mom at the mouth of the kitchen, one hand braced against the counter, her expression wan.

"Are you okay?" she asked slowly and suspiciously.

Oh no, that wasn't good.

"I have to pee." I made a wry face and imbued my voice with enough desperation to make it somewhat, if not wholly, believable. I did everything but place my hands in front of my crotch and dance.

Her face cleared. She seemed to buy the lie. Well, it wasn't so much of a lie since I really did have to pee, but it wasn't an emergency like I was playing it up to be.

I made it to my room and over to my desk where I saw my phone charging. I grabbed it and pulled the connector out as I walked to the bathroom. As I sat down gingerly, I pushed the button on the side to power it up. My good leg bounced as I waited for the white back-ground to fade into my lock screen.

Once I had done my business and washed my hands, I tapped out my code to open the phone and ... *holy moly!* My phone was lit up with so many notifications I was surprised it didn't just go ahead and shut back down.

I clicked on my Instagram account that had blown up and checked my notifications as I stumbled over to my bed and sat on the edge, taking the weight off my bad leg as I scrolled through them.

Evidently, my accident was the biggest news right now. I clicked one that someone had tagged me in and saw it was a video. I hit play then felt the little bit of food I had eaten this morning rise and threaten to escape. Someone had recorded my race. Someone had recorded my race, added circus music to the background, and posted it online.

Tears welled, hot and fast, as I watched in horror and embarrass-ment as the reason I was laid up this weekend played out on social media for the world to see.

My lungs were gripped in a vise, and I couldn't breathe. The walls were closing in on me. It felt like an elephant sat on my chest as the tears fell down my face like tiny rivers. I tried to suck air into my lungs, only able to get short hiccupping breaths before blowing them out. I needed to calm down, but all I could think was: who would do this?

I looked at the username and felt heat suffuse my whole body, hot and swift.

Sarah freaking Burns.

It looked like she had posted it right after they had left my house, waiting until the weekend of the party, which meant they were probably all in on it. No way they didn't know. My guess would also be that Laura orchestrated it, and all because of Miles. This whole situation was so jacked. Somehow, I was going to have to get myself out of it.

I finally got ahold on my breathing and cleared my Instagram notifications. From the glance I had of the comments, I knew I didn't want to go back and read them. I didn't want people to feel bad for me.

On the heels of my anger was the sting of betrayal and humiliation. My heart felt like it was beating a mile a minute, yet it felt hollow at the same time.

I wondered if Miles knew. One minute, he told me he loved me, and the next, he was partying with the same people who had humiliated me.

My body bucked with a sob. Wasn't there one person on earth who cared? Who genuinely loved or even liked me? I would take just *one* person. What was so wrong with me?

My fingers trembled as I closed the app, held the button down until the icon shook, and then clicked the X in the top corner. Instagram gone.

I held the phone tighter in my hand, tempted to chuck it at the wall.

Why did I think I could handle this? Why did I keep trying? There was no hope. No future. I would always be this …

I could feel the will leaking out of me, leaving me cold, as my eyes lost focus and my mind blanked. I just wanted to go to sleep and never wake up. I didn't want to exist anymore.

Wounds to the soul didn't just bleed; they ate at your very being. They fed on everything good, everything right, until you were hollow. Until you were a husk of the person you once were. Until you crumbled to dust and blew away in the wind. I was ready. I was past ready to leave this world on a breeze.

The phone vibrated in my hand, and I looked down to see a familiar gray rectangle on the screen, the yellow Snapchat icon in the top left-hand corner, and "from *perfecttragedy5*" in the box.

I sniffed and shakily wiped my face with the hand not holding the phone. Did I want to look? Heck, did I even care anymore?

I laid back across my bed, decision made, and went to the app.

The first snap was one of the ones I had missed earlier. It was a picture of a black ceiling fan in motion and the text strip read, "*Good luck @ doctor's! Your biggest fan.*"

A surprised giggle erupted from me. I didn't know what to do with it. Just moments ago, I was in a downward spiral of self-loathing, and now I was giggling at corny Snapchats.

But, how did he know I went to the doctor's?

Then I remembered. I saw Elodie Thomas in the school office when I was signing out. She must have overheard me tell the secretary where I was going and had told Sterling.

Elodie was a sprinter on the track team, and she was in theater ... with Sterling. She had beautiful almond skin, with freckles across the bridge of her nose and cheeks; large dark eyes; and short, fluffy hair that didn't know whether it was wavy or curly. I didn't know her well since she was always quiet and soft-spoken.

The next snap that followed was a selfie of Sterling with the puppy dog filter. I pressed both the side button on my phone and the center circle at the same time, saving the picture to keep for later. Then I froze when I realized what I had done.

He would know I saved his snap. The app would alert him. *Crap!*

Before I could work myself into a real panic, the next picture came on the screen. It was a picture of a white coat hanger lying in the grass, and with it read, "*Hang in there. It gets better.*"

My stomach dropped. He didn't know ... Sterling Chapman with his freedom, with his choices.

I rubbed my chest and wished for some control over the emotions swirling inside me. I was just so tired. I was tired of feeling ... everything.

I sighed then clicked out of Snapchat. After I did, a notification popped up that said *perfecttragedy5* was typing. I clicked on the app again and waited, a tingle of something fighting the tiredness I felt, and then the blue dialogue box showed up.

Perfecttragedy5: *Are you okay?*

AllyEver16: *No.*

Perfecttragedy5: *Meet me at Westbank Park @ the pier?*

Could I? I had never snuck out before. I was supposed to take it easy, but my dad *was* gone, and my mom, well, I didn't know if she was still in the kitchen. Would she go to bed after putting the groceries away?

Guilt sliced through me, sharp and deep. She had to be in pain, and I doubted she had refilled her Tramadol today. They kept track of those kinds of things since they were habit-forming and could be sold on the street.

I shouldn't try it. I didn't really deserve to.

Reluctantly, I typed ...

AllyEver16: *I can't.*

Instead of telling him what an awful person and daughter I was, I turned my phone off and positioned myself on my good side where I could lay my head on the remaining pillows. I stared at the wall that held my white wooden desk, blush pink chair, and the clotheslines of posed pictures of family and friends artfully arranged above it. I wanted to rip every single one of them down.

I both loved and hated my room. It was cute and girly, but I hadn't picked anything out for it when my parents had let me redecorate it my freshman year. Mom had called in her interior designer, Rosalind, and I told her a few colors that I liked. She ran with it and started working on it while I was at school.

My bed was plush with a white bed sheet and a blush pink blanket draped over the end. The accent pillows were different sizes in the same blush as the blanket and shades of gray. A couple even had fur, which I hated. My headboard was slate gray and padded. The night tables on either side were light pink and gold, with rectangular mirrors hanging above them. I liked the accent wall she had painted behind the bed. It was white with irregular-shaped gray dots and the words

"*Hello, gorgeous*" stenciled in gold. The top was in print caps and the bottom was a curving lowercase script that rested directly above the headboard.

As I lay there, trying not to think of the unfairness of my life or things I could have done differently, an insistent tapping started, coming from my window and drawing me from my dark state. My mom hadn't come and checked on me, so I assumed she must have crashed. Besides, she wouldn't be the one tapping at my window.

I peered over my shoulder toward the window, not expecting to see anything, yet there, framed in the glass, was Sterling Chapman. I rubbed my eyes to make sure I wasn't hallucinating as I carefully rolled to my belly, and then stared. Sterling was still there.

He lifted his chin, and then looked around like he was expecting someone to sneak up behind him. We didn't have blinds because my mother declared they messed with the design aesthetic, which I imagined was really Rosalind's words. However, we had a security system.

He lifted a finger and curled it in a "come here" gesture.

My mouth dropped open. Sterling Chapman beckoning me to him was one of the sexiest things I had ever seen in my life.

I gently got out of the bed and limped toward the window.

He made a gesture that I assumed was for me to open it, but I pointed at the little, white, rectangular box attached to the pane. If I moved it, the alarm would beep. If the alarm was armed, it would trigger the actual alarm and alert the police. I was surprised it hadn't beeped with all of Sterling's tapping.

He looked to the side, I guessed to make sure he wasn't seen, but there was a bush that partially covered my window since the air-conditioning unit was also next to it. Sterling stood in the space between them.

Inspiration struck, and I held up a finger. Then I slowly—not that I could move quickly—and quietly made my way back down the hall and to the kitchen. My mom was nowhere in sight. I could only assume she was asleep in her room.

I went to the drawer that contained the butter knives, and then to the drawer that held some basic tools. I grabbed a package of the big command strips and took them, along with the butter knife, back to my room. I hoped, even though I shouldn't, that Sterling was still there when I returned.

I sighed when I saw he was, and a little, fragile bubble of hope formed. He was dressed in a worn, dark gray tee that had *Hogwarts* written across the top. I might have fallen a little bit in love with him right there.

When he saw me, a little smile played at his lips, and he raised a brow.

I gingerly kneeled by the window and went to work. I took the butter knife and pried the sensor from the glass. When it beeped, I froze, and then I listened for movement coming from the hall. When I heard nothing else, I applied a command strip to the back of the box and pressed it to the wall next to its partner sensor. It only beeped when it moved away from the smaller strip of plastic attached to the window casing.

I opened the window and said, "Hi," suddenly feeling shy. A flush of warmth hit my cheeks.

"Hey." His mouth tipped up on one side, a wicked glint in his eyes.

"So ..."

"So ..." he said back.

There was this energy that snapped back and forth between us. The air practically hummed with it. I couldn't think. What could I say? I had so many questions I wanted to ask, but the only one that came out was ...

"How do you know where I live?"

He scoffed like that was a ridiculous question.

"Elodie told you, didn't she?"

He shrugged, but I caught the slight pink staining his cheeks. "I may have talked to her today ..."

Again, Elodie.

Elodie knew where I lived because we had thrown an end of season pool party for the whole track team last year. She hadn't shown up, but she could still have my address since we texted the invites.

"So, um, why are you here? You know I have a boyfriend, right?"

He was so handsome that it made me ache. I could stare at him all day. Yeah, I was really worried about having a boyfriend right now. I did intend on breaking up with him soon ...

He rolled his eyes, but then his face instantly sobered, and his unique eyes went intense. "I was worried about you."

I looked down at my fingers resting on the sill while my heart soared. While my supposed friends feigned concern, with Sterling ... I could *see* the sincerity written all over his face. He wasn't there for gossip or to lord over my injured state. Sterling knew my deepest, darkest secret and had yet to tell anyone or blasted it on social media.

"Why? Why are you doing all this?"

"What?"

"The snaps and this?" I gestured with my hand, moving it back and forth between us.

"It's all part of my plan," he said somewhat cryptically.

"Plan for what?" I was confused. What kind of plan did he have that involved me?

He didn't make me wait for the answer.

"My plan for saving you." This was said like it made all the sense in the world.

Was I a damsel in distress? No. Well, maybe ... I didn't really know. I was confused by what he meant. I was saved in the Biblical sense, but I didn't think that was what he was alluding to.

He wanted to save me from myself.

"Saving me? It's too late for that. I'm beyond saving ... I'm practically on life support."

"I know," he answered in a thick voice, and I watched as his Adam's apple bobbed. He lifted a curled fist and coughed into it like he was clearing his throat before changing the subject. "You know, you can add me as your friend on Snapchat and maybe send a few in return." The sly look was back in his eyes, and I had to keep myself from swooning out the window.

"How did you get my username, by the way?"

"Instagram."

Had I posted it on Instagram? Or had someone else?

"I don't remember posting it on Instagram ..."

"Maybe it was Facebook."

I had a feeling he was teasing me, but his face was so serious.

"I never get on Facebook."

"I have my ways." This time, a smile stretched his lips, showcasing his perfectly straight, white teeth.

"You're on Facebook?" Surprise leaked into my voice. I couldn't picture him on it. He seemed ... too cool.

"Isn't everybody?" There was laughter in his tone, though that wasn't exactly an answer.

I opened my mouth to tell him just that, but then he stood abruptly.

"Gotta jet."

Before I could say anything else, he flicked two fingers as he strolled away.

It didn't occur to me until a moment later that he couldn't have parked in the driveway. So, where exactly had he walked to?

HOPELESSLY DEVOTED

It was Monday, and I was still on crutches. Crutches sucked. My mom had read on the internet that you needed to wrap the tops so they didn't rub blisters or make the skin under your arms raw. Therefore, we did just that, wrapping the top bar with microfiber towels and securing them with rubber bands. I was grateful because, even with the extra padding, my underarms were sore.

This weekend hadn't gone well. I did too much last week with not enough ice and not enough rest. My mom fussed at me when she came into my room Saturday morning and saw that I had not elevated my injured leg or put an ice pack under myself. It was weird receiving her attention that way.

I knew my mother loved me, but over the years, a wall had formed between us. She had never spoken to me unless it was to instruct or relay a message, and she had never shown emotion. It was like she had been one of those robotic wives in that Nicole Kidman movie about that subdivision. Now she was acting like the wall had never existed. Again, weird.

Needless to say, I had spent all weekend iced and rested as my mother hovered in the wings. The only bright spot was that Sterling had kept to his plan. He had sent me two new snaps. One was a bottle of Naked Juice with the caption, *"My first naked selfie,"* which admittedly made me blush and giggle. The other was a picture of his half-eaten meal from Whataburger with the message, *"It's the little things, like Fancy Ketchup."*

Everyone in Texas knew that Whataburger had the best ketchup. Fancy brand ketchup was something the fast food chain served in little tubs that came in regular or spicy. I preferred regular, but I noted that Sterling preferred the black label spicy.

I knew what he meant by "the little things" and tried to think of some I enjoyed. Maybe if I could focus on the small, positive aspects of life, I wouldn't fixate on all the negatives.

I contemplated sending him a snap back, but chickened out. What would I send? I could pose for a selfie and use a cute filter that made anyone look perfect, but ... that felt lame. Therefore, I didn't send anything. I did, however, add Sterling as a friend.

At school, I got even more looks and whispers, more people asking if I was okay, and more awkward hugs than I did last week right after my injury, all probably due to the video. Though people continued to help me, I didn't see Miles or Sterling, which made me both happy—Miles—and disappointed—Sterling. I didn't go to lunch. Instead, I went to the locker room to turn in my uniform and talk with our track coach.

I was mad at everyone. I was mad at Laura and her crew. I was mad at Miles. I was mad at myself for letting this go on for as long as it had.

It was the end of the day, and I was at a loss. Athletics was my last class period, and I didn't think I would be able to go home yet. I didn't want to go out to the track because a) my armpits hurt, and it was a long walk out there on crutches, and b) I didn't want to talk to anyone, especially about my injury or when I was going to be competing again.

It was strange not practicing or training. I couldn't recall a day since seventh grade when I hadn't at least run laps, done agility drills, or hit the weight room. My life had revolved around track for five years, and for it to be gone so suddenly, it left me feeling adrift. I was a boat without a port.

This past weekend, I hadn't given much thought to what I would do with my afternoons. I didn't have homework, and there was nothing for me to do with any of the other organizations I was a part of. Prom committee had already raised all the money we would need, so I didn't have to do anything else for that until April.

What was I going to do now?

Well, right now, I was going to find Rick, the school trainer, and talk to him about my physical therapy. Maybe he could give me some insight into what else I could do to heal quickly.

I opened the door that led into the boys' locker room where the training area was located. The way the school had this set up was probably a violation of Title Nine, but no one really cared enough to say anything, though I wish they would.

The boys had a huge locker room with a training area in the middle that had a metal whirlpool tub, a couple of padded tables, an ice machine, and a kitchenette. It reminded me of a cell with the training area being the nucleus. The coaches' offices were at the gym side, toward the front. On either side were doors that led to two different dressing rooms for the boys where they had a laundry room, another ice machine, and an equipment room toward the parking lot/football field in the back.

The girls had a locker room on the other side of the gym that was behind the visitor bleachers. If we had use of the whole space, it wouldn't have been so bad, but they had split it into two locker rooms. One was for P.E. and the other was for girls' athletics. Again, it wouldn't have been so bad except the half we had was split into a dressing room, bathroom, equipment room with washer/dryer, no ice machine, and one coaches' office for five coaches to share. It was cramped and hot.

I walked through the door and noticed Rick wasn't where he was usually stationed. The space was empty, which wasn't surprising since everyone should be at their designated field by now.

I deposited my backpack on one of the tables, debating on whether to just wait for Rick to return or go sit in the gym, when I heard voices. I wouldn't have thought anything of it if it wasn't for the female voice I heard shouting from the dressing room.

I hurriedly made my way to the dressing room door, and as I got closer, I noted this wasn't some girl shouting for help; this was a very familiar voice shouting in anger.

As quietly as I could, I cracked the door open. When neither person noticed, I watched in fascination as what I knew all along played out.

"You son of a bi—" Laura hurled as she reared her fist back and hit

Miles in the arm. He was standing in front of his locker, dressed in his baseball practice clothes. He was in profile, so I couldn't see his face, but I could see all of Laura.

"Baby, it didn't mean anything." Miles' voice was smooth, conciliatory. He sure liked to use the word baby, didn't he?

He reached up to touch Laura, but she slapped his hand away hard enough that an audible *crack* echoed throughout the room.

"It didn't *mean* anything! Screwing some slut at *my* house, in *my* room, during *my* party didn't *mean* anything?"

"I don't know why you're mad, Laura. You know the score. You know the rules."

I could hear the blood rush through my head, and I gritted my teeth as I tried to control the impulse to march in there and slap the snot out of him. He treated girls like used socks. We were all interchangeable and disposable.

I didn't mean anything to him, not really. I was a status symbol as one-half of the golden couple of Oleander High. My father was the second richest man in town and owned his own law firm. In Miles' eyes, us being together was just the natural order of things.

"You don't know why I'm mad?" She sounded incredulous.

"We're not together. I'm not your boyfriend. I think you forget that I'm with Ally."

Laura laughed, the sound bitter. "You're with Ally? Goody-goody, straight as a board, wouldn't know what to do with a dick if it slapped her in the face, Ally? The girl who can't sneeze without her daddy's say so?"

Ouch. Tell me what you really think ...

"Don't talk about her that way." Miles' body was rigid, his tone hard and defensive.

My heart would melt, but he *was* currently arguing with my *former* best friend about having sex with someone besides *her*.

"What do you think Ally would say if she found out you've been screwing me and the rest of the female population at this school for years? Think she'd want to stay with you then?"

I wanted to laugh. I really did. Did people really think I was so clueless? Then the urge to laugh died as ... Yeah, people really thought I was that naive. That *stupid.*

The familiar feelings of self-loathing coursed through my veins like poison.

Miles leaned forward, getting in her face. "You breathe a word to Ally, and I'll make your life a living hell at this school."

I watched as Laura's face morphed from anger to something else. It made a sick knot form in my stomach as I watched her lift her hand and run her fingers from Miles' shoulder to his hand, and then to his thigh.

"I'm sorry, Milesy-poo. You know I get jealous." She even stuck her lower lip out.

"Well, don't. It pisses me off."

Her eyes flashed, but she hid it so quickly I doubted Miles even saw it.

She knew Miles would make good on his threat. He would mess with the one thing she wanted, the one thing she valued above anything—her popularity. He was the richest and most popular guy in town, and if he whispered the right words in the right ears, her reputation would be in tatters.

"Let me make it up to you," she purred as she brought her body closer to his.

Oh, yuck.

"You know what I like ..." Miles' voice deepened.

Before I could witness anything that would require eye bleach and a puke bucket, I closed the door. My breath was coming in and out in shallow pants. Anger and disgust churned in my gut. I wanted to smack them both.

I wasn't sure where I was going, and I didn't realize I was heading in the wrong direction until I was already through the gym and opening the doors to the cafetorium.

Music assaulted my senses as I looked into the dimly lit room, the only light coming from the overhead ones on the stage.

Our high school didn't have a true auditorium. They had simply added a stage to one end of the cafeteria and put the band hall behind it to one side, and the speech/drama teacher's room to the other.

Feeling lost and a little sorry for myself, I moved to the back of the room. I just wanted to hide for a little bit before I made my way back to the locker room to get my backpack.

I pulled a chair out as quietly as I could and parked my crutches against the table, then watched a girl's performance. The girl from the parking lot.

She was even more beautiful under the lights; her pale skin glowing, her black hair shining, making it look iridescent. She also had a decent voice. It was smoky and bluesy, but it didn't really fit the song. I was more jealous. I loved to sing and had a pretty decent voice. Not smoky and bluesy, but adequate.

The sound of a chair scraping along the floor drew my attention away from the stage. I looked across the table and saw a young boy with smiling eyes and an impish face looking at me. He didn't say anything, just pointed his finger at the girl and nodded.

I smiled and nodded back, not sure what else to do. Then I took in his facial characteristics and noted he had Down syndrome. I didn't know anyone with Down's.

I turned back to the stage and watched the girl finish the last lines of the Olivia Newton-John song.

When the music ended, and a small spattering of applause broke out, Mrs. Cook called, "Good job, Raven," and held out something for the girl to take.

I was even more jealous of her. She was beautiful, talented, had a cool name, and most of all, she knew Sterling better than I did. The sour feeling grew when I saw Sterling watching her from the wings.

I felt a hand on my shoulder and jumped. The boy was standing next to my chair.

He took my hand, pulled me up, and basically dragged me toward the stage, sans crutches.

"I have a hurt leg! Stop!" I cried to no avail as I limped along behind him, my hand captured in his solid grip.

I guessed no one had seen me come in earlier because the room suddenly broke out in whispers at my sudden appearance on stage. The boy—I needed to learn his name—mumbled something I couldn't understand and gestured to me. As the music started back up, he then bowed to me before disappearing, leaving me to stand there like an idiot.

"I bet she can't even sing," a catty voice said to one side of me.

I looked over in the wings to see Raven standing near Sterling, her arms folded against her chest, hip stuck out, and a smug smirk curled on her perfectly plumped lips.

Can't sing?

I was so freaking tired of everyone taking pot shots at me. I hated that my father didn't trust me enough to make my own decisions and had basically taken over my life. I hated that my mother let him treat me any way he wanted. I hated that my boyfriend didn't think I was worth the wait and screwed anything that moved. I hated that my friends weren't good friends and had stabbed me in the back ... repeatedly. And I hated that this girl thought she had one over on me and had expressed that in front of Sterling.

Something in me cracked.

If I had any nerves before, they were long gone, burned away in the heat of my anger. I was going to show them all. I didn't spend all those years in church choir for nothing.

I had already missed the opening verses. The song was now at the part where it was building to the pre-chorus. I caught the wave and started singing.

My lower half was stationary, but my top half? I could have joined the Supremes with the moves I was making. I was telling a story using my voice, my face, my hands. I just let the music flow through me.

I told the tale of sitting around, waiting for a boy, and then my heartache at my love being pushed aside. I built the momentum to where I unleashed all the emotions that had been percolating inside me through the pent-up longing of the chorus. I sang, and I sang my heart out. I poured myself onto that stage. I channeled Olivia Newton-John, and she took over.

As the song neared the end and the last strands of music played, I wound it down and finished strong. When I was done, the cafetorium was silent.

I stood there, panting, my heart sinking. Had I just embarrassed myself?

My chin hit my chest as I fought the tears that wanted to come, but then it happened. The room exploded into applause, and a male voice yelled, "That was *de-vine*." There were whistles and shouts.

I picked up my chin and looked around the cafetorium, seeing people who had been seated were standing and still clapping.

"Excellent!" Mrs. Cook practically squealed. She approached the stage with a bag of something in one hand and a clipboard in the other. Her hair was up in her trademark bun, wearing a floral print dress and sweater, and her cat-like glasses were perched on her nose. "Marvelous, Allison! I must have you as our Sandy," she breathed out, excitement laced in her tone. She clutched the items in her hands and did a little shake as she smiled so big I could see almost every tooth in her mouth.

Mine dropped open, and I tried to speak, to tell her this had to be a mistake, but I couldn't form the words. It hadn't dawned on me that I had walked in on the auditions for *Grease*. Maybe I was as stupid as everyone thought.

"I didn't know she had that in her," came from Blake, a boy I'd had a few classes with, and who I often saw hanging out with Sterling. He stood over to the side of the stage, next to Elodie.

She gave a shy wave when she saw me looking at her. Not sure what else to do, I gave her one in return, but it was in slow motion since shock was the main emotion taking over my body.

I turned my attention back to Blake, who was dressed in jean shorts; a short-sleeved, black, button-up shirt that had white diamonds all over it and was buttoned all the way up to the top button under a bolo tie; dark, round sunglasses perched on his nose, much like Mrs. Cook's; and a dark brown felt hat with a wide brim sat on the back of his head. He reminded me of Duckie from *Pretty In Pink*. I looked down and, sure enough, he also wore shoes that resembled Duckie's from the movie.

"Nice shoes, Duckman."

"Anthropologie®, baby. Bringing Duckie into the modern era," he said while still smacking his gum and flashing me a grin.

"Mrs. Cook, she's not even in this class," interrupted a snotty voice. Raven was still standing by Sterling, arms still crossed over her chest, but now she was glaring daggers at me.

My gaze flicked to Sterling, who was staring at her in consternation, before looking over to something in the audience area.

"Well, now—"

"And she's a gimp," Raven interrupted Mrs. Cook, making my head jerk up at *gimp*. Who the hell did she think she was? "She tore something last week. I saw the video of it on Instagram. How is she going to be able to do any of the choreography?" she asked with a superior smirk.

"I can do the choreography."

What was I saying? I couldn't do this. Could I?

Before I could take back my statement, Raven scoffed, "How? I doubt you could have danced before your bum knee."

"Hamstring," Elodie corrected quietly.

As something unpleasant moved through Raven's features that looked a lot like loathing, I decided she wasn't pretty anymore. If you could contort your face into something so spiteful, your beauty quotient dropped.

"Whatever." She rolled her eyes.

"I started physical therapy already. I probably can't do anything high impact, but I doubt y'all will have me sprinting and jumping over obstacles."

Mrs. Cook's mouth skewed to one side like she was thinking.

"Still, you're not in this class. You're in athletics," Raven broke in again.

We were all still standing around, but some had moved from their spots backstage, and others had come to sit on the steps that led up to the stage in the front. They were all looking at me with bright and hopeful expressions, all except Raven.

Mrs. Cook, who was in front of me on the second step from the top, said, "This is true." She looked disappointed.

"Is being in drama a requirement to be in the musical?" I asked.

"I'm afraid so," Mrs. Cook replied, her exuberance from before subdued.

"Then I can switch."

A few gasps rang out. Even I couldn't believe I had just said that.

That I had just committed to this without discussing it with my parents first—mainly Derek Everly.

Something foreign unfurled in my chest. It made me feel lighter.

"Are you sure?" This was from Sterling.

I saw he had moved closer, the boy with Down syndrome now standing slightly behind him, grinning big and wide. I couldn't help returning the smile. That fella was either mischief personified for getting me into this, or he could be an angel sent from Heaven. I was guessing the latter.

"Yeah, I'm done. My track season is over for this year, so this will work for me. I was just wondering before I came in here what I would do this period."

Sterling smiled, stealing my breath.

"Wonderful! Why don't you go to the office right now and get it straightened out so you'll be on the roll tomorrow?" Mrs. Cook instructed, the happiness back in her voice.

"Yes, ma'am."

Before I could move to try to navigate the steps, Sterling was there and I was lifted. He had one arm under my knees while the other curled under my back so I had no choice but to wrap my arms around his neck as he carried me down.

He was warm, the muscles I could feel against me were solid and strong, and that woodsy scent I associated with him flooded my nostrils. He carried me like I was lighter than a feather. All of it almost made me groan, yet it did make me shiver.

When we got to the bottom of the steps, I expected him to put me down, but he didn't. He carried me back to the edge of the cafetorium to where my crutches were still propped against the table.

I looked over his shoulder to see everyone staring at us, except Mrs. Cook, who looked oblivious. Blake was fanning his face, while Elodie looked like she was fighting a giggle. Then there was Raven who, if looks could do bodily harm, I would be on the floor in a pool of blood.

Sterling carefully set me down and handed me my crutches. "I didn't mean for you to make this so easy."

What was he talking about? I was pretty sure he made me stupid.

Either that or I was still in a stupor from being in such close proximity to his body.

"Wh-what?" I asked with no little confusion.

"When I shared with you that I had a plan, it wasn't to save you through musical theater. Even though, it doesn't hurt."

I just stared at him without comprehension.

His eyes were twinkling with humor, and his lips ... those awesome lips weren't curved up in a traditional smile. No, they gave a hint of a smile like he was fighting back laughter. It was a good look.

"Haven't you heard that music can rescue the soul?"

Huh?

"Oh, Allison! Here ..." Mrs. Cook hustled up and handed me a sheaf of papers and something wrapped in white plastic. I looked at the package that said *Cow Tales* in orange with a picture of a brown cow. She then patted me on the arm before hoofing it away, yelling, "Blake, get down from there!"

"It's candy," Sterling supplied helpfully.

"Oh." I was still staring down at the items in my hands.

"Don McLean, 'American Pie.'"

My eyes shot up, and my brows drew together. "Excuse me?"

"YouTube it."

"Okay ..."

He was giving me whiplash.

"Well, I better get back on stage and help Mrs. Cook wrangle this group." He motioned over his shoulder with his thumb.

I nodded, my voice stuck in my throat. I wasn't ready for him to leave, but I needed to get to the office, and he had to go.

He gave me a crooked grin before turning and walking away. I was still standing there, watching him, when he then spun around and started walking backward as he called, "I still haven't gotten a snap back from you."

I smiled. He probably wouldn't anytime soon either.

He winked then jogged the rest of the way back to where the class was gathered on the stage.

PRETTIEST GIRL
I EVER DID SEE

I was surprised by how easy it had been to change my schedule, but from the number of times the counselor had asked how my parents were, that probably had something to do with it.

When I was done in the office, I ran into Elodie, looking as tired as I probably felt. Whoever said crutches were helpful had lied. They were a pain.

She asked where my backpack was, guessing I had left it somewhere, and then ran and got it from the locker room for me. I met her in the gym as she came out, wearing her practice clothes and holding my bright pink backpack. Elodie wasn't in athletics, but she still participated in track. I was really beginning to like Elodie.

Now, here I stood, outside on the sidewalk, waiting for my mom to come pick me up. She had declared I wasn't driving today so I could rest my leg. My leg did hurt, and I was ready to sit down somewhere.

School had let out and almost everyone was gone. The buses had already loaded up and taken off for the day, too. The parking lot still held the cars of the kids who were at either track, tennis, softball, or baseball practice. I noticed Sterling's car was gone, but Miles' bright red flashy truck was still there, as well as Laura's white BMW. I rolled my eyes at the sight.

I was hunched over the top of my crutches, trying to take the weight off my leg, when out strolled Miles and Laura.

Have they been in there all this time?

Miles saw me first and stuttered to a stop that caused Laura to crash into his back.

"Hey!" she cried out as she looked up at the back of his head in confusion.

"Ally, baby," Miles greeted me with an uncomfortable smile and what looked like guilt etched on his face.

Laura's face showed irritation before she masked it and gave me a smile that reminded me of a cat who got its cream, which she had.

She stepped around him so they stood shoulder to shoulder. They looked like a matching pair with their golden hair and blue eyes. She was dainty and petite to his tall and athletic frame.

"Hey, Ally!" she said with a bright, fake smile.

Anger flamed hot in me. I couldn't stand looking at either of them. I couldn't live like this anymore. The game had finally come to an end and, dang it, I was going to be the winner this time.

"Look, I need to talk to you both." No forced smile. No greeting. Straight to the point.

Miles' face morphed from discomfort to wariness, and Laura's smile dropped as apprehension took over hers.

"What's up?" Miles grunted as he propped his hands on his hips and stared at me like he was trying to read my mind.

"I'm not stupid, you know," I blurted.

Smooth, Ally.

His brows furrowed, and his tone gentled as he replied, "I know. You're one of the smartest people I know."

Laura stayed silent, her eyes darting toward the parking lot like she was debating on making a run for it.

"You and Laura have been screwing forever."

I was tempted to pull my phone out and take a picture of their faces. Both were frozen, except for their jaws dropping open. Laura made a strangled noise, while Miles' mouth opened and closed like a fish. Then they both spoke at the same time.

"That's not—"

"Of course not—"

I cut them both off with a slash of my hand. "Don't bother lying. I heard you both when I was in the training area during athletics. I went to the door of the locker room when I heard Laura yelling at you."

They both paled then turned interesting shades of red.

"What did you hear exactly?" Miles asked as he took a step toward me.

I held up my hands to halt him. I *really* didn't want him in my space.

"You know what I heard." I looked him dead in the eyes, hoping to convey my meaning.

Their color deepened until they looked like a pair of tomatoes.

I decided to put them out of their miseries, though they didn't deserve it.

"I didn't hear y'all doing it, if that's what you're worried about. I left before someone's genitals were exposed." I cut my eyes to the side, not seeing anything, just not wanting to look at them.

When Miles blew out a breath, I turned back to them.

He was a step away from Laura, looking lost and unsure of what to do with himself. Laura just stood there and stared at me. I was tempted to wave my hand in front of her face.

"How long were y'all going at it, if you are just now leaving the locker room? And how did you not get caught?" I tried for a teasing tone, but it fell flat.

Their expressions changed, and both gave me a weird look.

What? Had they expected me to scream and cry?

"You're not mad?" Laura asked hesitantly and like I might be slow. Yeah, she had expected hysterics.

"Oh, I'm mad. I'm mad at both of you, but I'm more upset with myself for letting it go on this long."

"It was just the one time," Miles said like I was going to believe he hadn't been having sex with my best friend for almost three years.

Laura and I both snorted, and she looked surprised.

"You knew all along?" she whispered.

"Uh, yeah. You're not exactly great at hiding it."

"It didn't mean anything," Miles interjected quickly.

I stared at him. Then my gaze flicked to Laura. To him it might not mean anything, but with the way Laura's face had just crumpled, it meant something to her.

She brushed by him, and Miles leaned as if he would grab her, but he didn't. He rocked back as she speed-walked to the parking lot. Then we both watched her get in her car and drive off.

"Playing games of the heart," I stated quietly through my clenched teeth.

I was seething. How could he treat someone like that? She had shared her body with him not even an hour ago, and he had just discarded her like trash.

"What?"

"We're done," I told him frankly.

"*What!*" he bellowed, moving toward me. Putting my hands up didn't ward him off this time. In fact, it did nothing. They were crushed between our bodies when he grabbed me by the upper arms and tried to bring me closer to him.

"Let me go, Miles," I hissed as I tried to lean away from him while trying to keep the crutches under my arms.

"We're not through. We're supposed to be together. It's always been you and me, and it will always be you and me."

I shook my head.

"Those other girls never meant anything. I'm a guy, so yeah, I need to get some. That's just what guys do. I didn't promise them anything, not like you."

That's just what guys do?

A red haze came over me, and I tried to jerk away from him, which made my crutches crash to the ground. I wobbled, but he held me fast.

"You giving them you, physically, is a promise whether you said the words or not. Being with someone that way should mean something. So, every time you say, 'it didn't mean anything,' it makes me want to throat punch you," I told him hotly.

"It would mean something with you," he said softly, ignoring my threat.

I rolled my eyes. When they rolled back in his direction, he looked hurt.

"No, it wouldn't. I'd be just another name on your list. Another notch on your bedpost."

"No." His fingers dug into my skin, but I ignored them.

"Aren't you tired?" I asked exasperatedly.

"Tired?" He looked at me like I was speaking a foreign language.

"Yeah, tired. Tired of everyone expecting something from you or to be something. You don't love me. Not really."

This time, he was the one to shake his head, but I powered through.

"Listen to me," I said earnestly as I stared into those blue eyes that used to mean something to me, used to make me feel safe, comfortable. "Aren't you tired of sneaking around? Wouldn't you like to be a single guy for once, taking a different girl out each weekend without hiding it?"

He looked at me like he was seeing me for the first time. "You're serious?"

"Deadly." I paused before whispering quietly, "I don't love you." He winced, but I kept on going. "At least, not that way, and I don't think you love me either. I think you love the idea of us. I think you love that it would make your parents happy, and you like making them happy."

Though he looked at something over my shoulder, I knew my words had struck a chord.

"We don't have to be this ... You're playing games of the heart, and these girls are losing. Right now, you're ahead of the game, but sooner or later, all this playing is going to catch up to you, and then you'll be the one to lose, one way or another."

"I think it's caught up to me now. I'm losing you."

"No, you'll see, and you're going to thank me."

He closed his eyes and whispered, "I don't know."

I put my hands on his shoulders and squeezed. "I do. Now, aren't you way late for baseball practice?"

He opened his eyes, stared at me for a beat, and then let me go. I dropped my hands and rubbed my arms where his fingers had gripped me hard.

"Yeah ... Sorry about ..." He gestured in my direction then rubbed his brow.

I made to reach down for my crutches, but he beat me to it, picking them up and putting them under each of my arms in turn. Then he moved back, putting a few feet between us, but it might as well have been miles.

"What do we do now?"

"We move on."

His throat moved as his beautiful blue eyes searched my face like he was memorizing it. "Prettiest girl I ever did see," he whispered.

I smiled but only said, "Practice?"

He nodded then cleared his throat. "So, I'll see you around?"

"Yeah, you'll see me."

He gave me a small smile, a small wave, and then he was gone.

I turned back toward the parking lot and stared at the runners on the track in the distance. What a difference a few days makes.

My mother's black Range Rover pulled right in front of me, cutting off my view. So absorbed in watching the bodies of my teammates in motion, I hadn't seen her coming down the road.

I blinked then moved to the back seat to put my crutches away before getting in the front. I buckled in then looked at my mother who hadn't said a word, even though she was late.

Her eyes were covered by huge black sunglasses, but the telltale blotchy redness on her face and her sniffles let me know she had been crying.

"Are you okay, Mom?"

She didn't move her head, just kept looking straight ahead as she murmured, "I'm fine."

Now was probably not the time to tell her that I had made some changes to my life in the past couple hours ... without their consent.

"Okay." I watched her for a moment, deciding that, yeah, telling her about dropping athletics and breaking up with Miles was probably not a good idea.

I shifted forward and unzipped my backpack, pulling out my phone and headphones. A text lit up my screen.

Laura: *Tell anyone about today and you're dead.*

Nice. Real nice, Laura.

I cleared it and clicked on the YouTube app. I put Don McLean in the search bar, having no idea who he was or what he sang. The first video that showed up was titled *"Don McLean, American Pie (with lyrics)."* I wondered if it had anything to do with the movie, but paired with what Sterling had said, that made no sense. I put my earbuds in and clicked the video.

The slow piano music and opening lyrics caught me off guard. I eyed the screen again, making sure I had the right song. Then it picked up and the lyrics changed. My eyes widened when he mentioned the day he would die. Since Sterling was the reason I was sitting here and knew my secret, I found this ironic.

When the man sang the line that was similar to what Sterling had said to me, I could not keep the smile off my face. Then it died when he talked about her being in love with another man.

Did Sterling think I was in love with Miles?

I continued to listen and, despite my initial reaction, it grew on me. By the third chorus, I was swaying in my seat.

When it was over, I opened Snapchat, went to Sterling's chat thread, and typed:

Me: *Are you serious with those lyrics?*

I didn't have to wait. His Bitmoji, which was adorable by the way because it looked almost like him without the bicolored eyes, peeked over the chat line.

Sterling: *What? <#Wink emoji>*

I exited the app and googled the lyrics, reading until I figured out what I wanted to say, then sent it before I could talk myself out of it.

Me: *So, Don did mention something about dancing really slow ...*

Sterling: *He also mentioned something about her having a boyfriend.*

I knew it! Now what do I type?

I wanted to tell him that I had broken up with Miles without actually coming out and saying, "Hey, I broke up with Miles." I looked through the lyrics, but I couldn't find any inspiration. The Bitmoji peeping up at me seemed to mock me.

Me: *He didn't say that exactly.*

I winced because it sounded lame after I had typed it out.

Sterling: *?*

See? Lame.

When the car came to a stop, I popped my head up to see we were home. I pulled my earbuds out—the music had long since stopped—and peeked over at my mother.

She said nothing, just gazed straight ahead. I recognized the look on her face. She didn't want to go in. She was thinking about driving away and never coming back.

"Mom, you okay?"

She seemed to shake herself out of it, pivoted toward me, and said in a flat tone, "Allison, I'm fine."

Before I could refute that, since she was so not "fine," she changed the subject.

"You should be okay to drive tomorrow. Don't forget your physical therapy appointment at two p.m." She then heaved herself out of the car.

The mom from yesterday was gone. The robotic mom that I was used to had taken over again.

When we walked into the house, she went directly to her room. I didn't see her for the rest of the night.

FIRST DAY OF MY LIFE

Tap, tap, tap ...

I blinked awake. My room was still dark, and my phone alarm was silent. My mind in a fog, I wasn't sure what time it was or why I was even awake. I had been in a deep, dreamless sleep and was eager to return. It was hard most nights just to fall asleep, though that was all I ever wanted to do.

I closed my eyes again and tried to sink back down into that comfortable abyss.

Tap, tap, tap ...

My eyes shot open, and I sat up, letting the comforter pool around my waist. I surveyed my room, looking for the source of the dratted noise, and froze at the sight of a face in the window. I opened my mouth to scream, but then stifled it when I recognized the face peering into the room with his finger placed over his lips.

I grabbed my phone from the night table and saw it was two o' clock. Why was Sterling at my window in the middle of the night?

I slid from the bed and stumbled over to the window, forgoing the crutches that were propped against the end of the bed. Then I kneeled and opened the window, the chill of the wind making me shiver.

"What are you doing?" I whispered as I crossed my arms over my chest and rubbed my hands along the outside of my arms to warm up.

"You never messaged me back."

"So, you just decided to show up at my house?"

He shrugged like it was no big deal, but the smile he gave me was downright devilish. I could feel his eyes examining me, and I blushed since I was only wearing a pair of sleep shorts and a cami.

"Go put something warmer on and come with me."

Was he crazy?

"I can't."

Good girls didn't sneak out of their houses. My parents would have him arrested if they caught him at my window.

"Why not?"

I opened my mouth to list all the reasons this was probably a bad idea, but I couldn't get past one word. "Because ..."

I paused. Wait. Why couldn't I? I was a teenager. I was supposed to break the rules, right?

I had never done drugs, smoked, drank, or had sex with my boyfriend—well, ex-boyfriend. I had never broken curfew. I was in the top ten percent of my class, on the A honor roll, and had never gotten in trouble at school, not even a dress code violation. My picture was probably in the dictionary under "model student." I had worked myself into knots trying to be perfect that it was literally killing me. I deserved to have some fun.

I stepped away from the window, and Sterling's expression fell. I stayed him with my hand then went to my dresser to grab a pair of black leggings and to my closet to grab a sweatshirt. Then I limped to the bathroom to change. I didn't bother with a bra since the cami had a shelf bra and the sweatshirt covered my braless boobs anyway.

Texas in February was funny. You never knew what the weather would do. Tonight, it was cold and wintery. The grass, brown and brittle. Tomorrow, it could rain or the sun would be shining, making you think spring was early. Then, the day after, it would snow, or it could be in the nineties and feel like summer. Who knew?

I never followed the weather because it was always wrong. I just never put my winter clothes up and dressed in layers. It was easier to take something off or put something on than have nothing.

I came out, grabbed my tennis shoes by the bed, and stuffed sock-covered feet into them.

"Don't forget your crutches," Sterling reminded me.

I got up and grabbed them, handing them to him through the window.

"Do you need help?"

I started to shake my head, but then thought he might need to catch me. Although my room was at ground level, it wasn't like I climbed out of windows regularly. And with a bum leg, I didn't want to hurt myself further.

I crouched and reached for Sterling. His hands were large and cold in mine as he took my weight when I swung my good leg through then my injured one until I sat on the ledge.

"You good?" Sterling asked, handing me my crutches.

I nodded and got them under me before shoving off.

We slowly made our way to the small wooded area that separated my house from the next-door neighbor's. The moon was full, so it wasn't all that dark, more like someone held a flashlight above our heads.

I looked over my shoulder at the driveway and thought it was weird not seeing my dad's car parked in the circle driveway. Weird, yet not unwelcome.

I hadn't heard from him since he left. No phone call or text message, only radio silence. Which was again odd, but not unwelcome. It was freeing not having to worry about my every move and every word. I could breathe for the first time in years, and it was ... amazing. This was probably how inmates felt when they were released from prison.

My mother had been in her room all evening. Hopefully, she was asleep now. We should be in the clear unless my dad decided to come home right now, which was unlikely since it was after two in the morning. Still, a niggle of worry tickled the back of my mind. Not about getting caught, but that there was something very wrong happening between my parents.

We—more like I—had stumbled halfway through the wooded area when Sterling muttered, "This won't work." He stopped me with a hand to my arm, and before I could finish blinking, I was in his arms for the second time that day.

"My crutches," I hissed.

"You don't need them."

I gave my head a small shake as I replied, "Excuse me? I think *I* should be the judge of that."

"We don't have all night," he stated, still trekking through the wilderness—not much wilderness since we were in a subdivision—like I was inconveniencing him.

"Maybe you should just take me back to my house." I tried to cross my arms over my chest, but he suddenly dipped me low like he was going to drop me.

With a cry, I wrapped my arms around him like a clinging vine.

He chuckled. "Hush, princess."

"Princess?" I asked in outrage. I was *not* a princess. My parents might have bought everything any teenager would ever desire, but I hadn't asked for it. I hadn't even wanted half of it, but they had still bought it to keep up with appearances. It wouldn't do for me not to have something Laura, Sarah, and Ariel had.

"Yeah. Princess."

"Are you making fun of me?" I seethed.

"No," he answered in a voice filled with laughter.

I looked up into his face and saw that his eyes were dancing, and his mouth was caught in a self-satisfied smile.

"Sterling!" I whisper-yelled.

He stopped and tucked his chin down to look at me, eyes still twinkling, but the smile gone. "Ally, I just want to show you something, and then I'll bring you back, okay?"

I stared at him for a minute, thinking this whole situation was surreal. Every moment I spent with him felt that way. He was too ... everything to be real. He had to be a dream.

I quelled the urge to pinch myself as I gazed into his extraordinary eyes. They flared to life, going from a twinkle to a smolder.

"Okay," I responded breathily.

I could feel myself drawing closer to him like a moth drawn to a flame. I could feel his breath fan across my face as our eyes stayed locked to one another's. My body began to tremble in his arms, and that seemed to bank the embers that glowed in his eyes. He tore them away, and I immediately mourned the loss. Then he gave his head a slight shake before putting us back in motion.

When we got to his car parked on the street that ran behind my house and a few blocks down, he slowly set me on my feet. He reached in his pocket and unearthed a set of keys, then unlocked and opened the car door.

Before I could move to get in, he picked me up again. I saw this was becoming a habit with him.

"This really isn't necessary."

"I don't want you to get hurt worse because of me, so I'll just carry you if I need you somewhere."

I rolled my eyes rather than answer. I had a feeling anything I would have said in reply would have been pointless.

He ran around the front of the primer-colored vintage car, got in, cranked the motor, and put it in drive.

"Where are we going?" I was curious, and I had to admit, excited at the same time.

My heart pounded in my chest, and my skin tingled. I couldn't believe I was doing this. I had snuck out of my house. Not only that, I had snuck out with *a boy*. And not just any boy; it was *Sterling Chapman*. Sterling Chapman who had a lip ring and an old muscle car. I knew it was a muscle car because the engine growled like a beast. I practically vibrated along with the engine.

"You'll see," he answered, the smirk back.

I didn't want to creep him out by just sitting there and staring at him, so I tore my eyes away and focused on the scenery out the passenger window. I watched it fly by as we made it out of the subdivision and toward town.

"What did your last message mean?" Sterling's rumbly voice cut into my contemplation.

"What message?"

I knew what he was talking about; I just didn't want to sound too eager to volunteer the information about Miles and me, or the nonexistence of Miles and me. I honestly didn't know what was going on between Sterling and me, and I wasn't going to allow myself to hope this meant something to him.

"On Snapchat. You said something like, *He didn't say that exactly.* You trying to tell me something? Or were you being literal?"

"I broke up with Miles," I blurted.

So much for playing it cool.

I didn't look at him. I just kept my eyes trained on the passing landscape. I had read somewhere that silence could be deafening. In that moment, I understood the phrase. The silence was so loud I could hear every shift of his body and the rustling of his clothes. I didn't realize I had been biting my lip until the coppery tang of blood hit my tongue.

I rubbed my hands down my thighs and listened to the sound of the tires moving over the blacktop.

We turned off onto a road that led to the lake, giving me an idea of where he was taking me. He had mentioned Westbank Park a few days ago, so I wondered if he was taking me to the pier he had wanted me to meet him at the other day.

As we took another turn, I saw the sign declaring "Westbank Park" with a large, white arrow pointing in the direction we were traveling.

He pulled through the iron gate and into the graveled parking lot, stopping the car in the deserted lot. Then we just sat there, staring out the windshield at the lake in the distance, lost in our own thoughts.

"I'm glad you broke up with him. He was a douche, Ally," Sterling said, his tone carrying a bitter tinge.

I quickly cut my eyes to him and saw that he wasn't looking at me. He was still staring straight ahead, his jaw flexing. His eyes were distant, not like he was staring out at the lake, but at something else, maybe a memory? The harsh lines of his face were made more prominent by the moonlight that streamed through the glass. He looked older, more serious. There was also something different about his face that I couldn't put my finger on.

I searched, starting with his eyes, lingering on the blades of his cheekbones, and then dipped to his plush mouth and strong jaw, then back up again. It took me a minute, but I finally noticed the lip ring was gone, leaving a small hole where it had once been.

"Where's your lip ring?" I asked, sounding harsher than I had intended, but I was disappointed he had taken it out. I had always been curious about it, like what it would feel like against my own lips. Was it cool to the touch, or warm from resting against his skin? I had this recurring fantasy of testing it with my tongue.

The question must have jolted him out of wherever his mind had gone because his answer drew me from my not-so-innocent pondering.

"Mrs. Cook said it had to come out for the musical."

"Oh." I didn't try to hide my disappointment. Elodie had said Sterling got the role of Danny when we had talked after she got my backpack for me.

"Did you like it, princess?"

I narrowed my eyes, but didn't say anything. I wasn't going to give him the satisfaction of an answer.

"You don't have to answer that. It's written all over your face," he announced as he opened the door and unfolded himself from the car. Before he closed it, he stuck his head back in and looked at me from under his brows. "Don't even think about getting out without me. So, sit tight."

Had he read my mind? If so, I was in trouble.

I sat there like he had asked. It wouldn't do to hurt myself trying to get around just to spite him.

A moment later, he was opening my door and scooping me out of the passenger seat. I again found myself with my arms wrapped around his neck.

As he walked toward the water, I warned, "If you throw me in and leave me there, I will kill you."

"Now, what have I done to give you the impression that's something I would do?"

I said nothing as we headed, not for the pretty picnic area that was set up by the lake, but toward another wooded area. Sterling was definitely getting his workout in tonight.

"Do you need to rest? You've been hauling me around a lot today."

"Nah, I'm good."

And I guessed he was. He didn't sound winded as he moved along the wooded shore.

I didn't know how he could see where he was going since the canopy above had blocked most of the light from the moon. However, a few minutes later, we emerged into a small area that was cleared just enough to reveal a pier. It wasn't new, but it wasn't old. The wood was weathered, yet it still looked solid.

"I didn't know this was here," I whispered.

"That's probably because you and your girlfriends never moved past the picnic area," he replied sardonically.

He was right. They had roped off a small area for swimming at the picnic area, but the girls and I never swam. We just sunbathed in our bikinis on the shore. Lake water was beneath us, as Laura would say. The only time we came here was because the guys wanted to. We could swim at any one of our houses, but the lake had less supervision.

"How do you know that?"

Had he seen us? Had he been up here during the summer and I never noticed?

"Just a wild guess," he muttered.

His footsteps sounded hollow as he walked down the pier with me still in his arms. When we got to the end, he set me down, and I slowly untangled my arms from around his neck, resting them on his shoulders.

Sterling wasn't looking at me; he was concentrating on digging something from his pocket. When he pulled it out, I saw it was his phone. I started to lift my hands off him when his voice stopped me.

"Keep your hands there." The light from the screen illuminated his face as he moved his fingers over it.

It was chilly, and the sweatshirt wasn't doing much against the breeze as it came off the water. It was peaceful, though, with the sound of the water lapping the shore.

The soft sounds of music flowed from his phone as he reached behind him to put it away. Then he moved his now free hands under my sweatshirt, gently gripping my hips before swaying us.

"Um, what are we doing?" I asked hesitantly.

His fingertips were burning a hole through the material of my leggings. Then, when I felt his thumb brush my bare skin, it was like a shock of electricity.

"We're dancing really slow."

That wasn't what I meant, and he knew it. Was he interested in me? Was this a date? How could I be on a date and not know it? I always knew when I was on a date with Miles.

I didn't know if I wanted to laugh or cry. My heart felt lighter than it ever had in my life. If this was a date, it was the best one I had ever had.

I licked my lips and looked up to see Sterling gazing down at me. Neither of us said anything as we moved in motion with the song, the lyrics seeming to wrap around us.

I broke eye contact and leaned forward, resting my forehead against his hoodie-covered chest, breathing in the clean scent of him.

The emotions were too much, too intense.

I was born under a dark cloud. I had never been what you would call a happy person. Not even as a child. Happiness was always a fleeting feeling, tinged with inevitability. An inevitability that something would happen to snatch it away. But slow dancing on this pier, defying everything I knew to be *right*, I had a glimpse of true happiness. Of freedom. I wasn't thinking about the future. I was thinking about tonight. Right now. The lyrics of this unconventionally romantic song stirring something inside me.

When it was over, we stood in each other's arms, not moving, lost in the moment and in each other's presence and warmth. I wanted to burrow inside Sterling and never leave. I knew when I looked back on this, I would note it as one of those life-changing occurrences.

"What song was that?" I asked quietly, though there was no one else to hear me. The moment just felt too fragile, as if any noise would shatter its beauty.

"'First Day of My Life' by Bright Eyes," he murmured just as quietly. I didn't know if he was being quiet because I was, or if he was feeling all I was feeling.

"I love it." My voice was thick and sounded foreign.

"Good."

GETTING THE STORY STRAIGHT

I walked into the kitchen, surprised to see my dad, hair wet, seated at the bar with a bowl of oatmeal in front of him. I wanted to ask when he had gotten home and where he had been, but ... I wasn't sure I wanted to know. I had a feeling something was coming. It was looming over our heads like a guillotine. The atmosphere in the house was different. Where there had been no tension between my parents before, it was practically a corporeal thing now.

My mom was at the table on her laptop, but when I came into the room, she quickly shut it.

"Morning," I called, my eyes darting between the two adults in the room.

My dad grunted, while my mom greeted, "Morning, honey."

I saw Mom from this weekend was back.

"Do you want me to fix you breakfast? I can make bacon and eggs."

I stopped and stared at her. *Bacon and eggs?* I hadn't had either of those things in ... I didn't know how long.

My eyes darted toward my dad, whose face was like thunder. My father was a man who could communicate everything he wanted to say with a look, and the look he was shooting me and my mother said, "don't even think about it."

I opened my mouth to tell her "no, thanks," but my dad decided to reiterate his point by saying, "Ally, you're going to be down for a while, so it's important not to pack on the pounds. You—"

"Lay off, Derek." Mom gave him a look filled with warning.

My gaze shot to my mom then my dad, who shut his mouth then got up like his butt was on fire. He threw his still full bowl into the sink then stormed out of the room without another word.

"Mom ..." I swung my head toward her, about to ask what was going on. I might not have wanted to know before, but if she had Derek Everly on the run, I wanted in on the secret.

She just shook her head at me and said, "He has another business trip to get ready for, and he's in a hurry."

Sure. I squinted at her and tried to get a read on her expression, which was carefully blank.

I opened my mouth again to ask where he was off to and where he had gone the last time, but she cut me off again.

"So, bacon and eggs?" Her face transformed from blank to faux cheerful.

I nodded, hobbling my way to the table and sitting down. I watched her closely, looking for a sign of something that would clue me in on what was going on as she quickly and efficiently fixed me breakfast then set it in front of me.

I stared down at the bacon and eggs, suddenly wanting to cry.

"Don't forget you have physical therapy at two," she told me as she sat down with her own plate in the chair next to mine.

I searched her face again. She looked the same as she always did. No wounds or scars visible to indicate that aliens had invaded and swapped her brain out for another one.

Wait ... I needed to tell her about the change to my schedule. I didn't know if I could miss theater with the musical coming up.

"Um, Mom?"

Her eyes came up to meet mine, looking at me expectantly.

"I ... um ..." I wasn't sure how she was going to take me dropping athletics. I knew Dad was going to blow his lid, though I couldn't do anything with it anyway.

"What, Ally?" Her tone was soft, not impatient for once.

"I ..." I decided I should just treat it like a Band-Aid and rip it off. "Idroppedathletics."

"What was that?"

I took a deep breath, counted to five, and then said on the exhale, "I dropped athletics."

Her mouth dropped open, and her eyes widened.

I took advantage of her shock and explained, "See, I kind of stumbled into the theater class's auditions for *Grease* ..."

She was still staring at me, and her eyes had gotten impossibly wider, but at least her mouth had closed.

"And, well, I got the part of Sandy. And to participate in the musical, I had to be in theater ... so I switched."

I waited for her to say something, anything, and when she did, it was my turn to gape at her.

"Do I need to sign anything?"

That was it?

I swallowed hard. "Um, yeah ... I think there are some forms in the stack I got from both the office and Mrs. Cook."

"Okay." She then went back to eating her breakfast that wasn't on the approved list of diet foods for either of us.

I just stared at her. No comments or concerns?

"Um, do you think Dad—"

"Don't worry about your father. Now eat your breakfast before it gets cold."

With that, I dug in and savored every bite.

Before I left for school, I had all the necessary paperwork signed and ready to turn in. Maybe today really *was* the beginning of the first day of my life.

I breathed deeply, and it was easy as I navigated my car toward the high school; unlike before, when it had felt like I was fighting for every breath. A cautious hope had been planted yesterday, and today it was taking root.

❧

I pulled into my assigned spot in the parking lot to see Miles sitting on the large concrete base of the light pole next to it. My palms started sweating, and my stomach turned. Anxiety and awkwardness made my skin feel like it was too tight for my body.

I moved the gear shift to park, and before I even had the engine cut, he had the door open.

What in the world?

"You do realize we broke up, right? I don't think I dreamed that yesterday."

He chuckled as he helped me out of the car before opening the back passenger door and taking out my backpack and crutches. He handed me the crutches, but swung the backpack on the opposite shoulder from where his hung. "No, you didn't dream it."

"So, what gives?"

I scanned the parking lot to see Laura emerging from her car, glaring at us. I ignored her and started scooting toward the door. Several people waved and called out to both Miles and me. I gave small smiles in return, while Miles did that guy chin jerk thing. This was the usual for us, Homecoming King and Queen greeting their court, but it felt awkward today. Miles and I weren't a couple anymore. So, why were we greeting everyone like we were?

Feeling another pair of eyes burning a hole through my back as I crossed the parking lot, I stopped and turned just my head to look over my shoulder.

Sterling stood next to a black Ford Fiesta with Blake chattering away at him. I could tell he wasn't listening as his blue/brown eyes bore through me. The skin between his brows was furrowed, and the corners of his lips were turned down in a fierce scowl. I tried to send him a bewildered look, but his face went blank. Then he turned his attention to Blake, who was gesticulating animatedly with his hands.

My stomach sank to my feet.

I felt a hand touch my elbow and shifted forward again.

"Did you hear me, Ally?"

I shook my head, trying to ignore the sick feeling curling in my stomach. Miles and I were back in motion and on the sidewalk that led to the school's main entrance.

I kept my head down, ignoring the other students, and answered, "No, sorry. I spaced. So, why are you walking me into school?"

"Because I think we should get our story straight," he stated, like we were in on some big conspiracy.

Story? What story?

He opened the door for me and let me walk through first as I asked, "Sorry?"

"Yeah, I, um ... I suppose you didn't tell anyone we broke up? You didn't change your status on Facebook or anything. I just wondered ..." He hovered over me, keeping the other students from accidentally knocking into me or jostling me as they tried to get to their lockers before the bell rang. It was almost time for the first one.

"No, we're still broken up. I haven't been on Facebook in probably a year."

"Oh," he said, blowing out a breath. Then he opened the door that led to the locker area as the bell sounded.

"So, again, story?" My voice was impatient as I tried to avoid hitting people with my crutches, but the hall was a crush. People tried to stop and talk to us, but I avoided eye contact and kept moving, shutting them down. Plus, I was stuck on the fact that Sterling was mad at me.

"Yeah, people are going to ask why we broke up and stuff," Miles finally answered when we were at my locker.

I got it now. He didn't want me to tell anyone I dumped him. Pride was a large, yet fragile thing.

"I planned on telling people that it was a mutual thing. We both just wanted to be friends."

He handed me my backpack, and I was in the process of switching books when he asked, "Really?"

I fought the urge to roll my eyes.

"That's the way it happened, right?" I looked up after zipping my backpack and gave him my big-eyed, innocent look.

He looked at his shoes then back up at me from under his lashes with a half-grin playing at his mouth. It was an attractive look, but it did nothing for me. "I have to admit, I wish things could have been different."

A strangled sound came from the back of my throat. *Uh-oh.*

"But they are what they are, and I'm kind of relieved we're not stuck in that place anymore. Waiting is hard."

I didn't fight the urge to roll my eyes this time. He hadn't waited for anything.

"Turn, and I'll put your backpack on."

Again, I felt him before I saw him. I had been staring at the floor in front of me as Miles hefted my backpack on my shoulders, but when I lifted my eyes, I saw Sterling at his locker a little farther down the row from mine.

The way the school had their lockers set up was weird. The classroom area was behind two sets of double doors and was one big horseshoe. Before you got to the classrooms, there was a sectioned off area of lockers between the two halls. The back wall had your standard top and bottoms, but the rest of the lockers were island rows of just bottom lockers with a laminate counter on top. You could see from one end to the other. The back row was for seniors, and then worked its way to the freshman on the row before you entered the horseshoe hallway of classrooms.

Sterling's locker was closer to mine since our last names were not far apart on the alphabet, and we were both juniors, which meant we were the second row from the first.

Sterling was watching our exchange, something flashing in his eyes before I watched them completely freeze over. I shivered from the chill as he tore his eyes away from mine. Then I saw the flex of his jaw as he clenched his teeth. He shook his head and charged away, disappearing behind a swarm of teenage bodies.

I felt hands on my shoulders before I heard Miles ask, "What is up with that dude?"

I didn't say anything, because I didn't know.

"He giving you trouble again?"

"No!" I spun around and faced Miles, whose shoulders had drawn back at my cry.

"I think he's gay, babe."

What?

"Why would you think that?" I asked, flabbergasted. Sterling was *so* not gay. Last night at the lake was definite proof of that.

Nothing had happened, except dancing, but the tension that had built between us as our bodies brushed and swayed together left no doubt in my mind there was something between us. And it wasn't platonic.

"He's always hanging out with that gay guy."

Seriously?

"That doesn't make him gay, Miles," I said with a touch of laughter and disbelief.

"Whatever. He's not good enough for you."

That sobered me up.

"I don't think that's your call."

"He's not one of us, Ally."

Thank God.

"Thank you for helping me with my backpack," I said as I moved to go around him since the hall had cleared while we had been standing there, discussing something that wasn't his business and never would be. The tardy bell was about to ring, and I didn't need to be late.

He grabbed my arm, and I swiveled my head around to look at him.

"Just think about what your parents would say, okay? They wouldn't approve of him."

I wanted to laugh. Was he trying to keep me away from Sterling, or have me run straight into his arms?

"Sure, Miles."

He let go of my arm and just gave me a grim look. Probably because I hadn't sounded very convincing, even to my own ears.

I pushed off with my crutches and step-clanged my way toward my first-period physics class. When I was outside the door, the tardy bell sounded at the same time I felt my phone vibrate in my pocket.

I propped myself against the wall outside the door and pulled my phone out, hoping it was Sterling. However, the screen showed a text from my mom.

Mom: *Moved your physical therapy appointment to your lunch hour. Didn't want you to miss your first official day of theater, first impressions and all that. Be safe. Good luck. Love you.*

The excitement I had felt this morning had been dimmed after Sterling's reaction when he had seen me with Miles. Now I was both relieved and disappointed after my mom's text. Relieved I wouldn't have to miss theater, but disappointed it wasn't Sterling on the other end of the message.

I opened Snapchat and clicked on the chat icon, then clicked on Sterling's thread.

Me: *Everything okay?*

I then typed, "*Miles and I are still broken up,*" but deleted it and started again.

Me: *This morning wasn't what it looked like. We're still broken up, and that's why Miles was walking and talking with me.*

Me: *He wanted to "get our story straight." **rolling eyes emoji***

I waited a minute, hoping and maybe praying his Bitmoji would peek back at me. I was already late, so it wasn't like I was in a rush. When it looked like he wasn't going to reply anytime soon, I finally typed one last message.

Me: *Hope to talk to you in theater class.*

Gah, I was lame.

BEAR WALL OF FAME

The day did not improve. I never managed to catch Sterling's eye again, and he never responded to my Snapchat messages. It scared me a little that a boy I didn't know all too well was governing my mood.

I went to physical therapy and lay on one of the training tables with these electrode things hooked up to my thigh again after they iced it for twenty minutes. This only gave me time to obsess over all the reasons he had never replied.

My physical therapist, Jamie, declared my injury was in better shape than she thought it would be while she was taping my leg with something called KT Tape. This surprised me since I hadn't done everything like the doctor had told me.

The KT tape was supposed to help take pressure off my tear and make the muscles surrounding it do the work. She thought I would only need to finish the week out on the crutches, and then try walking with just the KT tape and no brace.

I made it back to school, note in hand, just in time for my last class. The step-drag sound I made echoed throughout the cafetorium as I scuffled in right before the late bell sounded.

I was lucky Mr. Tanner had excused my tardy from this morning. I had played up my injured leg. Did I feel bad about it? No, not really.

Everyone was already seated on the steps, most looking at me since I made such an awful noise with these things. Elodie hopped up and took my backpack from me while I propped my crutches against one of the tables in front of the stage. She tried to help me walk over to sit, but I waved her away and took the bottom seat in front of her.

I looked over to where Sterling was seated next to Blake, not sparing me a look. I darted a glance at Raven, who was seated on the other side of Blake. She was peeking at me from the corner of her eye, her lips twisted into a smug smile.

I stared at the patch of tile in front of me, not really seeing anything, wondering how I had gotten back to this point. Despair hung over me like a shroud, my arms felt like someone had beaten my armpits with a bat, my leg was sore, and I was trying really hard to see the point of being here. I was drawing in on myself again, retreating from the devastation his apathy made me feel.

"All right, class!" Mrs. Cook cried as she clapped her hands together like we were a group of unruly kindergarteners, making me jerk at the sound. "I have assigned the rest of the roles. They are posted on the wall backstage. Once you check that, please grab the scripts and CDs that are on that table." She pointed to one of the tables in front of the stage. "Then, let's get to practicing some of these songs." She clapped her hands, but this time in excitement.

I didn't move. I waited for everyone to get their copies and get settled before I slowly made my way to the table. I didn't even bother to see what Sterling was doing. I couldn't take him ignoring me.

What had I done that was so wrong? It wasn't like Sterling was my boyfriend. I could talk to whomever I wanted. I just wondered if it was something else. Maybe he had realized I wasn't worth the effort, or that I wasn't who he had thought I was.

I tuned out the sound of everyone talking and was reading through the script when Mrs. Cook's voice cut through the chatter.

"Okay, first, let's have our Danny and Sandy come up. Pink Ladies and Burger Palace Boys, follow along in your books on the steps, but you don't have to sing. We'll play the lyrical version so Danny and Sandy can perform along with lyrics." She delivered that in such a rush that she had to suck in air when she was through. I swore she gave that whole instruction on a single breath. "Everyone else needs to move to the tables and start reading through their scripts," Mrs. Cook added hastily and breathlessly.

The dull throb of an oncoming headache began to pound in my temples. I closed my eyes and rubbed circles there with my fingertips. Then I yanked the ponytail holder from my hair and did a quick finger-comb, trying to relieve the pressure.

"Ally?"

I looked up at Mrs. Cook, and then around the room, noticing everyone else had moved.

I gingerly got up, watched my feet as I walked up the steps, and stood in the middle of the stage as I waited for instructions. I knew he was there—I could feel him—but again, I was afraid to look at him. I wasn't strong enough to see the indifference in his eyes after what he had given me on the pier. I had hoped things would be different today, but I was back to being alone. Always alone.

"So, grab the lyrics for 'Summer Nights,' and let's try it out."

I flipped the book open, located the song, and kept my eyes trained on the lyrics in front of me.

The music began, and then Sterling started singing. When it was my turn, I sang, but my heart wasn't in it. I turned my body toward his, but focused on a spot above his head in the wings. Mrs. Cook sang the accompanying parts, the only one who sounded excited about a summer romance. Neither Sterling nor I were very convincing, though I was really impressed Sterling could hit those John Travolta high notes.

Once the song ended, the room plunged into awkward silence.

"Oh my goodness gracious, that was awful! You all sounded like you had a wet blanket thrown over yourselves." Mrs. Cook sounded horrified.

Heat hit my cheeks, my shoulders drooped, and my shoes were looking pretty interesting right now. I reached back and rubbed the tension from my neck, hoping she wouldn't make us do it again.

"I want you two to go in the back and work on this. If y'all can't get it together, I'll have to recast."

Maybe she should. Maybe I should try the work program and get an early release instead of theater.

I limped down the steps again and made it to my crutches, hastily jamming one under each arm. I winced as I put my weight on the pads. I was ready to throw these things to the curb. I guessed there would be no more carrying me around.

I glanced around the room and saw Sterling's back as he headed toward the spot in front of the gym doors. I step-swung my way over there, taking my time since I really, as in *really*, didn't want to do this.

I stopped a few feet away and kept my eyes on the gray brick wall by his left ear. Neither of us spoke. Tension, and not the good kind, sat heavy in the air. I was tempted to say screw it and walk around the corner to the parking lot.

He sighed, and then asked in an annoyed tone, "Will you at least look at me?"

I darted my eyes to his face, but then quickly back to the wall.

"Longer than five seconds."

I could tell he was getting impatient. I didn't know why he was acting this way. I didn't do anything to him.

I reluctantly took my eyes away from the wall. It was an exquisite sort of agony. I loved his eyes. They were usually warm, but even now, as they stared back at me, devoid of any emotion, they were still the most beautiful pair I had ever seen. The brown, the color of rich amber, looked to have bled out from the small portion of sky blue that had taken up less than half of the iris in one eye and just dotted in the other.

"Why are you acting like this?" I asked in accusation laced with hurt, which was pathetic, but I had to know. I could feel the sick churning in my stomach threatening to escape, but I couldn't stand this gulf that seemed to have come from nowhere. He had been the one sending me snaps, and he had been the one knocking on my window at night while I still had a boyfriend. Now, after giving me hope, he wanted to jerk that out from under me for no reason? No, I needed to know what I had done that had been so wrong.

He scoffed as he looked down at the floor while shaking his head like he couldn't believe I had just asked him that.

I pulled in a breath and held it, trying to control the burn in my chest.

"So, how's Miles? He good?"

Uh, did he even read my Snapchat messages?

I straightened out of my hunched position over the crutches and asked, "How would I know? Didn't you read the messages I sent you?"

He lifted his head a little and studied me. I could feel his eyes as they darted from my hairline to my eyes and finally settling on my lips. Then he reached behind him and pulled out his cell phone. He moved his fingers over the screen, his face a picture of concentration before it cleared. When he looked at me again, the expression on his face morphed into one of relief.

"So, that's why he was all over you this morning?"

"He wasn't all over me this morning," I shrilled.

"Uh, princess, he was touching you."

There he went with the princess thing again. I still wasn't sure I liked it. I didn't feel like a princess. I felt more like the unwanted step-daughter.

I grimaced and shifted my weight to my good leg. The usual ache had turned into an insistent throb of pain.

"You hurting?" The concern etched on his face eased the sting of his earlier hostility.

"Yeah, I went to physical therapy at lunch, and they did this elec-trode thing that made my muscles contract. It didn't feel too bad then, but I think it's catching up to me now."

He nodded, and then, before I knew it, I was in his arms, and he was striding over to the lunchroom tables. He deposited me in the closest chair then grabbed the one next to it, flipped it around, and straddled it. He folded his arms on the back and rested his chin on top of them.

"You don't have to keep doing that," I said as I stretched my legs out in front of me and winced. The insistent pain had dulled, but it still throbbed.

"I don't mind. You're light and probably weigh a buck twenty soaking wet."

He was wrong about that. I weighed one-thirty, and that was naked and dry. I wasn't too short, and I wasn't too tall; just average height. My body, however, was comprised mostly of muscle. My dad had had me lifting weights from the time I was twelve until the week of my injury. I wasn't about to tell him any differently about my weight, though. Not that there was anything wrong with my weight, but still ... I wasn't about to contradict him if he thought I weighed less. My mother would just about die if I did. I rolled my eyes and changed the subject.

"You think she'll recast us?"

There was a devilish twinkle in his eyes, and the corner of his mouth tipped up. "No," he replied like he had all the confidence in the world, and I guessed he did.

I wished I had that kind of faith in myself.

I chewed my lip as we sat there, not saying anything. There was music playing and people talking, but it didn't intrude on our little bubble back here in the corner.

Drawing up the courage, I decided to ask him what had been bothering me for most of the day. "So, why were you mad at me today?"

"I wasn't mad at you."

I made a rude noise, blowing air out through my lips in disbelief before I could check my reaction. My eyes widened to the size of platters, my cheeks felt like they were on fire, and I slapped my hands over my mouth. However, Sterling gave no reaction to the fact that I practically spit all over him.

Finally, he chuckled, but it held no humor. He looked toward the trophy case that lined the wall between the two sets of double doors that led to the gym.

"You were mad at me," I insisted. I knew it was true. It had been in his eyes, and the hostility that had just radiated from him onstage and after.

Only his eyes shifted back to me, and it was just for a moment, before he looked back to the wall. His jaw flexed, and then he said through gritted teeth, "It wasn't anger at you driving me, princess."

I ignored the princess remark and shook my head.

"I was jealous," he admitted so quietly I thought I must have misheard him.

Say what?

I wanted to laugh, but I knew that would probably not be a good move. I was getting lax in suppressing my reactions and emotions after not being around my father for a few days. I was slipping.

"Why?" The thought of Sterling Chapman being jealous of Miles Thorpe was ridiculous.

He didn't say anything, and I let him have that.

"There is absolutely nothing for you to be jealous of Miles Thorpe for ... unless it was me you were jealous of. Miles did tell me he thought you were gay."

His face twisted, and his lip curled. "Like I would want Miles Thorpe if I were. He has to have the worst case of FOMO I've ever seen. I'd be worried I'd catch something."

I snorted. Miles was the only person who thought his horndog ways were a secret.

In any case, Sterling wasn't the only one who had been feeling jealous. I had been wondering about Sterling's relationship with Raven since she had confronted him last week in the parking lot, and that curiosity had only increased with her attitude during theater class. I wanted to ask, but I wasn't sure I really wanted the answer.

Before I could reply, the bell sounded, and the room turned into a hive of honey bees. Students poured out from the halls, their noise a buzz of chatter.

"Memorize your lines! We'll work some more tomorrow. After-school rehearsals start next week," Mrs. Cook yelled shrilly over the din. The last was barely audible.

I looked at Sterling who hadn't moved. I decided I wouldn't either and just wait out the crowd so I could walk to my car without the hassle.

I could feel everyone's eyes on us and hear the whispers, some not even bothering to whisper as they discussed us like we weren't sitting right there. I thought this would be something that would piss him off, but his lips quirked upward like he was fighting laughter.

Did I care that people were talking about me? I looked for the tight knot that usually formed in my diaphragm that made it so hard to breathe, but it wasn't there, and I didn't have the urge to do my breathing exercises. I searched within myself to see if I really cared about other people's opinions. I already knew I didn't care what my old crew thought. I was over them. I did know I cared about what Sterling thought. Not even an hour ago, the thought of him thinking badly of me about brought me to my knees.

That thought made my breath catch, and I inhaled deeply to prevent the knot from forming.

"So ..." Sterling's voice brought me back to the almost empty cafetorium, where a few kids still milled about. Other than that, it was just the two of us.

I blew out a breath and replied, "So ..."

"You really through with Miles?"

"Yeah, I never ..." I shook my head, sure that Sterling didn't want to hear about my relationship or lack of one with Miles.

"You can tell me." His chin was still on his hands, and his expression was open.

I looked around to see if anyone was close enough to hear our conversation then lowered my voice. "We were going through the motions. I haven't had feelings for him in so long it's hard to remember when I did. There just wasn't anything there anymore."

"Dumbass."

"What?"

"Miles Thorpe is a dumbass."

"Why?"

He lifted his chin and looked at me like I was crazy. "You own a mirror, right?"

A blush stole over my cheeks, and I cleared my throat before replying, "Yeah, but that doesn't mean anything."

"I can see how you would think that, especially with where your head is at, but you have to know it isn't just because you're stupidly beautiful."

I felt my face go slack. He thought I was stupidly beautiful? Raven was stupidly beautiful.

Before I could stop myself, I blurted, "Not as beautiful as Raven."

I couldn't believe I had just said that. My face felt like it was on fire.

Sterling's lip curled, and his face darkened at the mention of the other girl. "Not in the same league as you, babe. Yeah, she's gorge, but she has nothing on you. Your beauty isn't just on the outside; you have this light inside you that you don't even realize you have. You're beautiful on the inside. I don't know how it all got twisted inside your head, but you are. Your beauty shines so bright that you practically glow."

My nose started tingling, and my vision was going wonky through the wet that had gathered in my eyes. He was so wrong. There was no beauty inside me. I wasn't a good person. I was a fake, a phony. The perfect persona I had worked so hard at was a farce ... and he knew it.

"I think that's the nicest thing anyone has ever said to me, even if it isn't true. You know it's not true. Yeah, I'm not ugly, but on the inside ... I'm hideous," I whispered.

He straightened, and his head shot back like I had dealt him a blow to the face. "I'm not blowing smoke up your ass—just stating facts. What you just said ... that's a load of crap." His nostrils flared and the grip he had on the back of his chair turned his knuckles white.

"You don't even know me. My friends and I, we're not good people. I may not do the mean girl stuff, but I don't stop it either. That makes me worse than they could ever be."

"I know you. I know you're not like those vipers you're friends with, and I'm hoping now that you've dropped Miles, you've decided to cut them loose, as well. And yeah, watching those girls tear into people wasn't right, but I imagine you had a lot more things to worry about than what those skanks were doing." He lifted his brows and gave me a hard stare.

I looked away and swallowed against the lump that had formed in my throat, knowing what he had alluded to.

I concentrated on the framed photos that hung above the trophy case. My dad's picture was there. I could see his familiar visage. It was like looking in a mirror. I was his reflection in female form, except I wouldn't ever be on that wall. It was the "Bear Wall of Fame," where the pictures of students who had competed on the state or national level hung. I was good, but I didn't have the talent he had possessed. My legs were a little too short, and the love for the sport just wasn't there to make up for the deficiency.

A lump formed in my throat and my eyes itched. So many hours wasted on something that didn't matter. Something I didn't even care about in the first place and would be forgotten ten years from now, and for what? Nothing. A dislocated hip and a torn hamstring. My chest burned at those thoughts, and I didn't realize I was crying until I felt a touch on my cheek.

I instinctively drew back, but Sterling didn't move. I hadn't even heard him get up, so lost inside my head. He was crouched in front of me, swiping the tears off my cheeks with his thumbs. His touch was so gentle, so soft that I felt everything inside me just crumble.

"Shh ... We'll fix this," Sterling murmured as he pulled me into his arms and I sobbed into his shoulder.

I faintly heard someone in the background ask, "Is she all right?"

No. No, I wasn't all right.

I felt Sterling nod, his cheek brushing against my hair.

"Should we call Derek?" That came from another voice, and it made me freeze.

Sterling must have read my body language, because he answered, "No, she'll be okay." He said this with so much confidence that I pulled away and looked at him in the face.

He was gazing right back at me, resolve etched over every feature, determination blazing from his eyes.

He tilted his head forward, and I shifted to see Mrs. Cook and Mr. Goddard, the principal, behind me. Mr. Goddard was a short man with thinning gray hair that he tried to comb over. He was as round as he was tall.

I nodded and assured them, "I'm fine. Um ... Just a little overwhelmed with the leg and all." I pasted on a watery smile, hoping they would buy the lie.

Mrs. Cook looked at us with both relief and delight. She reminded me of a 1950s housewife in her black and white polka dot housedress and cardigan. She even had on red lipstick that could often be found smeared on her teeth.

I guessed our current position assuaged her worry about having to recast the roles. We definitely looked cozy now.

Mr. Goddard, who normally could only be described as jolly, looked concerned, but there was something else in his face that I didn't like —disapproval.

"Well, young people, I advise that you take time to collect yourselves, and then move along. Students shouldn't be hanging around here after school without purpose." His glasses slipped down his nose, but he didn't bother to lift them, which made him look more disapproving.

I took in a deep breath and exhaled a shuddered, "Yes, sir."

"Yes, sir." Sterling's wasn't as deferential and held a note of sarcasm.

I shot a cut-it-out look his way, but he didn't even look at me. He just smiled a big, insincere smile at Mr. Goddard until the man toddled away.

Mrs. Cook was still there, examining us. Then she said, "You both might want to start working on your scripts on your own time together. I'll have some CDs made with the music. The more we practice, the better the performance will be." Her voice rose in excitement on those last words.

"I was just about to suggest that to Ally, Mrs. Cook." The smile he gave her was just a little less genuine than the one he had given our principal.

"Good, good." She nodded then sashayed her way back in the direction of her classroom.

"She has a point," Sterling said as he rose from his seat and grabbed my crutches.

"What?" I asked as I looked up at him, not bothering to get up just yet.

"We should get together on our own time to run lines. We can't today 'cause I have to be at work, but what about tomorrow? You wanna come to my house after school?"

My eyes rounded. "Are you asking me to come to your house?" I asked stupidly with no small amount of wonder.

He chuckled. "Uh, yeah ..." He drew the *yeah* out like I might not be all there upstairs.

"Where do you work?"

I didn't know he had a job. Then again, I really didn't know him at all, so I didn't understand why I was so surprised. I promised myself right then that I would remedy that. I was going to learn everything I could about him.

"I work at my gramp's auto shop when he needs me or when I need the extra money."

"Which is it today?"

He smiled a smile that made me tingle all over. "Extra money."

A smile formed on my lips.

"Your eye makeup's smeared." He reached out and wiped the remaining wetness from under my eyes, then rubbed his thumb on his jeans.

I covered my face with my hands so my voice was muffled when I asked, "Does it look bad?"

"Nah." He chuckled. "I got it pretty good."

I dropped them and looked up at him to see if he was being serious. His chin was tipped down, and he held me in his steady gaze.

"Okay." My voice was small and unsure, but I was going to take his word for it.

"Let's get out of here before Old Goddard loses the rest of his hair."

I laughed, but then winced when he helped me to my feet. We made the trek to the doors that led to the student lot and walked down the long sidewalk outside. His hand was firm and warm where it rested against my lower back as he guided me.

"Do you want me to carry you?"

My leg was really starting to burn, so I just nodded.

Sterling helped slip my backpack from my shoulders and donned it. Then he tossed my crutches in the grass before he lifted me in his arms. He was warm and smelled good, and I couldn't resist laying my head on his shoulder as he strode toward my SUV.

There, he set me down, swung off my backpack and gently dropped it to the concrete before opening the driver's side door, telling me, "Hang tight. I'll run back up and get the crutches."

I sat in the driver's seat with the door open, my legs hanging out of the car, as I watched him jog across the parking lot and up the way. It didn't escape my notice that he had a really nice backside in those jeans. The way he moved, you would think he was getting ready to go to baseball or track practice, but that wasn't him, I was learning. He wasn't like those boys.

I inventoried what I knew about him. Sadly, it was a short list. He liked acting, drove an old muscle car, worked at an auto shop for his granddad, was friends with Blake Davis, and he gave a crap about me. Oh, and there was something going on between him and Raven. I rolled my eyes at myself because that last part sounded like a nasally obnoxious twelve-year-old in my head.

He jogged back, carrying my crutches in one hand. "Where do you want them?"

"Just put them in the back seat."

He did just that then grabbed my backpack off the ground and stuffed it back there, too.

I smiled to myself because he was just so nice.

When Miles had helped me with my backpack this morning, it had been a surprise. To him, I was more background noise. He didn't think to do those kinds of things unless he wanted something, like this morning. I was the trophy that he took out occasionally and polished. Nothing more, nothing less, even if he didn't realize it.

"Thanks."

"No probs. Got your phone?"

"Um, it's in my backpack," I said as I limply gestured toward the back seat.

When he pulled his phone from his pocket, I noted he didn't carry a backpack or any books with him. Weird.

"Tell me your number."

I rattled off my cell as his fingers flew over his phone screen, and then I heard a buzz sounding from the vicinity of my backpack.

"That's me. Now you have mine."

I didn't know what to say. My first reaction was to squeal, but that would be embarrassing. Instead, we stared at each other for a beat before he leaned in. I felt his lips touch the top of my head and sucked in a sharp breath because the feel of his lips on my hair was a burn. I could feel its heat scorching from the point of contact all the way through the rest of my body.

He pulled back, but brushed his nose along my hairline, making me shudder. Then he backed away, while my heart pounded a rapid staccato in my ears.

"Pull your feet in, princess. I have to get to work."

I tried to regulate my breathing and not look like I was as shell-shocked as I was by his tender action. I figured I failed when I saw the smug look plastered on his face.

Once I was fully in the car and belted in, he gripped the top of my door as he told me, "Drive safe. Send me a snap." Then, dead serious, he winked and shut the door.

I might have melted into a puddle in the seat.

When I just sat there and stared at him through the window, he tapped the roof of the car twice. I shook myself out of my mini-stupor that was the power of Sterling's wink and watched him step away before I faced forward and put the car in gear. Then I slowly drove toward the exit, looking in the rearview mirror and finding Sterling still standing where I had left him.

For the first time in a long time, I looked forward to tomorrow.

THE GRAPES OF WRATH

Yesterday, after getting home, I had gone into a temporary coma. Not really, but that was what it had felt like. I had come home, laid on top of the covers on my bed, still fully dressed, and hadn't woken up until my mom shook me awake the next morning.

After a hair-raising trip across town, I was still late when I pulled into my spot in the parking lot. I shut the car off and blew out a breath. No point in rushing now. I wondered if I could just hang here until it was time for second period. That was something I normally wouldn't do, but honestly, the thought of rushing inside the building on crutches made me want to jab my eye with a pencil.

It was amazing how different the world appeared in just a few days. I had been ready to end my life not even a week ago, couldn't think about anything else, and now it was ... promising. The sense of dread I had lived with for so many years, that twisted and churned inside my belly, had just disappeared. I could breathe easier ... freer. My father's absent oppressive presence and the exit of my former friends and boyfriend had changed my life for the better. For the first time in a while, maybe the first time ever, I felt like there was a net underneath the tightrope I had been walking.

My mom had showed signs of actually being human and began acting like a mom. I took a leap and did something I had never thought to do, and was now starring opposite the boy who had intrigued me since the moment I had first seen him. Sterling had saved my life, and the relief I felt now at his interruption was indescribable.

I looked around the lot and saw his car parked in its usual spot. I felt a thrill at just the sight of it. Somewhere in that school was the guy who had taken over most of my thoughts.

He hadn't texted me again yesterday, and I wondered if he had to work late or maybe he was waiting for me to make the next move. I hadn't received any more texts from Laura or Miles either. It felt weird, yet oddly freeing not to be tethered to them anymore.

To kill time, I picked up my phone and opened Snapchat. Should I make the next move?

I clicked the icon that flipped the camera to my face and jumped. In my rush to get here, I had showered but hadn't bothered to do my usual hair and makeup routine. I was fresh-faced, and my hair was in a messy bun on top of my head. Who was this person looking back at me?

I decided it didn't matter because most of these filters included eye makeup and made your skin look flawless. Who needed makeup when you had Snapchat?

I quickly scrolled through today's options and chose one that had ears and eyelashes. I posed, forgoing the popular finger to pouty lip and head tilt, and let a small smile play at my lips before I pressed the button. It wasn't bad, so I hit the "*send to*" button and selected Sterling's name. Then I paused, a feeling of self-consciousness creeping over me. Before it could fully take root, I tapped *send* and blew out a noisy breath, tapping my fingers against the doorframe.

Still not wanting to go in, I pulled my backpack over from the passenger seat and got my script out, which was a teal book with a silhouette of a couple in a convertible against the backdrop of a full moon. Sterling and I had been the only ones to receive the actual book.

I hit play on the car's CD player, and the musical filled the car. I had popped the CD in on my way home from school yesterday.

I flipped through the pages, noting it wasn't exactly like the movie. We also had the school version of the script, so it was going to be different from the original musical, as well.

My phone sounded, and I looked to see that Sterling was typing, then it buzzed with a Snapchat conversation alert.

Sterling: *Where r u?*
Me: *Parking lot.*

His Bitmoji peeked at me from behind the text screen, and I smiled.

Sterling: *Why?*

Me: *Late. I overslept. *Sleeping emoji with zzz**

Sterling: *Emoji with hands to face and screaming*

I held the phone for a minute and waited for his Bitmoji to come back, but it never did, so I opened the script book and resumed reading.

I was halfway through it when I glanced up at the clock and noted it was time to go. I stuffed everything back into my backpack then carted it over to my lap as I opened the car door and got out.

I was halfway up the walk when the bell rang for second period, and by the time the tardy bell rang, I was seated in Mrs. Jones' AP English.

Mrs. Jones was a small woman with steel gray hair that rose from her head like a cotton ball. It looked like you could just pick her up and scrub your pots and pans with her hair. She wore no makeup, and her skin hung from her face, making her eyes slit and her lips look like a permanent scowl.

I actually liked her. She was stern but fair, and her love for literature leaked through into her lessons. Right now, she was lecturing on *The Grapes of Wrath* and the symbolism that could be found within its pages.

I heard a scrape of metal against my desk and glanced down to the side. A well-manicured hand with pink polish and rings on her fingers quickly moved her hand away, leaving a folded piece of paper behind my bent elbow. I kept my eyes to the whiteboard as I reached with my other hand under my arm and grabbed it, bringing it down to my lap. I then unfolded it and spread it out against my thigh.

Did you and Miles break up? Did he break up with you?

I looked at Sarah, who studiously kept her eyes up front, and wondered what her damage was. I mean, really? After posting that video on Instagram, she had the balls to ask me that, let alone talk to me? She could get bent. I wanted to text her exactly that, but cell phones were prohibited in Mrs. Jones' classroom. You had to take them out of your backpack and put them in a slot on a plastic shoe rack she hung by her desk.

I pulled the note up and wrote my reply. Then I reached out to drop it back on Sarah's desk, when it was snatched out of my hand.

My eyes shot up, finding Mrs. Jones next to my desk with the folded paper in her hand. I was sure my eyes were rounded in horror, because I never passed notes, knowing what would happen.

"You know the rules."

Yeah, I knew the rules.

She unfolded the note, saying, "I'm surprised, Allison ... and Sarah —I'd recognize that scrawl anywhere." She peeked up over the note, her gaze lasered in on the girl next to me. "Let's see what was important enough to interrupt John Steinbeck."

Her eyes darted across the page, and then she read Sarah's questions aloud before reading my reply. "*Seriously? This is none of your business, but since you spread*—I'm going to skip this part, ladies—*you might think it is. Before you get it twisted and start spreading lies, I'll tell you. Miles and I did break up. Happy? We both decided we were better at being friends. Now you can go tell Laura like the lapdog you are, and then get bent.*"

As the classroom erupted into whispers and laughter, my cheeks grew hot.

"Now, maybe you'll think twice before passing notes in this room again." That said, Mrs. Jones strode back to the front of the classroom and picked up where she had left off.

"Bitch. Miles is better off without you. You're nothing now that you aren't Daddy's little track star," Sarah hissed in my direction.

I didn't spare a glance in her direction. I focused on the little, gray-headed literary general. However, I did make sure to scratch the side of my nose with my middle finger. I was completely done with Sarah Burns.

❧

By the time lunch came around, I was conflicted on what I should do. Should I go into the cafetorium and eat by myself? Or maybe I could try to eat in the locker room? I didn't want to just assume Sterling would save me a seat.

As I hobbled my way down the hall, past the locker area, I felt someone close in on me from the side. I turned to look at the person who was so close I could feel their body heat against my left side and started at the sight of Sterling smiling at me.

"Why don't you eat lunch with us today?"

I just stared at him as he led us through the double doors and into the busy cafetorium.

"So, do you feel like"—he squinted at the standing dry erase board that stood behind Ms. Velma, the cafeteria lady who ran the register —"chicken fried steak in line one, or Salisbury steak in line two?"

"I'm not really that hungry."

Chicken fried steak was not an approved food. I usually packed my lunch, but with being late, that was something that hadn't happened this morning.

"Come on, princess. Let's go get a subpar chicken fried steak and find a place to sit."

I balked as a voice inside my head screamed, *"How many calories are in that?"* It sounded a lot like Derek Everly.

When Sterling placed his hand on my lower back, I felt it like a brand. As long as he was touching me, I was helpless against him moving me toward the first line.

Going through the line—a first for me—I then followed him to the steps of the stage where all the theater kids were seated. He carried my tray since I was still on the crutches.

I could feel every eye in the room on me as I tried to take careful steps. The last thing I wanted was to faceplant in front of the entire school. Sweat beaded down my back and along my hairline, but I did my best to act like it wasn't.

You would think I would be used to having attention on me since, for several years now, I had been nominated to every Homecoming Court, student group, and ran track in front of large groups of people. For some reason, though, this all felt different. I felt like people weren't just watching, but judging me.

Sterling went up the steps to the very top and deposited our trays.

Then he rushed back down just as I set the crutches against the side of the stage and started shrugging off my backpack. He took the bag from me before I had it all the way off and ran it up to where the other kids had piled theirs next to the pillar. Then he was on my injured side and helping me climb the steps.

Once I was settled at the top with my feet stretched out in front of me, he placed the tray in my lap and asked, "You want me to get you a Coke?"

I felt my eyes get large again and stuttered, "Um, no, thank you ... I, uh ... can't have those." A blush crept up my neck and deepened on my cheeks. I had the urge to fan my face, because I was still sweating and now my cheeks were hot.

"Why?"

I opened my mouth to repeat the evils of sodas that my dad had ingrained in me from the time I knew what they were, but then snapped my mouth shut. Why couldn't I have a Coke? I wasn't training anymore, and he wasn't here to see me drink one.

I shook my head. "Never mind. Yeah, I'd like one."

As Sterling's smile brightened, I had a feeling he knew what was going on in my head.

He jogged down and around the corner to where the vending machines were located as I looked down at the food on my tray and checked a lip curl.

I felt a tingle on the back of my neck and scanned the area, finding a pair of burning blue eyes glaring at me. At the bottom of the steps, surrounded by a group of girls I didn't know, sat Raven, and if looks could kill, I would be dead on the floor.

"She's just jealous," said a familiar, feminine voice.

I turned my head and watched as Elodie took the spot next to me, while Blake moved to my other side but a step down, looking up at me.

"She and Sterling had a thing," he stated bluntly.

I knew it!

I looked at Elodie, who was rolling her eyes.

Before I could ask either of them about it, Sterling was back and handing me my drink.

"Thanks."

"Raven the Maven is being salty AF, burning holes through your girl," Blake informed him.

Sterling scowled, but he didn't bother to look in Raven's direction. He just shrugged and opened his own drink.

"You know—"

"Don't," Elodie cut Blake off as my eyes came to him.

"Whaaaa?"

"You know," Elodie muttered.

"So ..."

Elodie blew out a sigh of resignation.

I shifted to look at her, and she cast me a commiserating look.

Blake pointed at his own face then twirled his finger in large circles. "You should follow my Insta. Fix your face." He then dug into his own steak like he hadn't just delivered that comment.

My mouth dropped open, and my face probably turned ten shades of red.

"What?" I whispered.

"Blake!" Sterling barked.

"Not cool," Elodie commented.

"I don't lie." Blake stuck out his chin and tilted his head as he defended himself.

I knew I looked rough. No makeup, hair on top of my head, and I was wearing track pants, a tee, and my trainers.

I examined what Blake was wearing—tight skinny jeans that were folded up way past his ankles, and a white tee with the sleeves rolled up. Over that was a leather vest that looked like the front of a motor-cycle jacket, and on his feet were neon yellow canvas shoes. His hair was styled and combed over to one side in a fashionable style that contradicted his edgy look. I loved it.

When I didn't say anything, because an idea was beginning to form, Elodie replied, "Yeah, we all know, but that doesn't mean you have to say any and everything that comes to mind."

My scrutiny turned to Elodie, who was dressed in cuffed blue jean short overalls with a black, stretchy-looking, wide-necked tee that was on her shoulders now, but could hang down to the tops of her biceps if she was feeling flirty. She also had a navy and white flannel with hints of red tied around her hips, and white Docs.

"Can y'all help me shop for some new clothes?" I blurted.

Elodie's eyes widened, while a squeal from my left had my eyes and many others' darting in Blake's direction. He reminded me of Mrs. Cook in that moment as he clapped his hands together excitedly.

"Dude," Sterling grunted.

"Makeover!" he cried, both hands raised in the air in glee, ignoring Sterling's admonishment. Then he brought his hands down in a "wait" gesture like inspiration had struck before he declared, "Leather leggings."

"No," Elodie stated.

"That could work." That surprisingly came from Sterling.

My gaze shot to him incredulously.

"What? I'm a guy. Leather pants are hot," he explained as he chewed a bite of something from his plate.

"Literally," Elodie muttered.

I giggled.

Sterling swallowed, and I watched his throat work. How could someone look so good just eating. He then smiled his half-grin at me, and I fought the urge to sigh dreamily.

"She needs an edge."

I tore my eyes from Sterling and to Blake, who was defending his leather legging declaration. Then my eyes moved to Elodie, who was inspecting me out of the corner of her eye.

"Yeah, she could rock an edgier look. Her usual clothes are sweet, but they look more like a uniform."

They felt like a uniform. If Elodie could sense that, I wondered what else she perceived when she looked at me.

As a knot formed in my gut at the thought, any chance of eating went down the toilet.

"She needs a newly-single-and-looking-to-mingle wardrobe."

Sterling glowered in Blake's direction.

"Hey! You think Miles—"

"Don't," Elodie stated firmly, cutting Blake off again.

"Ellie! I was just—"

Elodie shook her head. "I know what you were going to ask."

"He could secretly play for the other team!" Blake exclaimed.

Oh, gah! Laughter bubbled out of me at the thought of Miles, pro-vagina Miles, switching teams. *Never gonna happen.*

I chuckled. "I hate to kill the dream, Blake, but that will probably never happen."

My eyes were drawn to the spot I had been sitting at just last week to see Miles there with his buddies, but no Laura and her squad. Our gazes caught, and he looked dumbstruck. When I gave him a close-lipped smile, his face blanked before he turned to Gage, who evidently had been speaking to him during our silent exchange, and said something in reply.

Laura not sitting at their table surprised me. Even Ariel wasn't sitting with her boyfriend. Scanning the room, I found them in the corner closest to the gym. Laura looked her usual unflappable self, but Ariel looked ... depressed? I had to be imagining that. Sarah mimicked Laura's look, and as I watched their interactions, it looked as if Sarah was shadowing everything Laura was doing, which was straight-up weird, as always.

"So, after school, Ally?" Elodie interrupted my inner musings.

"Huh?"

Elodie's eyes widened a fraction, and she looked at me like I wasn't very bright.

"Shopping. You wanna go shopping after school today with me and Blake?"

"I—"

"She can't. She's coming to my house today."

Everyone went silent, while I kept my eyes downcast. I couldn't stop the curl of my lips.

"Well, okay then," Elodie stated the understatement of the year.

I played with my mashed potatoes as conversations swirled around me. Mostly, Elodie and Blake talked about the musical, with a few words from Sterling here and there.

"I can't believe I have to play a character called Doody," Blake groused. "Doody, Doody, Doody, Doody." He dropped his plastic fork in disgust then set his tray away from him.

"Yeah, keep saying it because that'll make it better," was Sterling's sarcastic reply.

"Our scripts are different from the movie. I don't know some of the songs that are in there," Elodie complained.

"You watched *Grease Live*, right?" Blake asked in a loud voice, but then continued in a much quieter one. "I remember some of the songs that weren't in the movie from there. If you didn't DVR it, I'm not sure we can be friends anymore."

She ignored him and went on like he hadn't spoken. "'Hopelessly Devoted To You' isn't even in there, Ally."

I noticed that this morning and was kind of disappointed. I was lucky to have grown up watching the movie.

I cleared my throat. "Then, why was that the audition song?"

Sterling answered, "Because it was the only solo Sandy had that most of the girls would know."

"How do you know that?" Elodie asked in surprise.

"I heard her talking to someone on the phone about it before auditions last week." Sterling cleared his tray then looked pointedly at mine.

"You can have mine if you want." I pushed my tray toward him then unscrewed the cap on my soda, took a sip, and ... *Oh, holy crap! It burned!* I choked, coughed, and spluttered. Some of it bubbled up my nose, which led to me scrambling frantically for napkins. I bent at the waist so I could hide my face as I blew my nose and wiped the mess from my face. My eyes watered, and my throat felt like I had just swallowed bubbling sandpaper. I didn't remember it being like acid!

"Are you okay?" Elodie sounded concerned.

"What was that?" Blake was not concerned. He evidently found my near-death experience funny.

"Princess, come here."

I lifted my watery eyes and peeked at him through my fingers. One of his hands was at my back, rubbing up and down soothingly, but the other held a bunch of napkins. *Um, what?*

He took his hand from my back, and I instantly missed the affectionate touch. Then he was peeling my fingers from my face. When he could see me, he proceeded to wipe me off himself. The gesture struck me as odd. It seemed almost fatherly in a way, which both weirded me out and exhilarated me.

"Been a while since you had a soda?" he asked quietly.

I nodded. I probably hadn't had one since elementary school.

"We'll break you in better next time."

I wanted to laugh. There was no way there was going to be a next time.

When he was done, he wadded the napkins and threw them on the closest tray, which happened to be mine.

Elodie and Blake were arguing over soft drinks in the background and not paying attention to my embarrassing reaction to carbonated beverages.

The bell then sounded, and Sterling collected our trays.

Blake reached for Elodie's as he muttered, "My turn." Elodie smiled as she handed it to him and giggled as he huffed then jogged away.

"Wait here, and I'll help you down," Sterling commanded.

"I can get her sorted, Sterling," Elodie offered.

"Okay."

Sterling was down the steps and striding toward the tray depository when Elodie whispered in my ear, "I think he likes you."

I jerked and looked at her. "Um ..." I wasn't sure how to answer that since I hadn't even been single for twenty-four hours. What was the etiquette on those kinds of things? Still, I hoped it was true, because my slight crush was swiftly moving into serious territory rather quickly.

Elodie stood and reached out to help me up before she bent to retrieve my crutches.

"You don't—"

"I really want you to play Sandy, and if you're going to be able to do that role, you need to be in fighting form. Raven really wanted that part—still does—and if she can take it from you, she will."

My mouth opened and closed like a fish out of water. Raven would try to take my part? How?

Elodie handed me the crutches, and then bent down again to get my backpack before helping me put it on.

"I don't think crutches are going to work on these steps."

She laughed. "Oh, right."

I tossed them down a few steps while a giggling Elodie grabbed my hand on my hurt side and assisted me down. When we were on linoleum, she went back for the crutches.

Once we were settled, Elodie got up on her toes, looked in the direction Sterling had gone, and then leaned closer to me as she said softly, "He was never like this with Raven."

Before I could ask what she meant, a familiar chest was in front of me, and I looked up into the unhappy face of my ex-boyfriend.

"Ally, we need to talk," he stated tersely.

Okay.

"Um ..."

"What do you want, Thorpe?" Sterling practically growled from my left. I hadn't seen him approach, but he was now plastered to my side and glaring at Miles.

"This isn't your business, Chapman," Miles growled back.

Both guys were glaring at each other with clear dislike, and it unsettled me. Yesterday, when Miles had talked about Sterling, it was like he barely knew him. But now, seeing them in each other's space and feeling the hostility that clogged the air between them, I knew I was missing something.

"I'm making her my business."

I felt my heart flutter at his declaration.

"Look, guys, we need to get to class or we're all going to be late," Elodie interrupted.

I peeked over in her direction to see that she, too, was freaked by the confrontation.

"I was late this morning. I really don't want to be late for another class today," I added helpfully, but neither male tore their gaze from the other. "My leg hurts," I added in a pathetic voice and reached behind me to rub my hamstring.

Both guys looked down at me at that.

Miles stepped closer and said, "We need to talk, Ally. Soon. There are some things you need—"

"Ally isn't your concern anymore." Sterling's arm shot out, and he pushed himself in front of me and closer to Miles.

I peered around Sterling's bicep—he was almost a foot taller than me. The position they were in reminded me of boxers before a fight, where they stood nose to nose and talked smack to each other while photographers flashed their cameras and cameramen recorded it. Something needed to happen before the actual fight took place.

I sighed in relief when I saw Mrs. Jones walk up with her empty tray, her short legs pumping when she saw the standoff.

"Boys!" she cried, nudging her tray and one hand between them. It was comical since she was so tiny yet acted like she was ten feet tall. When neither moved, she threatened, "If either of you raises a hand, I'll whomp you with my tray." She jiggled it threateningly.

I couldn't stop the giggle that erupted from me, and evidently, neither could Elodie. Two boys over six feet tall brained by a woman who was barely five feet tall.

The boys scowled at us and stepped back from the other.

Miles opened his mouth, but Sterling cut him off, "You really want her to know?"

Miles snapped his mouth shut and twisted his neck like he had a crick, then looked down at his shoes, his jaw working.

What didn't he want me to know?

I stared at Miles, but he wouldn't look at me, so I looked up at Sterling, whose blues eyes were like chips of ice aimed at Miles.

"Know what?"

Neither would look at me.

I grabbed Sterling's shoulder and repeated, "Know what!"

"Nothing," Miles murmured before he turned and stormed away.

I looked toward Elodie to see if she had any freaking clue about what was going on. However, she looked just as shocked as me and shook her head at what must have been the silent question on my face.

"Now, Miss Everly, Thomas, and Mr. Chapman, y'all need to get where you need to go."

I had forgotten Mrs. Jones amidst our drama.

I went to step around Sterling to go after Miles when a large hand clamped down on my forearm. I lifted my eyes to Sterling's and noted that the ice had thawed, but was replaced with something unidentifiable.

My fingers felt cold, and my skin was starting to feel clammy. The whole situation was leaving a sour taste in my mouth.

"What. Is. Going. On?" I gritted through my teeth.

"It'll work itself out." He tore his eyes away, and I watched the movement of his Adam's apple as it bobbed.

I didn't know if he was lying, or if he was hoping he was telling me the truth. Nevertheless, it still didn't answer anything.

"Miss Everly. Go. To. Class."

My eyes shot to Mrs. Jones, whose head was tilted down, giving me her *no funny business* look from above the glasses perched on her nose.

She shoved the glasses back up her nose with a finger and delivered, "All of you."

I squinted up at Sterling, but it was Elodie who grabbed my elbow and tugged.

"Let's go, Ally."

I reluctantly followed her toward my next class.

A GIRL WITH A PLAN

I fumed the entire period after lunch. My face full of thunder made everyone give me a wide berth, even Mrs. Lovelace, our art teacher, avoided me. Once the bell rang, it was time for theater class. I was ready, and I was going to find out what the hell was going on around here. I had too many questions and too few answers. Not only with Miles and Sterling, but when I got home, I was going to be asking more questions.

Where had my dad really gone? I had a feeling he wasn't on a business trip, so ... where was he? My parents were pretty insular, and the few friends they had were only "society friends." They brunched, golfed, shopped, and cocktailed together—nothing else. Neither of my parents were close to their families. My dad was an only child, and he hadn't been visiting my grandparents since both sets had passed years ago.

I clip-clopped—that was what I sounded like in my head—into the cafetorium and searched for the guy who was slowly driving me insane. He was sitting by the closest table, facing the hallway doors. When he saw me, he shot straight to his feet and prowled toward me. I tried to burn him to ash with the heat of my glare, but he was apparently heat ray resistant.

We stopped in front of each other, and I opened my mouth to let him have it, but he swooped me up in his arms so fast that I had to wrap my arms around his neck to keep from tumbling forward.

"Wait! Sterling!" I cried, my crutches falling to the linoleum with a clatter. I wiggled my backpack off, and it dropped in front of one of the tables with a *thud*. I hoped I didn't have anything breakable inside.

Sterling didn't even slow. He rounded the corner in front of the gym and passed the vending machines like he was going to the band hall. He stopped in front of a door that was to the left, set me down, and pulled out his keyring. He flipped through them until he found the one he wanted and jammed it into the lock. Then the door was opened, and he practically shoved me inside.

"Where are we? How do you have a key?" I asked in astonishment, unable to see anything in the darkened room.

"Don't be mad at me." He ignored my question, which reminded me of why I was mad in the first place. I could feel his breath on my face and the heat of his body as it barely brushed against mine every so often.

"Don't tell me not to be mad at you when you're ignoring my questions." I started to pant. I didn't know if it was from anger, or being in a dark, enclosed space with someone I was extremely attracted to.

"We're in the supply closet that the theater department shares with the music department." His cheek brushed against mine, his breath tickling my ear. "Mrs. Cullen gave it to me during OAP last year and never asked for it back."

I made a noise in my throat. He knew that wasn't why I was mad and was avoiding the issue.

"Did you just growl at me?" His voice held a tinge of laughter, something I could feel against the shell of my ear.

"What is going on between you and Miles? He acted like he barely knew who you were yesterday, and today you know something I don't know about him. It also wasn't jealousy you were throwing his way today. You lied to me." I tried to keep the hurt out of my voice, but I failed spectacularly.

"I didn't lie to you, princess. I *was* jealous yesterday. I explained why, and it wasn't anger at you that made me act like an ass. I don't like Miles. I never have. I think he's a douchebag."

"Then, what were y'all getting in each other's faces about?"

I felt him stiffen, but then he relaxed. "It's something that's between me and him. He's dealing with a situation."

What situation?

I started to interrupt him, but then his lips pressed hard against mine, and my brain just ... well ... it short-circuited.

His warm and surprisingly soft lips were a dose of pure electricity. I wouldn't have been surprised if the hair on my head stood on end. My whole body tingled.

I pressed in closer, absorbing his heat, the energy that flowed from his body to mine. I wanted more.

When I was about to deepen the kiss, he pulled away.

"Wh-wha ...? Huh?" I panted. His kiss had evidently made me stupid.

"Don't interrupt me." Sterling skimmed his nose along mine, making me shiver.

"Okay ... What were we talking about?"

He laughed, and I closed my eyes.

"Well, if you can't remember, I'm not going to remind you."

I had to think for a moment, trying to recall what we had been discussing before he had scrambled my brain. All I wanted to think about was kissing him again and the fact that I wished he had the lip ring.

No.

Miles. Sterling. Secrets.

"What's going on?" I asked softly, wishing I could see his face.

"Do you trust me?"

Did I trust him? Well, he was the reason I was standing in this broom closet. If he had not knocked the pill bottle out of my hand ...

I swallowed. The sting of tears pricked my eyes and burned inside my nose.

"Yes, I trust you," I whispered.

"Then trust me when I tell you that this is something you don't need to worry about."

I opened my mouth to refute his statement, but he again pressed his lips to mine in a quick kiss.

"Y'all broke up, right?"

I nodded, but then remembered we were in the dark and he couldn't see me. "Yes."

"He's not yours to worry about anymore, and it's not your business."

I felt my spine stiffen, affronted. It wasn't my business?

I paused. Well, he was right. Miles' situation wasn't mine to deal with anymore. The lying, the cheating, the ... everything—it was not mine anymore.

I felt a weight I hadn't realized I had been carrying lift from my shoulders. Miles wasn't a weight sinking me down anymore. But, what about Sterling? What did Miles want to tell me about him?

"But, what was Miles going to tell me about you?"

Sterling went still, and this time, he didn't relax. Again, I wished I could see his face.

"I don't know. Probably some more bullshit."

Why did that feel like a lie? Should I call him on it? I did just tell him that I would trust him.

Before I could decide, he said, "We should probably get out of here."

I heard the *clank* of the door opening and squinted at the light that invaded the room.

He then yanked me to him, and I yelped.

"You okay?" he whispered. Our bodies were pressed together, and his head was tilted down to mine. His unusual eyes were all I could see, and it made my breath hitch and heart stutter.

"I love your eyes," I replied in a breathy voice that made me inwardly cringe.

Said eyes lit up, and the skin at the corners crinkled. I felt a rumble come from his chest where my fingers were digging into the fabric of his T-shirt.

"Thank you," he said, still chuckling.

"They're two different colors," I went on inanely, like he didn't know and we had all the time in the world.

"Congenital segmental heterochromia iridis."

"Um, what?"

"That's the medical term for it. Don't know if it's genetic, or if I'm just a freak of nature. The doctor nixed the mutant gene when I was a kid. So, no hope of joining the X-Men, but less than one percent of the population has it."

"X-Men? What superpower did you want?"

A devilish look crossed his face, and I would know why when he said, "What kid didn't want X-ray vision?" He leaned back and trailed his eyes from the top of my head to my chest, and then he leaned to the side like he was looking at my behind. His eyes traveling over me was like a physical touch, and my body flushed with heat. I was both hot and shivery, which shouldn't be possible. It was like my body was at war with itself.

I covered my discomfiture with a giggle and smacked his shoulder, which was hard with muscle. I had the urge to let my hand linger and possibly squeeze it.

He smiled back unrepentantly, so big and wide that I was dazed by the sheer beauty of it.

"We should probably get back to class."

Class. Right.

I gave myself a little shake and said, "Yeah, I hope she hasn't done attendance yet. You better have a good excuse for us being late."

"I got it covered, princess. Can you walk without the crutches? I doubt it would look good to Mrs. Cook—me carrying you back to class with your face flushed and your lips swollen."

My hand flew up to my lips, and my eyes widened in panic. "My lips are swollen?"

"Not bad."

He took my arm on my hurt side as we slowly walked back to the stage area, him taking a majority of the weight off my bum leg. Mrs. Cook watched us from the corner of her eyes while instructing Elodie, who stood in the middle of the stage, "Elodie, you're really going to have to project. No room to be shy now. I want Raven, Lana, and Janet on stage doing the accompaniment." She then turned her body our way and snapped, "You're late."

"We were checking what props we had in the closet," Sterling stated coolly. Meanwhile, I had mentally crossed my fingers and hoped she didn't figure out he was lying. I really didn't need the school calling my parents. They were of the mind: if you got in trouble at school, you got in trouble worse at home.

"How did you get in there?"

"It was open," he lied again, evidently not wanting her to know he had a key.

"Did you find anything?"

"No, looks like Mrs. Cullen cleared it before she left."

Mrs. Cook's face darkened, and her mouth was slashed.

The news on the street was that Mrs. Cullen had been suspended last year after having the theater kids perform a play that wasn't the one she had registered at the district competition, or an actual published play. It was one she had written, which disqualified them. She had somehow been able to keep her job this year, but before the school year had even started, she ran off to New York to be a playwright, leaving Mrs. Cook, the speech teacher, to pick up all the pieces. Therefore, Mrs. Cook had missed all the deadlines for competitions, claiming she didn't know about them. Honestly, everyone thought she had done it on purpose, not wanting to do One Act Play. But she had to do something since they hadn't done a performance this year. And since Mrs. Cook was obsessed with the movie *Grease*, it wasn't a surprise when she picked the musical. Her classroom was literally decorated with *Grease* memorabilia ... *everywhere*.

While Mrs. Cook stewed, I scanned the room for my crutches and saw them propped up next to where Blake was sitting, along with my backpack. I tried to move away from Sterling to go get them, but he held my arm firmly. I tilted my head back to look up at him, but he was still speaking to Mrs. Cook.

"We're going to have to get donations and make the rest of the sets ourselves."

Her hands went to her hips while she stared at something on the floor. She was furious, I could tell. Her bun was even quivering on top of her head.

"Well, that just means we're in for some long days and probably some weekend practices," she stated to the floor.

No one said anything. The room had gone ominously quiet with the prospect of the work that lay ahead of us. In addition to learning lines, music, and choreography, we were going to have to make props and sets in our free time. Everyone else might be dreading this, but I was anticipating it. I had found a new purpose. A purpose that would require me to spend a lot more time with Sterling.

"Okay," she barked with a clap of her hands that cracked throughout the room. "Let's get back to this last song. Then we'll try to block out the first scene. If you aren't singing, you need to be reading your script in the audience."

Finally, Sterling led me to where Blake was with my things and pulled out a chair for me that was across the table from them.

"I need my backpack."

He nodded, but before he could move to get it, it was sliding across the table.

"What do you have in there, sister? Rocks?" Blake asked incredulously.

"My life."

He mouthed the word "*okay*" then bent his head back down to his script.

I heard the chair next to me scrape against the floor and peeked out of the corner of my eye at Sterling as he sat next to mine.

"Where's your script?" I whispered.

When he tapped the side of his head, I furrowed my brows. What did that mean?

Blake snorted and muttered, "Lucky bastard."

I looked between the two, not understanding what I was missing. Before I could ask, though, the music started and Elodie's voice cut through the air soulfully but hesitantly as she began "Freddy My Love." She swayed her body side to side, but other than that, she was ... awkward.

Raven, Lana, and Janet didn't help. They sang the "ah, ah, ahs," but did so in a way that was more mocking than complementary. Elodie knew it and got progressively worse. She fumbled some of the lines, even though the lyrics were in her hand, and looked more like a pendulum on a clock swinging back and forth than someone singing about a boy they loved.

When the song ended, she put a hand over her face, and my heart constricted. I was supposed to be going over my own lines, but I couldn't take my eyes off the uncomfortable show that had played out in front of me.

"Elodie, did you forget everything I told you to do five minutes ago?"

"N-no, ma'am."

"If you can't get over this shyness, I'm going to have to recast the role," Mrs. Cook stated in resignation.

Raven's hand shot up, and Mrs. Cook called on her.

"If Elodie doesn't feel up to being Marty, I'm sure Lana could switch with her," she said in a saccharine tone that made me want to gag.

I heard a noise come from behind me, and then Blake whispered in a horrified voice, "Dude, she can't sing," to which Sterling just grunted.

I had to do something because Elodie couldn't, wouldn't lose her part.

"Mrs. Cook!" I called out, thinking of something on the fly. When she twisted her torso to look at me, I went on, "I can help her. Give us the weekend, and we'll have it all worked out."

She studied me a moment, her gaze shrewd, and then she seemed to come to a decision. "Okay, I'll give you the weekend. But if she can't perform this song by Monday, I'm giving it to someone else." She turned back to the stage and added, "But not Lana."

Blake's muffled laughter drew my eyes to him.

He bent over, his face in his script book, and his shoulders shaking.

"You're helping me this weekend," I hissed at him.

His head shot up, and he looked at me like I was crazy. "Of course I am. You may be the girl with a plan, but you have no clue what you're doing."

I couldn't argue that. I didn't know how I was going to help Elodie. I just knew I couldn't let her part get taken by one of Raven's friends. They reminded me too much of Laura and her squad, who pounced when they saw someone with a weakness and tore them to shreds. In high school, weaknesses were blinking neon signs, and if you didn't hide them, it would be social damnation.

Maybe between Blake and I, we could figure something out to help Elodie gain some confidence.

"All right, thespians! Let's block out the opening scene."

I heard someone whisper, "What did she calls us?" but I drowned out the rest of the room.

Since I wasn't in the opening scene, I kept to my seat and stared down at my script book. My mind wasn't on the words, though. I was thinking of ways for Elodie to get her groove back.

BIG LIPS AND NO HIPS

When theater was over, Sterling walked me to my car. We had managed to block out one scene and had begun another before the bell had rung, signaling the end of the day.

I wasn't any closer to figuring out a way to help Elodie. It was something I was going to have to think on tonight, or maybe I should google it. Hopefully, Blake would have some idea of what we should do.

When we stopped by the driver's door, bodies close, Sterling reached up and tucked a loose strand of hair behind my ear.

"So, you still coming over tonight?"

I suddenly felt shy. I didn't know why. I'd had a boyfriend all my teenage life, but this was different.

"Tonight? I thought I'd follow you ..."

"Can't have girls over without my pops being home. He gets off work at six, so how bout six fifteen?"

"Oh, okay."

He smiled, and instead of the usual butterflies, it felt like a flock of pigeons were flapping in my tummy. That was the effect his smile had on me.

"I'll text you the address. Gotta pick up Jack."

Before I could ask who Jack was, he bent and kissed my cheek. My breath caught at the feel of his lips on me again, and my heart might have skipped several beats. By the time I had come back to myself, I was watching his back as he jogged over to his car.

I brought my hand to my cheek to hold the feeling of his kiss to my skin. I always thought it was stupid when girls said they wouldn't wash their skin after a celebrity or their crush touched them, but now I saw the logic of it. I never wanted to lose the feeling of his lips touching me.

"It won't last." A snide voice interrupted my thoughts.

I looked toward the voice and saw Raven at the other side of my car, glaring at me with so much bitterness that all the fluttery feelings in my stomach soured.

"He's *mine*. Always has been, always will be. You'll see. He's just—"

"Look, Sarah! Raven *can* do something with her mouth besides going down on a guy. You know, I heard she uses her teeth. I can see why ... She has fangs." Laura had leaned close to Sarah and whispered the last part loud enough for us all to hear. They were standing at the hood of my car in their identical throw-down poses of arms crossed, hips cocked, wearing lethal smirks.

"Yeah, I doubt they're retractable. I also heard she gave Jimmy Brown herpes last year. I think it's true since it looks like she's getting one of those things on her lip." Sarah didn't whisper; she said it loud enough for people in the row over to hear.

Raven's hand flew to her lip, her eyes wide with horror, probably since the parking lot was still pretty full and we were drawing quite a bit of attention.

"Nasty," Laura said with a shudder.

I felt like I was having a flashback. Laura was sinking her own fangs into someone while I stood there and watched. The right thing to do would be to stop them. The kind of person I wanted to be would do that, but with the way Raven and her friends had treated Elodie earlier, she needed a dose of her own medicine.

Raven's claws were a kitten's compared to the ones Laura and Sarah owned. Theirs were the size of a tiger's, and just as lethal.

Raven looked around at the audience we had amassed, shot me a hate-filled look, and then scuttled off without a look in Laura and Sarah's direction.

I looked to where my former friends stood, but they were gone, as well, strolling off toward Laura's red Mercedes. I didn't know what that was, but I guessed it was an olive branch of sorts, or maybe a detente of hostilities. I didn't know why else they would intervene. Maybe for old time's sake? Or maybe Raven had crossed them in some way? The only feeling I could summon was a twinge of gratitude. Overall, it reminded me too much of the person I had been around them, and I didn't like it. Not at all.

I blew out a breath. There was nothing else to do but get in my car and go home. I had things to do and a boy to see.

❦

Sterling said to come over at six fifteen, so there was time to kill. I clip-clopped my way into the living room to see Mom at the dining room table on her laptop. The floorplan was an open concept, which left the kitchen, living room, and dining room one big open space with lots of windows. It was decorated in white and cream, making it look more sterile than homey, but the effect made the room seem gigantic rather than just large.

Mom was dressed in a pink tracksuit. Her hair wasn't curled like it normally was, but down and straight, hanging past her shoulders. It struck me that she looked more like Regina George's mom from *Mean Girls* today than Marilyn Monroe. I giggled as I pictured my mom saying she's a cool mom and bringing me a drink that looked like a cocktail.

She looked up from her laptop and asked, "What's so funny?"

"Nothing," I replied as I shook my head. I didn't think she would find it funny.

"How was school?"

I had my head in the fridge, getting a water, but pulled back and peeked at her from behind the door. "Fine," I said cautiously. I wasn't used to her taking an interest in anything other than what my dad told her to take an interest in.

"Theater go okay?"

"Yeah."

I closed the fridge door and was heading toward the hall when she asked, "Just yeah?"

I semi-turned back to her to see her eyes focused on me. "It was good, Mom."

"What did you do?"

I shrugged. "We worked on some of the music and blocked out a scene."

"How is your leg? You need ice?" She carried genuine interest and concern in her tone.

"Leg is good. It's just sore, but the KT tape has helped, I think."

"Good." She nodded.

I pointed down the hall. "I'm just gonna go to my room now."

"Text me if you need me to bring you anything."

O ... kay. I wasn't sure we had ever done this routine before. Still, her interest made something inside me thaw a little. I was beginning to like this new mom.

I knew I was supposed to be asking questions about where my dad was, but after my ire had burned out, and she was being this kind of mom, I was hesitant to even mention him. So, I didn't. I wanted to preserve this a little longer.

I closed the door to my room, suddenly consumed with nervous energy. I paced the room, which I probably shouldn't do without my crutches, and tried to think of ways I could help Elodie so I wouldn't obsess over going to Sterling's house.

When I walked past the full-sized mirror attached to the closet door, I froze. I had to change clothes and do something with myself!

I tore my sweatshirt over my head, and when my arms were raised, I took a whiff of my pits. They didn't smell, but I should probably shower just in case. Then I got the rest of my clothes off and hobbled into the bathroom. While in the shower, I scrubbed my armpits and other various parts, then shaved everything.

I was in a towel in the closet, violently yanking hangers from side to side when I heard my phone buzz. I abandoned my search for the right outfit to see if the text alert was from Sterling.

Unknown Number: *415 Smith St.*

Unknown Number: *You'll see my car in front.*

Unknown Number: *Like pepperoni?*

The first thing I did was save Sterling's number. Then I answered his last text.

Ally: *Like, on pizza?*

Sterling: *Yeah.*

Ally: *Then yes.*
Sterling: *Cool.*

I guessed we were eating pizza.

I let out a quiet squeal, threw my phone on the bed, and then limped back to my closet.

I dressed in a pair of jeans that had faux rips and tears down the front, giving them a worn-in appearance, and a big, slouchy, baby pink sweater that wouldn't sit on both shoulders at the same time. It constantly slipped, exposing a bra strap and the skin at my shoulder. I usually wore a tank underneath it, since undergarment exposure, even if it was a bra strap, was prohibited at school.

I did the whole dry and curl thing with my hair, so it flowed in shiny waves over my back and shoulders. Then I applied the usual makeup, but added a light pink matte gloss that looked somewhat natural and smelled like strawberries. The color made my oversized lips look not so big.

I gazed at my reflection, confirming that I looked like my dad made over—brown hair, brown eyes, light olive skin tone, and his athletic build. I both loved and hated it.

My dad had good genes, but every time I saw my reflection, I was reminded of him. This was why I often wished I had my mother's traditionally beautiful features, not to mention her curves. The only thing I had gotten from her were my lips, which seemed too large for my face. Maybe one day I would grow into them. Mom always said I would, but I doubted it. I was seventeen, almost an adult, so if I was going to, I probably would have by now.

Still, I felt pretty, which was unusual. I normally dressed and styled myself by rote, not caring or putting much thought into it. Clothes were clothes, and hair was hair. I knew I was expected to look my part, but it was nothing I felt particularly proud of when presented with the finished product. Now I felt a spark of interest.

My clothes, while trendy, were things my mother or my friends had chosen. They weren't *mine*. It was past time to change that. Hopefully, Elodie and Blake could help me with that tomorrow.

I went to my desk and opened the middle drawer, pushing things around until I came across what I was looking for and pulled it out.

This past summer, Laura, Sarah, Ariel, and I had gone to the mall a few towns over. While they were at Starbucks, I had decided to run into Claire's to kill time. While there, a set of stretchy black chokers had caught my attention. I had picked them up, examined them, and then bought them on a whim. I had then come out of the store, bag in hand, and met up with the crew.

When asked what I could have possibly bought in Claire's because, evidently, it was a store that sold cheap junk for tweens—Laura's words—I showed them what I thought was cute. I had been so wrong.

Laura had thought I had bought them as a gag, and faced with her disapproval, I had played along. I toed the line again after that, letting everyone pick out everything for me, losing myself in the process.

I opened the package, took out the black band, and undid the clasp. I pulled all my hair to one side and put it around my neck before I swung my hair back around, gave it a tousle, and arranged it back in place. Then, feeling brave, I picked up my phone and pulled up Snapchat. Two snaps in one day? He wouldn't expect that.

I smiled evilly at myself in the mirror then proceeded to send Sterling his second snap from me.

"Where are you going?" my mom asked when I emerged from my room sans crutches. I thought I would test my leg out this evening. The therapist had said I would be able to ditch them after this week.

I leaned against the counter at the edge of the kitchen and answered, "I have to go study lines with a friend." I wiggled the script book in my hand, then set it back down on the marble.

"What friend?" Mom took her eyes off whatever she was doing on her laptop and peered at me from around the screen. "And where are your crutches?"

I hesitated, not sure how she would respond. "Sterling Chapman. And I thought I would test my leg out tonight." I stretched my leg a little then bent my knee just to prove my words.

"I guess I don't know him. Where does he live?"

"Um ..." I pulled my phone out of my pocket. I hadn't really thought about where I was going. "Smith Street?"

"That area isn't bad. What does Miles think about you going over to another guy's house?"

Oh crap. I had forgotten to tell her about the breakup.

"Um ..." I shifted my weight from my bad side to my good one. I really didn't want to tell her about Miles.

"Ally?"

Of all the times she wanted to get involved in my life.

"We broke up," I spat out. Like a Band-Aid, right?

"*What!*" she shrieked.

Uh-oh. That was a code red decibel. Dogs were probably whining in the neighborhood, and I was in trouble.

"Mom ..." I was going to try to stem whatever freak out she was about to have, but I was unsuccessful.

"What do you mean, you broke up? What happened?" she yelled.

I sighed. "We decided it wasn't working. It was a mutual thing."

"A mutual thing?" she said incredulously.

What? Was there an echo?

"Yes," I replied slowly, carefully, lest I poke the bear again.

"Well, wha—"

"Mom, just trust me." I pulled my phone from my pocket and checked the time. I was going to be late if I didn't get her settled. "Miles is okay, I'm okay, and we're still friendly." I wasn't sure about that last part, but I needed to give her some reassurance. I knew I had failed when tears filled her eyes and she choked on a sob. What on earth? "Mom?"

"But, he was such a nice guy. He was so good to you."

Good to me? Snort.

"I—"

"Doesn't anyone stay together anymore?" she wailed, cutting me off.

What. On. Earth? Who else broke up?

A chill ran through me. I wanted to ask her what she meant.

"Mom—"

"Don't pay attention to me." She sniffled and rolled her eyes upward to wipe the skin underneath them. Thank goodness she invested in expensive cosmetics, because if that were a cheap mascara, it would be all over her face right now. "It's just hormones. I don't know why I got all weepy," she continued with a forced chuckle.

I still didn't believe her.

I looked down at my phone again and saw it was six ten. I was running late.

"I gotta run, Mom. But maybe, when I get home, we can talk some more, okay?"

She cleared her throat and replied, "Okay, honey."

I tried to smile reassuringly, but I feared I failed. I felt anything but reassured. I felt like the foundation beneath my shoes had suddenly turned to sand and everything was about to crumble under my feet.

I turned to leave when my mom called, "Take your crutches with you and leave them in the car. You may need them later."

"Yes, ma'am." I changed direction to get them from my room.

When I came back out, crutches in hand, she asked, "Do I need to fix you something to eat for when you get home?"

"No, ma'am. Sterling texted me that they ordered pizza."

"Be sure to text me his parents' number, okay? Just in case of an emergency."

I sighed. I was for sure going to be late, but still answered, "Okay, Mom."

I hurried to the door and through it, and when I opened my car door and was about to get in, my dad's shiny black BMW pulled into the circle driveway. Not wanting to see him or have him give me the third degree, I slammed the door shut, cranked the engine, and pulled away.

He was walking toward the house with eyes on me as I drove by, his expression set to disapproval—his normal one for me. I gave him a little wave, and he stopped, those eyes narrowing on me, likely seeing my bare shoulder. The expression on his face turned murderous.

I sped my car up and burned rubber to get out of there, checking my rearview mirror to make sure he hadn't gotten back in his car and was following me. I wouldn't put it past him.

I prayed. I prayed that the only thing he did was send me an angry text later.

SOMETIMES, IT'S THE LITTLE THINGS...

I had to pull over a little ways from my house because I had forgotten to plug the address into my GPS. Oleander was a smallish town, but I never went exploring, so I didn't know the ins and outs like most citizens. All my friends lived in the same gated community growing up, Nerium Gardens, and we only left to go to school, church, or shopping in another city.

It also allowed me to see if my dad had followed me. When five minutes went by with no BMW in sight, I felt my shoulders relax.

Before I pulled back onto the road, I shot a text to Sterling, letting him know I was on my way and apologizing for being late. Right when I was about to pull back onto the road, my phone lit up with a notification. I glanced down and saw I had a Snapchat from Sterling. I quickly shifted to park and opened the app.

The picture showed a gas stove burner with a glowing blue flame, and the text across it read, *"Is it *flame emoji* in here, or is it just you?"*

A startled giggle slipped past my lips, and I lifted a hand to feel the grin that split my face. When had I ever smiled so much? Certainly not since I had entered high school, maybe not even junior high.

An unfamiliar warmth filled me up like a water tank filling me full to bursting, and my heart felt so light I thought it would grow wings and fly right out of my chest. I suddenly couldn't wait another minute to get there and see the boy who was changing my world.

The GPS took me to the neighborhood that surrounded the elementary school across town. The houses were the crackerbox style that were so common in the South. Most were in good condition with well-kept yards, yet a few were in disrepair and boarded up. Overall, the neighborhood wasn't bad, just like my mom had said.

I turned on the street marked Smith, and then, a couple houses in, Siri declared that my destination was on the right.

Parking at the curb in front, I studied the small, square, red brick house with white shutters and posts that held up the overhang of the front porch. I shut off the engine and leaned forward until the steering wheel dug into my diaphragm. The sun had set, so I couldn't make out much. Sterling's primer gray car was in the driveway next to a red vintage truck that gleamed in the porch lighting. I guessed there was no need to search out the house number.

I inhaled through my nose and blew out a noisy breath, drumming my thumbs nervously along the steering wheel and trying to get my racing heart under control. My mouth was dry, and there was an empty feeling in the pit of my stomach. I needed to get ahold of myself. There was no reason to be nervous. It wasn't like we were alone. He had told me his pops would be home.

I grabbed my script book, opened the car door, and walked carefully up the concrete walk. At the door, I pushed the glowing orange button that rang the bell and waited.

As footsteps approached from the other side, I sucked in a breath, mentally fortifying myself to seeing Sterling. However, when the door flew open and the air in my lungs escaped in a surprised *whoosh*, the person who answered the door wasn't the boy I had expected or was coming to see. It was the boy from auditions, the one who had dragged me up on stage.

He smiled at me widely and waved his hand with so much exuberance that my surprise melted away. He said something I couldn't understand, and then moved from the door and swung his arm out wide to invite me inside. I giggled at his gentlemanly gesture and stepped in. His grin grew, and he looked behind him.

I followed his eyes and found Sterling leaning against a counter, his arms and ankles crossed, a smirk tilting up one side of his lips. Why did my breath catch every time I saw him? You would think I would be used to his looks by now, but they disarmed me every time.

"Hey," I said breathlessly.

He examined me from the top of my head to the tips of my toes.

There was appreciation there, but also heat. The kind of heat that made me shiver.

"Nice sweater," he said, eyes stuck on my bare shoulder.

"Thanks." A blush warmed my cheeks.

"Where are your crutches?" The heat in his eyes cooled, replaced by concern. As the skin between his brows furrowed, I had the inexplicable urge to massage it away with my fingers.

"Decided to have a dress rehearsal without them. PT says I can ditch them next week." My tone was light, and I hoped it relieved his worry.

"Then, shouldn't you wait till next week?" His tone was hard, and the corners of his lips had turned down.

I opened my mouth to argue with him, when someone touched my covered shoulder, making me jump. I turned toward the boy I had yet to be introduced to, who had dark hair like Sterling's, but his eyes were ocean blue, no brown mixed in. The rest of his features resembled the markers of his genetics. He was speaking again, but I could not find a familiar word.

"Jack, why don't you get the plates? Sterling, quit giving her shit," came a deep, rumbly voice, and I shifted to look where it had come from.

A large, broad-shouldered man stood at the mouth of the hall. He was dressed in a vintage Grateful Dead tee, not unlike the kind Sterling wore, but his was larger due to his bulging biceps and broader shoulders. His hair was silver and combed to the side, his beard dark with silver streaks, and his eyes were the exact shade of Sterling's icy blue. He moved toward us, his hand outstretched.

"Silas Chapman, but you can call me Pops."

This was Sterling's pops? He didn't look like any pops I had ever seen.

I clasped his large hand and gave it a firm shake like I had been taught and said, "Allison Everly, but you can call me Ally."

He turned his head to look at Sterling from over his shoulder. "She's a beauty, son. Like this one better than the last one."

"Pops," Sterling growled.

Pops chuckled. "Okay, okay. Don't get your panties in a twist."

Jack started speaking again, and Pops' eyes went to him and warmed.

"Yeah, J, let's go eat, buddy." He clapped Jack on the shoulder and gave it a shake before they led us to the four-seater dining table where a pizza box sat.

As I passed Sterling, he came in close, his shoulder brushing mine, and directed me to the closest chair. He pulled it out, and I lowered myself down.

"Thanks," I said quietly.

Jack had gone and come back with plates, proceeding to pass them out. I took mine and nodded my thanks. He smiled a wide smile then sat in the chair next to mine. Sterling took the one to my right, and Pops sat at the one across from me. He flipped the box lid open and grabbed two slices.

"Don't be shy, girl," Pops called, and Jack nodded as he nabbed his own slices.

Sterling rolled his eyes, but it was good-naturedly, not in real annoyance. He reached in and tore off two pieces, but instead of putting them on his own plate, he deposited them on mine, and then got his own.

"How was school, guys?"

Jack answered in Jack-speak, and Sterling mumbled, "Fine," around a large bite of pizza.

"How's the musical?"

Sterling's mouth was full, so he tilted his head in my direction, which I took as a hint for me to answer.

"Good. Just have to figure out a way to get Elodie over her shyness by Monday."

"Why Monday?" he asked after he swallowed a scary-large bite of his own pizza.

I told him about what happened in theater class, and when I mentioned Raven and her actions, his mouth drew into a tight line, and his eyes shot to Sterling.

"Told you that girl was bad news."

Sterling's eyes were on his plate, his jaw flexing as he muttered, "Not now, Pops."

Pops cleared his throat and switched back to the subject. "So, how do you plan to get Elodie over her stage fright?"

I looked to Sterling, who was gazing back at me, and shrugged. "I haven't figured it out yet."

Jack cut in, sounding like he was asking Pops a question. When Pops answered, "Yeah, you can go watch your iPad," I found I had been right.

Jack scooted his chair back and was about to scamper off, when Pops said, "Plate."

Jack huffed out a breath, but grabbed his plate and took it into the kitchen. Then he hurried past me, and I assumed to the hall where their rooms probably were.

"I have an idea," Pops declared.

I cut my gaze to him and waited.

"Karaoke."

"Karaoke?" Sterling guffawed.

"Yeah, boy," Pops shot back with a thread of enthusiasm.

"Wouldn't that make it worse?" I asked.

"I used to be in a band in my younger years."

"Oh yeah?" I asked, genuinely curious. I looked to Sterling, who looked bored. Evidently, he knew his pops had been in a band.

"Yeah, I played rhythm guitar. Anyway, we had a great lead singer. Well, he became great. But when he first started singing gigs with us, he sucked."

A giggle escaped, and a small smile played at Pops' lips.

"He was stiff as a board and looked like he would piss himself any minute anytime we got on stage."

"So, you took him to karaoke?"

"Yep."

"How did it help him, though?"

"No clue. Maybe it just relaxed him. Lots of people getting up, singing whether they could or not, people cheering them on. I don't know. I just know it did the trick."

"That's great," Sterling cut in, "but how is that going to help us? There aren't any karaoke bars here, and we're all underaged."

"Let me think on it tonight and see if I can figure out a way around that."

"I'd really appreciate it ... Pops."

When Pops smiled, it became apparent where Sterling had inherited his stunning one from. Pops was hot for an old guy, which meant many good things for Sterling's future.

We finished up eating our food. Pops and Sterling talked about cars and the auto shop Pops owned in town. I was happy to just sit there and listen. I loved how Pops didn't discount any of Sterling's ideas or opinions. He listened, and I mean, he *really* listened. The total opposite of my father, who never listened, and if he did, he disregarded anything I had to say.

I wondered where Sterling's parents were for the millionth time. Was Jack his brother? Did he and Jack live with Pops? I knew he worked for him, but was it more?

"Welp, y'all should probably get to it."

Pops got up from the table, plate in hand, and reached in Sterling's direction. Sterling grabbed my empty plate and his then handed them to his grandfather.

"I'll be in the garage working. Y'all stay in here or the living room. No bedrooms. I'm not ready to set up a crib in your room yet, boy."

A strangled sound came from Sterling, and I knew my face was blood red.

Pops smirked as he strode into the kitchen.

"Sorry about that," Sterling said in a gruff voice.

I cleared my throat before I replied, "No problem."

Pops came out of the kitchen, and as he passed the table, he shot us a wink. As Sterling groaned, Pops then ambled through the living room and out the door.

"So ..." I drawled after I heard the door close, "we should probably start working through the script." I pulled my book closer to me from where I had lain it on the corner of the table. Then I looked to Sterling, who hadn't moved. "Aren't you going to go get your script?"

"Don't need it."

"What do you mean, you don't need it? How are we going to work on our lines if you don't know them?"

"I know them."

What? How did he know them already?

"I have an eidetic memory, princess."

My eyes rounded as I searched the depths of my memory for that definition, not wanting to ask because I didn't want him to think I was stupid.

"I basically remember everything I read, even if it's just once. A photographic memory."

Whoa. How lucky was he? But wait ...

"If you can do that, why aren't you, like, the top of the class? You should be up for valedictorian next year," I said incredulously.

He chuckled. "See, I'd have to actually read the material to ace the tests and assignments."

My mouth dropped open. Why wasn't he taking advantage of his skill? Maybe he really did have mutant genes.

"I just don't—"

"Princess, I'm in the top ten. I just don't have any interest in making speeches or having my picture in the newspaper."

"You're ahead of me?" I asked in surprise. He had to be because I was at the bottom of that totem pole.

He smirked then shrugged.

How had I not known this? Why wasn't he in any of my advanced placement classes? It just didn't make any sense. Sterling basically *was* the theater department.

"But, you're in theater?" I felt my brows drop and my mouth screw up.

"Yep."

"That makes no sense," I stated.

"How about this, then? I just don't want the extra work. I have theater and my job at the shop. I'd like to have a life somewhere in there."

My face relaxed. I could sympathize with that. I hadn't ever had a life outside of school and track. Yeah, I'd had a boyfriend and friends, but those relationships had felt like work. They were no different and certainly weren't any fun.

"That I can understand. I haven't had much of a life lately or, well, ever."

When his eyes turned sympathetic, my gut twisted. I didn't want pity. Not from him.

I dropped my eyes to the worn oak wood of the table and tried to control my breathing. I wanted to run, to flee. I couldn't stand the thought of him feeling sorry for me. It made me sick to my stomach.

Warm skin closed over my hand, and I looked up to where Sterling had one of my hands clasped tightly in his own.

"We're going to change that. I want you to have a life. I want you to have every teenage experience we're supposed to have. Even if it's just little things. Sometimes, those are the best things of all."

I stared at the way Sterling's large hand surrounded my smaller one, feeling the warmth of his skin, the tingle of electricity that seemed to travel from where our skin touched all the way to my heart. I had to agree. Sometimes, it was the little things that were the best of all.

❦

We managed to work through our lines for over an hour before I had to get home, questions bombarding me the entire time I sat at the table with Sterling.

We were on our way to the door, going through their small living room, when a picture on top of the entertainment center caught my attention. I paused, my eyes snared by the beauty in that picture. It was an eight-by-ten of a beautiful young girl with shiny dark hair and a wide, open-mouthed smile. Her face was in profile, and in her arms was a chubby little baby sporting his own wide gummy smile.

"That's me and my ma," Sterling said from behind me, his body heat warming my back as it brushed against me.

I looked over my shoulder at him to see him staring at the photo. "Where is she?" I asked quietly. I didn't know why. Pops was in the garage, and Jack hadn't emerged from his room, not once.

My heart was beating a heavy, sluggish beat, and cold crept into my fingertips. I didn't have a good feeling about what his answer would be.

"Don't know," he replied softly, his attention now focused on the bare skin of my shoulder. Then those lush eyes of his lifted and bored into mine.

My breath caught, and my heart started beating double time. There was a wealth of emotion in his eyes, and I knew, even if I lived to be a hundred, I would never reach the bottom of those depths.

"How can you not know?" The question wasn't accusatory; it was searching. I wanted to know him, everything that made him who he was, and that included his family.

Why was Pops raising him? The pictures that lined the walls and furniture were a testament to him living in this house since he was young.

He slowly lifted a hand and, with just the tip of one finger, he lightly stroked the skin of my shoulder. I shivered, feeling my body flush with heat.

"She split. I was fourteen months old when she dumped me with Pops and took off. She's only come back once, and that was when I was three. She dropped Jack off and was gone again."

"But, wh—"

"She's a junkie, princess." He said this like it wasn't a big deal, just a fact.

I sucked in a breath. How could he be so cavalier about that? And why would she do that? I just couldn't understand. My heart bled for him and Jack at the thought of having a mother who wasn't a part of their lives.

"What about your dad?" I asked, my stomach roiling. At the same time, I was tingling all over from his finger burning a path from the base of my neck to the edge of my shoulder and back up again. On the trip back, he dipped over and traced the ridge of my collarbone. Goose bumps prickled my skin. I didn't know how to feel. These conflicting emotions were strange and warred against each other.

He shifted closer. "Never knew my dad," he breathed against my hair, then brushed his lips through my hair and trailed down my neck.

I closed my eyes and felt my body shift back into his. The script I had been holding dropped from my hand as my backside nestled against his front and my shoulder blades planted against his torso.

He brought his other hand up and tucked my hair behind my ear, then smoothed it down and pulled the mass from my neck and over to the other shoulder. He trailed his large, warm hand down my side and lower until he gripped my hip. He was burning me up from the outside in.

"I love this sweater," he hummed against my skin.

I couldn't take it anymore. No one and nothing had ever made me feel this way.

I spun around so fast that Sterling didn't have time to brace himself. I winced at the pain that surged up my leg, but ignored it to fling my arms around his neck and plaster my chest to his, making him stumble back a step. If he wasn't so tall and strong, I probably would have knocked him to the ground.

I pulled down on his neck as I lifted onto my tippy-toes and smashed my mouth to his.

Once the shock of my attack cleared, he banded his arms tightly around my waist and probed at the seam of my lips with his tongue, seeking entrance. I opened, giving him access, and whimpered. He groaned when my tongue touched his and we began dueling.

His taste was addictive, and the feel of his lips and tongue became my new obsession. I had never felt so much in my life. It was warmth, electricity, happiness, lips and tongues, my heart's erratic beat ... The emotions swirling inside me were filling me to the brim and would burst out of me.

I didn't know how long we stood in his living room, making out, but the fog lifted when I felt a presence at our sides, followed by a throat clearing. We jerked apart so fast I would have stumbled if not for Sterling grabbing my forearms.

"Baby cribs, Sterling," Pops stated.

I wanted to sink right through the floor and disappear. My face must have been the color of a tomato—it felt that way—and I couldn't look at Pops. He had just caught me going at it with his grandson right in the middle of his living room.

"Jeez, Pops, I get it," Sterling snapped.

"Now, you better get home, Ally. It's a school night," Pops advised before he moved from the room. "It was nice meeting you, by the way," he called from somewhere down the hall.

I looked to Sterling, seeing his face was a little pale, but then he just shook his head.

I didn't reply. My mouth wouldn't even work. My lips felt swollen and tingly, and I had probably swallowed my tongue sometime during the last five minutes.

Sterling reached down and retrieved my script book from where it had fallen on the floor. Then he slid one hand to the small of my back and guided me to the door.

Once we were outside, the cool air cleared some of the remaining fog, and I muttered, "That was embarrassing."

Sterling's eyes crinkled, and he chuckled.

I shook my head, but smiled because, even though we had gotten caught, I didn't regret the kiss. It had been amazing; the best one I had ever had. I had only ever kissed Miles, but those kisses had been tame. Nothing like the fire that had burned between Sterling and me.

"How do you sneak out so much with him around?"

His grin turned into a cocky smirk. "Wouldn't you like to know."

Uh, yeah.

"For real, how do you? He doesn't strike me as someone who lets things get past him."

"He's not, but Pops is one of those men who, when he sleeps, he *sleeps*. The man has about five alarm clocks to get him up in the morning."

"Oh," I muttered, a little disappointed. I had imagined Sterling having his ninja skills honed to perfection.

We stood and stared at each other on the stoop in front of his door, the outside light casting shadows over his face and making it look almost sinister. Eventually, he leaned forward, and I watched as his face descended toward mine. My heart began pounding so loud I could hear and feel it in my ears.

When he was an inch from my lips, he whispered against them, "See you tomorrow."

His eyes were so close that they were all I could see. An ocean of blue with islands of amber. I fell into his multicolored eyes and never wanted to leave.

Sterling obliterated the remaining space between our lips for just a moment, then pulled back.

"Man, you're cute," he breathed, and his breath on my skin sent familiar tingles skittering over me. I knew I should leave, but I didn't want to.

I gave him a close-lipped smile.

"You need help walking to your car? It's dark out."

I shook my head, and then, before I could change my mind, I got up on my tiptoes again and quickly kissed his cheek. "Thank you for tonight," I told him, trying to imbue meaning into the words.

I meant that in so many ways. I was thanking him for sharing his family with me, for feeding me, for practicing with me when he obviously didn't need to, and for igniting something inside me that I thought I didn't have. I didn't know I could feel excitement like that. Miles had never gotten anywhere close. I was so grateful after considering myself broken since I could never drum up a physical response toward Miles.

Sterling was opening my mind and my heart to new experiences.

"You're welcome, princess. Maybe I'll be at your window tomorrow night. Can't tonight. Pops has a date with his woman."

"His woman?" I asked in astonishment.

"Yeah, he has a lady friend in town that he sees, and I have to stay in with Jack. Plus, I never know when he'll get home."

I mouthed the word "*wow*," and Sterling smirked.

"Apparently, the old man is a hot commodity."

I giggled. I was sure he was. Pops didn't look like anyone's grandpa, and he was in good shape.

"I better go."

"Yeah," he replied, a small smile still clinging to his lips.

I backed up slowly then turned and walked to my car, eyes to my feet to make sure I didn't trip over anything. My hand was on the door handle when I turned to look back at the Chapman's house. Sterling hadn't moved. He still stood on the stoop, hands jammed in his pockets, his eyes on me.

I gave a little wave, and he lifted his chin in return. Then I was in my car and on my way home. The clock on the dash said it was nine thirty, and I sincerely hoped my dad wasn't still home. I didn't know where he was right now, but I hoped it wasn't there and that, wherever he was, he wasn't stewing over the way I had left this evening.

BARBARA AND DONNA

When I had gotten home Wednesday night, Derek Everly's car hadn't been in the driveway, and he hadn't been waiting for me inside the house. Nor had there been a missed call or text. I had gone to bed for the first time with a smile on my face, reliving every moment of the kiss I had shared with Sterling until I fell into a peaceful sleep.

It was now Friday. Thursday had gone by without incident. Sterling had waited for me by the light pole and had walked me into school. I had sat with him, Blake, and Elodie at lunch, and we had discussed ways to get Elodie over her shyness. Blake was all for the karaoke idea, but we had to find a place that featured it. Then we needed a plan to get inside since most karaoke places were bars. Practice had been better, mainly because Raven had been absent. No one knew where she had been. Elodie seemed to have relaxed more and had done well on the speaking parts we had practiced.

We had to postpone our shopping trip since Blake had to fill in for the receptionist at his sister's hair salon last minute. Friday just ended up being a better day for everyone all around.

Since I couldn't do a lot of walking, we planned for Blake and Elodie to come over to my house and do some online shopping. Sterling had grumbled when Blake had told him in no uncertain terms that it was a "Blake and his bishes' date."

Sterling had explained that Jack had had a bad night last night, so he needed to stay in. My heart melted, and my hurt at being stood up morphed into understanding. I wondered, though, what a bad night for Jack meant. Was it a medical or emotional problem? I didn't know, and I hadn't felt comfortable asking Sterling about it at the time. He was tired. The purple smudges under his eyes and his constant yawning told me that he probably wouldn't be at my window tonight either. That was okay; he needed his rest.

"Okay, class, today we're going to run through 'It's Raining On Prom Night,' and that's"—she looked down to the paper in front of her —"Ally and Raven's duet. Then we'll block out the third scene."

"Duet?" I asked in a strangled voice. I must have heard her wrong.

"Yes, I'm the girl on the radio," Raven sneered.

Great. Just freaking great.

"Now, ladies," Mrs. Cook barked.

I slowly got up and made my way up the rest of the steps on one side while Raven did the same on the other. I could feel her spiteful gaze burning holes in the side of my face, but I refused to give her the attention she was craving.

I had the same feeling churning in my stomach that I had before a race—nerves, adrenaline, and determination. My competitive side was rearing its ugly head, ready to take on the girl who wanted Sterling.

Mrs. Cook ascended the steps, clipboard in hand, and pointed to the front of the stage on Raven's side. "Now, Raven, you stand down-stage right. We're going to have a standing mic set up here." She strode to the place she was discussing and tapped her pointed toe to the spot she wanted the mic.

Once Raven was where she had instructed, Mrs. Cook beelined toward me, grabbed me by the shoulders, and started moving me. "Ally, you're going to be perched on a bed we'll have set up ... here." She placed me at a point marked by a beige masking tape X. She then let go of my shoulders and hugged the clipboard to her chest.

I heard a snort, and my eyes zeroed in on Raven, who muttered, "Like she'd know what to do on a bed."

My spine shot straight, and I narrowed my eyes at her. She evidently hadn't learned her lesson this week. I changed my expression to one of boredom and deadpanned, "Ouch. You *really* got me there."

At the cackle of laughter, both mine and Raven's eyes shot to the sound. Blake was sitting in his chair, facing the stage, trying to restrain his laughter.

"Shut up, fairy," she hissed.

"Raven!" Mrs. Cook snapped.

"You calling me gay? I'm straighter than the pole yo mama dances on," Blake quipped.

"Children!"

Everyone's eyes went to Mrs. Cook, whose face was red, and her arms were straight down by her sides, fists clenched so tight the paper on her clipboard was wrinkling.

"No more. We have too much to do to be striking out at one another," she fumed in a quavering voice. She then focused her eyes on Raven and stated in a tone that brooked no argument, "You *do not* talk like that in this room ever again. Are we understood?"

"Yes, Mrs. Cook," she answered, her face red and sullen.

As always, my eyes searched out Sterling, who was sitting behind Blake. His posture was one of forced relaxation, leaning back with his hands tucked behind his head, elbows wide, and his ankle crossed over his knee. You would think he was just chilling, but I could see the strain on his face and the tenseness in his body. When his eyes met mine, they were riled. Despite that, he gave me a wink and a smile.

My body lost its own stiffness, and I smiled back.

I heard a weird noise and peeked over at where Raven was standing on the other side of the stage. Her face was twisted as she stared back and forth between Sterling and me. Finally, her eyes settled on mine, and the rage emanating from them made my skin crawl.

"Okay, ladies, let's get the music going and see what we have."

At Mrs. Cook's announcement, I saw the cruel smirk that tipped up one side of Raven's lips. This wasn't going to be some simple duet. This was a challenge. She wanted to out-stage me. I knew it like I knew she was a hateful skank.

As the opening piano chords filled the room, Raven's sultry voice rang out. I had to give it to her. She could sing.

When the time came for me to cut in, I didn't sound like the heartbroken girl I was supposed to. I let my voice fly.

Her eyes flashed, and she upped her volume, trying to drown my voice out. I saw her volume, and raised her in power and attitude. Soon, it became a head shaking, back and forth duel of sound. I practically shouted the speaking part. What we didn't know was, our audience was ensnared in the performance, our voices blended and flowed together in perfect harmony.

The song came to an end with us belting out the last words in perfect loud accordance.

The room was silent, and I cast my gaze around to see most of my classmates seated with their faces slack in shock or their mouths hanging open, except Sterling. He had a smug smile fixed to his lips, and when he saw that I was staring at him, he pursed his lips and gave me a nod. My eyes then went to Mrs. Cook, who for once wasn't instructing us after a performance. Instead, she just stood there stiffly, her eyes the size of saucers.

I peered over at Raven, who looked just as confused as me.

I cleared my throat and was about to ask what was going on when everyone broke out into applause.

Blake jumped up and cried, "That was like watching Barbara Streisand and Donna Summer duke it out in 'No More Tears.'"

I didn't know what that meant, but I knew I would have to YouTube it later.

Elodie, who was across from Blake, rolled her eyes, but said, "That was epic."

The surrounding students nodded their agreement.

I felt a blush steal over my cheeks and tried to swallow the lump in my throat at their praise.

Mrs. Cook became unstuck and declared, "You must perform it that way during the show!"

Oh boy. I was going to have to buy some throat lozenges. Mine felt scratchy after projecting so much.

I walked off the stage and sat in front of Blake, but then leaned back toward him and asked out of the side of my mouth, "Barbara who?"

Blake, who had been leaning forward, shot back in his chair and gasped, "What! I was sure you would've known the Streisand-Summer duet. You like classics."

"How do you figure?" I twisted in my seat to look at him.

"You knew who the Duckman was. Trust me, no one around here got it when I wore those shoes and that hat."

"I just like old movies. Music? Not so much, but I'm learning. Sterling introduced me to Don McLean."

Blake rolled his eyes. "Of course. Pops has him brainwashed with seventies rock music. I swear you need a proper diva education."

Sterling, who had evidently been listening to our conversation, leaned forward and clapped Blake on his shoulder as he stated, "Who better to give her one than you, Blake."

"Darn skippy."

Laughter bubbled in my chest, and I heard a matching one over to the right and caught Elodie's eyes. We tried to hold it in, but the sight of each other fighting it sent us both into gales of laughter. It probably wasn't as funny as we thought it was, but I needed the release. The drama onstage and the tension that had smothered the room had me feeling jittery. Laughing at Blake's antics seemed like a better solution than crying.

❧

I pulled into the driveway after school with Blake and Elodie following in Blake's black Ford Fiesta. The coil of dread that had been sitting in my stomach unfurled upon not seeing a black BMW anywhere. The last person I wanted to see was Derek Everly. I could hear his voice, full of recrimination, echoing in my head about my choice in new friends.

He was always adamant that the only people worth knowing were those who were white, straight, and financially well-off. He believed people with darker skin tones were too culturally different to have anything in common with, gays were perverts, and poor people were untrustworthy and grasping.

I could hear him now. "*If you want to be successful in life, Ally, you have to surround yourself with the right people.*" No matter how many times he said those words, they never took root. They were more like an abscess festering inside my brain.

His kernels of "wisdom" always caused revulsion to boil up inside me and feelings of loathing to crawl along my skin. I didn't believe any of that. I didn't ascribe to his philosophy. I didn't place value on skin color, sexual orientation, or money. Those things were surface. Those were just aspects of a person, not the whole. Value should be found in things that couldn't be seen. I knew this. We even learned it in church. It just seemed that Derek Everly had turned a deaf ear to anyone else's words but his own.

Living his way of life had me in the bleachers with a bottle of painkillers. Between the toxicity of the people surrounding me, my stagnant and oppressive environment, and the developing sepsis of that abscess, it had all turned into a lethal combination.

Now I was semi-free. Derek Everly hadn't been around lately, and I had been given opportunities to change my life, as well as my future. I was changing into the person I had always wanted to be. It was like feeling the warm, healing rays of the summer sun after living in a bitter cold winter. His specter still loomed like a gray cloud in my blue sky, but his shadow hadn't yet darkened over me.

I was interrupted from my thoughts by a knock on my window. I swung around and jumped back at the sight of Blake's nose pressed against the glass. He pulled back and wiped the imprint he had left with the sleeve of his shirt.

"Charming," I muttered as I closed the door behind me after getting out, then hauled my crutches through the driver's side door from the passenger seat.

I would be so glad when I could throw these in the lake. I fantasied about it all the time, especially when my armpits felt bruised and the skin raw.

"Love your digs," he said.

"Yeah, my house could probably fit in it three times," Elodie added as she slapped Blake's arm with the back of her hand.

I examined my house from their perspective. It was a large, Mediterranean-style house, one-story because my dad's knee couldn't handle stairs every day, with white stucco, trusses, a dark brown tiled roof, lots of windows, and an arched doorway. I had always seen it as a prison, a place where I simply existed.

"Yeah, I guess it's nice."

"Nice?" Blake sputtered.

I ignored him as we walked toward the door and let ourselves inside.

"Mom?" I called as I hung my backpack on the back of a bar stool and propped my crutches against the edge of the counter.

"O. M. G," I heard Blake whisper reverently.

I looked over at him and Elodie to see both were gawping as they took in the interior.

"Is your mom an interior designer?" Elodie asked.

I snorted. "No, she hired a lady to come in and decorate it. Rosalind did the overall design, but she comes every season to switch out linens, pillows, and seasonal decor."

Elodie's eyes widened, and she choked out, "There are people who actually do that? Around here?"

I nodded.

"I thought only celebrities and public figures did stuff like that."

An uncomfortable feeling slithered inside me, and the back of my neck itched. I scrutinized the luxury surrounding me, and the hot feeling of shame lodged itself inside my chest. We didn't need all this, not really. My dad hired Rosalind to make our house look magazine perfect, and then had Mom supervise her. We had a housekeeper who worked three to five days a week to keep everything looking pristine.

As if sensing my discomfort, Elodie put her hand on my shoulder and quietly said, "I think it's cool, Ally. I think I'd like a job like that someday."

"You could so do that, Ellie," Blake commented.

"Ally?" my mom called as she rounded the corner on the other side of the kitchen and came to an abrupt halt when she saw I wasn't alone. "Oh."

"O. M. G," Blake repeated, scurrying toward my mom and clasping her hands. "You are de-vine!"

Startled but flattered, my mom replied, "Why, thank you ..."

"Blake. I'm Blake, and that's my friend Elodie standing by Ally. We're her new friends."

Her eyes widened, and her mouth flapped open and closed.

I giggled, and Elodie hissed, "Blake, your mouth."

"Whaa? It's true."

My mom's eyes softened when they came to me, and I gave her a small smile.

"I hadn't heard that sound come out of you in so long," she said so quietly I barely heard her.

"She laughs like that all the time around us and Sterling."

"Sterling?" she asked with a little too much interest that I had to cut off whatever Blake was going to say.

"Blake and Elodie are going to help me pick out some new clothes."

"You probably shouldn't be out shopping with your leg, honey."

"Oh, we're going to do it online, if that's okay? I can use the credit card, right?"

"Oh, sure, that's fine. I paid down the balance this morning, so it should be good to go."

"So, we'll just ... ah, go to my room and hit up stores online." I grabbed my backpack to take with me because my wallet was in there, and then turned toward the hallway that led to my room. "My room's back here, guys."

They looked at each other before they both faced my mom.

"Nice meeting you, Mrs. Everly!" Elodie called out.

"Yeah, totes awesome," Blake added.

I opened the door to my room and escorted them inside.

"Your room is so Pottery Barn," Blake declared.

"Is that a good thing?" I asked, thinking it probably wasn't. I mean, they probably thought I was a rich, spoiled brat.

"It's sweet," Elodie replied.

"But it just doesn't seem like you," Blake finished.

I had already thought that, but hearing them confirm it had vindication soaring through my veins. This space wasn't mine. It was our interior designer's.

I looked over to the wall with the clothesline of pictures and thought about the life I had led just a week ago. This was the room that had belonged to that girl.

I shrugged the crutches from under my arms and threw them haphazardly in the direction of my bed. My backpack followed, crashing onto the mattress. I got close to the wall where the pictures hung and stared at the faces of me and Miles, of Laura, Ariel, Sarah, and me, and at a combo of the four. There were others of me with my parents or me just by myself.

It was like looking at a stranger, like the picture that came with a new frame. The photographs were a story of a girl who seemed to have it all—handsome boyfriend, beautiful friends, and doting parents. Problem was ... the story was fiction.

I reached up and caressed my track picture from last year. It was the one of me and my dad. I was in my uniform, hair blown straight, makeup perfect, and my smile had been stretched so wide that I looked ... unnatural. I stood behind a hurdle, hands on the plastic top, the track beneath my feet, the bleachers in the background, and Oleander High was written in big, black block letters across the top of the plastic. My dad was down on one knee in front, wearing khaki shorts and an Oleander High School polo that all the coaches wore. His smile was one you saw on billboards advertising used cars, class action lawsuits against trucking companies, or maybe for dental implants—perfect, insincere. There was nothing in those eyes that were an exact replica of my own. While mine were blank, his were ... nothing. Just two pools of emotional voids.

The bleachers in the background caught my attention, and I stared at that top corner of metal. That was the place I had worn the uniform I was wearing in the picture and tried to down a bottle of pills. I guessed the subconscious is a powerful thing.

I shivered.

"Ally?" Elodie's voice came from behind me.

I shook myself of the memories and ripped the picture from the clip. I stared at it a beat then tore it in two. My dad on one side, me on the other, and a gulf in the middle.

That didn't feel as satisfying as I thought it would, so I tore it again, and again, and again. Soon, paper was raining to the floor like confetti.

"What is she doing?" Blake whispered to Elodie.

"I'm cleaning," I answered.

"That doesn't look like cleaning," he replied.

When there were no more pieces to shred, I reached for another. Again, I studied the picture. It was a black and white close-up of Miles and me. His arms were wrapped around me from behind, and his smile was brilliant, while mine was ... not. It was small, close-lipped, almost looking annoyed because, well, I had been. He had disappeared with Laura at a birthday party, and then came back to me smelling like her perfume.

Without any more thought, I mangled the picture, its pieces joining the ones on the floor.

I felt a presence next to me and looked over to see Blake reaching for the picture of just Miles. Then, without a word, he started ripping it apart. After he was done, he threw them in the air like confetti.

He twisted his neck toward me and announced, "I get it now."

Tears burned my eyes, and my throat felt thick. I hadn't let the emotions I had been holding back surface. I had them locked tight in a box inside my brain, but at his words, his understanding, the locks started rattling. I stared into his brown eyes that were soft on mine in empathy, and let everything broken inside me surface.

"*I get it*," he whispered.

I nodded, and my chest bucked with a sob.

I felt an arm circle my shoulders from my other side, and my head fell to the female shoulder next to me. I knew my tears and snot had to be leaking onto her shirt, but she didn't pull away. She let me break on her.

Without thought, I let everything inside spill out of my mouth. I told them about my life, my dad, and how I felt suffocated by everything and everyone around me. How I had tried to end my life because I had felt like I had no other choice. And when I was done, we all just stood there and stared at the wall in front of us.

I didn't know why I had told two people I barely knew something so personal. In my experience, showing weakness would only get you hurt, but something inside of me whispered that I was safe with them. That they would understand. Maybe I was wrong, but sharing the darkest moments of my life had felt ... natural.

Freeing.

Blake broke the silence when he shared, "I thought about ending my life once. I was like you—trying to be something I wasn't and desperate for an escape. Sometimes, the bravest thing we choose is to be ourselves and live on our own terms."

I didn't feel very brave.

"I didn't choose to live, though. Sterling made that choice for me."

I couldn't look at either of them. I wrapped my arms around my middle as shame churned in my stomach at the admission. My eyes stayed glued to the picture of me with my former friends. We were in our bikinis, lying out on the loungers by my pool, all fake smiles, tans, and fashionable sunglasses.

"You're standing here, aren't you?"

Yeah, I was still standing here.

"You could have taken those pills if you wanted to. You wouldn't have cared if they were dirty if you really were set on killing yourself."

I thought about that and conceded he had a point.

"But Sterling—"

"Divine intervention," he stated.

I couldn't argue that.

I looked to Elodie, who had stayed quiet, and my heart broke a little at the sight of the tear tracks on her cheeks.

She moved forward and took down the picture I had been staring at, studying it for a minute. Then she unexpectedly crumpled it in her fist, dropped it to the floor, and proceeded to stomp on it.

A surprised laugh exploded from my chest, and I could hear Blake's, as well.

We watched as Elodie stomped, smashed, and jumped on the photograph, grunting as she did so. By the time she was through, Blake and I were leaning against each other, bent at the waist, laughing so hard our stomachs hurt. It felt good. Amazing.

Elodie turned to us and smiled, a huge dimpled grin that transformed her face from pretty to mesmerizing. Then she erupted into giggles.

Somewhere in the back of my brain, I wondered: is this what having true friends felt like?

For the first time in my life, I felt safe and like I belonged.

B & E

Hilarity over, every picture now destroyed but one—the one of my mom and me at a church banquet. Now we were sprawled on my bed, laptop open, browsing clothing sites.

"That skull top is cute," Elodie pointed out while she flicked her finger at the computer screen.

I looked to Blake, who wrinkled his nose at the picture of a Goth-looking girl wearing a dark gray shirt that was long enough to be a tunic. It was a cold shoulder style, meaning part of the sleeve that covered the bicep was missing, but it had a piece of fabric above the elbow. It also had silver studs designed into the shape of a skull on the front. I wasn't sure it was my style.

We were on Hot Topic's website, a store that had been forbidden to me before. We had already searched through most of the tops listed. I had looked at rock band tees, mesh tops, and skull designed everything. None of it fit my personality. I felt like, if I wore them, it would be like playing dress up. I would be pretending to be something I wasn't.

"I don't know why you want to change your style. Other than your yoga pants and T-shirt day, your clothes are on point," Blake said.

Elodie had her fingertips on the touchpad and was scrolling through the top selections as she said, "She wants to be different, Blakey. She can match Sterling in some of these tees."

"So, you want to turn her into Raven?" he replied sarcastically.

I shuddered. Yeah, I didn't want to be anything like Raven.

Changing the subject, I explained, "I didn't pick those clothes out. They are of my past. I want to figure out my style without someone telling me what to buy and what to wear."

"Then, girly, this site is not for you." Blake chuckled, reaching over and snatching the computer from in front of me.

"Hey!" Elodie cried.

He started typing, and then another site popped up. He moved the laptop back in front of us and started scrolling through what the site offered.

"Here, try this."

The site was one I had never heard of—Modcloth. My eyes trailed over the offerings, and several things caught my eye. Before I knew it, my cart was full of tops, tunics, leggings, skinny jeans, a couple of black pants, and even some skirts. Shoes ... Oh, the shoes. Booties, flats, vintage-inspired heels, and knee-high boots. I went a little crazy. When it was time to check out, I felt a twinge of guilt and a whole lot of self-consciousness. I looked to the people beside me to see if they judged me.

"Well, aren't you going to buy it?" Blake demanded.

I peeked at Elodie from the corner of my eye. When she felt my scrutiny, she just nodded.

"Well, let me grab the card."

&

Shopping done, we were lying side by side on the bed, staring up at the ceiling.

"You know," I started, "Sterling's pops had an idea on how to get you over your shyness."

Elodie turned over on her side, elbow to the bed, head propped on her hand, as she eyed me carefully.

Blake snorted, and Elodie made a gesture for me to continue.

"Pops thinks we should take you to sing karaoke."

"It's a brilliant idea," Blake agreed.

Elodie gulped, like I could hear it, and she turned a little gray.

"We haven't found a place yet, but he said he's looking into it."

Her eyes stayed glued to my duvet cover, but she nodded.

"It'll be okay," I told her quietly.

My phone sounded with an alert just as Blake gasped, "Ooo, I almost forgot!"

I reached above my head for my phone and pulled it down to face level. The yellow box on my screen told me I had a snap from Sterling.

It was a picture of him making a sad face, lip pout and all, with his arm around a stick figure he had drawn that had long brown hair and a smiley face. The text band read, "*Someone is missing.*"

I giggled, and when I did, the phone disappeared. I looked at the thief as she stared at Sterling's pathetic picture.

"I think he really likes you," she commented, eyes trained on my phone.

"You think?" I couldn't keep the note of insecurity out of my voice.

"Yeah." She hesitated for a moment but went on, "He was never this way with Raven."

"What's the story there?"

"I honestly don't know why they broke up, but when they were together, they fought a lot. They were just intense."

"Oh," was the only thing I could think to say.

The door to my room burst open, and then a panting Blake stood at the side of my bed by our feet.

"Where did you go?" Elodie asked.

"I had to run out to the car to get this!" He thrust a bottle of something into the air like he had found the Olympic torch and was raising it for us to admire.

"What is it?" I squinted at the bottle in his hand.

"It's the new you." He lowered it and put it an inch away from my face.

"I still don't know what this is." I couldn't read the label without going cross-eyed, so I didn't even try.

"It's champagne!"

"Um, no, it's not," Elodie told him flatly.

"Not the drink! It's hair color." He jerked it back to his chest as I felt my eyes widen. Hair color?

"Wh-what?" I spluttered.

"It's time for a change, Sandy."

"No."

"Do you even know how to apply bleach? Because that's straight-up bleach, Blakey."

"Of course. I got this from my sister's salon. Watched her do it a million times, Ellie."

"I don't think this is a good idea," I whined.

❧

"Oh. My. Gawd."

"Let me go back and read the instructions. Maybe I missed a step?"

I stared at myself in the mirror, hair wet and dripping on the floor. The room smelled of chemicals and possibly burned hair.

"Look what you did to her head!" Elodie yelled.

"Shh ..." Blake tried to quiet Elodie, but it was too late.

The door to my room opening made an ominous sound amidst the ensuing chaos.

"Hey, guys, what's that sme—" My mom abruptly cut herself off. Then I watched her face morph from mild curiosity to horror, the phone in her hand falling and clattering on the floor. "What did you do!"

"We were—"

"I told you this was a bad idea," Elodie hissed.

I could only stare into my mother's shocked eyes as she slowly reached down and collected her phone.

With one hand, she started pressing buttons, and with the other, she rubbed her back. Regret, shame, and guilt hit me like three consecutive punches to the gut. Had she been able to have her pain medicine refilled?

Once she was done with whatever she was doing on her phone, she flicked her hand toward me and said, "Grab a towel and a hat. Simone said she could fit us in before they close. You better start praying to Jesus now, thanking him for her having a last-minute cancellation. If she hadn't, you'd be dead."

I gulped.

"We'll just, uh ..." Blake started uncomfortably, but Mom speared him with her eyes.

"Oh, no. You two are coming along. Now, pack up and move out."
She turned around, hand still to her back, and half stormed, half
hobbled out of the room.

We all looked at each other for a moment, and then got to moving.

The car ride to the salon in my mom's Land Rover was awkward.
Nervousness and fear practically vibrated the car off its wheels.

When we pulled into the deserted lot in front of Salon Cheveux,
one moment I was looking at the graceful facade of the salon, and the
next, I was staring at the back of Blake's head.

"O. M. G.! I've heard of this place."

Elodie gave his head a shove as Mom clipped, "Let's go."

Salon Cheveux was in a strip mall close to the mall-mall a couple
towns over. The white bricked front stuck out amongst the other red
bricked stores, and the black letters declaring the name was clean and
simple.

We pushed in the glass-front doors and were greeted by a sea of
white. White receptionist desk, white chairs, white seating area, white
shelves holding white bottles. White, white, white.

"Mandy," Simone greeted Mom as she strode out from the gap
between two overlapping white walls that separated reception from
the workstations.

Simone was a statuesque blonde dressed in a tight, black jersey dress
and spike-heeled boots. Her hair, as always, was pulled back into a severe-
looking ponytail. I was pretty sure that was why her face defied gravity.

A strangled noise came from beside me, but before Blake could
make another noise, Elodie had her hand over his mouth, giving him a
look that told him to behave.

I shifted back to watch the two women exchange air kisses, and
then Simone leaned back, keeping her hands clasped to my mom's
biceps, as she asked, "How are you?"

Her tone made the hair on the back of my neck stand up, and the
concern on her face made my chest tighten.

Mom quickly cut her eyes to me, which seemed to snag Simone's
attention. Simone followed then jumped when she caught sight of my
appearance.

"Honey, is that orange I'm seeing under that hat?"

When I didn't answer, my mom snapped, "Yes, she and her friends decided to dye her hair."

"It was for her role as Sandy in the *Grease* musical we're doing at school," Blake blurted, not able to hold back any longer. "And can I just say—"

Elodie again slapped her hand over his mouth. "You're the reason we're here, so you might want to keep your trap shut."

He made big eyes at Elodie then scanned the room and noted the scowling faces of my mom and Simone. I watched his Adam's apple bob as he swallowed, but he stayed quiet, even when Elodie took her hand away.

Simone tsked but didn't say another word as she led us back to the workstations and motioned for me to take a seat in her chair. Once I was seated, she whipped a cape around my front and fastened it before tearing off my hat.

Her hands flew to her mouth, trying to cover her gasp, my hat falling to the floor.

My once shiny dark hair was now the color of a pumpkin.

"What did you do?" she asked as she pulled sections of my frizzy orange hair up and examined them.

I was trying to push the encroaching panic down and lock it away, but it was beginning to dawn on me how much I had screwed up. I shouldn't have let Blake talk me into coloring my hair. What was Sterling going to say? I was going to be a laughingstock!

I breathed deeply in and out like I had trained myself to do, but the panic was gaining ground.

"Can you fix it, Simone?" Mom asked as she appeared behind Simone's shoulder, grabbing my attention, which interrupted my mental breakdown.

I braced myself for the worst, but when Simone answered, "Am I Simone?" I let the trapped breath whoosh out of my chest.

"I think, if I apply some toner and a deep conditioning treatment, it should be okay. She's lucky that her hair wasn't damaged," she went on, still pulling sections of my hair up and watching me in the mirror.

Her face was one of censure. I knew she would let me have it before I left.

"Thank God," my mom breathed.

"She's got good elasticity, and I'm guess this was virgin hair, so again, very lucky."

"Well, I trust her hair in your hands. Me and these two will wait for her in reception." Mom patted Simone's shoulder then disappeared, taking Blake and Elodie by the back of the necks.

"What were you thinking?" Simone recriminated when they were gone.

"I-I—"

"You weren't. That's the only answer."

I closed my eyes, not able to bear the brunt of her glare.

"If you wanted to go blonde, then you should have come to me. I should've been the one to color your hair for the first time. I've been cutting it since you were a little girl, so it should have been me guiding you into the world of hair color."

"I know," I replied lamely.

She reached for a pair of gloves and snapped them on. "This is going to take a while," she muttered, looking through the cart at her side.

Hours passed, and I wished I had grabbed my phone before I had left the house. I was bored and caught somewhere between hope and panic. I didn't know what Simone's efforts would look like, but it had to be better than pumpkin.

SHE WAS THERE

Tap ... Tap ... Tap ...

My eye shot open, but I didn't move. My hand instinctively went to my hair, and I undid the loose knot I had tied to the front of my head before bed. Simone had said that "pineappling" would keep my hair looking styled rather than flat when I woke up in the morning.

Tap ... Tap ... Tap ...

Fear and dread ran through my veins like ice water. I knew who was at my window, but what if he didn't like my new look? What if he took one look at me and burst out laughing? I hadn't been able to snap him back earlier, so what if he was mad at me?

Tap ... Tap ... Tap ...

B & E, Blake and Elodie's new nickname that oddly enough my mother thought up, had assured me it was a good look. Blake had practically fawned over my "champagne" Sandy hair. I wasn't sure I liked it, but Elodie had said that now that my hair was blonde, I looked more like my mother. My mother was beautiful, so I took that as a compliment, but blonde was still very different.

Sterling had sent me a Snapchat while I was at the salon, but I never replied. I was too freaked out over my hair when I got home to think of anything to say, but the picture of him and Jack doing a puzzle at the kitchen table had made me forget about my hair for a moment, to smile at the beauty of them. Jack's smile was so big that it looked like it hurt, but even in a picture, he radiated pure happiness, pure joy. Sterling's wide, happy one evoked a different response. His took my breath away. It wasn't the practiced one he gave the world, but one that showed he was genuinely happy to be spending time with his brother. Where Jack's shone with the purity of a child, Sterling's made my ovaries quiver. The text band at the bottom had read, *"His smile is reason enough to get up in the morn."* I had to agree, but I thought Sterling's smile was enough, too.

The tapping stopped, and I didn't know whether to be relieved or disappointed. Then I heard the scrape and slide of the window opening. Did I forget to lock it last time? How could I have been so stupid?

I sucked in a breath and slid down farther into bed, bringing my comforter overhead.

"Ally?" Sterling whispered, and then I felt the bed dip beside me.

I screwed my eyes shut tightly as my heart raced a mile a minute. I prayed he would leave, thinking I was still asleep, but that just wasn't my luck.

I felt the covers lift and cool air hit my heated skin. The jig was up.

I rolled over and blinked up into Sterling's face.

"Who are you, and what have you done with my princess?" Sterling's voice vibrated with laughter.

"I heard blondes have more fun," I croaked.

"I'm going to kill him."

"You don't like it?" I whispered.

"It's not that." He reached out and brushed a curl off my face, tucking it behind my ear. The tender gesture made something that had frozen inside me at his words melt. Then, fingers still in my hair, he examined me from my hair to my face, and then down to my exposed neck as he said, "I just loved your brown hair, but I imagine I could get used to this new you. You could chop it all off, and you'd still be stunning."

He *loved* my brown hair, and he thought I was *stunning*? My face went soft, and my heart soared. It was too soon to feel what was rioting inside my chest, but I was learning that love wasn't something you could control.

My father had started the lesson, having been the first man to break my heart. Miles had killed my young love and faith in the emotion. Sterling? Sterling was teaching me something new. He wasn't trying to control or manipulate me to get something in return. Sterling seemed to just ... care. He cared about me—how I felt, what I thought. I wasn't a body without a brain. I was a brain who happened to have a body. A *person*. Or, that was how he made me feel.

I lifted my hand and cupped his cheek that was rough with whiskers. I rubbed my thumb along the edge where they ended and the smooth skin began, staring into his eyes and trying to convey everything I was feeling as I said, "Thank you."

The corner of his mouth lifted into a smirk, and it was so sexy it made my mouth go dry.

I licked my lower lip, and his eyes dropped from mine to the movement. He stared for a protracted second before leaning in and tasting it for himself, tracing his tongue along my bottom lip.

As my tongue came out to greet his, the kiss became languid, each exploring the other's mouth, and so hot I thought I would melt into a puddle on my bedsheets.

Scooting closer, he moved his hand from the bed to my hip over the covers. I moved my hands to his hair, dragging my fingers through his dark brown tresses, lightly scratching his scalp with my nails. He groaned.

I didn't know how long we spent making out on my bed before Sterling eventually pulled away, panting while I mewed at the loss of his mouth.

"We have to stop," he breathed heavily.

"Why?" I panted, trying to lean back in for another kiss, but he just caught my lips against his cheek as he brushed it past mine. His whiskers tickled as they scraped against my skin.

His lips were right under my ear, their softness caressing the skin there when he whispered, "Because we're in your bed, in your parents' house, and I want to slide under these covers and do a whole lot more than kissing right now."

I froze, my eyes got huge, and my heart felt like it stuttered to a stop, along with my brain. "Oh."

"Yeah, oh."

I just stared at him in complete shock. What did I say to that? I wasn't ready to do "that" yet, but I *wanted* to at the same time ... with *him*.

He stroked my hair away from my face then trailed his hand to the back of my head, cradling it. Sterling searched my face, looking for something. I didn't know what, but he must have found it, because he gave me a small smile and muttered, "cute," before he heaved himself off the bed and stood at the side. "Get dressed and meet me outside," he ordered. Then he was gone, and I was still in bed, trying to wrap my head around what had just happened.

I did as I was told and was dressed and outside in about ten minutes.

"Do you need your crutches?" Sterling asked.

I shook my head. I was going to try to walk to his car without the instruments of Satan.

"We'll go slow," he stated, then grabbed my hand and laced his fingers through mine.

We went slow, as promised, and made it to his car that was parked in the same spot it was last time. He opened the door for me, and then jogged around and got in himself. After he cranked the engine, music filled the interior, and I couldn't contain the laugh that seemed to explode out of me.

"What?" he asked, looking confused yet amused.

He took a second to listen then he started cracking up as "Look At Me, I'm Sandra Dee" serenaded us.

Fifteen minutes later, we pulled into the back of the gravel parking lot of the Lil' Slugger tee-ball fields that was down the road from the high school.

"What are we doing here? I'm not sure I'm up to playing baseball."

"You'll see," he replied. That dang smirk was back on his lips. The smirk that made me lose my mind and got me in trouble.

He again opened my door and helped me out. Then we were strolling hand in hand out of the gravel parking lot and away from the fields.

There was a playground adjacent to the tee-ball fields and behind the small community center. It was plunged in darkness, except for a single light pole on the edge closest to the community center's parking lot.

He led me to a set of swings that were in the darkest part of the playground and gestured for me to sit in one while he took the other, facing me. I gripped the chains with both hands and watched as he did the same. Then we just stared at one another, swaying slightly because it was hard to keep yourself still in a swing. I had the urge to push off against the ground and start really swinging, but I was scared it would be too much on my leg. Another night.

"So, why here?" I asked, piercing the quietness of the night.

He was watching his black boots drag through the gravel when he answered, "I used to walk here at night to think before I got the Chevelle."

He was sharing another piece of himself, and I felt the privilege of that nestle in my chest.

"It's peaceful." I lifted my face to the sky and enjoyed the cool breeze on my skin.

Soon, the weather would turn, and the nights would be muggy and stifling. We had hit that sweet spot between chilly and warm, between winter and spring in Texas.

I had always associated this weather with track season. It was something I could feel on my skin and smell on the breeze. Most days, I dreaded the feel of it, and often wondered if I would still be leaping hurdles if it was solely my choice. The freedom of choice was something I had so little experience with, yet I savored more with each passing day. It was exhilarating yet intimidating, and I wondered if it would still be so if I'd had it my whole life.

"Have you ever wanted to start your life over?" I asked out of the blue, taking my eyes from the clear, starry night sky to watch his expression.

His lips twisted to one side as he seemed to consider my question, then answered, "No."

"Not even to change some of the decisions you've made, or make some better choices?" My voice held a note of incredulity.

I would in a heartbeat. I wished I could go back and start over. I would do *everything* differently. I would make better choices, and it wouldn't have taken me so long to start living my life for myself, to take control.

"Nope," he answered, looking at me sideways.

"Why?" I just couldn't wrap my mind around that. "Don't you have any regrets?"

"Of course I have some regrets." His eyes dropped back to his boots, but then they lifted. "Why do you want to start your life over? What are your regrets?"

I tightened my grip on the chains and dropped my head back to stare up at the night sky as I considered his question.

"I've always felt like I was an outsider ... with my family, my friends, the people in their social circle—heck, even in my own life. My choices have always been made for me, from what to eat to what friends I could have, what clothes to wear, what sport to play, and lately, what college and career to go into."

"Who's making those decisions, princess, if not you? It's kind of hard to do that without your consent."

I winced. He was right. All the same, it was embarrassing revealing how weak I was to a guy who seemed to have it all together.

"I didn't even put up a fight," I whispered. "I was always on the outside looking in, yet it was my life I was watching play out before me. I was an observer of my own freaking life. How messed up is that?" Tears stung my eyes, but I kept them at bay. I didn't want him to see me cry again. I wanted to be strong. I needed to be strong.

He grabbed the chains and stilled the movement of my swing, then dipped his head down until all I could see were his fantastic eyes. I lifted mine to his, even though shame had me wanting to keep them on the ground.

"So, what are you going to do about it?" His eyes drilled into mine, filled with so much determination that I felt it bolster my own.

"What do you mean?" I whispered.

"Are you going to let that happen to you again?"

My eyes slid to the side and away from his as I thought about my life before I jacked up my leg. The thought of living that way again made me sick to my stomach. I couldn't go back to that. It wasn't a life.

It was a slow death.

"No," I answered, resolved that I would run away before I let myself get put back in Derek Everly's golden cage.

Panic crawled along the back of my neck, and my hands began to sweat. I needed to change the subject, so I choked out, "Your regrets? You never said what they were."

He leaned back, letting go of my swing's chains. I watched as he pushed his feet against the ground and lurched forward then back. "About what?"

I had a feeling he knew what I was asking and didn't want to answer, but I persisted.

"The past."

Sterling stopped his momentum and blew out a breath. He glanced at me, indecision flickering on his face. "I'm hesitant to talk about her with you. Not that I don't want you to know about my past relationships, but ... it's over."

I just lifted a brow and stared at him, not sure I really wanted to talk about the beautiful non-elephant in the room who could pass for a young Megan Fox lookalike.

He read my look and sighed. "I regret wasting so much time with Raven."

Hearing him say her name was like a punch to the gut, which was silly because, with anyone else, it was just annoying. With Sterling, though, I didn't like it. Not one bit. I didn't want any of her, even her name, anywhere near his mouth.

"What happened with her? B and E said that y'all used to date." I had tried to sound nonchalant, but I wasn't sure if I succeeded. I had probably sounded like the petty, jealous person I felt like.

"B and E?" Humor laced his tone.

"Blake and Elodie."

He chuckled. "That sounds about right."

"Raven?" I questioned.

His eyes strayed to the woods that surrounded the backend of the playground as he rocked his swing back and forth. Then his eyes swung back to me, full of seriousness when he said, "Raven and I are over. For good. I just want to make that clear."

"Okay," I stated, feeling all the tension that had been in my body since her name was mentioned release.

"We've been off and on since freshman year. Mostly off, but every now and then, she convinced me to give her another chance. I loved her, so I would. At least, until she would ruin it."

The tension was back, and my body had locked when he had used the word *loved*.

"How would she ruin it?"

"Being herself," he replied sardonically.

I snorted, and a faint smile tipped his mouth.

"So, why were you with her? What made you love her enough to keep taking her back?"

I *had* to know. I wanted to know what would hook a guy like him so deeply that he would give you years' worth of second chances.

"She's ... well ... she's beautiful."

My heart fell. That was it? *She's beautiful?*

My hopes popped like a helium-filled balloon, and disappointment became a weight crushing down on my chest. I was traditionally pretty in that girl next-door kind of way, but Raven? Raven was exotic and in your face kind of gorgeous.

"And ... she's damaged."

Damaged?

Something twisted inside me and bile surged up my throat. Was that why he was attracted to me? Because I was damaged?

I shot up from the swing and whirled to face him, the pain the movement caused lost in my fury. "Is that why I'm here? You like damaged, and I'm pretty freaking damaged, right? That's the only reason someone like you"—I pointed my finger at him—"would want someone like me?" I jabbed my finger into my chest. Then I stared at the space above his head and muttered, "Knew it was too good to be true."

"That's not what I meant," he said as he got up and moved toward me.

I held up a hand to ward him off, but he just pushed into my space anyway.

I kept my eyes trained resolutely on his black tee, my voice cracking as I asked, "Can you please just take me home?"

Tears blurred my vision, and this time, I didn't bother fighting them. I couldn't. The familiar sense of numbness slipped over my senses, and I began to retreat within. I couldn't deal with this right now.

He took my face in his warm hands and announced, "No, princess, I'm not taking you home. You're going to let me explain, *then* I'll take you home, and when we get there, we'll make out by your window until I have to get back home."

My mind blanked. I knew I should probably protest, but my cylinders weren't firing, like, at all.

He stroked the apple of my cheek, and I closed my eyes. When he spoke again, my eyes flashed open, and I stared into his fathomless blue eyes with brown flecks.

"She needed me ... and I needed someone."

My brows knitted. What did that mean?

"I don't understand."

"Jack had to have major heart surgery right around the time I hooked up with her."

My mouth dropped open. I'd had no idea. Was he okay now?

He continued, "We met in theater class, actually. She was new— her family had moved to Texas from Seattle—and she was the one who asked *me* out." He chuckled, but it wasn't one of humor. "I wasn't in a good place. I was scared, and I mean, *really* scared. Thought I was going to lose my baby brother." He closed his eyes, like the memory was too hard to bear, but then he opened them and finished in a somber tone, "I needed a distraction, and she was there."

Poor Jack, Sterling, and Pops. I couldn't imagine having to cope with something like that. I had no siblings or any close relatives. What struck me was that Sterling said Raven was there for him. That didn't sound like Raven. She seemed like someone who couldn't see past her own agenda. But, what did I know? I didn't actually know her that way, or at all, really.

"Is Jack okay now?" I whispered, instinctively moving closer so my softness was pressed to all his hardness, my hands at his narrow waist.

"Yeah," he breathed out. "They think they fixed it all on that last surgery, and so far, it's been true. For a while, though, I thought Pops and I would lose him."

"I'm glad you had Raven to get you through it." I hated saying it, but having her had to be better than being alone. Right?

He gave me a funny look that I didn't quite understand.

"I mean, she doesn't seem like the type now to be that way, but ... at least she was good to you."

Sterling started laughing, and my confusion grew.

"What's so funny?" I tried to pull away, but he brought his arms around me and held me to him.

"Raven is a crap girlfriend, then and now."

"Then, what—"

"Princess, Raven ..." he started then looked to the sky like it might tell him how to explain the situation. That was when something clicked, and I replayed his earlier words.

He had said, "she was there," not "she was there *for him*."

"Oh," I squeaked as it dawned on me.

"Mistook that for love." He shrugged. "I was hurting. She saw that, used it, and I let her. She wanted a boyfriend, and I gave her one until I couldn't. Couldn't watch her do stupid crap anymore." He mumbled the last part.

So, him and Raven ... The image of them together seemed to burrow its way into my brain. It hurt to imagine him kissing her the way he kissed me. Touching her ...

I shook my head to dislodge the picture and asked, "Like what stupid crap?"

"Drugs. Drinking."

I grimaced. "Really?"

"Really."

"You weren't into that?"

He gave me a look. "Hell no! My pops would kick my tail. Plus, Jack being sick ... I wouldn't have done that to him. I'll admit I've had a beer or two in the past ... but drugs?" He shook his head. "Nope. My mom's a junkie. I wouldn't do that to myself, and I especially wouldn't do that to my pops."

I nodded. "So, it's over?"

He looked at me, eyes burning with so much heat that I squirmed in his hold. "Yeah. It's over for me and her, and I don't want to talk about her anymore."

"Okay," I conceded, since a lot of what he had told me tonight was some pretty heavy stuff. He didn't need me to push him for more.

He smiled, and my muscles seemed to liquify.

I turned and laid my head on his chest, listening to his heartbeat. It was strong and comforting.

"And just for the record, I wouldn't have started things with you if I was still involved with her. I'm not that guy," I heard and felt him say, his lips against my hair.

"Good to know."

"And, Ally?"

"Yeah?"

"Your hair stinks."

We both laughed, and if I wasn't so emotionally drained, I probably would have remembered to be embarrassed.

TWENTY-NINE THOUSAND AND HOWEVER MANY MORE

The ringing of my phone woke me from what felt like a minute of sleep. I usually loved the sound since it was the theme song of my favorite show, *Gilmore Girls*, but Sterling had brought me home at four thirty, and then we had made out against the side of the house until five.

I rubbed the grit from my eyes and reached for my phone on the nightstand. The screen showed the picture I had added to Sterling's contact, the one of him with the puppy dog ears. I noted it was way too early to be awake yet.

I swiped my finger over the screen and put the phone to my ear. "Why are you awake?" I whined.

"Did you forget?" Sterling's humor was clear over the line.

"Forget what?" I barked.

"Set work today at nine."

Squinting at the window and seeing the sun was already up, I put the heel of my hand to my forehead and muttered, "Oh, crap."

"I'll be there in five."

When I heard nothing else, I pulled the phone from my ear and looked at the screen. He had hung up on me!

I flipped the covers off and hobbled to the bathroom.

My new clothes wouldn't be delivered until sometime this upcoming week, so I dressed in jeans and a lacy cami with a gray knit cardigan from H&M. I opted for black ballet flats since I probably shouldn't attempt to walk in boots or heels just yet.

The doorbell rang, and my tummy fluttered. No one was up yet. I wasn't even sure if my dad was here, which made me glad. I didn't know where he had gone, and I was scared to ask. Things weren't right with my parents. I wasn't stupid.

The bell rang again. I slowly moved to the entryway, flung the door open, and there he was. And *wow*. He was dressed in black jeans, a gray Henley with a leather jacket over it, and a slouchy gray beanie covering his messy dark brown hair. Seriously hot. I still mourned the loss of the lip ring, though.

"Ready?" he asked with a flash of white teeth.

"Yeah." I patted the purse at my side then turned and closed the door. Instantly, he grabbed my hand and led me to his car.

"Where are your parents?"

I searched the driveway. No cars.

Confused, I unzipped my purse and pulled out my phone, seeing a text from Mom.

Mom: *Had an appointment. Be back sometime this afternoon.*

I swiped open my phone and punched out a reply.

Ally: *K.*

Ally: *@ school 4 theater.*

Then I shoved my phone back into my purse and slid into the car while Sterling held the door open. Once I was situated and belted in, he leaned in and kissed me gently on the lips before pulling back an inch and whispering, "Good morning."

On the way there, we debated movies of all things. He asked me what my favorite one was, and I went into a spiel of all the movies I loved and how I couldn't pick just one. Most of my picks weren't even from this decade. I loved older movies, especially teen romantic comedies. He scoffed at my choices and declared that *The Fast and the Furious* franchise had the best movies of all time. I didn't know if he was just poking fun at me or if he was serious. The banter was something new, but it was fun and natural, both of us laughing at the other. My belly actually hurt from laughing so much.

When we pulled into the mostly empty school parking lot, I saw Blake's Ford Fiesta and wondered if Elodie had caught a ride with him. I had learned yesterday that Elodie didn't have a car, so she rode to most places with Blake. He even picked her up for school. I thought maybe I could help Blake out sometimes since he had to work three days a week at his sister's salon after school.

"Hey." Sterling got my attention, and I turned to face him. His brows were furrowed, and he had a serious expression on his face. "I didn't get much sleep last night—"

"No kidding? I didn't either." I smirked then added, "I wonder why."

He gave me a small smile, but it fell when he continued. "I couldn't stop thinking about what you said last night. I know I said I had regrets, but ... I'm not sure I would call them regrets anymore."

My whole body froze. What did that mean? Was he going to try to get Raven back? Had something happened? Had I done something?

"Relax, princess," he cajoled, squeezing my hand that he had held during the entire drive and rubbing his thumb between my thumb and pointer finger.

I blew out a breath and tried to relax my rigid muscles.

"Everything is supposed to happen for a reason, right? That's what everyone says. So, if everything happens for a reason, then my wasting time with Raven led me to where I am right now." He looked at our hands, fingers intertwined on his thigh. "I wouldn't trade any of those bad decisions, if it means I get to sit with you right here, right now, holding your hand."

My breath caught, and tears filled my eyes. If I hadn't already been half in love with him, I would have fallen head-over-heels in this instant. That said, I was all the way in love with him now. There was no turning back. Sterling Chapman owned me, heart and soul, and I couldn't tell him yet, if ever.

"Don't cry," he demanded softly, his voice achingly tender.

"I think that's the most romantic thing anyone has ever said to me," I hiccupped.

He reached over with his free hand and traced the tears that had spilled down one cheek. Then he trailed his fingers along my jaw until he rested the pad of his thumb on my lower lip.

A nervous habit had me licking my lips, brushing my tongue against his thumb. Sterling's eyes heated until they practically glowed. Then he pushed his thumb farther into my mouth until it scraped my bottom teeth. Not knowing what else to do ... I kissed it.

Sterling's eyes dilated, and his nostrils flared. If I thought his look was hot before, it was downright scorching as he watched my lips and his thumb. His hand tightened on mine, and my body flushed with heat.

"We don't have time to make out. We're already late," he rasped, pulling his thumb back but sweeping it back and forth over my lip, eyes never leaving his movements.

Neither of us made to move out of the car. The air was thick with electricity. Goose bumps pebbled on my skin.

Sterling groaned as he pulled away then closed his eyes and let his forehead bang against the steering wheel. Then he reached for the door handle and broke the spell.

I giggled.

As we walked into the cafetorium, Sterling had upgraded from hand holding to putting his arm around my shoulders. I was snuggled into his side, soaking up the affection. I hadn't had a lot of it in my life, so his PDA was something I liked. *Really* liked. He was warm and made me feel safe.

All eyes came to us, and then whispers broke out. I knew they were talking about my hair. I shrank farther into Sterling, wishing I could disappear.

"It'll be okay, princess. You're beautiful," he stated.

I wanted to believe him, but the looks of disbelief and stares had me wanting to murder Blake.

"You both are late ... again," Mrs. Cook barked.

I had never seen her wear anything other than a variant of a house dress and cardigan combo, but today she wore blue jean overalls, with a white, long-sleeved shirt underneath, and a red bandana tied over her hair. She even had on sneakers.

I stifled a chuckle and apologized, "Sorry, Mrs. Cook. It was my fault."

"I pulled into the lot this morning and didn't see her car. Thought I'd go by and see if she needed a ride, which she did, since her mom borrowed her car," Sterling lied.

I shot him a nervous glance. He was staring down at me with an amused smirk on his lips.

Mrs. Cook cleared her throat and looked down her nose at me, clearly not impressed with my apology or Sterling's explanation. "Don't let it happen again. And, by the way, you didn't have to dye your hair. We could've just bought you a wig."

I searched the room for Blake, plotting my revenge, and saw him sitting at a table with Elodie, avoiding my glare.

Mrs. Cook spun back to the rest of the room and stated, "Now that everyone has *finally* arrived, we're going to split up into groups and plan out what props and sets we need to create for each scene. More than likely, there will be paint involved, so I hope you didn't wear anything you don't want to get dirty."

As Sterling guided us toward Blake and Elodie's table, I looked down at my outfit and winced. I really didn't want to get my camisole covered in paint.

"Hey, B and E," Sterling greeted, his smile wide and teasing.

Blake looked up at us and replied with a grin, "Hey, liar, liar, pants on fire, and Ally." He was reclined in his chair, ankle propped on his knee, hands folded in his lap.

I eyed his pants, which were brown with striped, asymmetrical patches at the knee, zippers at the pockets, and had some gold button flap thing at the crotch. He had paired it with a gray V-neck tee and a black sweater that had thumb holes in the sleeves.

I glared at him, but before I could blast him, he declared, "Shut up. Your hair is fabulous, and everyone else thinks so, too."

"But the whispers—"

"Were ones of delight. The blonde is fierce and hot AF," Blake countered.

"I like your pants and sweater," I muttered, deciding arguing with him was a lost cause.

"Thanks, love. But I'm going to say it right now ... I'm not painting."

I glanced at Elodie who was unusually quiet. "Hey, Elodie."

She was hunched over the table, head in her hands, only her eyes moving to acknowledge me.

"Don't mind her. She's worried about performing her song on Monday. Raven already started in on her this morning, the thirsty witch, and she's freaked," Blake supplied.

I gritted my teeth and searched out Raven. She was on the other side of the room, laughing with Janet and Lana. She must have felt my gaze because she turned to look at me, took note of Sterling's arm around my shoulders, and sneered.

I decided to do something I had only done once in my entire life ... I raised my hand to my face, flipped up only my middle finger, and scratched my nose with it, blatantly flipping her off while glaring daggers at her.

Her eyes narrowed back at me like she wanted to murder me ... *violently*.

I felt Sterling's heat and his lips at my ear before he whispered, "I saw that."

I ignored him, watching hatred morph Raven's features. Then her face went funny. Her eyes widened in panic, and then she went pale as she quickly covered her mouth and ran for the nearest trash can.

The distinct sound of retching and gagging made everyone in the room turn and look at Raven bent over the trash can against the wall. Some gagged and others muttered "gross" and "sick," while Raven's two friends and some other girls went over there.

"Serves her right," Blake muttered.

Mrs. Cook hurried over to the group gathered around Raven and shooed them away. She took Raven by the shoulders and guided her to the hall that led to the teacher's lounge.

I looked up at Sterling to see his reaction. His face looked funny.

"You feeling okay?" I asked. Maybe he was one of those who got nauseous when he heard someone throwing up?

His jaw clenched, and his lips thinned. He didn't answer verbally, just nodded and averted his eyes.

I glanced at Blake, who was studying Sterling. Then I checked Elodie, who hadn't moved from her dejected position. I moved out from under Sterling's arm and went to sit next to her. Sterling took the seat next to mine and scooted in close, draping his arm over the back of my chair.

"It's going to be okay, Elodie. We'll figure something out," I said as I reached out and squeezed her shoulder.

She just nodded, but it didn't look like she felt any better or even believed me.

I sighed and thought this was going to be a long effin' day.

§

We were in Sterling's car, driving out of town, but not in the direction of my house. It turned out we didn't need to build anything today. Most of the props had been donated, and what we couldn't make, the shop class would. Therefore, we ended up just painting signs and banners for Rydell High, and then blocked out more scenes. I was becoming more confident in this theater stuff once I knew where to go and what to do. I knew we would need to practice more, but I could see the threads starting to weave themselves together.

I looked out the passenger side window, noting the sun would set at any moment. I didn't need to ask where we were going since, moments later, we were pulling into the lot of Westbank Park.

Sterling cut the engine and said, "Come on," before he got out.

I reached for the door handle and followed his lead, limping around to the front where he stood waiting on me. When I came in close, he grabbed my waist and hefted me up on the primer gray hood of his car.

"Wha—"

He let me go, and I scooted back farther so I didn't slide off. The warm metal felt good on my throbbing hamstring, dulling the ache. It probably would have burned if I hadn't been wearing jeans. I had done too much over the past couple days and was feeling the brunt of it.

He climbed onto the hood beside me and put his arm around me.

"What are we doing?" I whispered. I didn't know why. We were the only ones out here, and we were outside.

"We're watching the sun set," he replied, not whispering.

I cuddled in close to his body as we silently watched the bright orange orb sink below the horizon. The light blue sky streaked in oranges, reds, and purples, giving way to the navy of the oncoming night. Stars began to twinkle in the ever-darkening sky as the sun fell and all traces of its glow disappeared.

At one time, I thought there could never be a more perfect sunset, but I had been wrong. So wrong. This was the most perfect sunset I had ever witnessed and probably ever would for the rest of my life.

"Did you know," Sterling broke into my silent reverie, "if a person lives to be eight-five, they would see twenty-nine thousand and two hundred sunsets?"

I shook my head that was resting on his shoulder. "No."

"I think I could sit here and watch twenty-nine thousand and however many more with you." He rubbed his cheek against my hair, and my heart gave a little leap, probably trying to escape my chest and invade his. I could get used to this, but I had questions.

"What are we doing, Sterling?"

His cheek was still pressed to the top of my head when he asked, "What do you mean?"

I pulled back so I could see his face. Well, try to see it in the dark that had shrouded us.

"Are we dating? Boyfriend and girlfriend? What?" It came out snippier than I had wanted it to, but I was feeling a little panicked.

He was silent a beat, his face expressionless, almost guarded. Then he asked, "What do you want to be?"

I blew out a breath and turned to gaze out at the lake. I knew what I wanted us to be and who I wanted to be. Right now, I had the opportunity to try on this new Ally Everly, to be the open and honest person I never could have been before.

My insides quivered, and my palms started sweating, but I answered him.

"I want to be with you," I replied in a small voice, eyes still focused on the gentle motion of the water, trying not to wince at how weak it had sounded.

I felt fingers grip my chin, and then my face was turned back toward him. He was so close that his eyes snared mine. I couldn't look away. I was transfixed by their beauty, and it wasn't just the unusual color; it was the expression flowing out of them.

"Good," he said softly then started to lean forward.

Before his lips could touch mine, I blurted, "Why?"

This was something that had been plaguing me. Why was Sterling so interested? Yes, I was pretty, but that was basically all I had going for me.

His brows furrowed, and he tilted his head to one side. "*Why?*"

"Yeah, I mean, why do you want me?"

He paused, examining my expression, then asked, "Are you serious?"

Was I serious? Of course I was serious. Why else would I have asked a question that had the potential to destroy me? I mean, what if he couldn't think of anything? What if he answered it the same way he had answered it last night about Raven? I just didn't see what he could possibly see in me.

"Yeah." I sounded annoyed because I was, well, annoyed.

He shook his head and muttered, "I want to wring their necks."

"Who?" I asked. Now it was me who was confused.

"Your daddy and that douchebag Miles Thorpe," he gritted out. "Neither one of those assholes helped you see your worth. Your father more than Miles. A guy is supposed to show his woman, whether they're his daughter or girl, that they're precious. You tell them, but you also show them by treating them like gold."

He rested his forehead against mine and continued to stare into my eyes as he said, "Ally, you are amazing. You think you're weak, but you're not. You're strong—"

"No, I'm not," I interrupted, shaking my head.

"Ally—"

"I tried—"

"I know what you tried to do. I remember the last sunset we watched together, even if you didn't realize I was there with you. Strong people have moments of weakness, and that was yours. Even rocks crack and break over time with enough pressure. That doesn't mean you can't repair those crack and breaks." He paused to let that sink in. "You're also smart. And when you forget to be guarded and aren't bracing yourself for the worst, you're funny. I've been watching you for a long time, Ally Everly."

I pulled back and inspected his face, gauging whether he was just teasing me or telling the truth. His expression was completely earnest, and hope unfurled and grew inside me.

Sterling reached up and tucked a strand of hair behind my ear. "I also know you've been watching me for a while, too."

Heat rose to my cheeks, and my gaze dropped to Sterling's jean-clad thigh.

He dropped his hand from my hair then grabbed both my hands in his and started rubbing them between his own. "It's getting chilly. We should probably head back."

I nodded, mainly relieved because I was mortified that I hadn't been as stealthy as I thought in my Sterling stalking over the years, but also because it was getting cold. The wind off the lake was always chillier.

He continued to warm my hands, bringing them to his mouth and blowing on them before letting them go and sliding off the hood. He then captured my hips and pulled me forward until his legs were between my own. Tilting his head down, a devilish look on his face, he said in a smug voice, "So, it's official. You're *my* girl."

I smiled shyly and nodded, my gaze never leaving his.

He dipped forward and brushed his lips against mine. It wasn't an open-mouthed, tongue kiss; it was a slow, soft kiss. A reverent one. A kiss that, if I had been standing, it would have brought me to my knees.

He moved up and pressed another one to my forehead before he moved away and helped me down from the hood and into his car.

He didn't have to say words. His actions, his kiss, they showed me he thought I was worth something. That he thought I was precious. It was the little things. It was everything.

Sterling walked me to my door, his kiss brief and his face haggard. He had to be exhausted after our late night, and then being gone all day with no sleep.

"I'm gonna go home and crash. Night, princess." He flicked two fingers, and then he was in his Chevelle, the glow of his taillights disappearing down the road.

The porch light was on, and my mom's car was in the driveway, so I knew she was home. Dad's car was still mysteriously absent. The new Ally Everly would get to the bottom of what was going on.

I straightened my shoulders and marched—more like limped with determination—into the house, finding Mom curled up on the couch, watching *Grey's Anatomy*.

I strode to the couch and plopped down next to her. "Where's Dad?" I demanded.

"Why?" She didn't look at me, her eyes remaining fused to the screen.

Why? Did she think I wouldn't notice the grand master puppeteer who constantly pulled our strings had suddenly disappeared?

"Um ... Because he's been home at night almost every night for the past seventeen years, yet he hasn't been home in almost a week?"

"Business trip. He's having to take lots of business trips," she said in a tone that was devoid of emotion, her eyes still not straying from the medical drama playing out on the television.

"But—"

She suddenly reached for the remote and clicked off the TV. She still didn't look at me when she declared, "My back hurts, so I think I'll take a pill and head off to bed."

My stomach dropped, and my chest got tight. It got worse with her next words.

"I had to call Russell to get another prescription since I can't find my bottle of pain meds anywhere."

My gaze dropped to my hands, and my breath started sawing in and out of my body. It was good she wasn't watching, or she might have caught my impending panic attack.

"Night, Ally. Love you," she called, her voice fading.

"Night, Mom. Love you," I whispered.

I dropped my chin to my chest and squeezed my eyes shut. I was an awful, horrible daughter, and if I could manage it, she would never know.

On autopilot, I got up from the couch, cut off all the lights, and checked the door. Then I staggered to my room and numbly got ready for bed. When the lights were off and I was alone in the darkness of my room, I let the tears of shame and guilt leak from my eyes.

Never. She would never find out what had happened. No one would, except for Sterling, Blake, and Elodie, who already knew. The incident was going in a box, and I was going to bury it so far inside me that it never came out.

And that was how I forgot ...

MAGIC OF KARAOKE

Sundays were church days, so I was shocked when I rolled out of bed that morning and it was *way* past time to be there. Like, it was over. And Mom wasn't anywhere in sight. I even knocked on her bedroom door, but nothing. No sound. No nothing. Weird.

So, here I was ... foraging for sustenance since it was after twelve, when the doorbell sounded. Confused, because I didn't know who would be here, I padded to the front door and looked out the peephole.

Sterling.

I jerked the door open and gaped at him. "What are you doing here?" Belatedly, I realized I was still in my pajamas and no bra.

He smiled. "You didn't get my text?"

"Crap," I muttered. I hadn't checked my phone since I had gotten up. It was sitting on my desk in my room.

I invited him to come in, but he shook his head and gestured behind him where a black Ford Explorer was idling in the driveway, Pops in the driver's seat. His black aviators were trained on us, and he lifted his finger from the steering wheel in a wave. I lifted my hand back.

"You need to hurry and get dressed, and you won't be able to do that if I come inside." Sterling raised his brows. Yeah, I got his meaning.

"Just give me a minute." I turned, not even bothering to close the door, and hobbled quickly down the hall. I pulled the first thing from my closet, which was a thick, white, long-sleeved shirt with two black horizontal stripes, and black skinny jeans. I tied my hair up in a pony-tail, not even running a brush through it, just finger-combed it. I did, however, brush my teeth and wipe my face with a facial cleansing cloth.

This was not the Ally Everly of before. That Ally would have felt self-conscious leaving the house without makeup or even her hair down. I was embracing the new me. The blonde Ally who was up for adventure.

I slipped on my shoes, grabbed my purse, wrote Mom a note, and then met Sterling at the door, since he hadn't moved since I had left.

I kissed his cheek and whispered, "Hey."

"Hey, princess." His returning smile was wide and happy, and I loved it. He was so handsome standing there, looking back at me with warm eyes and a relaxed expression, like everything was right in his world.

Hand on my lower back, he guided me to the back driver's side door and opened it. I jumped at the sight of B & E.

Blake was practically vibrating in his seat, and Elodie looked like she was going to be sick.

I turned to Sterling. "What is go—"

"Got no time. I'll explain on the way," Pops barked.

I looked at him and saw that he had twisted his neck so I could only see his profile while he spoke to me.

In a softer tone, he said, "Hey, Ally, darlin'."

Sterling closed the door while I replied, "Hey, Pops."

Once Sterling was back in the front seat and we were motoring out of the driveway, I leaned forward and whispered to him, "Where's Jack?"

Sterling twisted back and answered, "Jack doesn't do too well with noise, so he's with a friend today."

Sitting back, I watched Pops open his mouth to say something, when Blake burst out, "We're going to karaoke!"

Elodie groaned.

I leaned forward to place my hand on her knee. "You okay?"

"She's just nervous," Blake interjected.

"It's going to be just like singing in class," Sterling said from the front.

"I think that's the problem," I gritted out to him from the side of my mouth, my focus on Elodie's ashen face.

"We'll have it all sorted by tonight. I got a friend back in the town I grew up in; she owns a diner and agreed to host an impromptu karaoke night for us. I got the equipment in the back," Pops boomed.

"A lady friend?" Blake asked in a sing-song voice.

Elodie whacked him on the shoulder and gave him an "are you crazy" look.

Pops' rumbly laugh of disbelief filled the cab as he said, "Shit no. Sally is old enough to be *my* mother." When Sterling sent Pops a look, he amended, "Okay, maybe an *older* sister. But don't tell her I said any of that. I like my balls right where they are."

I giggled and noticed that Elodie had cracked a smile, the first one I had seen since Friday.

An hour later, we pulled in front of a small diner aptly named Sally's and all got out of the Explorer. As Pops, Blake, and Elodie headed for the door, Sterling moved to the back to unload the machine and mic. It was a lot smaller than I thought it would be, just a medium-sized white stereo with a rainbow-striped speaker, a small screen on the front face, and two mics attached.

"Where did y'all get that?"

"Pops got it at Best Buy this morning. It'll be Jack's next birthday present when we're done." He handed me two CD cases. One read "Party Time Karaoke," and the other was from our musical.

"It's a nice thing your pops is doing for Elodie," I said quietly. I couldn't remember any of my former friends' parents ever doing anything remotely this nice for me or, well, even their own kids.

"He's known Elodie since she was a baby. Her dad is a hobbyist. Owns a Stingray."

"Oh." I hadn't known that. The only things I knew about Elodie's parents were that her mom was white, her dad was black, and they both had been in the military.

As we walked through the door, a bell jingled overhead. I saw Pops by the counter, talking to a tiny, elderly woman whose hair seemed to make up the majority of her height. Pops caught our eye and motioned us over.

"Sterling, Ally, this is Sally Lafayette," Pops introduced.

Sterling let go of my hand and reached out for a shake. "Ms. Lafayette."

She knocked his hand aside and wrapped her frail-looking arms around him for a quick squeeze, saying in a scratchy smoker's voice, "Family don't shake hands around here."

Sterling made an uncomfortable yet amused face and patted her back with his free hand, the other still holding the machine.

She leaned back, hands still attached to his arms, and declared in a hoarse cry, "Woo-ee, you are the spittin' image of Silas at that age."

When she let go, he then hooked his arm around my waist and pulled me forward. "This is my girlfriend, Ally Everly."

I couldn't stop the smile that stretched my face. This was the first time he had introduced me publicly as his girlfriend. I could feel B & E's eyes on us, but I didn't care.

I, too, reached forward to shake her hand, but she accepted mine and gave it a vigorous two-handed shake.

She looked at Sterling and proclaimed, "She's a looker, honey. Pretty like my Sunny. She's at culinary school right now in Dallas with her handsome boyfriend."

"Oh. Um, well ... thank you." I didn't know who Sunny was, but she was evidently important to Sally.

"Love the hair color." She flashed a perfectly straight, dingy, *bedentured* smile.

"Told you so," I heard Blake hiss from my left.

"Can we set up anywhere?" Sterling asked, evidently ready to get the show on the road.

"Pretty much, but that spot would probably work best. There's a plug and everyone can see you over there." Sally gestured to an area in front next to a wall.

The diner started to fill as we set up the machine—well, as Sterling set up the machine. The rest of us stood around and watched.

Pops dragged over a barstool from the counter so the machine didn't sit on the floor and so everyone would be able to see the screen when their turn came. Then he went back to his own stool at the counter and his coffee.

It was decided on the way over that everyone, except Pops of course, would get a turn. We were going to be like the commercial breaks in the Elodie show.

Once Sterling had it set up, he held his hand out for a CD.

"Which one?" I asked.

"Let's do the party CD and end on her *Grease* solo," Blake said.

Sterling nodded his agreement, Elodie made a funny noise, and I just handed Sterling both CDs.

"I'll go first," Blake volunteered.

The three of us moved to the red faux leather booth next to the machine, me and Sterling on one side and Elodie on the other.

Sterling handed Elodie the CD case and instructed, "See what songs on there you want to sing, and then we'll pick. It's your show."

The bouncy opening beats of "Fancy" by Iggy Azalea came out of the little speaker surprisingly loud, and Blake's hilarious imitation of the female singer had everyone alternately bobbing their heads and chuckling. Once he was done with his over-the-top performance, the sparse crowd applauded, and he moved to the side.

I glanced at Elodie, who hadn't moved from her seat and seemed to be mumbling to herself.

"Ellie?" Blake interrupted what looked to be her pep talk. "Your turn, doll."

She sucked in a breath then blew it out, repeating this action over and over, reminding me of a pregnant lady in labor. Then she surged from her spot, snatched the mic awkwardly from the machine, almost knocking it over, and stood in front of the crowd ... frozen.

I tapped Sterling's leg and tilted my head in her direction. She had forgotten to choose a song and start the music.

I slid out, letting Sterling by so he could help her.

"Love Me Like You Do" by Ellie Goulding started playing, yet Elodie wasn't singing. Or, I should say, her mouth was moving, but no sound was coming out. She looked like one of those blinky-eyed china dolls—eyes and lips moving, but no one was home.

Meanwhile, the crowd was losing interest and had gone back to their food and conversations.

Without a thought, I grabbed the second mic, glanced at the screen, and started singing. I moved in close to Elodie and started bumping the side of my good hip softly against the side of hers and bobbing my head. Elodie's eyes got even wider at my antics, so I upped my game. I progressively got louder, sillier, and eventually, maybe even miraculously, she loosened up enough to sing loud enough so everyone else could hear.

I knew we couldn't let her sit after this one—she didn't need time to build her fears back up—so I motioned to Blake to come up and sing with us for another song. We trapped her up there with us as Sterling selected another song, which happened to be a fun one—Meghan Trainor's "All About that Bass." I didn't even need to see the screen for the words.

The diner began to fill with more patrons, and Sally came from somewhere in the back to watch our performance. By the end of the song, Elodie had relaxed enough to not only sing, but bust some moves. I was giggling so hard I bent double. I couldn't remember the last time I had laughed so hard. The rest of the diner guests were having a good time right along with us.

I was wiping a tear from under my eye and going to sit down when Sterling halted my movement. He stared down into my face, his eyes full of warmth and amusement, and said, "I love watching you laugh. I don't think I've ever seen you giggle so hard."

"I don't think I ever have," I replied with a watery chuckle. My sides hurt, and my belly felt hollow from the hilarity.

"Kiss for luck?" he requested, using my favorite sexy smirk.

I lifted onto my tiptoes and pressed my lips to his, then pulled back and whispered, "Good luck," against them.

Sterling, ever the gentleman, escorted me to my seat before he went up and set his music up.

When it was his turn, Sterling chose "Sugar" by Maroon 5, which made me giggle ... again. How fitting?

As always, his voice was impressive. His range was amazing. He could not only hit John Travolta's pitch on "Summer Nights," but he was Adam Levine worthy. I noticed, especially with the women, that his voice ensnared them all. It was like he was born to perform.

After he was done, we sent Elodie up to perform on her own. I instantly recognized the song she had picked and thought it was perfect for her. I looked at Blake and noticed that he, too, looked pleased.

The shy wallflower from before was gone. Elodie rocked Sara Bareilles' "Brave" and had everyone in the diner up on their feet, swaying and singing along to her vibrant vocals.

"Brave" broke the seal because, after that, it became the Elodie show.

I looked toward the counter and saw Pops still parked on a stool with an empty plate in front of him, looking very pleased with himself. I made a note that the rest of us should probably eat before we left.

After two more songs, which Elodie had sung solo, I gave Sterling the high sign. He switched the CDs out and set her up for "Frankie, My Love."

It was like a different girl was singing it. Elodie had diva flair and was pouring it out into the audience that had filled out to a Sunday night dinner crowd.

I swayed against Sterling as I listened, every so often glancing up at his face to find him watching me with a small smile on his lips. When the last notes of her final song played, she finished to the sound of thunderous applause with a big smile on her face. Pops was a genius.

After Sterling packed up the machine and we were all seated at a booth, Sally came over with another waitress and delivered a round of milkshakes and burger baskets "on the house." We all thanked her and ate some of the best food in the county. I didn't know if they were the best because I hadn't had a hamburger in several years or if they were just that delicious.

When we were on our way home, darkness had already fallen, so everyone in the cab was bathed in the neon glow of the dash. We had rearranged to where Elodie sat in front, Blake sat in the seat behind her, asleep against the window, and I sat in the middle, with Sterling behind Pops.

I was leaning against Sterling, snuggled under his arm that was draped over my shoulders, half-asleep, when I heard Elodie say quietly, "Thanks, Pops."

"No problem, darlin' girl," he replied.

"I think that was one of the best nights of my life," she whispered.

"The magic of karaoke," he stated matter-of-factly like that was all there was to it.

"Yeah."

If they said anything else, I didn't know, because I was soon fast asleep, curled into my new boyfriend.

⁂

When Pops pulled up my driveway, Sterling having just woken me up, the house was dark except for the front outside lights. Sterling walked me to the door and unlocked it for me before giving me a chaste kiss on the cheek. Mom had already gone to bed; the note tacked to the fridge confirming that.

> **Gone to bed. Hope you had fun!**
> **Love you and sweet dreams!**
> **Mom**

It was nice not being interrogated by my father upon coming home after dark. I was afraid to hope that this would be my new normal and that he would just stay gone.

My phone went off in my pocket, and I pulled it out, seeing a Snapchat notification from Sterling. I quickly opened the app, pressed the small red square, and loaded the snap.

It was a picture of Blake asleep in the car. I chuckled at how peaceful he looked in sleep. He was such a bundle of energy that it was strange seeing him not in motion.

Another photo followed, one of Elodie asleep, as well. At the bottom, the text read, "*True friends are a reason to stay.*"

Tears welled in my eyes. That was what I had now—true friends. Sterling had given me that. The realization floored me.

The tears fell and flowed down my cheeks in rivulets. How could I ever repay him for this?

I couldn't.

I fell asleep with that thought tormenting me.

GETTING HERS BACK

Monday morning was ... interesting. I didn't know whether people were staring at me because I had emerged from the passenger side of Sterling Chapman's nineteen-seventy Chevrolet Chevelle—I knew what it was because he had told me—if it was that he had his arm around me, or if it was the hair. I would say it was a combination of all three. Either way, I felt like I should have had one of those musical intros like they did in the movies. The staircase scene in *She's All That*, or maybe the parking lot one from *Twilight*. However, with everyone's eyes on me and all the whispers, it felt more like the Emma Stone scarlet-letter-black-bustier hallway scene from *Easy A*.

On the way to my locker, I noticed Miles' face turn red when he saw me, but he didn't approach. Just stared, stony-faced, at us from his locker before one girl or another—because there were several gathered at his locker—gained his attention.

Laura just looked shocked when she passed me in the hall, eyes wide and mouth open. Then she gave me a knowing look before patting her own blonde tresses and whispering furiously with Sarah and Ariel. Whatever. I didn't like that her eyes lingered on Sterling a little too long and with too much interest.

I would know the meaning of her hair patting and whispering later when Sarah flicked a square of paper on my desk in English that read, "*Fake AF Laura wannabe.*"

I guessed that answered my question about what happened in the parking lot. I wondered what Raven had done to get on Laura's bad side.

I crumpled the note and, when Mrs. Jones' back was turned, pelted her in the head.

She gasped and swore, gaining Mrs. Jones' attention.

"Miss Burns, we don't speak like that in my classroom. Detention."

I didn't think I had ever seen Sarah's face turn so red, not even when she had been caught naked on the football field that one time with Jesse Spear.

She fumed the rest of the period before practically running from the room when the bell rang.

I had managed the day without crutches. I still moved slow, but I believed the KT tape was actually working. I had PT tomorrow, so I guessed I would find out then.

When the bell rang for last period, I met Sterling outside my classroom door, like every period before, and he walked me to the cafetorium for theater.

We took our seats on the steps and waited for Mrs. Cook to appear. One thing I thought was funny was Mrs. Cook wouldn't need a costume for her role as Miss Lynch. Her plethora of vintage-inspired skirts and dresses were performance ready. Exhibit A was swish-swishing around the corner from the speech room. Mrs. Cook emerged in a light blue housedress ensemble with a cream sweater draped over her shoulders.

Anticipation hummed through me because Elodie would get hers back today. It was deadline time.

I searched the room for her and Blake, but they weren't there, and the late bell would ring any minute. I turned to Sterling to ask where our friends were when a door slammed from the left.

Everyone's heads swiveled toward the sound, and a moment later, a panting Blake and Elodie jogged around the stage. The crowd broke out in whispers when they noticed what Elodie was wearing.

"Wha ...?" Mrs. Cook, who evidently had no clue what was going on, started right as the bell sounded and Blake and Elodie practically did a baseball slide to the steps in front of us.

I leaned forward and whispered, "Where did you come from?"

Blake leaned back, propped one arm on my knee, and whispered back, "The little girls' room."

"You're a little boy, though."

He rolled his eyes and made a rude noise as he sat back up.

Mrs. Cook's hawk gaze gave us a reprimanding look before she cleared her throat and commanded, "All right, thespians, today we're going to hear 'Franky, My Love' ... again." She gave Elodie a meaningful look, then remarked, "Love your ensemble, Miss Thomas."

Elodie had changed into a tight, Kelly-green sweater tucked into a black, knee-length bell skirt with a black, shiny, patent leather belt. She also had on a pair of black and white lace-up Oxfords. She looked amazing.

I peeked at Sterling from the corner of my eye. He must have felt my stare because he caught my eye from the corner of his. I bit my lip to contain my giggle. He looked as if he was restraining his hilarity, as well. This was going to be good. I just knew it.

"After that, we'll start working through the play from the beginning. I hope you've been memorizing your lines. Oh, and after-school practices start today, so I hope you've made arrangements for that." When no one made any comment to the contrary, she gave a nod and declared, "Right. Now, let's get on with it."

We all got up and moved to the tables, except for Elodie, Raven, Lana, and Janet. They took their marks on stage.

Raven must have gotten over whatever sickness she'd had over the weekend because her snotty attitude was back. The superior look on her face and the derisive looks and rolled eyes exchanged between her, Janet, and Lana were like a bad rerun.

"Waste of time," Raven whispered loud enough to the other girls to be heard where we were sitting. Then they all cackled, which set my teeth on edge.

"If I didn't know better, I'd think we were watching *Macbeth* with those witches," Blake muttered from beside me.

I swallowed a laugh. I hadn't seen *Macbeth*, but those girls were definitely witches.

I examined Elodie to see if their attitudes were rattling her newfound confidence, but her face was set and determined.

It was funny how theater wasn't much different than sports. These antics weren't any dissimilar than the intimidation tactics that took place on the starting line. It was just as much of a competition on stage as it was on the track, field, or court. At the same time, it was a team effort. If one player wasn't performing well, it could bring the whole team or, well, cast down.

When the music started, Elodie came alive. Her voice was soulful and rich, her movements graceful. Not the stiff, awkward girl who had let Raven and her friends upstage her. She engaged everyone in the audience, and when Raven "accidentally" knocked into her, she played it off. When that had happened, though, I had reached over and gripped Sterling's thigh to keep myself from marching up there and "accidentally" knocking Raven out.

When the song ended, everyone jumped to their feet, clapping. Blake ran up to the stage like he had just scored the winning goal in a soccer game and picked Elodie up, swinging her around. Raven, Lana, and Janet looked like they had sucked on lemons as they watched the scene, before stomping down the steps, not saying a word to Elodie.

I glared as they passed us, and they glared back until their eyes caught on Sterling behind me. Raven's expression turned calculating then morphed into flirtatiousness.

She lifted a hand as if she was going to touch him, and I clipped, "If you want to keep those fingers, I suggest you keep them to yourself."

"Sweetheart, these fingers have already been *all over* that. Isn't that right, Sterling? Remember all the *good* places they've been," she purred.

I felt my mask slip into place, the impassive one that held no emotion. The last thing I wanted was for her to see she had scored a hit.

Of course I knew they had had a physical relationship—Sterling had told me—but having it thrown in my face was like a punch to the gut. I should have been prepared for it. I mean, I'd had *loads* of practice since my ex-best friend had screwed my boyfriend for two years. I was the master of indifference. It just wasn't as easy because Sterling wasn't Miles.

In the short time we had been together, I had felt more with him and for him than in all the years I had spent as Miles' girlfriend. I was falling fast and hard. So, yeah, I wanted to claw her eyes out.

"You know, I really can't remember." Sterling's voice and his hand rubbing up and down my back broke me from my violent contemplations. I looked up and saw him put a finger to his chin and scrunch his face up in an exaggeratedly thoughtful expression. "The only person who comes to mind is *my girl*. Ally is the only person I remember or *want* putting their hands on me." His tone held a sarcastic edge, but eventually disintegrated into something almost lethal.

He leaned his upper body forward and got in her face before saying loudly, "In case you haven't figured this out, even though I've told you a million times ..." He leaned back then looked around the room as he announced, "Maybe I should just tell you in front of everyone so that maybe it will sink into that warped mind of yours." His eyes came back to her, filled with so much loathing when he said, "We. Are. Done. We have been for a *long* time, so quit with this stuff."

The scene had drawn every eye in the room, and people were talking in hushed tones all around us. For a minute, I wondered where Mrs. Cook was. Knowing her, she loved drama, so she often let it play out in her classes as long as curse words and violence weren't involved.

Raven's face screwed up into something ugly. There was so much wrong with this girl. She was beautiful, yes, but she was damaged. It was written all over her face right now.

"You're going to be *very* sorry, Sterling Chapman," she whispered through clenched teeth. Then her eyes darted to me. "You will be, too. You can't keep him. *You* can't have *everything*." Those last words dripped with so much venom I was surprised I didn't fall over dead. Then she stormed away.

Sterling watched her go with an uneasy look on his face.

"She's going to be trouble, isn't she?" I asked hesitantly.

He turned back to me, the uneasiness gone. Now determination filled his features. "No. I won't let her be."

I opened my mouth to ask how he planned on accomplishing that, when Elodie and Blake floated over to us.

"That girl is so thirsty that the ocean wouldn't be enough to fill her up," Blake commented.

Elodie just nodded, her gaze on someone, presumably Raven, over our shoulders.

Mrs. Cook clapped her hands, gaining everyone's attention, and instructed, "Now, no more drama."

She must not have realized how ironic her words were until we all busted up laughing. Even she couldn't keep the chuckle from her voice when she continued, "Let's set up for Act One, Scene One, kids."

We spent the rest of class and into the evening rehearsing for the musical that we had a little over a month to get ready for. *Grease Lightning* indeed.

THE SWEET LIFE

In one week, my life had changed, and it looked as if those changes were going to stick. In the past month, I had set up a routine of sorts. I was busy. I went to school, practiced lines, did homework, rehearsed for the musical, went to physical therapy once a week, and when I wasn't doing any of those, I was with Sterling or B & E.

Mine and Sterling's late-night adventures continued. We spent lots of time at the pier, talking and kissing. We were inseparable. Even when we weren't together, we were connected through text or Snapchat. I was in love, and life was just about perfect.

I still hadn't confessed my feelings to Sterling, and he hadn't for me either. They were on the tip of my tongue every time we were together, but we were too new, and honestly, I was scared. I didn't want to rock the boat or scare him away. I loved being with him and kissing him.

Our make-out sessions had gotten heavier and hotter, but something was holding us back from taking it all the way. It wasn't just my insecurities, but something on Sterling's end was in the way, too. Physically, we might have been ready, but emotionally, I guessed we both needed time.

My dad, according to my mom, was out of town for court cases. Those business trips had turned into a job out of town. It didn't sit right with me, and I had a feeling she wasn't exactly being honest. I wasn't going to rock that boat either, though. Our relationship had changed, and I felt like we were building a regular mother-daughter bond, yet it was still too fragile. The ground underneath me was starting to firm, but there were still cracks that could crumble at any moment. I wasn't going to be the earthquake that destroyed it.

The musical was looming in the not-so-distant future. We were working non-stop to make it possible. My leg and hip were healing. I was able to do choreography and light exercise. Nothing jerky or strenuous, but I was able to move without pain, and Mrs. Cook made it to where it worked with my songs and scenes. Jamie, my physical therapist, had said I was lucky I was a quick healer.

I had ceased to exist for Miles, Laura, and their friends. I had been excommunicated. This didn't bother me. I was actually happier not existing on their radar. I was just plain happy. I felt like I was seventeen with my whole life ahead of me, instead of older beyond my years and ready for it all to end.

Life was sweet ... I just didn't know it would sour so soon.

It was Thursday, the night before our first performance, and we were running our dress rehearsal. I had everything I needed organized and my costume changes were planned and in order, the last being my black, skintight "bad girl Sandy" outfit.

My mom had donated a portable professional makeup studio for backstage, which was just a big suitcase with a mirror and bulb lights installed into the lid, makeup trays, and retractable legs. I had complained I would have to run all the way to the band hall bathroom to do my makeup for the finale, and two days later, a large box from Amazon had showed up on our doorstep.

Everything had gone off without a hitch so far. I was surprised. Raven, who I thought would have been a problem after all the stunts she had pulled during our early rehearsals, had just ... *faded* over the past month. Sure, she still sneered and glared, but it was subdued. She seemed preoccupied, pale, and had lost weight.

I asked Sterling what he thought was going on with her, since he knew her, but he had just shrugged and changed the subject. She was his ex, and he despised her. End of.

I was backstage, dressed in skintight, shiny, black spandex leggings, a black belt around my waistline, a black Lycra off-the-shoulders top, leather jacket, and bright, candy apple red slingback heels. My hair was huge, curled and teased out like a cloud around my head, and the mic was hidden in its mass. I had lined my eyes black, painted my lips red to match my shoes, and wore gold hoops in my ears for the finishing touch.

I shifted side to side, nervous anticipation tingling along my skin and making my insides vibrate. I shook my body, starting from my hands and up my arms, then rolled my shoulders and neck. I didn't know why I was so nervous. We had practiced this for what felt like a million times. Nevertheless, my heart was pounding, a fluttery feeling filled my tummy, and a breathless feeling had overcome me.

I heard my cue and, without thought, I strutted onstage like I was supposed to, hips swaying and face full of attitude.

I actually *felt* it when Sterling caught sight of me, because the energy on stage changed. What was an act, a drama, had blended into the real thing. His face held genuine shock that gave way to an inferno. His eyes devoured me from the tips of my red toes up my legs. And as I slung the leather jacket away from me, they moved to my upper body and finally to my face and hair. His stare was like a physical caress that I felt ... *everywhere.*

Sterling bit his lip, and his hands fisted at his sides. For a moment, I worried he wouldn't be able to perform and was preparing to throw me over his shoulder and haul me away. Finally, he delivered his line, and I returned with mine—breathlessly and shaky, I might add—and then it was the scene with Erin/Patty.

I was so distracted I almost hit her in the face for real. I tried to give her an apologetic look, but I couldn't keep my eyes from Sterling for very long. I was like a moth to a flame, instinctively drawn to his heat.

We finished out the scene, and then the music started to play. His eyes were so intense and focused on me. It felt like we were the only people in the room as he sang the opening lyrics and prowled toward me. When he came in close, the air between us grew thick, and my heart started beating double time in excitement. I stuck my hip out and bounced in time with the music as I rolled my shoulders just like I had practiced, but it felt different this time, like we were playing a seductive game of cat and mouse.

He threw his letterman sweater, never taking his eyes from mine, and skimmed his hand down my side. The feel of his fingers burned me through the material of my clothes, and I shivered at how close he was to some places that were probably not appropriate to explore on stage.

Feeling like a predator, I moved around him, grazing my fingertips across his chest. I watched his eyes close and his body shudder at my touch, and smiled. He was just as affected by me as I was him.

We sang and danced, our bodies brushing, touches lingering. I was flushed and out of breath, wanting nothing more than to be alone with him and not in front of our classmates and teacher. Sterling was building a fire within me, and I was scared it was going to burn me alive on the spot.

The song came to a close, and we struck our final pose—me tucked into Sterling's side, his arm around my back, and the other behind the knee of the leg I had hiked up to his hip. Then he leaned in close, breath hot on the shell of my ear, his lips brushing my skin, and whispered, "Later."

That caused a full body shiver. It took everything I had in me not to turn my face to his and stick my tongue into his mouth.

I finished the dress rehearsal in a daze, listening with half an ear as Mrs. Cook called out instructions and suggestions. My mind was firmly planted on thoughts of Sterling and our plans after we were done tonight.

We watched each other, an awareness flowing back and forth between us like a current. I knew, and he knew, that tonight was going to be *the night*.

‹❧

Sterling pulled into the parking lot of our pier at Westbank Park. It was fitting since it was the first place he had taken me that night over a month ago. The moon was full, illuminating everything around us in an almost preternatural glow. The weather had changed from the chilliness of late February to the muggy warmth of early April. Everything that had been brown and dead back then had awakened to the living verdant green of spring.

"Are you sure?" Sterling spoke into the quiet stillness of the cab.

I nodded. I was sure. Everything inside me had shifted tonight. I loved Sterling. I loved him so much that it made my chest ache. I wanted him to be my first, my only. I wanted forever with him, and I wanted to start it today.

I knew I was young, and a small voice whispered that maybe I wasn't ready, but I needed to be close to him. I wanted to make him happy because: how long would he be satisfied with make-out sessions?

It occurred to me tonight that a guy like him, a guy whose every movement screamed sex, wouldn't be mine for long if I didn't meet that need in him. And I wanted to keep him. I didn't want what we had to turn into what I'd had with Miles. Because it could.

Sterling had already been with someone. Had shared that experience with her. I couldn't stand the thought of her having something with him that I didn't.

I felt his fingers brush my temple as he tucked a stray curl behind my ear. "We can wait, princess. I'm okay with what we have. I could kiss those pretty lips of yours forever." I could hear the hint of a smile in his tone.

I knew he meant that right now, but what about a month from now? Six months? A year? Would my lips be enough? Was *I* enough?

I turned, and my breath caught at the sight of him, like always. Would I ever get used to his beauty?

Sterling's features looked as if an artist had chiseled them—smooth skin, high cheekbones, a square jawline, and a full mouth. His hair was wet and messy, and his blue/brown eyes were searching, questioning. He had changed out of his Danny clothes and was in just a tee and jeans. He was easily the most beautiful boy inside and out that I had ever known, and I couldn't imagine him looking any better than he did in this moment.

Funny, how that worked. I knew I would remember everything about this night for the rest of my life, committing it all to memory.

"I love you," I whispered hoarsely, emotions building inside me to the point I thought I would burst with them. I stared into those ocean blue eyes with islands of brown and confessed, "I love you so much that I can't stand the thought of not sharing everything I am with you. I need this, and I need you. Only you."

Sterling reached out and dragged me to him, crushing me against his chest. Then he pressed his lips to mine for a hard kiss before he pulled back and rested his forehead to mine. "I love you, too, princess ... so much," he breathed, sounding winded, but he went on in a voice laced with wonder. "You amaze me every day, and you don't even realize it."

His words healed something inside me, something I hadn't even realized could ever be healed—the brokenness so a part of me that it had ingrained itself into my DNA.

I let my hands dive into his hair, gripping the soft strands as I dragged his face back to mine, pressing my lips to his and trying to convey without words everything I felt for him.

He met my lips with equal fervor and, for a moment, let me control the kiss. Then he cupped my jaw almost violently as he dug his fingers into the skin there, not enough to hurt, but it got my attention.

He lashed his tongue against the seam of my lips, seeking entrance, and I immediately opened, welcoming his taste. The kiss was wet, hot, and so full of passion and longing that I almost felt like crying.

He drew away an inch from my mouth and panted out, "Let's go to the pier."

I had no words. All I could do was nod and follow his lead.

The breeze off the water felt good against my heated skin as Sterling and I lay tangled on a quilt at the end of the secluded pier. My head rested against his muscular chest as I listened to the sound of his racing heart. He trailed his fingers softly up and down my spine in a lazy rhythm.

"I love you," he murmured, his lips moving against my hair.

"I love you, too," I rasped then kissed the skin above his nipple.

"You okay?" His voice was quiet and held a note of concern.

I smiled against his skin and nodded.

"Good." He pressed a kiss to the top of my head.

We lay there, listening to the sounds of the water as it lapped the pier, the serenading cicadas, and amphibian mating croaks. I committed it all to memory. I never wanted to forget this, not a single moment.

"Best night of my life," Sterling said so quietly I wasn't sure I heard him.

I lifted my head and looked down into his relaxed face. "What?"

He raised his head, eyes burning into mine. "Best. Night. Of. My. Life." Then he fell back to the wood with a *thunk*, like the movement was too much in his exhausted state.

My cheeks flushed, and I tucked my head back down to his chest, which now rumbled with laughter.

"I can't believe I lost my virginity with bad girl Sandy hair," I muttered.

"I like it," he said with a chuckle, his fingers sifting through it. "It's so fluffy."

I squeezed my eyes shut and tried my hardest to contain my giggle, but I couldn't. My shoulders shook, and I lifted a hand to cover my mouth.

"It's awful," I choked.

He continued to pet my hair as he argued, "Nah, it's beautiful because it's a part of you."

My breath caught, and I instantly sobered. Would his words ever stop taking me by surprise? He meant that. I could hear it in his tone.

My vision blurred, and a peacefulness I hadn't known existed calmed the constant storm that raged inside me. I snuggled closer into his side and rubbed my foot against the hairy surface of his leg, holding my tears at bay.

"I love you."

"I love you, too," he whispered into my hair.

THE LAST CURTAIN CALL

We had opened Friday night to a packed house. I thought I would have been nervous since I hadn't performed in anything other than Christmas pageants in elementary school and we had thrown this musical together in little over a month. Strangely, I hadn't been. I had been excited. The buzz of the crowd, the music, the hot stage lighting —they had fed the energy surging throughout my body.

I hadn't felt this kind of confidence since ... well ... ever. When I had performed on the track, it had been different. Yes, there had been adrenaline, but there had always been a sense of expectation. No excitement. I had been confident in my ability, but never to the point of pride, because it wasn't something I had really cared about. Also, my father had always been right there, ready to tell me what I had done wrong. If I ever went back, would I feel that confidence again? I doubted it. I dreaded the thought of running again.

Working with Sterling was as easy as breathing. We played off one another seamlessly, the energy and tension making the atmosphere pulse with electricity. It didn't help that we could hardly take our eyes from one another or keep our hands off each other. Even Blake and Elodie had commented last night after our first performance on the changes in our body languages.

"Y'all did it, didn't you?" he had asked point blank.

My cheeks had flamed, but I had played ignorant and asked, "Did what?"

"You know what," Elodie had chimed in.

I had simply shaken my head and gave them my big, innocent-eyed look.

"Yeah, the innocent act won't work this time. You actually have to be innocent to pull it off." Elodie had cackled.

That was when my whole face had gotten hot, and I knew I had been blushing crimson, so I had ducked my head and avoided their eyes when I had replied, "I have no idea to what you are referring."

"Yeah," Blake had said. "Deny, deny, deny."

I was the last one packing up my stuff backstage Saturday night when I heard muffled voices toward the back curtained area. Both shows had been a hit, and I knew there was no going back to hurdling after this experience, even if my hip was stable enough to go back. I loved the lights, the stage, the ensemble of people coming together to play their different roles. I knew I had fallen in love with the theater.

The voices grew louder as I screwed the lid back on the eye makeup remover I had just liberally used all over my face. Literally. Nothing could remove stage makeup like this stuff.

I slowly got up from my cross-legged position and crept my way back toward the sound. It was a guy and a girl arguing, but then it went quiet just as I had my hand on the blue velvet fabric of the curtain. I pulled it aside to reveal a guy and a girl in an embrace, but what almost brought me to my knees in agony were the identities of the people.

Raven.

Sterling.

They said hearts couldn't physically break, but that was a lie. Mine had just freaking shattered. The shards stabbed into vital organs as they fell. That was the only explanation for why I felt the hurt all over my body.

I tried to suck in a breath, but I couldn't. It was stuck in my lungs. The pain in my chest was so sharp, so agonizing my eyes watered.

I pressed my hand hard against my chest to see if I could feel a heartbeat, because it shouldn't be possible. You couldn't have a heartbeat if the organ wasn't even in your chest anymore.

I didn't know if I stood there for seconds or even hours as a silent observer before Sterling's eyes darted to mine then widened in horror as he tore his mouth away. He jerked back and put his hands between their bodies to get Raven, who had practically climbed him, away from him.

The scene was achingly familiar. I had heard the arguing; had he kissed her to shut her up, too? Was that something he did with every girl?

"Sterling?" Raven asked in a breathless voice that was like fingernails on a chalkboard. Then she must have noticed where his gaze had gone because she looked over her shoulder. Her eyes didn't widen in horror like his had. No, they glinted with *victory*.

Had she heard me coming? Had she planned this? Did it matter? Or had they been carrying on together all this time behind my back?

I shook my head at the thought. It would have been impossible. We had spent almost every waking moment together.

Raven laughed as she turned to face me. A hand on one hip, she tilted her head to the side, making a face of fake concern, pouty lips and all. "You didn't think your relationship with him was real, did you?" Her tone was patronizing, and she ended her question with a cruel smirk. If I hadn't been so numb, I probably would have flinched.

My eyes automatically went back to Sterling. It hurt to even look at him. His face was pale, and his eyes looked dazed. Dazed by Raven's kiss? His lips did look slightly swollen.

Disgust churned in my stomach and bile rose in my throat.

After a moment, he seemed to shake himself out of it. "Princess—"

"Tell her, Sterling," Raven cut him off, her voice hard. "Tell her how I'm knocked up with your kid."

Sterling's mouth went flat, and he closed his eyes. He didn't move toward me or refute her words. He just stood there stiffly with his fists balled at his sides.

Shock had me rooted in place, so I couldn't escape her next words.

"Yep, *princess*"—she popped the *p*—"Sterling was just using *you* to get back at *me*." She said this like she was trying to explain quantum physics to a kindergartener.

"What?" I whispered.

"That's not true." Sterling finally found his voice, but it was gruff with emotion.

I looked at his tortured expression and knew what she was telling me was the truth. He had used me, and I had let him. Was I just so desperate for love and acceptance that I hadn't seen the signs? I *gave* myself to him on a silver platter, thinking it was love, when it was nothing but a game between him and *her*.

"Come on, Sterling; it wasn't a coincidence that the week before you started things up with her, you broke things off with me because you caught *me* with *her* boyfriend."

Horror washed over me, and my eyes shot back to Sterling. Oh no. *No. No. No.* Please tell me that Miles and his wandering penis wasn't responsible for another of my life's disappointments.

When Sterling's face twisted, I knew.

Miles *freaking* Thorpe.

"That's not what—"

"Then what was it? You caught Miles and me going at it in his truck, and then the next week, you steal his girl and rub that in my face? Puh-lease."

I couldn't breathe. That oh-so-familiar storm I had finally gotten rid of was back with a vengeance. I dug my fingernails into the fleshy part of my palms until I broke skin and sucked back air. I drew it into my lungs and held it for the count of five.

Sterling took a step toward me, hand outstretched, and I shrank back from him, not wanting his hands anywhere near me.

"Ally, baby, please—"

"D-don't touch m-me," I stuttered on the exhale ... One, two, three, four, five.

He was moving closer, both hands in front of him like he was trying to get close to a wounded animal.

I looked frantically around the backstage area for a door, a hallway, an escape ... I had to get out of here.

"It's over, Sterling. You played your game, and now it's time to come back to where you belong. She needs to go back to her own people and quit pretending she actually belongs here when all she's doing is slumming."

If she had stabbed me with a knife, it wouldn't have hurt as much as the words that were spewing from her mouth.

I shook my head violently before I turned on my toes and took off, running for all I was worth. My leg was probably not ready for such strenuous movement, but I didn't care. My stupid hamstring be damned. I was a fool.

I ran blindly, not sure where I was going. I just knew I couldn't stay here.

"Ally!" I heard yelled in the distance.

I had to move. I had to leave. However, I didn't realize until I was outside and in the parking lot that my keys were still in my bag.

Freezing with that realization, I then took off running to the only place I could think of, hiding in the shadows and behind the cars that were still in the parking lot.

I made it inside the fenced-in area of the football field and behind the bleachers, still tucked into the shadows. At one time, this was going to be the last place on earth that I ever saw. Now I was using it to take refuge.

I knew I couldn't go on the bleachers because that would be the first place he would look, so I crept along the fence, past the home bleachers, and to the side gate behind the scoreboard. The rodeo pens were toward the wooded area behind the field, down the path, and across another field through there.

I ran through the gate and made it halfway across the small field when I started to get winded. Me winded? I wanted to laugh and would have if I didn't feel like my insides were on fire and being torn apart at the same time.

It was so dark I could barely see, the stars and moon hidden behind an overcast night. Or maybe my tears were obscuring my vision?

I tripped over the uneven ground and sprawled in the grass. I lay there a moment, forehead pressed into the pillow of new grass, and wondered how my life had come to this.

Inhaling the scents of earth and pine, I inventoried my body, noting my hamstring felt fine, but my knees and hands stung. Then I rolled over onto my back and tried to look at my palms, but it was too dark. I ran my fingers over one and winced at the torn, sticky skin.

Dropping my head back, I stared up at the night sky that looked how I felt. The light inside me had been overtaken and held hostage by the murky dullness of self-loathing and shame.

Why was I so weak? I should have known he was too good to be true. That his love hadn't been real. It had been too easy.

When I heard a deep voice yelling my name in the distance, I wanted to fuse to the ground beneath me and disappear. Why did the bottom always drop?

With the back of my hands, I wiped at the wetness that was still spilling down my face in torrents. That was when an odd thought struck me. Should I follow through with my plans from before? Wasn't I back to square one?

I searched within myself and found the answer surprised me.

Did I want to die?

No.

No, I did not.

I didn't want to die, even though it felt like I was right at this moment. The hurt in my chest was so acute.

I took a moment and tried to put it all in perspective.

So ... my life wasn't the musical we had just performed come to life. Rizzo was pregnant with Danny's baby, and it didn't matter that Sandy had become a greaser's dream girl—she was still crying on prom night.

The one thing I hadn't given to Miles, knowing he wouldn't value it for more than a moment, I had given to a guy who hadn't valued it at all. *Stupid, stupid Ally.*

A feeling of hopelessness sat heavily on my chest, making it hard to breathe. It was time to review. How did I survive this? Was there anything I could salvage?

Everything with Sterling might have been fake, but the lessons I had learned weren't. He and Raven might have gutted me, but I wasn't the girl I had been before. I had real friends now who weren't just Sterling's friends anymore. They were mine.

Had they been part of the plan? No, I didn't think they had any clue what was going on. I felt that in my bones. Blake was too honest for subterfuge, and Elodie just didn't have it in her. She was too good, too sweet.

I had family, even if it was just my mom. And she was actually my mom now, and not a robot. My dad wasn't in the house anymore, but that also meant his shadow didn't cast over all the good I had built over the last month and a half. I also had a million other little things to live for. Twenty-nine thousand, one hundred and eighty-three more sunsets to see. Sterling had shown me that, even if it had been part of some nefarious scheme. That was all I needed. It was a brilliant moment of clarity that helped the fog clear and reignited my will.

I felt my pants for my cell phone so I could text my mom at least, but I quickly realized I was still wearing my bad girl Sandy costume.

I dropped my head back on a sigh. She had come to watch both performances but had left right after the final curtain drop tonight. She wouldn't be looking for me unless Sterling called her. Just thinking about him made my heart hurt again, not that it had stopped.

I heard a crashing sound and lifted my head to see a dark form moving toward me ... fast!

"Stop!" I cried before they ran over me.

"Ally?" Sterling gasped.

I dropped my head back and closed my eyes.

"You have to let me explain," he panted.

I wiped the wetness from my cheeks with my fingertips. I couldn't look at him. It just hurt too much, so I kept my eyes closed and concentrated on the sounds around me, like the cicadas and leaves rustling in the wind.

I heard movement to my left, and then felt his body next to mine in the grass. He tried to lace his fingers through mine, but I instantly jerked my hand out of his and glared at him.

"Princess ..." he started hesitantly.

"Do not call me that."

"It wasn't what it looked like—"

"Says every two-timing dirtbag."

"She kissed me, and I froze."

"With your eyes closed?" I scoffed.

"Reflex? I don't know. It wasn't that long, and I was in shock. One minute I was yelling at her, and the next, she was on me."

"It looked like you were participating," I seethed.

"I wasn't," he reiterated firmly.

"You still lied to me." I couldn't hide the hurt that laced my tone.

"When?"

I shot up to a seated position, twisted, narrowed my glare, and yelled, "What do you mean *when*? Everything you did and said to me was a lie!"

He sat up, too, and even though I couldn't see him well, I could feel the heat of his burgeoning anger meet mine.

"How could you think that? How could you even say that to me after *everything*? You would trust *her* word over *mine*?" His voice was harsh and had progressively gotten louder until the last word came out as a yell.

"I don't know what to think!" I cried as I flailed my hands out and hit the ground. "You haven't explained anything to me. All I know is that you're going to have a baby with that ... that ... *ugh*! I don't even know what to call her. She's awful," I spat as tears welled in my eyes again.

I clenched my fists and relished the sting of my wounds. It distracted me from the nausea that churned in my stomach at the thought of them having a child together. It was unbearable because everything inside me rebelled at her having any piece of him, even his baby.

For a moment, the only sound was that of our rapid breaths. Then Sterling asked in a much quieter voice, "Are you going to let me explain?"

Was I? Well, it didn't look like I was going to get up anytime soon, so I replied, "Yes."

He again reached for my hand, lacing our fingers together, and I winced. The skin was still tender and bloody. When I went to pull away, he stopped me.

"Don't. I need to feel you; have some kind of connection to you while I try to explain this twisted mess."

"My hands are a mess," I muttered in a watery voice.

"I don't care. We'll get them cleaned up in a minute."

I quit tugging at my hand and reveled in the warmth of his hand in mine. I didn't want to, yet I craved it at the same time. Would this be the last time we held hands like this? The thought sent a pang through my hollow chest.

"I didn't think the baby was mine," he stated.

"So, you knew?" I hissed.

"Shh ... let me finish."

I swallowed whatever I was going to say, and even though I doubted he could see me, I nodded for him to continue.

"The reason I didn't think the baby was mine was because I always used protection. Never forgot, not even once, and never had a condom break."

"Okay."

"On the day ..." He paused, and I heard him swallow, then his voice hitched when he tried again. "On the day you tried to kill yourself, I caught Raven with another guy. That's part of the reason I acted so rude to you on the bleachers."

I remembered his parting shot at me that night. It had been harsh yet effective. It had lit something inside me, reignited my will. Now I didn't know if the emotion in his voice had been for me or because he had caught *her* with someone else.

"Miles." It wasn't a question, but a statement.

"Yes," he replied matter-of-factly.

"So, you started sending me Snapchats for revenge?"

"No," he said quickly.

"But—"

"I started sending you snaps because I wanted to help you. People take their lives because they're depressed and don't think they have a choice. It's an act of desperation. I probably should have told an adult that day, but ... I wanted to be the one ... I wanted to be the one to give you reasons to live. To show you how beautiful life can be."

My breath caught, and a lump formed in my throat. He had done that, but then he had taken it away ...

"And I always ..." He stopped, and I heard him swallow before continuing, "This is going to sound lame, but ... I always had a thing for you," he confessed.

A spark of hope lit, dispelling the blackness that had overtaken me, but I smothered it out. We had to finish this.

"So, you caught her and Miles that day?"

"Yeah, and Miles and I almost got into a fight. What stopped us was the fact that Raven started crying and saying she was pregnant, and she didn't know who the father was ..."

A light bulb lit in my brain, and the pieces of the puzzle started coming together. I squeezed his hand lightly, mainly in reflex, and shifted more toward him. "That was what you and Miles were talking about in the cafetorium that day when he wanted to talk to me! When you asked him if he wanted me to know ..."

"Yes."

"So?" I urged, leaning forward, needing to hear the rest.

"So, I knew it wasn't mine since I used protection and, well ... Miles is known to like not using it."

My head rocketed back, and my mouth dropped open. *Say what? Ew.*

"Is he stupid?" I asked incredulously because, I mean, what the heck? It was modern times. Everyone knew to use protection.

"You have to ask?" He chuckled, but his voice held no trace of humor.

"He could catch something!" I cried.

"Uh, yeah."

"Thank God I didn't do anything with him!" My lip curled in disgust at the thought, but then another struck me ...

"Have you been tested?" A sick feeling knotted my insides.

"Yeah, I went to the walk-in clinic the day after I caught them. It had been a while since I was with her, but still ... I got tested. I'm clean."

I blew out a relieved breath. *Thank God.*

We were both quiet, lost in thought, and I was thinking that things still weren't adding up.

"So, wait, why was Raven saying you were the father of her baby if y'all used protection? When was the last time you were with her? You said it had been a while."

He sighed, and I knew I wasn't going to like what he was about to say next.

"She said I was the father because"—he pulled in a breath—"she poked holes in all the condoms she found in my car when we were together."

Oh. My. Gosh. I felt my eyes widen, and I rolled to face him.

"Does that mean ...?" I choked out.

"I don't know. I haven't checked."

"So, she could be lying?"

"Who knows?" He sounded tired.

I was going to be sick. My heart felt like it was going to pound straight out of my chest.

"Let's go look. Now," I demanded, impatience drumming a chaotic beat over my nerves. I had to know, or I was going to lose it right here behind the football field in the dark.

I hauled myself to my feet and was about to leave him there, but I couldn't. He had the keys.

When I heard him get up, I practically jogged back the way we had come. Sterling caught up, and we raced back to the student parking lot. We had done it only the one time, but once was enough to get someone pregnant.

Sweat was dripping down my back and wetting my hairline. When we got to Sterling's beat-up old Chevelle, I wiped my damp hands down the front of my shiny black leggings, disregarding the pain it caused.

Sterling dug in his pocket for the key as I shook out my hands and danced on the balls of my feet. Then he was in the car and had the glove compartment open. I glanced surreptitiously around the parking lot to make sure no one was outside who could see us doing this. Still, I moved closer to Sterling, hoping to shield what he was doing from sight.

I was never having sex again after this. Nope. Never. I wasn't prepared to be a mother. If I didn't have sex, I wouldn't have to worry about becoming a teen mom or catching something I couldn't get rid of.

He grabbed a couple of the foil packets and handed one to me. I examined the square, flipping it over to check both sides, but I couldn't see a disruption in the package.

"I don't see anything."

"I don't either."

I handed Sterling the condom, and he set it on the seat.

"Let's check them all to make sure."

We then proceeded to check every condom in his glove box, and he even pulled the ones out of his wallet. Neither of us could find anything wrong with them.

I leaned against the car and slid down until my butt hit the concrete. He sat in the passenger seat, his elbows to his knees, wrists loose, and his head bent.

"So, she lied," I muttered, feeling a measure of relief.

"Looks that way. Or she just poked holes in the one. I don't know." Exhaustion seemed to coat every word.

We sat in the parking lot with the bugs buzzing and congregating around the still lit light poles, not saying anything, lost in our own thoughts. I wasn't in a good place. I'd had a lot of information thrown at me, and I didn't even know how to start processing it.

Did I want to get tangled up in this mess? Would it be wrong not to want to wade in and support Sterling during this time? He had hurt me, but he had lifted me up at my lowest point. Shouldn't I do that for him, as well? I didn't know if I had it in me. If I was strong enough or secure enough. I needed time. I needed to think.

"You know ..." he began, but stopped.

I turned my head in his direction and saw he hadn't moved.

"Know what?" I asked, wondering if I had actually heard him say anything or if it had been my imagination.

"Nah. I probably shouldn't say this," he muttered almost under his breath.

"What?"

"I should ..." he started, but then stopped again.

"Just tell me." My voice relayed my impatience. I was tired of this game and not in the mood to play it.

He lifted his eyes to me, and they roamed over my body. I had forgotten, again, amongst the current meltdown, that I was still dressed in the spandex outfit of sexy bad girl Sandy.

"I should probably be hot for you right now, dressed like that and holding a condom"—I looked at my hands, and sure enough, I was still holding the square packages—"but I don't think I could get it up if my life depended on it at the moment."

I laughed, but my heart wasn't in it. I really hoped no one walked up on us dressed like this, at this time of night, surrounded by a bunch of condoms. Speaking of.

I tossed the condoms I had been holding in his direction and missed. They landed at his feet.

He reached down and picked them up, holding them between two fingers. Then he twisted and threw them in the glove compartment before slamming it closed.

"I need time," I whispered.

"What?" he asked just as quietly.

"I need time," I stated more firmly, unable to look at him.

"For what? Are you breaking up with me?"

Was I? The thought of breaking up with him made my heart seize. But, could I be with a guy who had a kid, if the child Raven carried was his? How would that work? I believed him when he said our relationship wasn't about revenge, but I couldn't get the sight of him and Raven kissing out of my head. It was burned there, playing on a continual loop.

"I don't want to break up." I knew that down to my bones, yet I needed time to get my head on straight. "I don't think I could end it, even if I wanted to," I told him softly, lifting my eyes to his and seeing his face was soft yet sad. He knew I was in deep with him.

"You probably should," he said in a husky voice. "Or I should probably let you go, at least until I figure things out. But, like you, I can't. I just can't give you up." His voice cracked, and I saw the wetness fill his eyes. An answering wetness filled my own, and my body bucked with a restrained sob.

"What's going to happen if you do turn out to be the father?" I asked brokenly.

He rubbed the tears off his cheeks with the butt of his hand and answered, "I don't know."

Hesitantly, I asked, "Have you told Pops?"

"No, and he's going to flip his lid when I do." Sterling blew out a breath and stared off into the distance, probably envisioning how that conversation would go.

"I'm sorry," I whispered, and I was. I hated this situation. I hated it for me, but mainly I hated it for him. It wasn't fair.

"Me, too."

I sucked in a breath and pushed myself up. "I better go."

He nodded, not looking at me, his eyes still fixated on whatever was across the parking lot, or maybe something across the street.

"How much time are you going to need?" He sounded resigned.

"I don't know."

He turned back to me, his face anguished, and said one of the most tragically beautiful things I had ever heard in my entire life.

"I love you, Ally. I love you more than I've ever loved anyone. I'll give you time, and when you're ready, I will be right here waiting for you."

I nodded, mouth dry and throat tight. It felt like there was a gulf separating us now, and I didn't know if we were ever going to be able to close it. Right now, it felt almost impossible.

Tears were rapidly falling down my face. I didn't know a body could produce this many tears. Shouldn't I have run out by now?

I took off, running toward the building to get my things, sobbing the entire way there. I was glad everyone was gone. I was sure Mrs. Cook or maintenance were still around, but I didn't run into anyone.

When I came back out, Sterling's car was gone. I stood there and stared at where it had been as a bleakness I had never felt had me wrapping my arms around my middle. I felt lost and so utterly alone.

When I finally got into my car and was on my way home, I lost it. I screamed out my anguish so loud that it hurt my own ears.

NOT SO PRETTY IN PINK

Before lunch on Monday, I found myself seated in the waiting area outside the principal's office. An office aide had come and gotten me from Physics, telling me to grab my things, but not why I was being summoned.

When ten minutes had gone by, and he still hadn't called me in, I pulled out my phone and opened my Snapchat. I scrolled through all the ones I had saved, and a pang came from the left side of my chest. It had barely been two days, but I missed him.

I missed his voice, his touch, his smell. I missed his blue eyes with specks of brown, and him calling me "princess." I missed that cocky grin, and the way he made me blush with just a look.

I had pulled out my phone several times already today, just to remember what it was like before it had all gone wrong, but also in hope that maybe he would ignore my wishes and contact me.

I wondered if Sterling was calling and texting Raven—making plans to go to the doctor or to meet up to discuss their future. My stomach turned at the thought of the two of them together. They matched in their beauty, and now they could be sharing that with a child they had created. A happy little family.

My nostrils started to burn, and tears threatened to fall for the millionth time since it had happened.

I had made it home on Saturday in one piece and had gone straight to bed. Sleep had proved elusive that night. I had tossed and turned, haunted by the scene I had walked in on with Sterling and Raven backstage, Sterling's tormented face, and the nightmares of Sterling holding Raven in his arms as they gazed down lovingly at a dark-haired baby bundled in blue blankets.

When I was awake, I was in misery. I had stayed abed most of yesterday, gazing helplessly down at my phone. Blake and Elodie had texted and sent several snaps, but I had ignored them, not having the energy or inclination to explain what had happened the night before.

Fortunately, or unfortunately, I couldn't decide which, it appeared that Sterling was honoring my request of time and was leaving me be. For the millionth time, I questioned my decision, but there were too many unanswered questions. I wasn't sure I was strong enough to take on the responsibilities of having a teen father as a boyfriend, or if he would even have time for a relationship. I knew my parents would not be thrilled with me being involved with someone who had impregnated another high school girl. So, even if I wanted to be with him, it would probably be forbidden.

My mom had come to my room yesterday morning and felt my head since, these were her words, "you look like death." She had then come back several more times to check on me and had brought me soup that I'd had no appetite for, thinking I was sick. I hadn't disabused her of the idea. I had just poured the soup in the toilet when I had gotten up to use the bathroom.

I had been late to school this morning after another night of interrupted sleep and unwanted thoughts. When I had pulled into the parking lot, I still had no answers for our predicament and had slipped deeper into the depression Sterling's absence had caused.

His car had been parked in his assigned spot on the row in front of mine, and I'd had to fight back the ache of unshed tears. I hadn't thought my body had any more to spare. My chest had ached, and I had thought that maybe being late was a blessing.

I didn't know how I would react to seeing Sterling in the wake of Saturday night's revelations. I was hurt, and my emotions were all over the place. I hated being vulnerable, and that was what he had made me.

I heard the front office door open and looked to see my mother hustling through.

"Mom?" I asked, confused as to why she was here.

"Hey, honey," she greeted as she walked to the desk and signed in. She was dressed in bootcut jeans that flattered her curvy figure; a pastel pink, flowy top that was Boho chic; and a pair of dove gray ankle booties. Her hair was styled and curled to perfection, as always, and she wore silver jewelry at her neck, wrists, and ears. I liked this look on her. Usually, she dressed stiffly and formally when she came to the school. Clearly, that had been at my father's insistence.

"Do you know why they called me?"

"No. They pulled me out of class twenty minutes ago, and no one has told me why either." I bit my lower lip and tugged at the hem of one of the tops I had ordered from ModCloth.

We both had changed in the past month and a half, inwardly and outwardly. My father's "extended business trips" had lent us the freedom we were rarely granted when he was home, as evidenced by our change in style.

The door to Principal Goddard's office opened, and he stuck his head out. "Mrs. Everly and Miss Everly? Would y'all mind stepping into my office?" He looked behind my mother, obviously searching for my father, then reverted his attention back to her. "Do we need to wait on Derek?" he asked, his tone deceptively nonchalant, making the hairs on the back of my neck stand up.

Mom straightened her spine and said in a forbidding tone, "No, he's out of town for work, so it'll just be me today."

Mr. Goddard's face turned grim, and he avoided my gaze. I had a very bad feeling about what was coming next, even if I didn't have a clue as to what it was.

"You may want to call him now. We can possibly delay this meeting."

She shook her head.

Mr. Goddard let out a weary sigh, resigned. "Okay, then."

He stepped back, and my mother and I followed him through the door. He gestured to the two open chairs in front of his desk as he rounded it.

I sat down, but then froze when I noticed the police officer standing in the corner. Icy cold fingers of dread gripped my throat, making it hard to swallow the excess saliva that had filled my mouth. What was going on?

Mr. Goddard sat in the office chair behind his desk and rolled it forward. He slowly placed his hands on the desk and folded them. The good-natured man who always had a joke and a smile was gone. This man was one I wasn't familiar with, never having reason to be on his bad side. Now he was stern and official looking. Needless to say, I was freaking out.

"The reason I've called you both in here is because the drug dog detected something in your vehicle, Ally. Officer Michaels would like consent to search."

I looked to the stone-faced Officer Michaels. He was a tall, muscular, African American man of indeterminate age, with a shiny bald head. In any other circumstance, I would think he was attractive in his crisp black uniform with its shiny gold badge. Right now, though? Not so much. I couldn't think past the adrenaline pumping through my system and the frenetic beat of my heart.

"Normally, we don't call the parents in for vehicle searches, but since you and your husband are very involved with the school and community, I decided to give you this courtesy."

More like he didn't want my dad to launch a lawsuit against the school district. I wasn't sure he could, since they hadn't violated any of my rights, but it would be something my dad would threaten, no matter what. Fear was a currency my dad used liberally and often.

My stomach started to cramp, and I could feel myself sweating under my top. In a startling moment of clarity, a box that I had sealed, locked, and buried in the back of my mind burst open and I knew what this was about.

Did I confess? Or should I chance it, and maybe they wouldn't find anything? Fear paralyzed me. I couldn't bring myself to tell them what they would find and why. Shame and self-loathing burned and knotted my insides.

"Thank you, James. I'm sure this is all just a misunderstanding."

He didn't reply to my mom's statement, but turned to me and instructed, "Ally, hand your keys to Officer Michaels."

I swallowed thickly and fumbled with the zipper on my backpack as I got my keys and handed them to the policeman who closed his hand over them.

"Be back," he stated brusquely then strode from the office.

I was going to be sick. It was like watching a car wreck about to happen and being powerless to stop it. This was going to be bad.

I pressed my hand to my stomach and swallowed convulsively to keep the sick at bay.

My mom reached over and patted my hand soothingly. "You should have stayed home if you're still sick."

I couldn't even look at her. She didn't know what I had done, but she was about to find out. I pulled in a breath, held it for five, then pushed it out for the same count.

What felt like hours, but was probably only half an hour later, Officer Michaels came back into the office, holding a baggie. My eyes zeroed in on the contents, and then they dropped to my hands in my lap.

"What?" Mom whispered.

"Allison Everly, you're—"

"Those are mine," Mom cut Officer Michaels off as I heard him moving toward me to cuff me. "I left them in Ally's car when I borrowed it the other day. Derek had mine since his was in the shop."

There was a pause, then, "Your husband can corroborate that? Because, ma'am, I don't feel like you're being truthful right now," Officer Michaels replied in his deep, grumbly voice.

"Do you know Derek Everly, Officer Michaels?" my mother asked in a friendly but not really friendly tone.

I looked up at him from under my lashes and saw that his mouth was set in a grim line, and his jaw was so taut it looked like it had been carved from stone. Evidently, he knew my father. He should. Dad was one of the best defense attorneys in the county.

When he didn't say anything, she went on, "See, he'll tell you the same thing. You can call and check with DFW BMW dealership. They'll tell you that my husband took his car in last week, and his secretary came to pick him up. So, why don't you give him a call?" my mom finished softly, but if I wasn't wrong, it was said almost menacingly.

The officer heaved a huge, audible sigh then turned toward Mr. Goddard. "I'll let this go and not charge her since it's her mother's name on the prescription and the kid has no priors. Could be that what Mrs. Everly says is true. I don't think so, but I am *not* calling Derek Everly."

His dark eyes came to me. "Young lady?"

I looked up into his face and held my breath.

"Don't do this again, because next time, there will be charges, understood?"

I nodded furiously and answered, "Yes, sir."

There wouldn't be a next time.

My body wilted in relief.

He cut his eyes back over to Mr. Goddard. "We're through." And without another word, he spun around and strode out the door, the sound of his utility belt creaking.

I blew out a sigh. I could feel my mother's stare on me, but I still couldn't look at her.

Mr. Goddard got our attention when he cleared his throat.

"Allison, you may not have been charged with a crime today, but you still violated the district's zero-tolerance policy, and I'm going to have to suspend you ... for two weeks."

I sucked in a breath.

"But they weren't her pills," my mom argued.

Mr. Goddard just shook his head. "Doesn't matter. They were in her possession. We can't make an exception."

For the first time since I realized what was going on, I looked up at my mother and whispered, "Prom." Not that I really cared, but it was something every girl anticipated since she was old enough to know what it was, and I had seen *Pretty In Pink* eleventy-billion times since I was eight.

"No prom. Suspended students aren't allowed to attend." Mr. Goddard's words were firm, yet they held a small amount of sympathy.

I let my gaze fall to my hands. I didn't know what to think about missing my first prom. Sterling and I were taking some time apart, so I didn't know if that was something we would have attended, but I guessed at least one of the many questions I had been asking myself had been answered now. Was I sad to miss my first prom? Kind of.

THERAPY

Mom and I walked into the house after our meeting and dismissal from school grounds. My suspension was effective immediately. A school representative would collect two weeks' worth of my schoolwork, then call my mother to pick it up at the office. I was not, for any reason, to step foot on school property until my suspension was over.

As we walked through the entryway, I felt as if I was a criminal walking to the gallows. It was time to confess, probably past time. I bellied up to the elevated bar at the kitchen counter as Mom rounded it toward the fridge.

"Mom?"

She held up a finger, opened the fridge, pulled out a bottle of white wine, and uncorked it. She then went to the cabinet that held the stemware and pulled a large bowled glass down. Once she was situated, one arm braced on the counter, and the other fiddling with the bottom of her glass, she lifted her eyes and asked, "Are you on drugs?"

I swallowed and shook my head, examining the black veins that were ingrained throughout the sparkly white marble surface of the bar. Black and white. If only life was that simple.

I wanted to explain, to come out with it, but my tongue felt too big for my mouth. Sweat drenched my hairline and the back of my top, and I couldn't stop the tremor that ran through my limbs and practically vibrated my insides. I was not making a convincing case for being drug-free.

"Then, tell me, Allison Marie Everly, why my back pills were in your car? Were they for your leg? You could have just asked."

Again, I just stood there, not meeting her eyes, and shook my head.

My heart raced. I had the urge to flee. To take off running as fast as my body would allow. I wanted to be anywhere but here, explaining to my mom why I had stolen her pain medicine.

An uncomfortable silence filled the room. I could hear the tick of the clock that hung on the living room wall. Then I heard her glass crash to the counter as she yelled, "Answer me, dammit!"

She had finally lost it.

My head shot up to see her glaring at me, red-faced.

"Tell me why the *police* found prescription pills that did not belong to you in your car and you're now suspended from school. Please, tell me why, because right now, it's hard for me to believe that you're *not* using drugs."

I should just let her think I was an addict. I mean, wouldn't it be better for her to think that than for her to know the truth?

"Well, if you're not going to talk, I'll call the doctor right now and set up a urine test. That will answer my question."

Panic seized me, and my heart beat so loud it had to be audible in the quietness. It was either tell her the truth now, or her learning the truth later, because those tests would all come up clean.

I cleared my throat and settled my eyes back on those black veins. "I didn't take any of your pills." My voice was scratchy like I hadn't used it in years.

"Then, what were you doing with them?" she asked, exasperated.

I focused on the little speckles of reflected light that made the white marble sparkle. "I tried ..." I paused to take a deep breath, and confessed on the exhale, "Well, I was going to kill myself."

An unnatural quiet fell over the room. I continued my study of the bar top, cursing myself for being a coward. Shouldn't I at least look into her eyes and apologize?

Shame, an emotion that was my constant companion of late, burned in my gut.

"Wh-what?" my mom finally asked brokenly.

I sucked in a huge breath and lifted my eyes to look into hers. Her face was ghostly pale, and her eyes were filled with tears.

She shook her head and denied, "Impossible. Why? Why would you want to do that?" She hiccupped a sob, her shoulders hunched, and brought a hand up to cover her mouth. "No."

My vision blurred, my nose stung, and my throat ached. I was crying yet again, but this time it wasn't over a boy. It was a release borne of guilt and shame.

"I was tired, Mom," I explained, my voice cracking.

"Tired of what? You're seventeen years old, for goodness' sake! You have your whole life ahead of you!"

"You wouldn't understand," I muttered forlornly, feeling helpless. It felt like there was more than a kitchen counter that separated us; it might as well have been the Grand Canyon. She wouldn't understand just how soul weary I had been for years. How I couldn't take another day of being under someone's thumb.

Fat tears lazily rolled down my cheeks to drip off my jawline.

"Explain it to me, because I really want to," she implored, her eyes searching mine, her own tears falling.

"I wanted to escape. I was just so tired of not having a choice. Everything ..." I breathed in a shuddered breath and tried to compose my thoughts. When I actually took a moment to think about it, my reasons sounded petty and childlike.

"Everything what?"

"It sounds foolish now, but everything was decided for me without my input. Who my friends were, what I ate, what activities I was to participate in ... I felt like I was in the passenger seat of my own life." I slid my gaze to the side. "I just wanted it all to stop."

"Thank God you changed your mind! Honey ..." She started to sob and went on brokenly, "I don't know what I'd do without you. I love you, baby." She came around the counter and crushed me to her. We both shook with the power of our sobs.

I breathed the familiar clean scent of my mom's perfume and mumbled, "I'm so sorry," into the now damp fabric of her shirt.

I felt her stroke my hair as she breathed out, "Oh, honey, I'm so sorry I wasn't there for you. That I wasn't the mom you needed. That I wasn't strong enough to be. That's going to change."

We stood there for a while, our tears waning, and for the first time since I was probably a kid, I felt safe in my mother's arms.

"I didn't change my mind," I whispered. If I was going to confess, I might as well confess it all.

She pulled back and looked at me quizzically.

"Sterling ... he, ah ... he saved me."

Her mouth formed an *O*, and as I went on to tell her about that evening at the football field and how he had knocked the pills from my hand, she moved back around the counter to her glass of wine and took a drink.

"I'll have to hug his neck the next time I see him," she muttered as she wiped beneath each eye with a finger.

My mom had met Sterling briefly when he had picked me up for weekend rehearsals, but she had never given an opinion on him. She knew we spent time together, but between my schedule and hers, we never had an in-depth conversation about him.

I stayed silent, not wanting to tell her that Sterling and I weren't exactly speaking at the moment and why.

When Mom had gotten herself under control, the only evidence of her crying jag were the slight pink splotches around her eyes and on her cheeks.

She lifted her glass to her lips and leveled me with her gaze. Once she had taken a drink and set the glass back on the counter, she asked, "So, do you still feel that way? You still having suicidal thoughts?"

I shook my head. "No, Sterling helped me with that, too."

"Still, baby girl, you're going to have to see someone. I'm grateful to Sterling—don't get me wrong—but I'm not putting your mental health into the hands of a seventeen-year-old boy. He should have told someone."

I nodded my agreement. She was probably right—that was the smart move—especially since that seventeen-year-old boy kind of broke my heart over the weekend.

"I'll call the doctor here in a minute and get a recommendation," she added, then took another long drink, and when she was done, her expression made the hair on my arms rise and a sense of foreboding stole over me.

Her eyes dropped to her glass. "I have a confession, as well."

I gripped the edge of the marble as I waited, breath trapped in my lungs. I knew she was going to tell me what I had been suspecting for a while, but wouldn't let myself think on.

"Your father ... well ..." She looked to the side, as if something in the hallway would give her inspiration, then turned back to me. "He's not on a business trip. He moved out."

I stilled, the words echoing in my head, and my grip on the bar became white-knuckled. "Are you getting a divorce?" I asked.

She nodded then gave me a look that was so infinitely sad that it made my chest ache. "I don't even know how to say this ... but I know I won't be able to shield you from it for much longer." She looked away again, pain etched into her features. Then she turned back to me and confessed, "Your father had an affair with Tina ... and she's pregnant. He's living with her."

My mouth dropped open, and my hands went lax. "Tina? His secretary, Tina?" I choked out.

"Yep. Good ole Tina," she muttered sarcastically then took a deep drink from her glass, finishing it off.

Tina was a young blonde who had boobs the size of cantaloupes—the IQ of one, too. I had wondered how she had kept her job at Dad's firm. Now I knew.

"I'm going to be a big sister?" I asked in disbelief.

I was both elated and horrified. I had always wanted brothers or sisters, but I wouldn't want them to be subjected to the kind of parenting my father had practiced on me.

Mom nodded. Her normally flawless face looked older, the lines around her eyes and mouth more noticeable, and the blueish-purple rings under her eyes testified to sleepless nights and worry.

"So, how is this going to work? Don't tell me I'm going to have to stay with him and Tina every other week or weekend!" The thought was horrifying.

"Oh, goodness no!" she exclaimed, mirroring my abhorrence. "I've banned him from contacting either of us until we figure something out. I even threatened to take him to the cleaners if he didn't give us time!" She sighed tiredly. "So, for now, we're hammering out an agreement. You'll have to see him, so there will be some visitation, but you won't have to do any overnights or anything like that."

I blew out a relieved breath. Still, I felt disoriented and kind of numb. Things were changing too fast, and I felt like I was running to catch up.

"So, what now?" I asked, still feeling a little lost.

"Therapy," she answered on a sigh then reached for her phone.

ॐ

Mom, who was one to never let the grass grow beneath her feet, had me in a therapist's office the next day. It was decided that I would meet with Dr. Keller twice a week.

Dr. Denise Keller was relatively young with dark brown hair pulled back into a bun at her nape and trendy, hot pink glasses perched on her nose. She was supposed to be one of the best therapists for children and teenagers in the county. I sure hoped so.

Mom had also decided to start seeing someone. Her therapist was in the same building, so we would be carpooling. Most daughters had mani-pedi appointments with their mothers ... I had therapy sessions. I felt like we had finally turned into the modern American family.

It was also decided that my actions couldn't go without conse-quences at home. Therefore, I was grounded. I hadn't ever been grounded by my mother before. My dad? Lots of times. With him, I was grounded for just about everything, like a pound gained on weigh-in day or a bad track practice. Her taking my car keys, phone, and laptop was strange. It was also going to be a hellish two weeks.

Worst of all ... if Sterling did message me, I would never know.

PUT IT ON
A STICKY NOTE

The next two weeks were the most boring, yet the most enlightening of my life. With nothing better to do than to think and watch television—I did a lot of both—I found out there was only so much cable television I could watch, so I switched to Netflix and had gone through all the seasons of *Gilmore Girls*, *Stranger Things*, and was currently working my way through *Supernatural*.

Even when I was in front of the TV, I did nothing but think about my situation with Sterling and what I could have done differently. The conclusion was always the same: nothing.

I missed him so much I ached with it. I felt like I was missing a limb. I couldn't eat, and I couldn't sleep. I lay awake at night and stared out the window in hopes he would come to me. He never did.

I was eaten up with questions. Was he okay? Did he think about me? Was he missing me like I missed him? Or had he moved on? Was he reconnecting with Raven?

My thoughts repeatedly spun with endless questions. I couldn't even ask Blake or Elodie about him.

One day, it hit me like a bolt of lightning while I was watching *Gilmore Girls*. I loved Sterling. Like, I *really* loved him. It wasn't infatuation or puppy love. I *loved* him. I would love him even if he was going to be Raven's baby's daddy. You just didn't give up on the people you loved.

My dad had given up on me. He didn't have to say it. He hadn't been here in over a month, and he hadn't called. I didn't know if it was that he had screwed up so royally, or if it was because he couldn't live vicariously through me on the track anymore. It was probably both. Derek Everly hated mistakes, especially his own, so he pretended like they never happened. I guessed I had ceased to exist in his world.

What else was I supposed to think? He wasn't trying to make it right with me or Mom, so he must have just cut his losses.

One thing I knew for certain, I wasn't going to give up on my relationship with Sterling. We would figure this out. I was willing to try. I just hoped he hadn't quit on me. The thought made my heart clench, but I had to hold on to what he had told me that night—that he would wait for me and loved me.

I wanted to tell him all this, but unfortunately, I was without a phone, a car, and a computer. Unless he could read smoke signals, I wouldn't be able to tell him until my punishment was over in a couple days.

❦

I stood in the hall and stared at row after row of gray metal lockers, a veritable sea of them, each one representing a classmate. It was Saturday, my suspension would end on Monday, but Mom had gotten a text from Laura—yes, I know, shocking. She had gotten special permission for me to help decorate for prom since they needed all the help they could get. Despite not being able to attend, I was still on the prom committee.

I figured this was Laura's way of rubbing salt in the wound. I still wasn't allowed to attend, yet I had to come up here and decorate for it. I didn't want to, but Mom had given me *the look* and a lecture about honoring my commitments.

So, that was how I ended up in the hall, staring at lockers. I was hiding. I had snuck away from the insanity that was Laura and her minions in prom perfection mode.

Some of the lockers had footballs pinned to the front or pompoms. Mine had a track shoe, a gavel for Student Council, and a newly added drama mask. So boring. So plain. However, it made me think ... The outside of the lockers was a superficial representation of our role or who we were in school. They touted our extracurricular activities, but weren't we more than that?

I thought of all the kids who could be struggling with the same issues I had. Who yearned for an escape or a reprieve from the life they had been shoved into without their consent. The kids who were told who they were or who they were going to be by their parents, their friends, or even by society. My life had been a tragedy averted, but that didn't mean there wasn't another one in the making.

Sterling stood in the gap. He had been my intercessory, the person who stopped me from making a decision I could not unmake. He had also guided me back to myself and helped me discover who Ally Everly was outside of all the external influences that had been battering me my entire life.

I worried for those who didn't have a Sterling, a person who would come into their lives at the right moment, at the right time. And that was when it came to me. I could be that person ... Or, well, try to be.

A trip to the teachers' supply closet and a sharpie later, I was walking up and down the rows, writing notes on multicolored squares of sticky notes. If I knew the person, I wrote something I liked about them. I did this with everyone, even my old crew. Laura, her strength; Sarah, her outgoingness; and Ariel, her ability to have fun doing anything. I even left a sticky note for Miles, telling him that his charm was lethal. If the locker wasn't marked, or if I didn't know the person that well, I just left *"You matter,"* or *"You are important,"* or *"You are loved."*

My favorite notes were the ones I left for the friends I had made over the past couple months. I told Elodie she had a good heart, because she genuinely did. I also wrote that her freckles were my favorite feature, and her innate goodness was a thing of beauty. I wrote on Blake's sticky note that his artistic eye was beyond compare, and that his shoe collection was legendary. I also left one for him that said, *"Savage AF."* They were easily the bestest friends I had ever had.

When I neared Sterling's locker, the song "It's Raining on Prom Night" came to mind, and I started singing it under my breath. How fitting. And Sterling's note? Well, Sterling didn't get just one; he got several. I couldn't tell him about my revelations in the conventional methods, so I improvised. I plastered his locker door until the metal was no longer visible. The most important one, I placed right in the middle, and it was the only neon pink note up there.

And I did love him, even if he turned out to be the father of Raven's baby. He was the best person I had ever known, and I told him that, too. I told him that I wanted to try. I told him he was the best part of my day. I told him that he had the most incredible eyes I had ever seen. I told him I would slow dance with him forever. I told him I couldn't picture my future without him in it. The list went on and on. I just hoped I wasn't too late.

It took forever, and I was surprised no one had come looking for me.

I left the Sharpie and leftover stacks of sticky notes on the tabletop that covered the low-lying lockers. I really hoped maintenance didn't take down all my hard work.

I thought it was dumb I had to participate in the prom preparations when I had been banned from attending. I wondered if Sterling was going, and if he was, would he take Raven? The thought made bile rise in my throat, and my eyes stung.

I made my way back into the cafetorium where Laura was working with one of the men hired by the parents to have these huge columns swathed in purple and silver glittery gauze placed throughout the room. No one said anything or even looked at me funny. I wondered if they noticed where I had come from or that I had left earlier.

I went over to Laura and asked, "Do you need me to do something?"

She gave me a look that was kind of insulting, like I had been dropped on my head as a baby. "Uh, look around. There are tons of things that still need to be done." She cut her eyes back to the short man who was wiggling the pillar into place before shrieking, "You're going to tear it!"

Whoa. I backed away slowly and searched the room for a job that would not put me in her path.

The stage area had been fitted with strand after strand of white lights that came down as a curtain. The podium had been moved next to a red carpet that stretched backstage and rolled down the steps to the floor. Supposedly, there would be an MC who would announce the couples when they arrived, like a mix between a royal ball and a Hollywood event.

I went over to the team that was trying to pin or staple the red carpet down to the steps.

"Need any help?"

"Sure. Come over here and hold this down," was Gage's reply.

And that was what I did until it was time for everyone to leave and get ready for prom.

The room had been transformed into something out of a movie. I felt a small pang that I was going to miss it all. It was my first prom, after all.

As I left, it felt like everyone's eyes were on me, pitying me. No one had mentioned my suspension—probably because I had hidden for most of the day—but I still felt like a pariah. The people who I had belonged to were strangers to me, and my friends weren't there.

I was so busy staring at my shoes as I walked to my car that I didn't notice the boy leaning against my door. So, when I heard a familiar voice call, "Hey, Ally," I jumped a foot in the air. My head jerked up, and I saw Miles leaning against my SUV.

"Hey," I greeted, confused as to why he was there.

He pushed up from the door and stood in front of it, blocking my path. "How are things?"

He looked like his usual self—styled blond hair, ocean blue eyes, dressed in jeans and a button-down, and I could smell his cologne from where I stood a couple feet away. *Bleh.*

I nodded in short movements and replied on a sardonic chuckle, "Just peachy." Then I jiggled my keys in hopes he would take the hint.

I guessed my hint wasn't received because he still stood there and sighed out, "Yeah." He didn't move, his gaze caught on something over my head.

We stood there awkwardly for a moment until I couldn't stand it anymore. I was incredibly tired.

"What do you want, Miles?"

He lowered his eyes back to me and just stared, like he was looking for signs of something. Then he seemed to make up his mind about whatever it was. I would know what when he stated, "He told you."

I was too exhausted to pretend I didn't know what he was talking about, so I replied, "Yeah, he told me."

"The baby's not mine," he stated, his voice cracking on the word "baby."

I knew he wanted to believe that, but his tone, along with the look on his face, revealed his fear. He looked like a lost little boy. A lost little boy who was probably going to be a daddy.

"Are you sure about that?" I asked with a gentleness I didn't feel. I really wanted to smack him. I wanted to maim him for being so stupid by not having condoms and for screwing everything with a vagina without one.

He didn't say anything, so I did. I stared him straight in the eye and gave him some truth. "You need to do the right thing. For once."

He flinched. "What is the right thing, Ally? Tell me, and I'll do it." His shoulders hunched as he jammed his hands into the pockets of his jeans.

"You need to talk to Raven, you need to find out if the baby is yours, and then you need to tell your parents."

His head shot up, and he cried out, "I can't do that!"

"You can't go on pretending like your actions don't have consequences. You are probably the father of that baby, if the rumors about your condom aversion are true."

He ignored me, his face turning mulish as he declared, "I'm not marrying her."

Okay, I had tried to be patient ...

I threw my arms out and admonished loudly, "You don't have to! It's the twenty-first century, for goodness' sake!"

"I won't be able to play college baseball." He matched my volume in his panic.

I dropped my hands, closed my eyes, and sucked in a huge breath. Then I blew it out noisily and counted to ten before I opened my eyes and stated calmly, "Maybe. Maybe not. Do you honestly think your parents, with all their money and influence, won't take care of you and the baby? They love you. Y'all will figure something out."

He stabbed his fingers through his perfectly styled hair and grumbled, "This wasn't the way my life was supposed to turn out."

I chuckled, but it held no humor. He didn't know the half of it.

"Life rarely turns out how we plan it, Miles. It's funny that way. How well it turns out depends on how you accept those changed plans and live the life you're meant to, not the one you expected."

It was like Dr. Keller had spoken to him through me. I guessed therapy really was changing my inner voice.

He squeezed his eyes shut, and I could see his throat working.

I was done. If he took my advice, great. If he didn't, it wasn't my problem. I had enough of my own to deal with at the moment.

"Don't you need to get ready for prom?" I asked quietly.

His eyes popped open, and he nodded.

"Who are you taking?"

"Laura," he croaked out.

I smiled, knowing why she so readily took Miles back. She was vying for a position in the junior court. There was no question Miles would be the junior candidate, and whomever he brought as his date had the highest odds of being the female choice.

"Well ... y'all have fun." I kept my smile in place, hoping he would take the hint and move.

"Thanks." With that, he finally moved in the direction of his vehicle, which happened to be next to mine.

I bleeped the locks and was opening my car door when he called my name. I paused and rolled my eyes before twisting my neck to look at him from over my shoulder.

He was already in his car with the window down. His face was sad when he said, "I wish it was you."

He wished it was me, what? Did I want to know?

Before I could make up my mind on whether to ask or not, he rolled the window up and took off.

Maybe some things were better left unknown.

PROMTASTIC

"Mom," I called as I walked through the door. Her car was parked in the driveway, so I knew she had to be home somewhere. Maybe she would be up for a spa night while we watched *Supernatural?* I didn't feel like being alone.

No answer.

Exhausted and a little bummed, it looked like the only date I was having was with Sam, Dean, and a tub of Halo Top.

I strolled into the kitchen to get that tub and saw a note on the fridge.

> ***Ally,***
> ***Out with friends. Be back late. You got a package today. It's in***
> ***your room. Have fun!***
> ***Kisses!***
> ***Mom***

I sighed, wondering what package I had gotten. I hadn't ordered any more clothes. I guessed I would find out in a minute, thinking I would skip the Netflix and ice cream and just go to bed.

Feeling dejected and alone, I wandered down the hall to my room and flipped on the light.

On the bed was a box, and on top of the box sat my phone. A trill of excitement raced through me. I wanted to run over and snatch it. I could finally message Sterling!

As instantly as that excitement came, it was doused by the thought of the possibility of him being at prom tonight with a date. Again, I thought: would he have taken Raven? My gut twisted as I stared at the device like it was a snake coiled to strike.

I moved to the bed and set the phone aside, not glancing at the screen. Instead, I focused on the box.

It wasn't a regular brown cardboard box used for packing. It was a white gift box with a shiny emerald green ribbon. I fingered the fabric between the pad of two fingers, feeling its satiny softness, before I yanked and unraveled the bow. Then I lifted the lid of the box and gasped.

Inside was an emerald green dress and a matching pair of heels. *What was going on?*

The light from my phone screen caught my eye, and I saw that I was getting Snapchat notifications. I reached for the phone, my heart beginning to race at who the snaps were from and the butterflies in my tummy *swarming*. Forget fluttering.

I clumsily opened my phone and went to the app, my breath catching at what I saw.

It was a picture of the pier, but it had white Christmas lights tacked around the edges of the rickety wood. The text band read: *"Wear the dress and meet me at our place."*

O.M.G. Was I getting my *She's All That* promtastic ending?

I clutched the phone to my chest and let out an excited squeal that would have put a tween girl to shame.

"I have to get ready," I whispered into the empty room. "Fast."

§

The dress fit perfectly. I smoothed my hands down the soft, floaty overlay of the almost Grecian-style, maxi dress. It had black and gold rope-like straps. The double bands of them wrapped around the waist. It was a little risqué with its deep vee of exposed skin that went from my neck until almost my belly button. If my boobs were any bigger, I would probably be exposing myself every time I moved.

I knew who was responsible for the dress and felt a smile twitch at the corners of my lips. Of course Blake would pick out a dress that was both classy and sexy.

I left my still blonde hair loose with soft curls, and kept my makeup simple but dramatic. I lined my eyes with black liquid liner, creating a winged effect at the corners, and pulled out the extra set of fake lashes that Blake had given me weeks ago for the musical. The last thing I did was smooth red lipstick over my lips and put on my gold Kendra Scott dangling earrings my mom had given me for my sixteenth birthday last year.

My hands shook on the steering wheel as I drove toward our place at Westbank Park. Anticipation tingled all throughout my body as I barely drove the speed limit all the way there.

I pulled into the lot and saw Sterling's Chevelle, but no sign of the guy himself. I parked and barely had the engine off before I flung the door open and got out. I left my phone and purse, but bleeped the locks. Then I wetted my lips, my heart beating a mile a minute, and lifted my skirt as I hurriedly journeyed toward the pier.

I could see the soft glow as I picked my way through the tall grass and came to the small clearing. And there he was ... Tears blurred my vision, and my heart practically flew out of my chest at the sight of his beloved form.

He was dressed in a royal blue tux with a snowy white shirt, black bowtie, and dress shoes. His overlong hair was brushed back from his devastatingly handsome face, making him look debonair.

I let out a long sigh. Then I noticed the glint of something on his lip and pressed the back of my hand to my lips to contain the cry of joy that wanted to escape my lips.

His eyes devoured me in return, a small smile playing on his lips. Then he called out, "Are you going to just stand there?"

That was my cue to move, and I did. I practically ran and threw myself into his arms, inhaling his woodsy, clean scent. I basked in the warmth of his body since I had felt so cold for those two weeks without him. I savored the strength of his arms as they wrapped around me and the smooth, just shaven feel of his cheek as it rested on the skin of my shoulder.

"I missed you," I whispered in a watery voice.

He squeezed me tighter and replied gruffly, "And I missed you, princess, so much."

We held each other, needing to feel close after being apart for so long and after the scene that had occurred the last time we had been together.

Finally, we pulled back, and I looked up into his beautiful bi-colored eyes that were so warm I thought I would never feel a chill again. Smiling, I gently tapped the ring that was in his lip with one finger.

"I figured I'd need every weapon in my arsenal to get you to give me a chance ... to give us a chance."

The corner of my mouth tipped up as I stared at the silver hoop. "You didn't need it. I was going ..." I looked up into his eyes and hoped that everything I felt for him was there, easy to read. "I was going to tell you that I wanted to try. I mean, I want to try. I want to stand by you no matter what. Even if ..." I trailed off, not wanting to bring it up right now when everything was so perfect. "I love you, and that's what matters. I was going to tell you all this last week, but I guess you know what happened."

He nodded.

"Mom took my cell, and I figured you probably couldn't read smoke signals, so I knew I would have to wait ..." I remembered the display I had made at his locker, and my cheeks went hot. "And I may have tried to communicate all this to you ... on your locker."

His smile was brilliant, but then his brows crinkled. "What did you do?

I gave him a sheepish smile. "Let's just say I'm handy with a Sharpie and sticky notes." I needed to change the subject, so I leaned around his shoulder and asked, "So, what's all this?"

"Prom."

If I wasn't already in love with him, I would have fallen right then. Therefore, all that was left for me to do was fall even deeper.

I felt like I was in the final romantic scene of a movie, the grand gesture, the stereo over the head, the lit backyard, the birthday cake on the table, the Gibson guitar, etc. I expected a soundtrack to start playing at any moment.

He pulled away and took my hand, leading me down the wooden

planks of the pier. My heels made a *click-click* noise that sounded loud in the peaceful quiet of the lake.

"Hand me your keys," he ordered.

I automatically placed them in his hand, and he pocketed them.

"Don't want you to lose those or have them get knocked into the water."

"Good idea," I muttered. That was a real possibility.

Once we were in our spot, the place we had danced the first time we had come here and the spot where he had made me his, he reached into his pocket and pulled out his phone. After he pressed a few buttons, a song started playing that I didn't recognize, which was nothing new. Then he extended his hand and asked, "May I have this dance?"

When I placed my smaller hand in his, he pulled me in close. Our bodies melded as I laid my cheek against the fine material of his suit jacket.

We swayed to the music, his breath tickling my ear as he whispered, "Did I mention how gorgeous you look in that dress?"

"No," I answered.

"You're so beautiful it hurts my heart to look at you."

I snuggled deeper into his chest, feeling shy at his sweet words. I felt it rumble as he chuckled.

"Never thought you could be shy."

"Shut up," I mumbled.

Our bodies moved in time, rocking side to side, my softness to his hardness. I listened to the lyrics of the song with excitement and longing that created an ache in my chest, in my soul. This boy was so much a part of me now, and I wanted to be absorbed by him, to live in his skin as he lived in mine.

"What song is this?"

"'Skin and Bones' by Eli Young Band."

"I love it," I whispered.

"Me, too," he said against my hair before I felt him press a kiss there.

"Love you."

"Love you, too, princess."

And we danced in the glow of our pier under a velvety night sky filled with stars. I couldn't have envisioned a more perfect prom night, not even in Hollywood, or even in my dreams.

Sterling just kept on saving me, and I hoped he never stopped.

LABELS

It was the night after prom, and I was officially ungrounded. Sterling had wanted to do something, but I needed to reconnect with my two best friends. So, Elodie, Blake, and I were in the kitchen, baking cupcakes while my phone played Taylor Swift's "Look What You Made Me Do." We danced around the kitchen, swinging our butts side to side and singing into a couple of wooden spoons while Blake wore oven mitts and was doing something he called "Vogueing." We were having so much fun that no one heard the front door slam or see my father storm into the house. At least, until Blake caught sight of him and screamed.

We all turned to see what had him clutching his oven-mitted hands to his chest, and my gaze landed on the familiar form of my dad.

I hadn't seen him since before the musical rehearsals and was shocked to see him in such a state. His suit was wrinkled and looked slept in, his tie was loose and hanging from his neck, and his hair was overly long and wild, like he had torn his fingers through it recently.

I scrambled over to my phone and hit pause as my dad propped himself against the back of the couch, arms crossed, staring at us with hard eyes.

"Uh ... Hey, Dad."

"Can I talk to you for a minute, Allison?" His lips barely moved. He was grinding his teeth so hard I feared for his back teeth.

"Sure."

I glanced at my friends, who both looked concerned, and tried to give them a reassuring smile, but I didn't think it worked. The frowns didn't leave their faces.

Elodie reached up and gave my shoulder a squeeze as I wiped my hands on a dish towel, and I could feel Blake watching me closely.

I moved around the counter toward my dad. He stood from his position and, without a word or look, stalked back the way he had come.

When we were in the hall, he swept his arm out toward the kitchen and bellowed, "What is that?"

"What is what?" I asked, sincerely confused.

"You have a homo in my kitchen."

A *what?* I jerked back, reeling. The word seemed to echo throughout the hall, or maybe that was just inside my head? I could not believe he had just called my friend that.

"Wh-what?" I asked, not sure I had heard him right.

"What is wrong with your mom? I can't believe she let him in my house."

Heat coursed through my entire body, and my muscles began to tremble in outrage.

"Not only that, you've got some mixed mu—"

"Do not finish that sentence." I leaned forward, going so far as to stand on my tiptoes to get closer to his face.

He turned red, and his body tensed. I was so far beyond angry that I wasn't concerned that he looked like he wanted to haul off and hit me.

"How dare—"

"You come in here and start insulting my friends when I haven't seen you in weeks—no, *months?* After what you did to Mom? You didn't even come see me perform!"

He took a step back, the color draining from his face. I had never spoken to him that way. The girl I used to be would have been horrified right now, fearful. But the new Ally? The improved Ally? I felt strong, empowered. I was finally taking mine back from the man who had almost stolen everything from me.

"Yeah, Mom told me. I've had some pretty big things going on in my life, and you've been MIA."

"That's what I came here to talk about. I just heard your mom's voicemail about the suspension. What the hell were you thinking?"

I opened my mouth to tell him exactly what I was thinking for the first time in my life, but he cut me off.

"It's that boy," he stated with so much hostility that the hair on my arms stood on end and my skin prickled. "I mean, look at your hair! It's bimbo blonde! This is not my daughter! Him with his long hair and facial piercings ... He's a bad influence on you.

"He knocked someone up, Ally. Did you know that? It's all over town! How he's carrying on with *my* daughter while his baby is in another girl's belly! And you can probably kiss law school good-bye—they don't take druggies. But I'll try to fix it. I'll take care of him, too, and then you won't have all these ... issues." On that last word, he jabbed his finger toward the kitchen. "Now, I'm going to have a word with your mother. I'm not sure you should be in her custody."

He went to move around me, but I stepped in his way and, in a low voice, said, "You won't be doing shit." Before he could cut me off like I was sure he was about to do, I continued, "You don't *know* shit." I lifted my chin higher. "First of all, Blake, the 'homo' in your kitchen, is the most honest and giving person I have ever met. You could probably learn something from him."

My father was a formidable man, and in the face of his fury, I usually quailed. But this time, his anger did nothing but bolster me and harden my resolve to finally share what I thought with him.

"Elodie, the girl you were about to call a disgusting name, is one of the best people I know. She became my friend when she had no reason to. Those girls you made me be friends with treated her like crap for no reason."

"Ally—"

"Let me tell you something. Skin color is just that—skin color. It's something no one has any control over, other than God. We're not color-coded, white being good and dark being bad. We're all just people. Her having a black dad doesn't mean she doesn't come from a home with two parents who love and respect each other and share that with their kids. Unlike this house ..."

He snapped his mouth shut and just stared at me. All anger gone. The hostility that had seeped from his pores moments ago, a memory.

"Sterling? 'That boy'? He saved my life. The reason the dog found those pills isn't because I'm on drugs; I tried to kill myself with them."

He sucked in a sharp breath, his face portraying his shock at my words.

"Sterling knocked them out of my hand. I gathered them up, put them back in the bottle, then hid them in my car. I didn't want you or Mom to find out what I did."

He shuddered, ran a shaky hand through his hair, and then dropped his chin to his chest.

"After that, Sterling did everything he could to pull me from that place. See, I didn't think my life was worth very much. Everyone treated me like I was invisible, like I was a fixture. A lamp in the corner of the room that people thought they could just turn off and on when they wanted me to do something. I'm not a lamp! I'm not a possession or a prize. I'm just a person. A person who needed to feel loved and accepted. I hadn't gotten that from anyone ... until Sterling. Until those people you just insulted in that kitchen.

"And by the way, the boy *you* wanted me to date is probably the father of that baby. Miles can't keep it in his pants, like you, and he screws anything in a skirt ... *without protection*. Also, evidently, like *you*."

I took in a deep breath. "And the mother you want to take me away from? She has me in counseling. We're both in counseling. See, the males in our lives tend to let us down, so we're learning to be dependent on our own damn selves."

I wanted to yell, "What do you think about that?" but I didn't. I thought I had said enough.

He didn't move, and he didn't speak. I watched him as he just stood there with his head bowed and his shoulders drooped. He seemed so much smaller in that moment than any time in memory.

When he finally lifted his head, my breath caught. His face was ravaged, tears were pooling in his eyes.

"You're wrong, Ally ... You are a prize, and I'm sorry if I never made you feel like one. I just wanted ..." He swallowed. "I just wanted the best for you."

His words healed some of the hurt I had been carrying and brought back a memory of after my accident.

I remembered feeling myself being lifted and carried after I had fallen. I had looked up into the face of my father, whose expression was hard yet worried. His mouth had been set in a grim line, and I remembered how prominent the lines around his eyes were, making him look older than his forty-seven years. He had been so worried ... about me. Still, things were going to have to change if the gulf that separated us was ever to be breached.

He was going to have to change, and I hoped he did. My little brother or sister deserved a better father than the one I had. I still deserved better, and hopefully, I would get it before it was too late.

"I get it. I just think ... you need to rethink your way of expressing it. Mom said Tina is pregnant?"

He nodded, and his eyes looked so bleak that it made my gut twist. I didn't know if he was happy or sad about being a father again. I knew it was something that wounded my mother. She had shared that in one of the sessions we'd had together with her therapist, Dr. Fuller. She had wanted more kids, but he never had. Now he was fulfilling her dream without her when she couldn't anymore.

"Maybe you'll do better with my little brother or sister."

Tears filled my eyes as I thought about the little life my dad had created with his secretary. I hated the situation and his actions, but I couldn't find it within myself to transfer that to a little baby. Thoughts of one baby led me to ones of the baby Raven carried.

"I hope so ... I didn't do too bad with you, though," he whispered, his eyes traveling over the entryway like he was memorizing it. Then he looked down and to the side. He rubbed over the stubble on his jaw and said, "Well, I need to get back."

I held in a sigh of relief and just replied, "Okay."

He stared at me for a moment then sighed before he pivoted toward the door. When he got there, he stopped, hand on the knob, and twisted his neck to look back at me from over his shoulder.

"I do love you, Ally. I may not have shown it very well, and you might not think much of me, but you'll always be my baby girl." His parting lines delivered, he quickly left before I could say anything in return, closing the door behind him with a soft *snick*.

I felt an arm curl around my shoulders and another curl around my waist.

"Did you hear?" I asked hesitantly, hoping they hadn't.

"Yes, doll," Blake answered quietly.

Embarrassment and shame burned a hole in my gut. I turned my head toward him and said in a pained, quiet voice, "I'm so sorry. He shouldn't—"

"It's okay," Elodie interrupted.

"It isn't," I protested.

"No, it isn't," she conceded. "But he should be the one apologizing, not you."

"You know," Blake started, and I swung back to him, "I feel sorry for your daddy."

My mouth dropped open, and Elodie spluttered, "Why?"

"He lives in such a narrow world full of labels. The only labels I prescribe to are found in my clothes."

Elodie and I both giggled, but then sobered at his next words.

"When you put labels on someone, it's like sticking them in a box with no air holes until they slowly suffocate. People aren't just one thing. They're many things. So, why do people like your dad think they can just slap a label on someone and that's all they are?"

Good question.

"That's deep, Blakey," Elodie remarked.

"I have hidden depths, Ellie. I'm not just another pretty face."

A smile stretched my lips so wide it almost hurt, and my body shook with silent laughter.

Things were going to be all right. I had friends who stood by me, a boyfriend who loved me, and a family ... that was healing. Yes, this might not have been the life that had been planned for me, but it was the one I deserved.

LET THEM SINK

Tap ... Tap ... Tap ...

I smiled at the sound and feigned sleep. I *knew* he would come.

Tap ... Tap ... Tap ...

I slowed my breathing, even though my heart was racing, and made my body go completely still.

A moment later, I heard the window being opened, then felt the side of the bed depress. That was my signal to move.

I sprung up and tackled the large body that was kneeling on my bed. He fell to the mattress with an *oomph* as I straddled his waist, placing my hand over his mouth. He immediately gripped my thighs and gave them a squeeze.

"Shh ..." I whispered as I raised my finger to my lips.

He kissed my palm then nodded.

"What are you doing, princess?" he asked after I removed my hand, his quiet, husky voice making me shiver. I could see the flash of his white-toothed smile in the moonlight.

"I have a plan." I leaned down and pressed my lips to his, then swung off him and the bed in one fluid movement.

"I can see that since you aren't wearing your sleeping clothes," he whispered on a chuckle.

He was right. After Blake and Elodie had left, I knew Sterling wouldn't be able to stay away. Therefore, after I had changed into some shorts and a tank, I laid in wait.

After the confrontation with my dad, a plan had begun to formulate in my mind. Something that would help me close the door on my past and help me to live fully in the now.

I reached for the larger cardboard box that was beside my desk then turned and shoved it into a rising Sterling. He let out another *oomph* and stumbled, clutching it to his middle.

"What do you have in here? Rocks?"

I lifted the other smaller box, walked over to the widow, and slid my feet into a pair of flip-flops. I chucked the box through the window and had one leg over the sill when I turned and told him, "Come on, we have somewhere to be."

I was standing outside the window, bouncing from foot to foot when Sterling emerged. My skin itched, and I bit my lip as I waited for him to shut the dang window.

"So, where are we going tonight?"

"The pier."

We were in his car on the way to the pier and had stopped at the stop sign outside of town. When he didn't move after a minute, I turned to look at him and saw he had his phone up, and then I heard the distinctive sound of a shutter clicking.

"What are you doing?"

He didn't answer. He just kept pressing buttons on his phone.

My phone dinged in my pocket, and I narrowed my eyes at him before lifting my hips to slide it out.

Surprise, surprise, I had a Snapchat notification.

I sighed because, really, I wanted to get to the pier and get this over with.

I clicked the app then the little blue square in the corner. The picture he had just taken appeared, but what made my breath catch and my vision blur was what he had written at the bottom.

You are reason enough to stay

"It's true," he said in a way that I knew, down to my soul, he believed.

My eyes lifted to his, and I saw the love he had for me burning brightly in his unusual eyes.

"I'm beginning to see that now," I whispered. Then I was across the car and in his lap a second later.

I pressed my lips hard to his, moving my hands to touch as much of him as I could, trying to convey the depth of my love and adoration for him. I parted my lips, and his tongue invaded my mouth, deepening the kiss, making it hotter—wetter.

He was the first person in my life to show me that *me*, as a person, was worth something. That I didn't have to *do* anything or *be* anything other than myself to be loved and valued.

A honk blared behind us, interrupting the moment, and we broke the kiss.

"I hate that we have to stop, but I should probably get us to the lake."

I nodded and moved back to the passenger seat, my heart so light it could probably float right out of my chest. I reached for his hand, and he intertwined our fingers together as we rode hand in hand toward our spot.

❧

I stood at the end of the pier, a gold trophy in my hand, and a box filled with the rest I owned at my feet. I looked down at the plaque that read *100-meter hurdles - 1st place* and examined the golden girl figure mid-run at the top. I felt the weight of it in my hand, unable to believe that one stupid trophy could mean more to a man than his own child. It wasn't even real gold or marble based, just a piece of weighted plastic. Resentment burned in my gut and up my throat.

Never again.

I would never allow anyone or anything to rule my life again. I would fight to my last breath to protect the slice of happiness I had found with Sterling, my friends, my mom, and theater. My days as a track star were over.

Without another thought, I reared my arm back then swung it forward, letting the trophy fly, relishing the sound of the *plop* as it hit the water. I didn't even wait to watch it sink before I had my hand back in the box and hurled another trophy, then another, and another.

Plop.

Plop.

Plop.

I could hear Sterling behind me, clapping and cheering me on.

When I had told him about my plan to sink every last trophy I had ever won in the lake, he hadn't called me crazy or tried to talk me out of it. He had just said "*okay*," carried the bigger box to the end of the pier, and stood back to let me do what I needed.

When I was done with the trophies, the last little figure bobbing at the surface—that one must have had a wooden base—my arm was sore.

I kicked the large box behind me and reached into the smaller one, pulling out a blue ribbon. I didn't even pause to read the gold lettering. I just pulled out the lighter I had put in my pocket earlier and flipped the lid. As a small flame appeared, I watched it dance in the warm, muggy breeze. Then I took the ribbon, held it over the flame, and watched the material burn. When it burned to the spot where my fingers held it, I tossed it into the water.

The satisfaction I felt at destroying the physical representation of my old life was liberating. I wanted to shout or dance. It felt like I was shedding an old skin and was now free to move as I wished.

I glanced down at the number of ribbons in the box and sighed. I didn't want to stand here all night and burn each ribbon one by one, so I grabbed a handful and started running the flame over the ends until they caught. Then I tossed them into the box, left the lid open on the lighter, and dropped it into the box. I kicked my foot back then shot it forward, sending the cardboard sailing. It floated and drifted away from the wooden dock.

"You okay?"

I looked over my shoulder at my boyfriend who was the most beautiful person, inside and out, that I had ever met and nodded.

He jammed his hands into his pockets and asked, "What do you want to do now?"

I thought about it for a second, then a slow smile spread over my face. He returned the smile and took a step forward.

Anticipation and excitement mingled and fluttered in my belly as I grabbed the bottom of my tank and jerked it over my head. He froze and watched as I next reached behind me and unsnapped my bra. I caught it and held it to my chest with one hand while I moved to the snap of my blue jean shorts with the other and undid the button. Then I turned and faced the water before I kicked off my shoes and shimmied out of my shorts and panties.

I shivered when I heard his footsteps on the wood, and it had nothing to do with the weather since it was a balmy almost-summer night.

I quickly let the bra slide from shoulders then flung it over my shoulder. I heard him curse before I dropped feet first into the water.

The tepid water closed in over my head before I propelled myself back to the surface. I wiped the water from my face and eyes then looked to see a shirtless Sterling standing where I had been a moment ago. Saliva filled my mouth. My eyes were riveted to the sight of his bare skin.

"You know you're in trouble, right?" he purred.

My eyes lifted and caught his smoldering ones. They were so hot they practically glowed as he stared down at me.

"I sure do hope so," I stated matter-of-factly. "But you're going to have to catch me first." With that, I dove underwater and hoped he caught me soon.

EPILOGUE

The sticky notes were a hit. No one had guessed who had done it, except the people who really knew me—Sterling, Blake, and Elodie. Even the faculty had loved the idea and kept stacks of the neon squares and Sharpies in ready supply in the locker area. You would think there would be a few idiots who would abuse the privilege, but surprisingly, no one had done anything ugly with the notes yet.

Raven, at the insistence of Pops and the Thorpes, had an amniocentesis done once school let out for the summer. If there was a possibility the baby was Sterling's, the doctor wanted to check for chromosomal abnormalities. It also provided an excuse to have an earlier than planned DNA test done. Raven still claimed Sterling was the father, so she couldn't exactly refuse the procedure without looking like she wasn't confident of the outcome.

When the results came back that the probability of paternity was 99.9998% Miles Thorpe was the father of a healthy baby girl, Pops clutched his chest and collapsed in a chair, muttering, "No baby cribs." Meanwhile, Sterling grabbed me around the waist and swung me in a circle right there in front of Raven and the Thorpes, which was admittedly awkward.

When he set me back down, Jack patted Sterling on the back. Then, before I had time to gain my equilibrium, Jack grabbed me around the waist and spun me around, giggling like a little boy. I wasn't sure how much he understood of what was going on, but I figured he was just happy that his pops and big brother were happy.

Raven screamed and cried until Ella, Miles' mom, offered to let her move into their home. That dried her tears up pretty quickly.

Evidently, Raven didn't have a great home life, something Sterling had told me once. She had gone on all morning about how her parents were on the verge of kicking her out and she was about to be homeless. That her getting pregnant was the last straw for them, and now they didn't want anything to do with her or the baby. As she had said this, her eyes had never left the Chapman men, who had studiously ignored her.

Her words had the desired effect, though. She was getting a new address; it just wasn't her first choice. In the end, I imagined she wouldn't be too sad with her new accommodations.

During the commotion, Miles had disappeared. I hadn't seen where he had run off to, nor did I particularly care.

My parents' divorce had gone through rather quickly. They had signed the papers before school had ended. Mom got the house and primary custody of me. Dad got visitation and took me out to dinner a couple times a week, alone. I wasn't sure what his relationship was with Tina or if he planned to marry her.

My little brother, Derek Everly, Jr., was born the following September. He was absolutely perfect in every way. Even my father said so ... which was a good start for Junior.

Who knew that the worst moments of your life could lead you to the best? If I had followed through with the decision to end my life, I would have missed out on so much.

One thing that therapy had taught me was that life was comprised of seasons. We just had to weather the storms and take joy in those moments we found in the sun. Nothing ever stayed the same. Circumstances changed, and people changed. Life moved on despite the best-laid plans.

I had found love in the least likely of places, though I couldn't give Sterling all the credit. I had worked hard to get to a place where I finally accepted myself and found joy in the little things life offered. Even so, on a cold day in February, he *had* saved my life. He would deny it, but it was true.

His love was my anchor. My lifeline. He didn't realize this, but after that day, Sterling just kept on saving me ... and I hoped he never stopped.

ACKNOWLEDGMENTS

First and foremost, I have to thank *God* for blessing me with this life and the opportunity to do something I have always dreamed. Without my faith in Jesus, I wouldn't be here, writing stories.

To *my husband*, thank you for your endless support. I don't know how I'd be able to navigate this life without you. I love you more than words. Marrying you was the best decision I've ever made.

My children, thank you for being patient with all the takeout food and movie days. I love you more than my own life. You are my greatest accomplishments.

Thank you to *Kristin Campbell, Amanda Vance, Kat Kenyon, Deanna Strother, Raj Billa, Jennifer Simon, and Judy Zweifel* for all your feedback and support. Y'all are amazing! I don't know what I would do without y'all.

ABOUT THE AUTHOR

Sadie Allen lives in Texas with her husband and three small children. When she's not writing, she's reading, catching up on her favorite shows, or chasing her family around the house.

Connect with her online:
Website: www.authorsadieallen.wixsite.com/books
Facebook: https://www.facebook.com/authorsadieallen/
Instagram: www.instagram.com/authorsadieallen
Twitter: www.twitter.com/writersadie
Pinterest: www.pinterest.com/writersadie
Goodreads: https://www.goodreads.com/SadieAllen
Email: authorsadieallen@gmail.com

Sign up for my newsletter and never miss an update!
www.authorsadieallen.wixsite.com/books
or
https://goo.gl/forms/73wk5aLauoBUJprV2

Want to know when I have a new release?
https://goo.gl/forms/B8FsjOKbxuIQKXtV2

Other novels by Sadie Allen:
Maybe Never
Killing Devon Peters (2018)
Maybe Molly (2018)

**Keep reading for an excerpt
of Sadie Allen's debut novel,** *Maybe Never*.

MAYBE NEVER: EXCERPT

Judd

I slammed the locker door harder than necessary. It was just another day in hell, otherwise known as my life these days. Asher and his crew were at it again. Just when I thought they had forgotten about me and maybe I could breathe again, they did something like this. Well, it could be worse.

I balled up the fabric in my hands as I walked toward the trash can to toss away the offending floral dress that had been hanging up in my locker. Then I glanced at where Asher and his group were watching from the other side of the hallway. He flashed me that smirk that was becoming so familiar while his buddies—my former buddies--laughed it up.

Why hadn't I realized he was such an asshole back when we were best friends? Had he always been like that, and I was just oblivious?

Hitching my backpack up onto my shoulder, I walked down the hall to my next class, Culinary Arts, otherwise known as the cooking class.

My life sucked. I dropped out of athletics to take this class because it was the only one available this spring. No other openings. No other options. I knew because I had tried everything. At least I wasn't finding used condoms and K-Y jelly in my gym locker anymore. I doubted my hall locker surprises were far from over, judging by this afternoon.

When had I become so emo? Why was I asking myself rhetorical questions?

I gave my head a shake and prayed that the next hour passed quickly.

I walked through the door of Mrs. Shannon's room and stopped dead. The room was set up unlike any other class I had. There were long, faux wood tables with plastic chairs that made up one-half of the room, and the other half had mini-workstations with small oven/microwave combos lining the outer walls, and two islands floating in the middle with the same. There was an actual line taped between the classroom and the workstations, but that wasn't what had me standing in the middle of the doorway.

All the seats were taken except one, and I would rather take a seat in a car speeding over a cliff than the one that was open.

"Good afternoon, Mr. Jackson! Why don't you take the seat next to Miss Klein, and we'll get started," Mrs. Shannon's overly cheerful voice snapped me out of my contemplation of looking for that speeding car.

Sighing because, really? Why should I be surprised? My luck hadn't changed in two months, so why should it now?

I made my way over to the chair next to Ashley Klein, my ex-girl-friend and the twin sister to my ex-best friend, Asher. Yes, they were really named Asher and Ashley. And before I even put my butt in the seat, she rolled her eyes and curled her lip.

I was seriously questioning why I ever thought she was attractive. Yes, she had the classic blonde hair and blue eyes with a perpetual tan that lasted even through the winter. Not to mention, she had a banging body that I had seen up close and personal. Her attitude, however, was spoiled princess. I guessed the physical benefits made it easier to over-look the snotty brat that she was showing me now.

Ashley made a choking/coughing sound that suspiciously sounded like "fag," and then went silent while Mrs. Shannon went on to explain today's lesson that would lead into our new project. Part one was baking. Great. Something that I only knew how to do in a microwave with one of those pre-made cakes in a coffee mug. She wanted us to get with our partner from last class and take notes, beginning the planning process.

I pretty much tuned out the rest of her lesson when she started talking measurements, pre-heating, and greasing. My eyes were beginning to glaze over as she went on and on ...

I must have fallen asleep or went into a small coma, because I jumped when she clapped her hands together and announced that it was time to get with our partners for the remainder of the class. Next week, we would practice baking with the ovens. *Joy.*

I looked around the room, hoping that Ashely wasn't the odd person out who needed a partner.

Before I could ask Mrs. Shannon what I should do, she called out, "Mr. Jackson, you'll pair up with Miss Blackfox."

I was too focused on Ashley and ways to avoid her that I hadn't looked at the people across from us. One, who I recognized as a girl from the drill team. She was moving her stuff to sit next to Ashley, thank God, and the other was Sunny Blackfox.

I had been in school with Sunny since elementary, but for the life of me, I couldn't remember ever talking to her. She was pretty. Actually, very pretty, with long, shiny black hair; high cheekbones; and dark eyes. However, she always kept to herself and was quiet. Our paths hadn't ever crossed since we never hung out with the same crowd. I had always been busy with sports, even as a little kid, and when I hadn't been playing a sport, I had been with my friends, talking about sports, bikes, or hunting. Later on, as I got older, all that shifted to girls. Sports, my buddies, and girls. I didn't know anything about Sunny outside of her and I going to the same school.

I looked at her and found dark, almost black, serious eyes looking at me. They weren't filled with disgust or discomfort, not even curiosity, just ... expectant. I knew why when she asked, "Are you moving, or am I?"

"Right."

I grabbed my blank notebook and chair, and moved over toward her side of the table. Once I was settled, neither one of us said anything. I just stared at the blue lines on the paper in front of me while she seemed to be doing the same, except her pages weren't blank.

I snuck a peek at her through the corner of my eye. She seemed to be reviewing her notes.

At least one of us had paid attention. I couldn't tell you anything Mrs. Shannon had said after the first five minutes of class.

After a few more minutes, she finally looked over at me.

I quickly turned my eyes back to my paper, playing off the fact that I had been watching her. The last thing I needed was to be accused of being a creeper.

"So, have you ever baked anything before?" she asked. Her voice pretty much said she knew the answer.

"Uh ... no. I can't say that I've baked anything before, but I can heat things up in a microwave." I cringed. How lame was that? Anyone could press buttons on a microwave. I should get a gold sticker for that one.

"Well, then you can be in charge of melting the butter."

"Okay ... So, what am I melting butter for? I thought we could bring a box of Duncan Hines or Betty Crocker, and make a cake or something."

When she made a face, I figured that wasn't going to fly. Really, though? What did she expect? I had just admitted to microwave cooking, which was something I did all the time at home for breakfast and dinner. I didn't even know how to heat a frozen pizza in the oven, so I zapped pizza bites on a paper plate in the microwave.

"I was thinking that I'd make ... Well, that we would make miniature pineapple upside down cakes."

"I don't like pineapple."

"You'll like these," she said in a voice that held no doubt, which was the wrong thing to do. I liked a challenge, and Sunny had just unknowingly placed one before me.

"I doubt it."

Her eyes flashed in irritation, and I felt the corners of my lips curve upward in response. When was the last time they had done that?

I opened my mouth to tease her a little more, just to see that flash of emotion again, but Ashley's loud laughing froze me mid-speak.

"Then I said, I don't know whether Coach Jackson shops in just the women's section or the plus-size!"

That was followed by a peal of high, feminine laughter from the drill team girl.

The corners of my mouth that had previously been turned up thinned into a tight line. I counted to ten and focused on the clock on the opposite wall, trying to get ahold of the heat that was scorching through my veins.

"Hey, Judd! Do you know the answer?"

My dad had taught me many things. One of those being never hit a girl. Kind of ironic looking back at that now, when I had never been so tempted to lay my hands on a female until now.

Before I could do or say anything, Sunny's voice cut through their laughter, strong and clear.

"What is your problem? Did your brain absorb some of that bleach on your head or what? You might want to get that checked out. Just saying ..."

I looked over at the two blondes. For once, it seemed like someone had shut them up. No one--and I mean, *no one*--talked to Ashley Klein like that. She was too hot, rich, and more importantly-- at least to her--popular. Girls either fell in line with everything she did or said, or they were crushed under the toe of her high-heeled shoe. Not that anyone ever did anything to contradict her, but the threat was always present.

It was in the superior tilt of her chin and the slight smile that was ever present on her gloss covered lips. She was feared, and she fed off that. Again, why did I put my dick in this chick?

I looked over at Sunny, expecting to see regret written all over her face because, really, she had just jumped into the ocean with a bleeding wound, and Ashley could smell blood from over a mile away.

What I saw on her face, though, was far from regret. She was steady. Her eyes never left the two girls as she stared them down, and her face was again expectant, like she really thought they should answer her question. I wanted to laugh. Sunny had balls.

I looked back at Ashley and the drill team girl. It was like watching a tennis match. I watched as Ashley's eyes narrowed and saw the cogs begin to turn in her head. She was gearing up to throw down.

I had spent the past two months mute, taking in all her and her brother's venom, letting it infect my blood and blacken my heart, letting it cause almost as much damage as my parents had inflicted on me. And in the past two months, no one had stood up for me. When Asher and Ashley, plus all their friends, had spewed their garbage at me, no one had said a word or blinked an eye. Sure, when their backs were turned, a few students would look at me in sympathy, or maybe pity, but to say anything, they would have committed social suicide.

I got it. I really did. Still, every pity-filled look tore a huge chunk out of my soul, which had been pretty battered to begin with.

Though I would take every nasty word that Asher, Ashley, and everyone else said over pity, I had to stop Ashley before she used her whip of a tongue on Sunny.

I looked over at one of the bravest girls I had ever met and said, "She's not worth it, Sunny."

"But, Judd--"

"No, she's nothing to me, except a bad memory that left a nasty taste in my mouth."

I heard the shocked gasp from across the table and knew my barb had hit its mark. I would probably pay for that one later, but it felt good to lash out for once.

"But, Judd ..." she tried again, confirming something I had guessed about Sunny earlier. Like myself, or well, my old self, she didn't back down from a challenge. I respected the hell out of her for that.

Still, I wasn't about to let her stick up for me, so I shook my head, about to tell her to just shut up, when Ashely recovered and spoke before I could.

"No, Judd, I want to hear what trailer park has to say. Not that I care. I mean, why would I?" She chuckled and glanced over at Little Miss Drill Team, who wasn't giggling or smiling for once.

No, drill team girl looked like she wanted to crap in her pants. I expected her to break out with the sign of the cross. She knew by the look on Ashley's face, and that tone of voice, that she was in the presence of Satan.

Ashley might look like a little naughty angel, but as I had learned recently, that girl was filled with nothing but brimstone. I was surprised she didn't smell like sulfur.

"I mean, she's that drunk Indian's daughter ... What do they call him?" She looked back at Sunny, returning the expectant look Sunny had shown her a few minutes ago. When Sunny didn't say anything, Ashley snapped her fingers. "Oh, that's right! Laughing Lonny. Isn't that, like, his Indian name? I heard he sounds like a donkey when he laughs. Maybe he should change it to Laughing Ass."

What. The. Hell? I could feel my face turn red. I had to clench my fists to keep from reaching over and snapping Ashley's effin neck as anger boiled in my gut and my muscles tensed in preparation for action. I wanted to hurt her.

Then I felt a cool, soft hand touch my forearm.

I looked down to see Sunny's hand gripping it. Then my eyes traveled up her arm to her shoulder, and then to her face that was leaning toward me. It was blank, but there were no tears or hurt in her eyes, or anything akin to pain.

"Judd, relax."

With those two words, I did just that. I exhaled a huge breath and closed my eyes.

Sunny again had come to my rescue. I barely knew her, but in the span of ten minutes, I felt like she was one of the realest people I had ever met, and I couldn't stand the thought of her being hurt.

"Like you said, she's nothing," Sunny continued. "My dad _is_ Native American, and he _is_ a drunk." Sunny then straightened up to her full height.

I couldn't believe what I was seeing. Instead of absorbing Ashley's hate-filled words and running away, she was doing something better. Something I should have done all along. Sunny was taking back her power.

She faced Ashley down and said, "Why don't you tell me something I don't know? I agree with you that he sounds a little bit like a farm animal when he laughs, but what's your point? Do you have daddy issues, in addition to being a bigot? Because you can't seem to leave ours alone."

I couldn't help it. I laughed out loud.

I could feel the eyes of the whole class turn in our direction, but I couldn't care less.

Then, before any more words could be exchanged, the bell rang twice, signaling the end of class and the end of the school day.

As Ashley got up and walked past us to leave the room, she hissed at me, "If you thought things were bad before, Judd, you just wait. They're about to get so much worse for you"—her eyes went to Sunny, looking her up and down in disgust—"and your girlfriend."

I never had a doubt.

Funny that she assumed Sunny was my girlfriend, when I hadn't even spoken to her before today.

"Bye, Ashley! It was fun chatting with you!" Sunny called out in a too cheerful voice that made me chuckle. The girl had a pair, and they were made of titanium.

"You probably shouldn't have done that," I told her as I closed my notebook and stuck it in my backpack.

"Why? She's a terrible human being."

I couldn't argue with her there. Still, Ashley's threat wasn't something to ignore.

"If you thought she was bluffing a minute ago, you're wrong. She's going to look for a way to make your life miserable. You stood up to her today, stood up for me of all people, and she's not going to let that go. Not that I'm not appreciative, but why would you do that for me?"

Sunny was quiet for a minute, concentrating on putting away her notebook and various pens and highlighters. My chest started to ache when I thought she wasn't going to answer my question. That maybe she was thinking going against Ashley on my behalf had been a mistake. Not that I needed anyone to fight my battles, but for once, someone might actually care about my situation. That maybe she thought treating me like the school's punching bag was wrong since I hadn't done anything to deserve it. That maybe I was a victim of this mess, too.

I was about to get up and head for the door when she spoke.

"What Asher and Ashley are doing to you is wrong. I was never in a position to say or do anything before since you and I never seem to be in the same place, but I've heard. Even a nobody like me hears gossip. Today, Ashley handed me the opportunity to finally say something."

I couldn't look at her. Too many emotions were swirling inside me. I didn't know whether I wanted to laugh or cry because of this girl. This girl who I never even paid attention to before today, who had had my back against a person I used to think I loved. Someone who should have stood by me when my life fell apart.

Though I had been Ashley's boyfriend for over a year, I had been her friend long before that since Asher had been my best friend from the time we started Pee-Wee football. I thought she knew me. I thought we were close. However, one thing this whole mess had taught me was that people weren't who you thought they were, and blind faith and trust were for fools.

You only really knew who your true friends were when you were at your lowest with nothing to offer. After the smoke cleared, that was when you finally saw who was left standing beside you. Unfortunately for me, I found myself alone when everything had been said and done.

"We're not responsible for our parents' actions, good or bad. If your friends couldn't see that, then they were never really your friends. You and your mom are the victims in this situation, not Asher or Ashley, or even the football team.

"For them to treat you this way says more about them than it does about you. All the people who are standing by and letting them do this are no better. We're not extensions of our parents, or even reflections of them. We're separate people with minds of our own, who may or may not agree with all the decisions that they make or have made for us. Yet, here you are, shouldering the blame for something you are not responsible for, and frankly, that's none of their business. It's not fair."

By the time she was done speaking, her chest was rising and falling so fast you would have thought she had just finished running a race. I had a feeling that some of the things she said weren't just about me, and that maybe having "Laughing Lonny" as a father hadn't been such a great experience. I also learned that Sunny Blackfox was quickly becoming one of my favorite people in the whole world.

"So, pre-law for you after graduation?"

Sunny let out a breathless chuckle, and I instantly wanted to make her do it again. I didn't think I had ever seen her smile or laugh.

"Why would you say that?"

"Because it seems like you have a strong sense of justice, or fairness—or whatever you want to call it. You were very passionate in that speech there."

She blushed, which was another thing I hadn't ever seen her do.

"Shut up," she said without any real heat. "Actually," she continued, "I want to go to culinary school. So, no pre-law for me ... Which reminds me that I need to get going, or I'm going to be late for work."

She then turns to her backpack and starts rooting around before finally pulling out a torn piece of paper. Taking a pen from one of the front pockets, she starts to scribble numbers on the torn piece of paper. When she's done, she hands me the paper.

"Since our planning was interrupted and we still need to go over what we're going to do Monday, here's my number. You can text me if you can come up with something better than box cakes or cookies. If not, I will send you my recipe, and we can divide up the supplies."

I looked at the scrap of paper in my hand and, sure enough, it had Sunny written in loopy, girly print with her number underneath it.

I took my phone out of my pocket and swiped my thumb across the screen, opening my contacts before entering her info. Otherwise, I would probably forget about it and lose that scrap of paper. Then I opened up my text messages and shot her a text.

When her phone dinged, I said, "Now you have my number, too."

We stood there, smiling at each other longer than necessary.

"Well, I better get going. I'm already on my way to being late for work. I'll either text you tonight once I finish my shift or tomorrow morning."

I watched her put on her coat and grab her backpack before she headed toward the door. When she hit the doorway, she stopped and looked back at me from over her shoulder, her face serious again.

"Don't let those people get you down, Judd. A year from now, this will all be a memory. Not a good memory, but a memory just the same." And then she was gone.

She was like a teenage Yoda, I could swear. I definitely had a lot to think over this weekend.

<<<<>>>>

Made in the USA
Middletown, DE
16 March 2018